LIVING W

A Year of Bible Discovery
With Christians of Ireland

EDITOR Rev. Frank P Sellar
Minister of Adelaide Road Donore Presbyterian Church,
Dublin 2.

SUB EDITOR Helen Geoghegan
Co-ordinator of The Road Ahead Project,
16a Palmerston Park,
Dublin 6.

Printing and Origination
Fodhla Printing Co. Ltd.
44 Hill St., Dublin 1.

Front Cover Illustration
Centre Cut from a N.Antrim
Oil Painting by R.G. Sellar

Formatting by David J. Temple

First Published 1999
ISBN 0-9515637-5-0

OUT OF THANKFULNESS
For Robert (80)
And Roberta
And their generation

OUT OF PRAYERFULNESS
For Rebecca (8)
And Robert
And their generation

ARTIST'S NOTES ON THE PICTORIAL WORKS

The plate for January is from a 14" square composite papercut with transfer lettering. The originals for all the other plates are known as 'relief prints'.

Relief Prints are made direct from plane surfaces generally of wood or linoleum, which are hand-crafted by use of knives, gouges or gravers.

To such a crafted surface, sticky black printers' ink is applied, usually by use of a rubber roller. The ink can adhere only to those areas of block surface that remain upstanding (i.e. in relief) after the cutting away of those surface parts removed by the artist's tools.

The block, so inked, is applied under controlled pressure to a suitable printing-paper.

When the paper is peeled away from the block, ink first imparted to it's uncut surface will then be seen transferred back to the white paper; but the artist-craftsman's tooling, not being inked, shows up in those paper surfaces that remain white and clean. For example, in the December print, the vertical stone walls correspond to the uncut surfaces of the lino block, whereas the snow, the hoarfrost on the trees and the light in the sky behind the tower all show up white where the gouges have been active.

As the December print is a pure block-on-white linocut, so also are the prints for April, June, September and November.

Plates used for March, May, July and October are also made from linocuts, but these original prints are additionally individually coloured with opaque gouaches or permanent transparent watercolours.

The print for August is from a block of plywood, the white parts being cut away by use of a sharp craft knife. The side grain of the wood surface shows up in the print and this is truly a 'wood cut'.

For February the plate shows an enlargement from a print made from a 3" X 4" wood engraving. Distinct from a wood cut which is incised on the plank, a wood engraving is made into the end grain of a slow-growing wood such as Box. The tools used are very fine chisels, seldom broader than 'an eighth of an inch', or fine-line gravers akin to those used in chasing on silverware.

The artist is asked at times why he is interested in the making of relief prints. The answer to this is twofold:-

Firstly, in the making of prints he can more widely share record of the joys in his experiences of life and thought than he ever could in the producing of 'one-off' paintings or sculptures that might end up in the collections only of the few.

Secondly, there is a constant and ongoing challenge in the action of decision-making. In the cutting or engraving of a block there is no room for shillyshallying. Work must be well considered before a knife, gouge or gravers be put to use. There are many fields in life where decisions must be taken and these must be taken to good purpose.

Robert G. Sellar. A.R.U.A

Contributors

Noel Agnew	The Word of God
Des Bain	Repentance
Robert Bell	Self Denial
Alistair Bill	Christmas
Derick Bingham	Life and Death
William Bingham	Assurance
Russell Birney	Rewards
David Boyd	Social Action
Douglas Bradley	The Church
David Bruce	Guidance
David Burke	Comfort When Afraid
James Burnett	Temptation
Mervyn Burnside	Faithfulness
Aiden, Carroll	Worry
Arthur Clarke	Caring
Ken Clarke	Encouragement
Dave Clements	Anger
Tom Conway	Confession of Sin
Willis Cordner	Illness
David Cupples	Bereavement
Tony Davidson	God as Reconciler
Rosemary & John Dunlop	Sex
John Faris	Unity
Joseph Fell	Eternal Life
Jim Frazer	Fellowship
Gordon Fyles	Prayer
Helen Geoghegan	Listening
Drew Gibson	Gossip
Stephen Gillespie	Work
Edgar Gilpin	Work
Ferran Glenfield	Witness
Jim Hagan	Doubt
Norman Hamilton	Freedom
David Hewitt	Work
Richard Hill	Friends
James Hyndman	Family / Husbands
David Johnston	Justice of God

Stephen Johnston	Greed
Neil Kennedy	Obedience
Brian Kingsmore	Conversion
John Kirkpatrick	Joy
Howard Lewis	Offices of Christ
Alvin Little	Holy Spirit
Peter Lyle	Failure
Douglas Mark	Persecution
Samuel Mawhinney	God's Love
Robert McMullen	Easter
David McCarthy	Praise
Alison McCaughan	Stress
Cecil McCullough	The Trinity
Graham McGeown	Healing
Paddy Monaghan	Christ likeness
David Montgomery	Neighbourliness
David Moore	Holiness
Trevor Morrow	Grace
Vivienne Murtagh	Grief
Gavin Pantridge	Work
Derek Poots	The Goodness of God
Stephen Rea	Forgiveness
Cheryl Reid	Good Works
Fergus Ryan	Avoidance of Sin
Joanna Samuel	Tiredness
David Searle	God's Glory
Frank Sellar	Honesty
Joan Singleton	Depression
Marisine & David Stanfield	Marriage
Roz Stirling	Youth
Steve Stockman	Humility
Paul Symonds	Obedience
John Thompson	Money
Ken Todd	Renewal
Clifford Tughan	Work
Andrew Watson	Children
John Woodside	Faith
Sandra Woodside	Hospitality
Sam Workman	Heaven

JANUARY

The elders of Adelaide Rd Donore Presbyterian Church have given thought to our aspirations, hopes and calling as a congregation in the new millennium, and more specifically within the inner city Dublin context. We have summarised our purpose in 5 words, all beginning with the letter 'W':

WORSHIP of God, Father, Son and Holy Spirit is our highest calling and chief end. Everything we seek to do is based upon truth as revealed in the Bible which is the **WORD** of God. Jesus is the "Word made flesh" who came down from Heaven and 'dwelt among us, full of grace and truth'.

The outworking of our faith is expressed through the twin wings of good **WORKS** (social outreach) and verbal **WITNESS** (evangelism). One without the other leads to imbalance and ineffectiveness.

At the centre of our congregation must always be a **WELCOME** for visitors, new members and strangers, 'Outsiders' encouraged to become 'insiders'.

Together these 5 vital elements of church life form the shape of a Celtic Cross, which encapsulates the essence of our faith in Jesus Christ within Ireland.

The Bible verses in this collection of devotions have thus been carefully selected to do justice to the indispensability of balanced **WORSHIP, WORD, WORKS, WITNESS** and **WELCOME** within the church and within our personal lives.

1st January — Worship

John 4 : 23

"True worshippers will worship the Father in Spirit and truth, for they are the kind of worshippers the Father seeks."

☞ What's the most important thing in my life?

That's not a bad question for the start of this particular New Year. To discover the answer, all we must do is ask ourselves two simple things;

> About what do I spend most of my time thinking?
> On what do I spend most of my money?

Perhaps we think most about another person, sex, our children, our stocks and shares or the state of my bank account? Maybe we think most of our money or redecorating our home, or food and drink or holidays, or my car or 'myself'?

What we think about most and what we spend the greatest amount of our money on is likely to be the thing that we worship, for worship is the giving to something or someone 'first place'.

When Jesus spoke to the woman of Samaria beside a well, He told her that the Father God seeks people who will first and foremost worship Him. 'Spiritually and truthfully', is the way He describes it.

After six unfulfilled and unfulfilling relationships, we can only assume she craved friendship more than anything else in the world, but these experiences had brought nothing but heartache, emptiness and unhappiness.

This coming year, may we find fulfillment in the activity for which we were in fact made...worship of the Father of Our Lord Jesus Christ. That alone can fill our deepest yearning.

✝ *Dear God, help me discover that when I put You first, everything else fits in to its proper place. Amen.*

♥ Our souls are restless, until they find their rest in you. (Augustine)

2nd January **Word**

📖 John 4 : 26

"I know that Messiah (called Christ) is coming. When He comes, He will explain everything to us.Then Jesus declared, 'I who speak to you am He'."

☞ In Nicolai Gogol's play *'The Government Inspector'*, the disreputable characters in a corrupt Tzarist Russian town expect an official from St. Petersburg to arrive; but in their frenzied panic they choose the wrong person!

Similarly, the Samaritans had an expectation that the Messiah was coming; God's anointed servant would unexpectedly appear, to sort out all their old problems and usher in a new era of peace and well being. They were looking for a Moses-like character to return, who would be their liberator...saviour. There was nothing wrong with their anticipation...but they chose the wrong person!

Years before, Moses had indeed led the twelve tribes of Israel out of Egypt to the Promised Land, but now another, greater than Moses, had come to establish His kingdom along with twelve disciples. The law had been given through Moses, (John 1 : 17), but grace and truth came through the Word made flesh ...in Jesus Christ. Moses had lifted up the snake in the desert, (John 3 : 14), but now the Son of Man would be lifted up, so that everyone who believes in Him may have eternal life.

The Samaritan Woman was right when she declared, "I know that the Messiah is coming...He will explain everything to us."

Jesus said: *"I who speak to you am He."* Let us not make a tragic mistake and chose the wrong person!

✝ *Gracious God, Thank You that we didn't have to go searching for You, but You came looking for us. Amen.*

♥ Greeting Card wording: 'Congratulations and Happy Birthday on your Anniversary this Valentines Day, Barmitzvah boy. Hope you feel better soon.'

3rd January Welcome

📖 John 4 : 9

"You are a Jew and I am a Samaritan woman. How can you ask me for a drink? (For Jews do not associate with Samaritans.)"

☞ A little girl answered the doorbell of their house in South Africa, "Who is it?" asked her Mum. "A smiling lady," replied the child. "Was she black or white?" "I forgot to look" came the reply.

Most people do however look very carefully at differences...colour of skin, quality of clothes, style of hair, closeness of eyes! They were no different in Jesus' day. No self - respecting Jew would be caught dead talking to a Samaritan. When the Assyrian's conquered North Israel in 722 BC and deported many Jews, they also imported numerous foreigners from Mesopotamia and Syria who inter married with those who remained. These became the 'Samaritans', and the returning Jews under Nehemiah in 445 BC refused to have anything to do with them.

Relationships deteriorated so badly that in Jesus' day Jewish pilgrims were sometimes waylaid in Samaria, and for most Jews there could be no such thing as a 'good' Samaritan.

Jesus, the Jew, therefore broke all conventions, engaging not just with a Samaritan, but a female, and an immoral one at that! He knew that she too needed a Saviour; and those who follow Jesus must also cross barriers that traditionally divide, in order to share the good news of salvation with those who are different from us.

✝ *Heavenly Father, I feel more comfortable with people who are just like me. Help me not to be scared, but, like Jesus, to reach out to all who need the Saviour's love. Amen.*

♥ A ship is safe in the harbour, but that's not what it was made for.

4th January — Witness

📖 John 4 : 14

"Jesus said, 'Who ever drinks the water I give him will never thirst. Indeed, the water I give him will become in him a spring of water welling up to eternal life'."

☞ Rev Jim Rea tells the true story of Rev Milton Cunningham, who was sitting in the middle of three seats on a plane flying from Atlanta to Dallas. On his left, at the window, sat a girl with Down Syndrome. On his right was a businessman.

"What's that sign?" asked the girl to the minister, while they were still on the runway. "That's the seat-belt sign. You have to wear your seat belt when you take off." "My mum says its good to wear a seat-belt," the girl replied. "Can you ask the man on your other side if he's wearing his seat-belt?" Mr. Cunningham did as he was asked; "Excuse me, but this little girl would like to know if you are wearing your seat-belt?" "I am," replied the businessman.

A little while later after take off, the girl again asked Milton; "What's that sign?" "That's the No Smoking sign. You are not allowed to smoke on an airplane." "That's good," said the girl. "My mum says it's best not to smoke. Can you ask the man on your right if he smokes?" Rather put out he turned to his neighbour and said; "Excuse me, but this little girl would like to know if you smoke?" "No I don't." he replied.

A short time after, the girl once again turned to the Rev Milton Cunningham and asked; "Do you love Jesus?" "Well, as a matter of fact I do," replied the minister. "That's good," said the girl; "My mum says its good to love Jesus." ("Oh No" thought Mr Cunningham, I know what's coming next! Sure enough...)

"Can you ask the other man beside you if he loves Jesus?" "Excuse me...this is rather embarrassing," said the minister to his business neighbour, "But this little girl would like me to ask if you love Jesus?' "Well, interesting you should ask that," he replied; "I don't ... but I've waited a long time to meet someone who could show me how I **can**." By the time they reached Dallas, he **did.**

✝ *Help me Heavenly Father not to keep the life giving news of salvation to myself, but enable me to share it with those who spiritually thirst, for Jesus' sake. Amen.*

♥ Salvation is free, but never cheap. (Deitrich Bonhoeffer)

5th January **Works**

John 14 : 39

"Many of the Samaritans from that town believed in him because of the woman's testimony. He told me everything I ever did."

There is nothing more powerful than a changed life. When the immoral Samaritan woman recognised in Jesus the "Christ who could explain everything," (v.25) she left her water jar and went back to the town. There she exhibited such a compelling picture of transformation that crowds of people came out to have a look, not only at her, but also at Jesus who had been the source of her new forgiven life!

It's tragic when the lives of those who claim to have had an encounter with Jesus fail to authenticate their words, but there is nothing more attractive, than when they do. Not only does it lead to the interest of others, but naturally and unaffectedly it draws many to the Saviour, so that as John 4 : 43 says; 'We no longer believe just because of what you said; now we have heard for ourselves, and we know that this man really is the Saviour of the World.'

This is Living Well!

Heavenly Father, may my words and actions so authenticate my faith, so that other people might be drawn to the one who alone can save. Amen.

"I don't believe all this stuff about blind people regaining their sight," scoffed an unbeliever! "Well I do," replied a wife and mother. "Once my husband was a drunk, but since Jesus came into his life, now he has become a considerate provider; our house is now peaceful; the children are happy and there's money to put food on the table! I still believe in miracles."

Frank Sellar

6th January — Witness

📖 Isaiah 6 : 8

"Then I heard the voice of the Lord saying; "Whom shall I send? And who will go for us?" And I said, "Here am I. Send me."

☞ How big is your God? Isaiah's vision of God in the temple was one of the formative things in his life. Isaiah was a prophet, with a direct line to the kings of Judah, a mover and shaker in the nation. But his whole ministry was shaken by his encounter with the eternal God. The wonder of God provides the motivation of Isaiah's response: 'Here am I! Send me'. A lesson can be drawn from this: serving God is no substitute for knowing Him. Like Isaiah, our knowledge of God is too limited and our service for Him too confined. We need a vision of a big God, a sense of wonder to sustain our lives. For many of us our God is too small.

✝ *Lord, lift our eyes from ourselves and give us a vision of Your greatness. Amen.*

♥ A little boy returned home from Sunday school and asked his mother, "Is God everywhere?" "Why yes." she replied. The little boy asked again, "Is God with us now in the kitchen?" "Why yes" his mother replied. "Is God in that empty milk bottle?" His mother paused. For the sake of consistency she replied "Yes." The little boy lifted the bottle and put his small hand over the top. "Got You!"

There is so much of the little boy in us, fascinated by God, but wanting to confine and control Him.

7th January — Witness

Matthew 4 : 19

"Come, follow me," Jesus said, "and I will make you fishers of men."

☞ *"Follow me,"* Jesus said to two fishermen on the seashore. This changed their lives and also altered the shape of the world. It was an invitation to discipleship, a call to a shared task: "And I will make you fishers of men."

In one sense, when Jesus walked in Palestine, there was a certain simplicity to being a disciple. Essentially it meant to go with Him, to learn, to obey and to imitate Him. The situation is not quite the same today. We cannot literally be with Him in the same way as His first disciples could. But the heart of a disciple of Jesus Christ desires above all else to be like Him, and to draw others into His way.

✝ *Lord, above the clamour of many voices, let me hear You and follow in Your way. Amen.*

♥ A traveller in Africa complained to his guide in the rainforest. "There is no path, we have lost our way." The guide replied, "There is no way, I am the way."

8th January — Witness

Matthew 9 : 37 – 38

"Then Jesus said to his disciples, "The harvest is plentiful but the workers are few. Ask the Lord of the harvest, therefore, to send out workers into his harvest field."

☞ We are all in the numbers game, whether it is in church, TV audiences, votes cast or spectators at a game. We tend to be impressed by big numbers and large crowds. In the Gospels, Jesus was generally uneasy with crowds. He wasn't into the numbers game. Instead He saw the crowds who followed Him for what they were, confused and aimless. They were, in His words, "like sheep without a shepherd". Jesus reacted to the crowds with compassion, His heart went out to them. How we see and react to people is important for Jesus' followers. The numbers game is a non-starter; compassion, love in action is the name of the game.

✝ *Lord, help us to see people, through the eyes of Christ. Amen.*

♥ In 1934, David, the young Prince of Wales, was being shown 36 injured veterans of the 1st World War. He chatted to all that were shown to him. "But I have only seen 35 patients, nurse," he said. "I understood there were 36." He was informed that no one was allowed to see the remaining patient as he was hideously disfigured. The Prince insisted and with a white face and drawn lips he looked down on what had been a young man. The tears broke out and the Prince with lovely impulse bent down and reverently kissed the cheeks of the broken man.

The Prince of Glory, stooped far, far lower to kiss worse ugliness. There has never been a story to equal it.

9th January — Witness

📖 Acts 1: 8

"You will receive power when the Holy Spirit comes on you, and you will be my witness in Jerusalem, and in all Judea and Samaria and to

the ends of the earth."

☞ Our world is obsessed by power, be it political, financial, military, or personal. Power counts, for power gets things done. The first followers of Jesus were not powerful people. The promise of power made to them by their risen Master Jesus was power to achieve one thing. They would receive the gift of the Holy Spirit; their lives would be invaded by the presence of Jesus, in order that they would present Jesus to an unbelieving world.

The same Spirit invades our lives today and gives us power to witness, just as He did to Jesus and His first followers. What happened to them when they received the Holy Spirit? They turned the world upside down. All the political, financial and military power will not change lives. Only the presence of Jesus, in the power of the Spirit, through His people can achieve that. Now **there** is a powerful thought!

✝ *Come Holy Spirit, and breathe Your life into our powerless lives. Amen.*

♥ "I like your Christ but not your Christians because they are so unlike Christ." (Mahatma Ghandi.)

10th January **Witness**

📖 Acts 13 : 47

"For this is what the Lord has commanded us: "I have made you a light for the Gentiles, that you may bring salvation to the ends of the earth."

☞ It is often said that as one door closes, another opens. This truism seems to have been at work in the Acts of the Apostles. Here in the city of Antioch, Paul and Barnabas face a closed door in the shape of Jewish unbelief in the Gospel of Jesus Christ. God opens another door, as non-Jews, people like us, receive the word about the Lord Jesus.

With great irony, Luke recalls the words of the prophet Isaiah to God's people many centuries before. Their vocation is to be a light to all nations, that salvation would come to all people through them.

It's tragic when God's people in whatever age close the door on their vocation. It is a timely reminder that God has the key to open other doors.

✝ *Lord, forgive our unbelief and keep the door open. Amen.*

♥ In the new millennium, there will be two types of church; fortress church and pilgrim church. The fortress church will have its doors firmly closed to God and the world. Pilgrim church will have open doors, on the move with God, reaching out for Him, beyond the walls.

Ferran Glenfield

11th January — Good Works

📖 Micah 6 : 8

"He has showed you, O man, what is good. And what does the Lord require of you? To act justly and to love mercy and to walk humbly with your God."

☞ Easier to say than do. It's easier to do things for people than to listen to them; easier to give money than address the cause of their suffering; easier to buy flowers than share the housework; easier to talk about God than to walk with Him. Cheap glory, cheque book charity and superficial sympathy are just a few of the methods we humans use to escape the serious business of enjoying God. We must *abandon* our superficial worship; we must go deeper, trust more radically, and take more risks with our safety and less with our sanctification!

Our sin traps us in a web of complications: Longing for the way things were (which they weren't!); fearing all the things that *might* happen...Trapped in the past and the future, unable to live in the present.

God says: My grace is sufficient for you. Let us walk humbly with Him today.

✝ *Trustworthy One, like a little child, I put my hand in Yours: Feed me, lead me, protect me, teach me... as only You are able. Amen.*

♥ A donkey with its eyes open is wiser than a prophet with a closed mind. (Numbers 22 : 21-31)

12th January — Good Works

📖 Matthew 5 : 16

"In the same way, let your light shine before men, that they may see your good deeds and praise your Father in heaven."

☞ What we are, determines how we live. Our job as the church worldwide is to be God's people; that means we need to start acting like our Father in Heaven - loving people that hate us, giving generously to people that would steal from us, doing extra work cheerfully and unasked, even though it won't be appreciated. That's what God is like, so why aren't we? Afraid to be put upon, afraid we won't have enough for ourselves, afraid, in the end, that God can't or won't provide for us, when we take Him at His word, and start trusting Him.

Do you ever wonder why so few people take Christ seriously? What would happen if *we* took *H*im seriously? Certainly, some would nail us to a cross, offended at our liberty *not* to join the rat race, *not* to say the same platitudes we hear on TV. (Too much light shows up the dirt!) But others might realise for the first time that they have a choice to make: the kingdom of this world, or the Kingdom of God; darkness or light…and they might even praise the God they see in our love for one another.

What have we got to lose?

✝ *Shine, Jesus, shine! Fill this land with Your Father's glory. Fill our lives with Your Spirit of love, humility, wisdom, self-control, and peace, so that we bring your light to your world. Amen.*

♥ Half a candle doesn't give half a flame: but it won't give light half as long, or as steadily, if it's burning at both ends.

13th January — Good Works

📖 Ephesians 2 : 8 – 10

"For it is by grace you have been saved, through faith – and this not from yourselves, it is the gift of God – not by works, so that no one can boast. For we are God's workmanship, created in Christ Jesus to do

good works, which God prepared in advance for us to do."

☞ Faith is faithfulness. We live by what we really believe; and we believe the people we trust, we trust the people we love and we are faithful to them. Unfaithfulness is what happens when we stop believing or trusting or loving. God is never unfaithful; He always believes in us – in spite of our sin, in spite of always looking at ourselves and never learning to love another for his own sake - because God gives Himself to us. Now that's grace - a gift - generosity. Call it what you will; Jesus, the eternal Son of God, is God's gift to us, and we'd be mad not to appreciate it!

† *Loving Father, thank You for loving me, far more than I could know. I want to trust, believe and love You today. What good have You prepared for me to do? Will You give me all I need to do it? Amen.*

♥ The world's population divides into two types - depending on how I'm looking at them: for example, my garden is either occupied by a hoard of marauding invaders (on my self–centred days) or a friendly caravan park for touring snails (God's other wonderful creatures).

14th January — Good Works

📖 James 1 : 22

"Do not merely listen to the word, and so deceive yourselves. Do what it says."

☞ Bills arrive, needing to be paid, until eventually the bailiffs arrive, and find the pile of bills. There's no point in arguing. " Oh, but I've received all your demands for payment, and I read them all, even the small print!" There is a time for acting on what we read.

The good news is that the word of God tells us what we owe, but it also tells us that it has been paid. Jesus covered our debts when He paid with His life. But we would be fools to read that in the Bible, and then go on living under a burden of guilt, as if we might still have to pay. And we would be fools, too, having been told that our debt has been paid, to treat with contempt or indifference the person who paid. If there is Someone that generous, I want to know Him, to express my gratitude, and to offer my friendship to Him. I also want to learn from Him how to manage my affairs better, so I can live in credit like Him, instead of constantly running up new debts to be dealt with.

Let us learn to live LIFE to the full. Listen to the Word of God, and let Him come to life in all you are and do!

✝ *God, You made us, You know what's best for us, and You love us. Teach me to hear Your voice in the Bible, and to find joy in doing what You say. Amen.*

♥ A minister preached on the same passage of Scripture several weeks in a row. Eventually, a member of the congregation, concerned that the minister was becoming forgetful, plucked up the courage to challenge him: "Do you realise that is the fourth time you've preached that sermon. Is there not a whole Bible to choose from?" The minister replied, "I'll stop preaching on this passage when you start to put it into practice."

15th January — Good Works

James 2 : 26

"If anyone thinks he is religious and yet doesn't keep a tight rein on his tongue, he deceives himself and his religion is worthless."

☞ Training an animal means giving it exercise within boundaries, giving it good habits, and preventing it from developing bad ones. We train a horse not to panic in traffic, not to over-react to loud noises; we train it to carry its rider where the rider wants to go, at the right speed, and stopping in the right places. What if we were to train our *tongues* to serve us as faithfully? What we say can do harm or good; but we can learn . 1Corinthians 13 says, "If I speak in the tongues of men and of angels…but have not love, I am like a clanging gong or a crashing cymbal." Do you love anyone enough to tell them about Jesus?

The first Christians couldn't stop talking about Jesus. Most of us talk about what fills our lives: family and work - even soap operas, cars and football. But not Jesus. Why?

† *Christ above me, Christ below me, Christ beside me on my left and my right. Be in the heart of each to whom I speak, and in the mouth of each who speaks to me. Amen.*

♥ Keeping a rein on our tongue doesn't mean locking it in the stables! It needs healthy exercise – and discipline!

Cheryl Reid

16th January — Fellowship with the young

Acts 2 : 42

"They devoted themselves to the apostle's teaching and to fellowship, and the breaking of bread and to prayer."

☞ My first experience of a real sense of loneliness was as a student, right in the middle of New York, at Christmas. It was there that I realised in a new way that it is possible to be lonely, right in the middle of a crowd.

It's also possible to be lonely in church. One of the privileges, and one of the greatest opportunities that some of us have, is to minister to young people and students who are away from home, and who visit our churches.

Sometimes all they hear is 'the apostle's teaching' and no more. They do need teaching, but they need more.

We don't only need to share our belongings, as the early Christians often did; more often it's our friendship, our love, and sometimes maybe even a place at our tables that's needed more.

✝ *Heavenly Father, help me share not only all that I have with others but my time. Amen.*

♥ Religious education teacher asked her class to write a note to God. Here is a sample of what she got: -

Dear God, "Instead of letting people die and having to make new ones, why don't You just keep the ones You have?" - Johnny

17th January — Fellowship with the young

📖 II Corinthians 13 : 13

"All the saints send their greetings."

☞ Years ago, young people went to school, and then to college or university nearby, and often travelled daily from home. Now they travel far, and younger and younger step out from the home environment to study or earn a living.

Those early days away from home, sometimes living in poor conditions, can be desolate and lonely. If you know of any such, have you ever considered dropping a note to them, and letting them know you care? *'As cold water to a thirsty soul, so is good news from a far country.'* Proverbs 25 : 25

An effective pastoral ministry can be fulfilled without ever leaving your home, or even your bed, by sharing your love, and showing you care, in a letter, or just a card, or even an e-mail with chit- chat.

✝ *Lord, thank You that You are always near me. Amen.*

♥ Dear God, "Maybe Cain and Abel would not kill each other so much if they had their own rooms. It worked with my brother." - Larry

---

18th January — Fellowship with the young

📖 Philippians 1 : 3, 5

"I thank my God every time I remember you. Because of your partner-

ship in the Gospel."

☞ It's good to look back and remember the people who have helped us along the way in life; the people who loved us; the teachers who encouraged us; the people who showed kindness; and all those who showed patience and offered us opportunities in our earlier years.

Are there young people to whom you could show the same encouragement in turn? If there are, don't just think about it. Do it.

If you do, in years to come, they may thank God every time they remember you.

What a beautiful memorial that would be!

✝ *Heavenly Father, help me to encourage others as I have been encouraged. Amen.*

♥ Dear God, "If You watch me in Church on Sunday, I'll show You my new shoes." - Mickey

---

19th January — Fellowship with the young

📖 1 John 1 : 6 - 7

"If we claim to have fellowship with him, yet walk in the darkness, we lie and do not live by the truth. But if we walk in the light, as he is in the light, we have fellowship with one another. And the blood of Jesus Christ, his Son, purifies us from all sin."

☞ To be in the dark is to feel alone and vulnerable. If we close our eyes to others on the way, coming on different paths, we might as well walk in the dark.

If we open our eyes however, to greet whoever else is on the way, then just like Pilgrim in Pilgrim's Progress, we can enjoy the fellowship and friendship of God's other children, and one day be a part of the reunion of all the Father's family in heaven.

Up on the North coast, there is a group of clergy from all denominations, who meet together monthly, in each other's homes, for fellowship and Bible study. They call themselves 'Friends of the Way'.

We should all make a point of being 'friends of the way'.

✝ *Lord, thank You for the many friends I have met on my way. Please let me be a friend to others. Lord, protect me from walking in darkness. Amen.*

♥ Dear God, "I bet it is very hard for You to love everybody in the whole world. There are only 4 people in our family and I can never do it." – Nan.

20th January — Fellowship with the young

📖 Acts 2 : 44

"All the believers were together and had everything in common."

☞ It's lovely to be spoken to, and greeted in a strange place.

It's even more joyful to be spoken to and greeted as a visitor in a strange church. It doesn't always happen, even in a time of welcome and fellowship after worship.

Church members can be so engrossed with greeting each other. And sharing the latest news, and enjoying fellowship with each other, that the stranger can remain unnoticed on the sidelines.

More often the adults are greeted and made welcome, but the children are ignored. But young people are part of the church, too, and are among some of its most devoted believers. Isn't it good to have them with us also, and let them know we are glad to have them there?

The members of all the believers in a church is not complete unless the children are included; for of such is the kingdom of heaven.

✝ *Dear Father, open my eyes to the strangers I meet and may I always greet them as I would like to be greeted. Amen*

♥ Dear God, "I read the Bible. What does 'beget' mean? Nobody will tell me." – Love, Alison

Jim Frazer

21st January — The Word of God

📖 Isaiah 55 : 10 - 11

"As the rain and the snow come down from heaven, and do not return to it without watering the earth and making it bud and flourish, so that it yields seed for the sower and bread for the eater, so is my word that goes out from my mouth. It will not return to me empty, but will accomplish what I desire and achieve the purpose for which I sent it."

☞ The people of Israel were a dreadful disappointment to the Lord. He'd sent His love to them and given His promises, but time after time they failed Him, presuming on His goodness and love. The prophets were the men appointed by God to bring His word to them. Often there were harsh words to be said, but there was always a balance. The people many times had to suffer for their wrongdoing but God was never vindictive, and ultimately His purpose was to bless them. Isaiah's words sum that up. Whatever God has said will happen. There may initially be times when the people simply won't be able to take in what's going on but ultimately God's promises will bring the life He intended for the people, and others will have to admit that only Israel's God could do such a work.

✝ *Sovereign God, forgive me that so often I will not allow You to make me what You want me to be. Amen.*

♥ We've learned how to make a living but not a life; we've added years to life, not life to years.

22nd January — The Word of God

📖 John 14 : 26

"But the Counselor, the Holy Spirit, whom the Father will send in my name, will teach you all things and will remind you of everything I have said to you."

☞ Today I bought a strimmer to try and tidy my back garden. The machine is covered in little signs. I pulled out an instruction book to find it was written in languages I couldn't understand. What good is an instruction book you cannot understand! Impatience was on the verge of taking over when I looked at another booklet. It was written in

French, Italian, Spanish and ...English. What a relief! I was able to decipher the signs.

How good we've got a God, who understands us. Jesus' promise, given here to the disciples, became a reality when the Spirit came at Pentecost and achieved His purpose. Under His guidance the Bible was written and today He guides those who teach it as to how best to explain it to those who listen. He enables the listener to take and apply what is heard into their lives, so that they increasingly understand great truths about God and His love for His people in Christ.

✝ *Dear Father, let Your Holy Spirit teach me more and more. On my own I'm going to be in trouble. I need Him to guide me along the way. Amen.*

♥ If the me I live with were changed, it might be easier to live with me.

23rd January — The Word of God

📖 Colossians 3 : 16

"Let the word of Christ dwell in you richly as you teach and admonish one another with all wisdom, and as you sing psalms, hymns and spiritual songs with gratitude in your hearts to God."

☞ Paul is writing to young Christians, who are in danger of being misled by people teaching what could so easily be taken to be the truth. How are they to resist this? 'Use the Bible' is the apostle's advice. How? As a weapon to defend themselves against those, who would damage their faith?

That's not Paul's way. To have the 'word of Christ' in their lives needs teaching and correction. Paul makes it clear that it is not as negative as many might conceive it to be, as he couples it with singing, 'psalms, hymns and spiritual songs'. How is that to be done? With thanks to God for what He has done in our lives.

The Christian without this gratitude will seldom make much progress in the spiritual life. This will only happen when, in Michael Wilcock's words – ' the cross has to dominate your horizon'.

✝ *My Father, help me to see more clearly the love of the Lord Jesus for me. Help me to be a good learner, for Your glory. Amen.*

♥ The thesaurus suggests an alternative for 'admonish' as ' lay into'. I wonder if many of us practice that, rather than being encouraging and positive as we should.

24th January — Word of God

📖 2 Timothy 3 : 15 – 17

"...and how from infancy you have known the Holy Scriptures, which are able to make you wise for salvation through faith in Christ Jesus. All scripture is God-breathed and is useful for teaching, rebuking, correcting and training in righteousness, so that the man of God may be thoroughly equipped for every good work."

☞ What a privilege it was for Timothy to have a grandmother and mother such as he did. He was given a great start in life. He was taught the Scriptures. What a high opinion Paul had of them. He saw them as the bringer of God's word to His people. He was sure that the Bible was not simply a compilation of men's ideas. It came directly from God.

Vitally too he didn't use them as a topic for discussion but as central to the development of the life of this young man. Using them would shape him to be someone useful in the work of God's kingdom. Paul's concern was always for Christians to be 'well rounded', able to live in harmony with their Heavenly Father and with the other members of the Christian family and to present a message to those still not Christians, that would draw them to meet and know the Saviour.

✝ *Heavenly Father, thank You for the greatness of Your Book. I want its teaching to shape my life more and more each day. Amen.*

♥ When you're lonely and your friends are too busy even for a telephone call, remember God is by your side.

25th January — The Word of God

📖 Hebrews 4 : 12

"For the word of God is living and active. Sharper than any double-edged sword, it penetrates even to dividing soul and spirit, joints and marrow; it judges the thoughts and attitudes of the heart."

☞ The late G.B.Duncan spoke of many Christians seeing Christianity as a 'feather bed existence'. A friend once bought me a promise box for a present. The verses were always so positive I ultimately threw it out. I didn't want a Bible that only made me feel good. The writer of this letter to the Hebrews is emphatic that the Bible will never produce ' feather bed' Christians. It isn't a book to be used to help the Christian to settle down and have as their theme tune, 'Merrily we roll along'. No, it's like the surgeon who wants to get to the root of the problem, maybe causing pain as he does so, but all the time wanting to restore the patient to full health. The Bible has the answers for all the situations of life. It will strip away all our misconceptions but it will also help us be like Jesus.

✝ My *Father, I want to be like the Lord Jesus. Use Your Book to show me where I need to change and at the same time show me what potential there is in me when I give the Holy Spirit freedom to do His work. Amen.*

♥ 'For one look at yourself, take ten looks at Christ.' (Robert M. McCheyne)

Noel Agnew

26th January — Life and Death

📖 John 11: 1, 3, 5 - 6

"Now a man named Lazarus was sick. He was from Bethany, the village of Mary and her sister Martha...So the sisters sent word to Jesus, "Lord, the one you love is sick"... Jesus loved Martha and her sister and Lazarus. Yet when he heard that Lazarus was sick, he stayed where he was two more days."

☞ The ways of God are strange and mysterious. Being thrown into an empty well leads to Joseph becoming Governor of Egypt. Being good-looking leads Esther to save the Hebrew people from genocide. Being blind leads Samson to his greatest victory over his enemies. Being rich leads Joseph of Arimathea to give his sepulchre to the crucified

Christ. Being poor leads the widow by the treasury in the temple to becoming the epitome of how God views giving. Christ's refusing to respond immediately to Mary and Martha's call to come and see their sick brother leads to the greatest of Christ's miracles.

We want the Lord to respond immediately to our calls, don't we? When will we ever learn that not only does prayer change things, prayer changes us! It teaches us to be patient. It teaches us over and over again that things are not always as they seem. You may be on the verge of the greatest time of your life but at this precise moment you would argue that this is the worst time of your life. Take heart. What often seems worst is best.

✝ *Lord, when things seem so dark...help me to trust in You for the coming of the dawn. Amen.*

♥ In Genesis He is the Seed of the Woman, In Exodus the Passover Lamb, in Leviticus, the High Priest, in Numbers the City of Refuge, In Deuteronomy, the Prophet like Moses, in Joshua, the Captain of Salvation and in Judges the Deliverer.

27th January — Life and Death

📖 John 11: 14-15

"So then he told them plainly, "Lazarus is dead, and for your sake I am glad I was not there, so that you may believe. But let us go to him."

☞ Why did our Lord have to go to Bethany in person to raise Lazarus from the dead? Did not the Saviour save the nobleman's son by healing him from a distance? In this miracle the Lord deliberately stayed where He was until Lazarus died.

Why, then, did He have to go to Bethany in person? Because the rest of the New Testament teaches that when it comes to the resurrection of the dead our Lord will remain on His throne and speak the word and summon the dead to arise. Note carefully the words of Paul in 1Thessalonians 4:1; "For the Lord Himself will descend from Heaven with a shout, with the voice of the archangel, and with the trumpet of God, and the dead in Christ will rise first." Every move Christ made in the miracle of the raising of Lazarus from the dead was filled with signs for us all. Again, note that the sign of Christ to believers in the raising of Lazarus is teaching us that if we die in Christ He will, at His second calling, raise our bodies in person. Coming to Bethany in person was the portent of the next great event that millions of Christians are waiting for. Even so Come, Lord Jesus!

✝ *Help me to live, as if You were coming back today. Amen.*

♥ In Ruth, He is the Redeemer, in Samuel, David's Greater Son, in Kings and Chronicles, the Reigning King, in Ezra, our Faithful Scribe, in Nehemiah, the Rebuilder.

28th January — Life and Death

📖 John 11: 20-22

"When Martha heard that Jesus was coming, she went out to meet him: "Lord", Martha said to Jesus. "If you had been here, my brother would not have died. But I know that even now God will give you whatever you ask."

☞ There is a strange mixture of emotions in Martha's statement.

There is a touch of scolding that seems to blame the Lord for being late. There is very deep faith that believed that Christ could certainly heal. There is absolute confidence that if Jesus asks His Father to raise Lazarus from the dead, the prayer would be answered. There is a touch of forgetfulness that Christ did not need to be present to heal. There is also an element of deep love and awe for Christ because Martha called Him Lord.

Are you having a day of mixed emotions? You are perhaps frustrated, even angry. You are, nevertheless, deeply devoted to the Lord but are forgetful that He has, as the man said, "Not brought you across the Atlantic to drown you in a ditch." So, in the flood of mixed emotions swamping you today, try not fall into a pining for what might have been. What good does it do? If God's will has been done, submit to it. In acceptance lies peace.

✝ *Help me know that in all things God works for the good of those who love Him, who have been*
Called according to His purpose. Amen.

♥ In Esther, He is our Mordecai. In Job He is the True Comforter, in Psalms our Shepherd, in the Proverbs our Wisdom, in Solomon the Bridegroom, in Isaiah the Prince of Peace, in Jeremiah the Righteous Branch. In Lamentations He is the Weeping Prophet.

29th January — Life and Death

📖 John 11: 43 – 44

"Jesus called in a loud voice "Lazarus, come out!" The dead man came out, his hands and feet wrapped with strips of linen, and a cloth

around his face. Jesus said to them, "Take off the grave clothes and let him go."

☞ The greatness of this miracle cannot possibly be exaggerated. Here is a man four days dead who is restored to life in a second. Here is a Christ who not only has absolute power over the world of spirits in that He calls a soul back from Paradise to join it again to its owner's body, not only has power over death itself, but has power over decomposition. No matter where bodies are buried or cremated, no matter in how many far-flung places, no matter under what conditions, the voice that called Lazarus will call them and put their bodies and souls together. No corruption or flame can finally separate them from resurrection. The resurrection of Lazarus is but a pale reflection of that coming resurrection. Lazarus was raised to face further sorrow but believers will be raised 'incorruptible and we shall be changed' (1 Corinthians 15:25). Our friends may bring us to the grave and leave us there, but God will not.

✝ *Lord, I praise You for the gift of life, and more, for the gift of eternal life. Amen.*

♥ In Ezekiel, He is the Four Faced Man, in Joel the Baptiser, in Amos our Burden Bearer, in Obadiah He is the One mighty to save. In Jonah He is the Compassionate One, in Micah the Messenger with beautiful feet, in Nahum the Avenger.

30th January — Life and Death

📖 John 16 : 2-3

"Jesus said, "They will put you out of the synagogue; in fact, a time is coming when anyone who kills you will think he is offering a service to

God. They will do such things because they have not known the Father or me."

☞ I sat one day with Gerald Grosvenor, the Duke of Westminster, in his office at Eaton Hall near Chester interviewing him about his life and times. It was an absolutely fascinating conversation. It turned to spiritual things and, as a soldier; he pointed out something I had never known before. "Every German soldier in the Second World War," he said, "carried a slogan on his belt, which stated, God is with us." He then went on to point out that more atrocities have been carried out in the name of God than anything else.

He is right. Jesus pointed out that people would be so twisted they would kill some of His followers and think they did God a service. They mistakenly think they have a monopoly of truth and would kill to preserve it. The curse of such thinking is still with us. "It is," said Abraham Lincoln, "not so important that God is on our side as it is that we are on His."

✝ *Forgive me for expecting You to be on my side, Lord, instead of me on Yours. Amen.*

♥ In Habakkuk, He is the Reviver. In Zephaniah the Saviour, in Haggai the Restorer. In Zechariah the Opened Fountain, in Malachi the Son of Righteousness. **And that's only the Old Testament.**

Derick Bingham

31st January — Conversion

📖 Matthew 18 : 3

"Jesus said, " I tell you the truth, unless you are converted and

become like little children, you will never enter the Kingdom of Heaven."

☞ You want to go to heaven? A noble aspiration and one obtainable for all who, in the words of Jesus are 'converted'.

But how are we converted? In placing a little child in the forefront of the disciples Jesus was teaching all would-be disciples the need for humility and trust.

To think like a child for adults with some degree of intellectual ability is a humbling process. To trust with child - like faith goes beyond our human limitations and an acceptance that God alone can supply that power to trust.

The widowed mother of James and John (Matthew 20 : 21) and indeed all the disciples (Luke 22:24) in wanting pre-eminence in Heaven were behaving quite the opposite of being child-like, they were being child-ish. Jesus wants us to trust Him today for our Salvation and eternal security. We are required to humble ourselves, confess our inadequacy and throw ourselves down at His feet in trust and obedience. In other words to be converted from sin and self to Christ and His Kingdom.

✝ *Lord, today in Your mercy, save me. Help me to trust in a child–like way and deliver me from behaving childishly. For Christ's sake Amen.*

♥ He who marries the spirit of the age soon becomes a widower.

FEBRUARY

This illustration of Barnacle Geese is from a wood engraving, original size 3″ x 4″. It is based on a number of pencil sketches drawn in Ward Park, Bangor, Co. Down, where these wild birds, flying freely at will, overwintered for several years in succession.

In the engraving they are depicted in a Strangford Lough setting.

1st February — Conversion

📖 Luke 22 : 32

"But I have prayed for you, Simon, that your faith may not fail. And when you have turned back, strengthen your brothers."

☞ Immediately after the breaking of bread in the Upper Room, the master started to warn Peter as to the problem that lay ahead of him and the rest of the disciples, starting that very day. Jesus calls the disciple "Simon", not (until verse 34) Peter, the rock. The repetition in v.31 - "Simon, Simon, behold (or take note)", emphasises the deep concern Jesus had for Simon Peter and all disciples. Watch out for Satan!

Peter was about to fall and deny Jesus and the Lord charged Simon Peter after he had been restored
(Converted or returned to Jesus) that he had a job to do.

Simon's fall was bad. He was headstrong and impetuous yet, when he returned to Jesus, he was to use his bitter experience of failure to strengthen and win others for Christ.

A person, who has gone into the depths of sin and then tasted the forgiveness of God, will speak first hand of their experience.

Its only when we have been truly converted (turned around) that we will be able to minister to others. Now is that not worth thinking about?

✝ *Help me dear Father not only to resist the Devil but trust in Your might and strength to do so. For Your glory and my ultimate good, Amen*

♥ A little girl saw a donkey with its head over a fence. She walked over to the donkey and said, "Don't be sad, my Aunt has religion too." Smile, the joy of the Lord is your strength!

2nd February — Conversion

Acts 26 : 18

"......Turn from darkness to light and from the power of Satan to God, so that they may receive forgiveness of sins and a place among those who are sanctified by faith in me."

☞ The Apostle Paul is here bearing witness to the saving and keeping power of Jesus Christ, to King Agrippa. With clear-cut conviction he first tells of his conversion experience on the road to Damascus. Then he recounts the commission he personally received from the risen Christ to go and tell the good news to the Gentiles.

This good news is still the same today for all mankind. The forgiveness of sins was and is available upon repentance and faith in Jesus Christ. D.L. Moody said, "Man is born with his back toward God. When he repents, he turns right around and faces God." Repentance is a change of mind followed by a change of behaviour. Have you repented and trusted in Christ Jesus? A man said to me " If I am going to hell at least most of my friends will be there." Later in private he confessed he was afraid, "scared to die". There is no fear for the believer. (Titus 3:5.) It has been said, "They slumber sweetly whom faith rocks to sleep." Are you resting today in Him?

✝ *Thank You Father for the assurance given that we who are redeemed by God's mercy have the imparted righteousness of Christ. Amen.*

♥ Count sheep? Why count sheep when you can count blessings! A Christian once said, "I guess I must have rolled, tossed and fretted for a full 3 seconds before I fell asleep".

3rd February — Conversion

1 Thessalonians 1: 9

"They tell us how you turned to God from idols to serve the Living and True God."

There it is - that same thought of turning to God (Conversion) which runs all through the Bible. Paul's letter to the young church at Thessalonica praises God for the faith exhibited by the newly born Christians, how they were good examples throughout all Macadonia, Achaia and even further afield.

Being 'born again' is like that. True conversion by repenting and trusting in Christ Jesus alone for a new life will inevitably call us to witness for Him by the words we say and the quality of the lives we live. Both are essential for witnessing. The early believers turned their thoughts and lives to the whole country. What about our life and witness? Is it bringing glory and honour to God? Do we really trust in Him? Remember that there is a God. Indeed as Voltaire wrote, "If there is no God, it would be necessary to invent Him". Trust Him today and keep trusting as we work and witness for Him.

Help me dear Lord to be more aware of my responsibilities to You and Your cause and to leave the rest of my every day affairs of life to Your care and control. Amen.

When life becomes all snarled up, offer it up to our Lord and let Him untie the knots.

4th February Conversion

📖 1 Peter 2 : 25.

"You were like sheep going astray, but now you have returned to the Shepherd and Overseer of your souls."

☞ These are sentiments of great comfort to all believers. They are fitting words reflecting not just our history or past lives as unbelievers but where we are today and the goal towards which we are expected to travel.

The sheep metaphor reminds me of the back lanes and hillside paths of North Antrim where I live. There to be seen any day are the stray sheep which are not where they should be. They are outside the fence trying to get in, illustrating my spiritual condition fifty years ago. A lost sheep looking in at the Christian way of Life. I was found and brought into God's fold when I told God I was sorry for my sins , abandoned my self–life and turned in believing faith to Jesus. Oh what a day that was. Knowing the burden of sin rolling away. Assured in my heart and mind that now I was a child of God through faith in Christ alone. Do you know anything about this experience? Do you travel alone or do you travel with him, to Glory?

✝ *Forgive me for going my own way in life, dear God. By Your spirit give me grace to turn to You and to trust You for all eternity. Amen.*

♥ If you would master temptation, you must first let Christ master you.

Brian Kingsmore

5th February — Hospitality

Hebrews 13 : 2

"Do not forget to entertain strangers, for by so doing some people have entertained angels without knowing it."

☞ In Middle Eastern countries hospitality to strangers has always been a priority. This was especially true for the Old Testament people of God. 'For you ,too, were once strangers in the land of Egypt' (Deuteronomy 10 : 9) Today's verse tells us of Abraham's hospitality to two unexpected visitors who turned out to be messengers from God. As Christians we have a special responsibility to open our homes to those who are 'strangers', especially those who are far from home. Perhaps not angels, but how many overseas students or medical personnel, now in leading positions in their own country, came to Christ through the warmth of Christian hospitality when they were 'aliens and strangers' to our shores?

✝ *Lord, thank You that You come to us as strangers and bring us into Your family. May we show that same welcome to others. Amen.*

♥ Enjoying the warmth of Arab hospitality as a visitor to the Middle East, I was offered particularly strong Turkish coffee, which I just couldn't drink. Not wanting to offend my hostess I waited till she left the room and poured the coffee onto a nearby plant. On her return she immediately refilled my cup. I discovered that to empty your cup or plate is a polite request for seconds!

6th February Hospitality

📖 Luke 10 : 39 - 40

"Mary sat at the Lord's feet listening to what he said. But Martha was distracted by all the preparations that had to be made. She came to him and asked, "Lord, don't you care that my sister has left me to do the work myself? Tell her to help me!"

☞ Jesus visits the home of two good friends, sisters Mary and Martha. They loved Him dearly and were delighted that He dropped in to break His journey. I feel for Martha, for I would be just like her, fussing in the kitchen, trying to make a very special meal for a very special visitor. She was fuming for, instead of helping with the preparations, her sister was in the front room chatting with Him. Jesus gently reminds her that what He really looked forward to on this short visit, was time to chat.

A good meal, no matter how simple, takes time to prepare, but the lesson here is that at heart 'hospitality' is opening the door to friendship and fellowship, and not to a show case home or cordon bleu cookery. Maybe we need to scale down our elaborate plans that make us 'fuss in the kitchen', so that we can give our time and ourselves to those we welcome into our home.

✝ *Lord; help me to make the right choices about how I spend my time and energy in the home. Help me to put people first. Amen.*

♥ The difference between 'entertaining' and 'hospitality'? Hospitality meets the needs of the guest, entertaining serves the reputation of the host!

7th February — Hospitality

📖 1 Peter 4 : 9

"Offer hospitality to one another without grumbling."

☞ An American evangelist was preaching in small village communities in the South American Andes. He arrived late one night, exhausted and looking forward to a good meal at the home of the local pastor. He was welcomed in, seated at the table and the pastor's wife brought in a small boiled egg on a plate and set it before him. He waited, wondering if this was all he was getting. As the rest of the family didn't seem to be joining him he enquired of his hostess. She answered vaguely that they would be eating later. No more food arrived and he felt inwardly angry. Then it dawned on him: this small egg was all the food they had, and they had given it to him! He asked the family to join him as he sliced the egg in six, and wept as he led them in a prayer of thanksgiving.

Here was costly hospitality such as he had never experienced.

✝ *Help me to be generous in my hospitality, not always thinking about the cost. Amen.*

♥ The art of hospitality is making people feel at home when you wish they were!

8th February — Hospitality

📖 Luke 14 : 16

"Jesus replied, "A certain man was preparing a great banquet and invited many guests."

☞ Jesus likens God's offer of salvation to a host welcoming His guests to a great dinner party with lovely things to eat. The invitation was not limited to the 'right sort' of people. In fact, many were in no position to return the invitation. The only condition was to wear appropriate dress, and even this was supplied.

Surely generosity should be **the** mark of the Christian, not from duty, but an overflowing sense of gratitude to the God who welcomes us into His family and eternal home. Someone has said "Hospitality is walking with Jesus, responding to friend and stranger alike with the compassion, forgiveness, acceptance and extravagant love with which we have been blessed".

Freely you have received freely give.

✝ *Thank You God for Your great kindness to me. Amen*

♥ After we said grace at the meal table, our young visitor piped up "We do that in our house too – But only when we have visitors!"

9th February Hospitality

📖 Matthew 25 : 35 - 36

"For I was hungry and you gave me something to eat, I was thirsty and you gave me something to drink, I was a stranger and you invited me in. I needed clothes and you clothed me. I was sick and you looked after me, I was in prison and you came to visit me."

☞ Jesus is not teaching that we will get to heaven by doing good, but that the mark of true faith is practical kindness shown to His brothers. What's more, to neglect to show hospitality is to neglect Christ Himself and deny the Gospel of grace. We seldom consider cooking meals, washing dishes and making beds as the really spiritual work of the church. Jesus reminds us that true faith is demonstrated in the smallest kindness and in it we express our love for Him. It is as simple as that! We don't need to be a good cook; we don't even need a home. Our 'cup of cold water' could be a telephone call, a cup of coffee and a listening ear; our 'prison visit' to someone confined by illness, depression or loneliness.

✝ *Lord, show me in what practical way I can love and serve You today. Amen.*

♥ The wine waiter approached a group of Presbyterian clergy dining together after a synod meeting. "Would you like to order some wine?" There was an embarrassed silence until the Clerk said: "Oh, no thank you, we're Presbyterians, we don't drink in front of each other...."

Sandra Woodside

10th February — Friendship

📖 Psalm 25 : 4

"Show me your ways, O Lord; teach me your paths."

☞ We pitched camp late at night. Woke at dawn and set off to climb one of the snow-covered peaks above the Drumochter pass in Scotland. After an hour we met other walkers coming down saying the weather was getting worse up top. We pressed on. The rain of the valley gave way to snow higher up. The wind pushed it hard into our faces. Having reached the summit it was time to turn back. But which way was back? The weather was worse, we couldn't see more than 5 metres ahead. My friend took out his map and compass and led me out of the lostness of the white-out. The small magnetic compass needle and his skill gave me the comfort of knowing which way to head home.

Christ shares our humanity, He has dwelt in our midst so that we might know His pathway out of our lostness and walk home with Him to the Father.

✝ *Lord give me Your direction each day and help me stay on the track. Amen.*

♥ On a very cold, snowy Sunday, only the pastor and one farmer arrived at the country church. The pastor said, "Well, I guess we won't have a service today?". The farmer replied. "If even only one cow shows up at feeding time, I give it food!" The minister gave him the full 25 minutes sermon. The farmer left disgruntled, "I said I would give it food … but not the whole lot for all the herd!"

11th February — Friendship

📖 Proverbs 27 : 6

"Wounds from a friend can be trusted, but an enemy multiplies kisses."

☞ "Rick! Your shirt does not go with those trousers!" – You can always rely on a friend to tell when you look ridiculous. "Are those grey hairs?" – You can always rely on a friend to identify what you would like to ignore. "Rick, you are putting on weight?" – You can always rely on a friend to tell you what you would rather not hear. "Rick, I have been hearing good reports about you" – You can always rely on a colleague, who is looking for something, to butter you up just before the big ask.

Real friends will tell it like it seems to them; hopefully they will do it gracefully! You will not hear them flatter you. Praise will have a more lasting effect, as will a cautionary note. Trust is the key. My friends tell me I have a poor dress sense, I am going grey, and in danger of middle age spread. They are right. Maybe there is still time... I am wary of flattery!

✝ *Thank You for my honest, loving friends and the difference that they make to my life! Amen.*

♥ When you tell a secret; it may go in one ear and then in another, and then in another...

12th February Friendship

📖 Matthew 11 : 19

"The Son of Man came eating and drinking, and they say, "Here is a glutton and a drunkard, a friend of tax collectors and sinners". But wisdom is proved right by her actions."

☞ "That is her husband," I was told, "You know of course that she married beneath herself." I listened but could only see a man. Yes, his background and hers were not similar, but this marriage was better than the advice I had just been given. Their love shone through! She grew ill and his love shone brighter still! She died and his love shone through his loss.

She married well, and the woman who engaged me with her 'helpful' advice revealed that she had said something that ought to have been beneath her. Where the wisdom lay was proved right in actions! Everything Jesus did was beneath Him – it was for us. To Him we are all the same. His love still shines through!

✝ *Lord Jesus thank You that You love all of us sinners. Amen.*

♥ Let the wife make the husband glad to come home, and let him make her sorry to see him leave. (Martin Luther)

13th February — Friendship

📖 John 15 : 13

"Greater love has no –one than this, that he lay down his life for his friends."

☞ "O.K. lets get two Captains to pick teams for football." I remember the dread that I used to have that I was going to be picked last – I was one of the smallest boys in first year and not a footballer! If one of my friends were chosen to pick teams then I would be ok. I mightn't be first choice, but I wouldn't be last – the one nobody really wanted. I remember the relief at being chosen by a friend. I remember making sure to choose that person when it was my turn to pick teams.

The message of the Gospel does not leave us with the dread of being unwanted, or accepted reluctantly. We are chosen. Jesus is the friend who has given everything to us. He has come to make God known to us as our Father. He's not accepting us reluctantly. He has given His life to demonstrate what we are worth to Him. He is serious about the choice! Good news now, no dread! I'm chosen!

✝ *Lord thank You for revealing that the Father has chosen me! Amen.*

♥ Sign on church notice board; The Low Self-Esteem Support Group will meet next Thursday at 7pm – 8.30pm. Please use the small entrance at the back of the church.

14th February — Friendship

📖 1 Peter 4 : 8

"Above all, love each other deeply, because love covers over a multitude of sins."

☞ The roast was marked down in price; being a thrifty student I bought it and set about cooking dinner. My fiancée arrived and the meal was served. Beef in a mysterious sauce. Years later my wife still laughs about that roast beef or was it leather? Why was beetroot in the sauce? She reminds me that I froze some of it and served her more on another occasion!

I am glad that her love still does not depend on my cooking. We can laugh together about the humorous things, cry over the painful things, work hard at the important things and decide on those things that don't matter. Love puts things into perspective! Christ's love is self–giving, life-giving, sin–covering. He gives us His love's perspective.

✝ *Thank You that I am Your beloved. Amen.*

♥ Don't question your wife's judgement – look whom she married!

Richard Hill

15th February — Anger

📖 Ephesians 4: 26 - 27,31

"In your anger do not sin. Do not let the sun go down while you are still angry, and do not give the devil a foothold. Get rid of all bitterness, rage and anger, brawling and slander, along with every form of malice."

☞ Anger is not necessarily a sin, but it's hard not to sin when we're angry. We know that anger itself is not a sin because the Bible is full of instances where we read about God's anger, the story of Jesus cleansing the Temple is a good example. There are times when it is right for us to be angry about the cruelty, injustice and neglect that we see all around us. However, it takes special grace to be able to deal properly with our anger. One important thing is that we must not allow it to fester. Issues that are not dealt with give the devil opportunity to lead us into sin. Unresolved anger easily turns into bitter rage.

✝ *Lord, if there's something that has made me angry today, grant me the grace to see it resolved before the sun goes down. Amen.*

♥ The anger of today is the remorse of tomorrow.

16th February **Anger**

📖 James 1: 19 - 20.

"My dear brothers, take note of this: Everyone should be quick to listen, slow to speak and slow to become angry, for man's anger does not bring about the righteous life that God desires."

☞ We noticed yesterday, that anger itself is not necessarily a sin for there are times when God Himself is angry.

However, as this verse tells us, human anger and God's anger are often very different. Rarely, does human anger produce something that is good. For this reason, we should be slow to anger, and instead make every effort to listen and to understand the other's point of view. It is often the case that when we take time to listen and understand there is no reason to be angry.

✝ *Lord, please help me today to be quick to listen and slow to become angry. Amen.*

♥ I have noticed that sometimes the speed at which we do things is significant. When my young daughters are going to do something mischievous, they can move at a tremendous rate, but when they are being obedient they move at a snail's pace.

17th February **Anger**

📖 Proverbs 14 : 29

"A patient man has great understanding, but the quick-tempered man displays folly."

☞ The writer of these Proverbs is known as a man of great wisdom. He must also have been a man of great patience who learned to control his temper. How many of us have got ourselves into trouble because we have jumped to the wrong conclusions in a fit of temper. Mr. Angry is also very often Mr. Foolish.

✝ *Lord; grant that today my temper will be overcome by patience, so that I might display understanding rather than folly. Amen.*

♥ Thomas Jefferson said, "When angry, count ten before you speak If very angry, count a hundred."

18th February — Anger

📖 Matthew 5 : 21-22

"You have heard that it was said to the people long ago, "Do not murder, and anyone who murders will be subject to judgement. But I tell you that anyone who is angry with his brother will be subject to judgement..."

☞ In the Sermon on the Mount, Jesus reapplies some important Old Testament Commandments. He deals with the attitudes and intentions of the heart and not simply with the external actions. The Pharisees said that righteousness consisted of performing certain actions, but Jesus said that it is centered in the attitudes of the heart. If we allow anger to become hatred against our brother then we have already broken the spirit of the sixth Commandment. This does not mean that we should go ahead and murder him anyway, since we already sinned inwardly. Obviously, sinful feelings are not excuses for sinful deeds. Sinful anger must be faced honestly and confessed to God as sin.

† *Lord, forgive me for the anger that has led to hatred of my brother or sister, and give me the grace to deal with its cause. Amen.*

♥ Anger is just one letter short of danger.

19th February — Anger

📖 1 Corinthians 13 : 5

"Love...It is not rude, it is not self-seeking, it is not easily angered, it keeps no record of wrongs."

☞ The chief antidote to anger is love. The word 'easily' is interesting, because it underlines again for us that anger is not always wrong. The anger Jesus felt that day in the Temple came from a heart that loved His Father and felt the disgrace that the traders brought to His Father's name. John tells us that before driving the traders out, Jesus made a whip out of cords, something that clearly took some time. His response was carefully considered. Jesus was angered, but not easily so, He didn't just 'fly off the handle'. We too, must allow the love of God to control us, so that we are not easily angered. This should be our pattern of life in the world, in the church, and perhaps most difficult of all, in the home.

† *Lord, may my life demonstrate the love that is not easily angered. Amen.*

♥ People who fly into a rage always make a bad landing.

Dave Clements

20th February — The Church

📖 1 Corinthians 12 : 27

"Now you are the body of Christ and each one of you a part of it."

☞ At the end of His time on earth Jesus left the first disciples to ascend to heaven. He left them His ministry. From now on the ministry of the risen Lord Jesus could be carried out by His new body the Church, in the power of His Spirit.

This is a wonderful privilege yet an awesome responsibility. We need God's grace to find our role in the body of Christ and each one of us has a God-given role. We also need His power to carry it out as we work with others in His body, the Church.

From now on we are the hands, the feet, the voice, the heart of Christ. May others see something of Christ in us when they encounter us as His body.

✝ *Lord, help us become a united, living and loving Body to reflect Your nature. Amen.*

♥ Would your congregation pass a Spiritual Fitness test as the Body of Christ?

21st February — The Church

📖 Revelation 21 : 2

"I saw the Holy City; the New Jerusalem, coming down out of heaven from God ,prepared as a bride beautifully dressed for her husband."

☞ The Bible uses many striking word pictures to help us understand the nature of the Church. The 'body' picture reminds us of our vital role in the ministry of Christ. Now the Church as the 'Bride' reminds us of the love God has for it ,and the love we should have for Him.

It is the most intimate portrait of the Church. John in his wonderful vision of heaven sees the Church as the perfect bride for God's Son.

In the Old Testament, Israel as the Bride of God was called to a relationship marked by faithfulness, devotion and love.

Surely these qualities should still be the hallmarks of the Church today as the Bride of Christ. It portrays a relationship of intimacy and commitment that is one of the great privileges of Christian faith.

✝ *Forgive us O Lord for our unfaithfulness in thought, word and deed. Amen.*

♥ If the Church is the Bride of Christ, are we true to our vows?

22nd February — The Church

📖 Ephesians 2 : 21

"In him the whole building is joined together and rises to become a holy temple in the Lord."

☞ In the New Testament and particularly in the writings of Paul the focus is usually on the Church as the people not the building.

Even here the building is not one of bricks and mortar but of people. People who as they are joined together in fellowship became the place where God now lives.

In the Old Testament, God's special dwelling place was the temple in Jerusalem. Now with the death and resurrection of Christ, He dwells in all His glory where people meet together in His name.

We are now the Temple! John Stott in one of his books says that in the Old Testament God was tied to the holy places whereas in the New Testament he is tied to holy people. Is our Church life fit to be a place, where as one translator puts it, God by His Spirit can 'feel at home'?

✝ *Lord make us a people where You can dwell and feel at home. Amen.*

♥ The Church is a building always under construction.

23rd February — The Church

1 Timothy 3 : 15

"If I am delayed you will know how people ought to conduct themselves in God's household, which is the church of the living God, the pillar and foundation of the truth."

☞ One of the most wonderful changes that happen when a person puts their faith in Christ is that they become a member of a new family, the family or household of God.

Before we were outsiders, strangers, even seen as slaves to sin. Now we are sons and daughters with God as our Heavenly Father.

As members of the family of God we need to ask God's help to reflect the family likeness and to conform to the family's new code of behaviour.

We also need to learn how to relate to one another in the Church not solely as fellow members but as brothers and sisters in Christ.

The family ties of the Church of Christ are eternal so let us learn on earth how to love one another!

✝ *Our Father in heaven we thank You for the privilege of being able to know Your fatherly love and care. Amen.*

♥ You can choose your friends but you cannot choose your family!

24th February — The Church

1 Peter 2 : 9 - 10

"But you are a chosen people, a royal priesthood ,a holy nation, a people belonging to God, that you may declare the praises of him who called you out of darkness into his wonderful light. Once you were not a people, but now you are the people of God..."

☞ Today in our society there seems to be a lack of belonging, a loss of identity among many people.

As a follower of Christ I have been given a new identity as well as a new family. I am now a member of God's people.

This is the purpose of God right through scripture. To have a people, a community who owe their allegiance to Him alone. The famous Old Testament verse, "I will be their God and they will be my people," emphasises this covenant relationship.
He called the Israelites from Egypt and made them His people. He calls us in Christ to make us His people today.

One of the problems the Children of Israel had was that they were tempted to compromise their allegiance to the Lord. Today that temptation still remains, particularly in Ireland, where only Christ can have our total allegiance.

It is a wonderful gift of God's grace to be part of His people, the church. In an era where so many people feel isolated, let us learn how to show the tremendous sense of belonging that is part and parcel of the People of God.

✝ *Lord thank You for calling me into Your community. May my behaviour be worthy of that calling. Amen.*

♥ I'm so glad that the Church is not perfect, for if it were I could not be a member of it. (Richard Wurmbrand)

Doug Bradley

25th February — Avoiding Sin

Genesis 2 : 8-9

"Now the Lord God had planted a garden in the east, in Eden... In the middle of the garden were the tree of life and the tree of the knowledge of good and evil."

☞ The human story begins with two fruit trees. One produced *life* in the unimaginable beauty of a world where God and man were in close intimacy and every longing of his heart was fulfilled. The other bore the bitter fruit of an impoverished existence, where evil is mixed in with good, where dreams never come true, and life always ends in *death*.

We're still faced with the same two trees. And it's a matter of belief. Are the things I long for found in a relationship with God, or will I listen to another voice that says *'Pssst! Over here! Don't listen to God. I have what you're really looking for'*. Millions realise too late that Satan doesn't deliver what he promises; he has nothing at all but death and destruction. Sin is a great deal more than breaking God's law; it's spurning His invitation to feast on His love. We're on the way home when we realise that the 'goodies' are all back in our Father's house.

✝ *Father, I'm sorry I've been looking for life in all the wrong places. I want to come home. Amen.*

♥ Adam pointed to the Garden of Eden: "We used to live in there, son, but your mother ate us out of the place."

26th February Avoiding Sin

📖 Revelation 18 : 2; 21: 10

"Fallen! Fallen is Babylon the Great!... And the angel carried me away in the Spirit to a mountain great and high, and showed me the Holy City, Jerusalem, coming down out of heaven from God."

☞ The frenzied semi-clad dancers whirled in the hot night below the Citadel of David. The TV's Eurovision commentator sounded apocalyptic: 'This is more like Old Babylon than Old Jerusalem.'

The Bible is a story of Two cities. The precious building materials for the first were buried in Eden – gold, precious stones and pearls (Genesis 2: 11-12). They symbolise the values of God's kingdom, the 'Jesus' actions and attitudes from which He is building a wonderful new society, the 'bride' of Christ, the New Jerusalem. That 'city' is fashioned from Eden's treasures – foundations and walls of precious stones, streets of gold and pearly gates! The second city is Babylon, symbolising the world's system as it opposes God. It is built from baser materials: pride, selfishness, self–righteous religion and sinful choices. But terrible destruction awaits Babylon. When God's people 'lived Jerusalem', they were blessed; when they 'lived Babylon' they became captives there. It's still the same, Every deed and word in Jesus' Name is a *Jerusalem choice* and is a building block in the eternal city. Every sinful act is a *Babylon choice* in a doomed city. Choose carefully which city you build today.

✝ *Lord, lift me up to a high mountain and help me glimpse the beauty of Your new society. Fill me with Your Spirit today so that I may make Jesus- choices that last forever. Amen.*

♥ The old song says: ' Dublin can be heaven...there's diamonds in the lady's eyes and gold dust in her hair.' Bring a little bit of heaven's gold and jewels to your town today.

27th February Avoiding Sin

📖 Genesis 2 : 10

"A river watering the garden flowed from Eden; from there it was separated into four headwaters."

☞ The rising voice of Martin Luther King gripped the downtrodden crowd: "'There is a river, the streams whereof make glad the city of God!' (Psalm 46 : 4)". The life-giving river began in Eden where God walked with man. When sin had made of life a parched wasteland, God repeatedly promised a coming day when He would pour out His Spirit like a refreshing river. (Isaiah 44 : 3; Ezekiel 47; Zechariah 14 : 8). The Jews expected the river of God's Spirit to spring up at Jerusalem's temple, which they regarded as 'the belly of the earth.'

The rising voice of Jesus the King gripped the downtrodden crowd. "If anyone is thirsty, let him come to me and drink...for out of his belly will flow rivers of living waters!" It was the feast of Tabernacles and the priests were at that very moment reading out the passages about the longed for river. Jesus was offering people the Spirit (John 7 : 37 – 39). Without the filling of the Spirit, sin easily overwhelms us and all we have is the shell of a religion with no power. In the New Jerusalem, the river of life (the Spirit) flows through the City from God's throne.

Jerusalem people are not just those who believe certain truths; they are those who are immersed in the Spirit which flows from the One who is the Truth.

✝ *Lord Jesus, I want to drink deeply of the refreshing river of Your Spirit so that I will have no taste for the enemy's mortal cup. Amen.*

♥ Worship in heaven is not so sober as ours; they've done a lot more 'drinking'!

28th February — Avoiding Sin

📖 Genesis 3 : 1

"Now the serpent was craftier than any of the wild animals the Lord God had made. He said to the woman, "Did God really say you must not eat from any tree in the garden?"

☞ The first thing God says about His heart for people was that he wanted to bless them (Genesis 1 : 28). The serpent, on the other hand, put a doubt into their minds. God was actually keeping something back from them. The serpent could supply what they were looking for.

Mankind got a snake's eye view of God and the deception has been almost total, even for 'religious' people. Heaven, it seems, is really a boring old place (like a big version of church), light blue, with about 50 metres visibility in golden fog, eerie choral music in the background and angels floating by stiffly saying "Hi!" Hell on the other hand is more like a good night in a pub – red lights, singing, laughter, and camaraderie. Naughty, but nice.

Our images have been successfully reversed. Sin is believing the lie. The reality is that God brings the blessing of true relationship, laughter, song, fun, wholeness. Real Christianity is more exciting than *Riverdance*. Hell is numbing loneliness, selfishness, and isolation and devastating loss. That's why the Old Testament ends, not with blessing ,but with the word 'curse'.

✝ *Lord, I believed the lie many times and I ended up with nothing but pigs' food. Please forgive my stupidity and rebellion and sin. Amen.*

♥ All the best pubs are in heaven.

29th February — Avoiding Sin

📖 Genesis 2 : 25

"The man and his wife were both naked, and they felt no shame."

☞ Nakedness is intended to be all about intimacy and total openness. However, I used to dream that I had shamefully turned up to fly an Aer Lingus 747 without my uniform and in my underwear!

When Adam and Eve sinned, their intimacy with God was spoiled and they hid from Him for fear of exposure. We still hide from each other, building layer upon sinful layer of stupid behaviours, attempting to avoid the pain of 'nakedness'. Our self-effort at covering is pretty transparent; however, it does little to hide our shame.

God graciously made a suitable covering of skins for Eden's hiding couple. It was the first sign that one day another lamb would die so that sin could be covered up. Sin and death entered the world through the first Adam. The second Adam – Jesus, the 'seed' of the woman, would, by His sacrificial death make a 'full, perfect and sufficient sacrifice for the sins of the whole world'. He is waiting to give a 'robe of righteousness' to every sinner who will come to Him in repentance and faith, and to restore true intimacy in the beauty of His eternal kingdom.

✝ *Lord, I feel exposed and ashamed. Cover me quickly with the covering I could never make myself, and please take me back to the place of not being ashamed in your presence. Amen.*

♥ Eve would have looked rather ridiculous if her covering had been a hat, don't you think?

Fergus Ryan

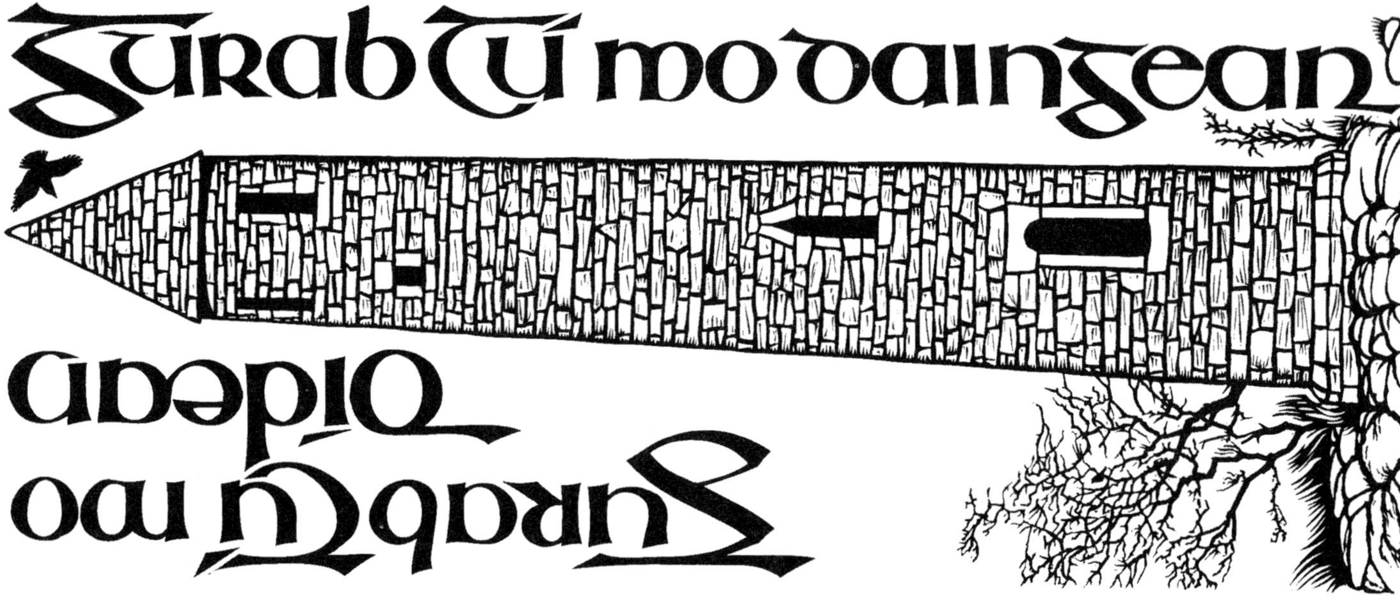

MARCH

The original is a linocut 19″ x 8″ to which gouache and water colours are added.
Its title, "Be Thou my Soul's Shelter, be Thou my High Tower" is a line from the hymn "Be Thou my Vision".
The lettering that flanks the tower is the Ancient Irish original of which the picture title is the equivalent.

1st March Work

Genesis 2 : 15

"The Lord God took the man and put him in the Garden of Eden to work it and take care of it."

☞ Even for those who don't know roses from rhubarb, there can be something uniquely restful about being in a garden. You don't get the same feeling about watching the production line in a component factory, for somehow there is a feeling of being more 'at home' amidst shrubs and tree, flowers and vegetables. Where does this come from? Surely from the home of our first ancestor, whom God placed, not in a city, nor in a wilderness, but in a garden: Gardening surpasses all other pursuits as the nation's favourite pastime. Gardening magazines outsell all others, and gardening programmes always draw good viewing figures. And all because when God made man He first of all made him into a gardener.

We know (v9) that the secret of the garden's appeal lies equally in its appearance and in its provision, but even in this paradise of sights and tastes man's task was much more than static admiration, but active participation in the processes which produced beauty and bounty. It's worth thanking God for His genius in making us this way, provided we see 'work' as much more than just having a job. All of us who are too young, too old or too infirmed to get a job can still find ways of caring for our 21st century garden now, alas, overrun with 'thistles and thorns' (3 : 18). We are not at our created best when we treat life as one long party!

✝ *Lord God, forgive me for neglecting the world in which I live, with all its pain. Show me where I can enhance your world by caring for others, and give me perseverance until I see fruit for my labours. Amen.*

♥ Which matters most? The exertions of the labourer, the richness of the soil, or the climate conditions – don't we need them all?

Gavin Pantridge

2nd March Work

📖 Genesis 3 : 19

"By the sweat of your brow you will eat your food until you return to the ground, since from it you were taken; from dust you are and to dust you will return."

☞ What a prospect as we face a new day! This is not the verdict of a merciless God but one of the sad outcomes of peoples' desire not to follow God's way (v.17). God formed our bodies out of the dust (2 : 7) and into these shells he breathed life and we became living beings. The original intention that man should till the ground and raise crops and animals for a livelihood remained, but because of disobedience, pain and distortion were introduced and a limited time span for the shell was set.

These shells will crack, crumble or decay but the essential me (soul, spirit) will continue to exist. So the burdens of the short-term, whatever they may be, should not be allowed to overshadow the possibilities of the long term. The God who has to punish sin is the God who has on His own initiative provided eternal life – a life that can begin from now.

✝ *Thank You that through knowing You, You can help me cope with the burden of life and taste something of a great future ahead. Amen.*

♥ We have not been promised a rose-garden but a special relationship with the gardener.

Edgar Gilpin

3rd March Work

Exodus 20 : 9 -10

"Six days you shall labour, and do all your work; but the seventh day is a Sabbath to the Lord your God. In it you shall not do any work, neither you, nor your son, or your daughter, nor your manservant or maidservant, nor your animals, nor the alien within your gates."

☞ Rabbi Meiv says that a one-legged man may wear his wooden leg on the Sabbath, but Rabbi Jossi prohibits. (The Talmud: Shabbath C 200AD)

Hardly a positive approach to keeping the seventh day! The Pharisees in Jesus' day had a similar attitude to giving, even to tilling their herb plants! Time is as valuable a resource as material wealth and God expects us to set aside regularly a quality day for Him. Paul in Galatians says we are no longer like minors obeying school rules to please God, but mature men and women with the full revelation of God and His Spirit within us. So we do not approach the first day (Sunday) negatively, with a strict and detailed application of the commandment, but as a day set aside for the worship of God as well as for our own rest and recreation. Surely we ought to give God the best and as Isaiah says "call the Sabbath a delight"

✝ *Thank You God that You have made the Sabbath for man (and not the other way round) Enable us to protect it from the creeping demands of a busy working life. Amen.*

♥ Economy is frequently a way of spending money without getting any fun out of it.

Stephen Gillespie

4th March Work

📖 Proverbs 16 : 3

"Commit your work to the Lord and your plans will be established."

☞ Even the humdrum routine of living has to be planned. Trivial matters of little consequence, like when to cut the grass or do the ironing, still have to be planned. More careful planning is needed for bigger issues which affect the lives of others – allocating sufficient time for family relationships and church fellowship. This verse tells us that the plans are **ours**. It is we who make the decisions. We are not God's puppets. Yes, we ask for guidance, but we get on with what opportunities come our way with whatever gifts and abilities we have.

But whatever plans we make, we then commit them to God. That can often involve some refinement of the plans, if it dawns upon us that our ideas are not consistent with God's ways. God's 'upside down' principles for a full and satisfying life in this world run counter to the predominant secular mindset of this world. So, planning for ultimate fulfillment will have to take seriously, for instance, that true greatness is in serving, not being served – that caring relationships are better than the things money can buy. Since we only have one life, it has to make sense to plan it with our Creators' advice in mind.

✝ *Lord help me to plan this day, and the rest of my days, conscious that my life can have no lasting value unless shaped by Your values. Amen.*

♥ "I don't want to achieve immortality through my work, I want to achieve it through not dying." (Woody Allen)

David Hewitt

5th March **Work**

📖 1 Timothy 5 : 8

"If anyone does not provide for his relatives, and especially for his immediate family, he has denied the faith and is worse than an unbeliever."

☞ Are we in the business of wanting to live each day in a way that pleases God? If we are, then Paul instructs us that the life that is pleasing to Him, is a life that will show consistent genuine love and concern, and will give practical help to all those in need (who is my neighbour?), but particularly those closest to us by ties of nature. Even if there were no other reasons for going to work (and there are) here is one which is reason enough.

John reminds us "For anyone who does not love his brother, whom he has seen, cannot love God whom he has not seen." (1 John 4:20). James warns us that for a believer to ignore wantonly the physical needs of others is to render our faith impotent. (James 2:16).

Paul, here, goes further. He condemns in the strongest language those who profess to know and love God but who make no practical provision for those who depend on them for the essentials of life. To behave in such a way is to deny the faith, and to be worse than an unbeliever – in other words, such failure and blindness is a gross sin.

✝ *Lord, touch my eyes that I will see, not only the distant needs of the world, but those needs on my very doorstep; Touch my heart, to respond to need wherever it may be, generously and cheerfully, out of a heart full of thanks and praise. Amen.*

♥ Faith comes by hearing. Love comes by serving.

Clifford Tughan

6th March Illness

Job 2 : 7

So Satan went out from the presence of the Lord and afflicted Job with painful sores from the soles of his feet to the top of his head.

☞ In Zomba market Malawi, I was intrigued to see the stall of the medicine man. All sorts of strange objects in jars, dried herbs, leaves and bones were attributed with magical properties. I found it difficult to get my head around the widely held view in Africa that if you were ill it was because some one has put a curse on you. The only way to combat magic was with magic. In the West we believe infections, viruses, bacteria etc cause illness. There is a biological explanation.

We struggle with a text like this one from Job. Job was tested, he lost his wealth, his family and his health and this was attributed to the work of Satan. Illness is more than a biological affliction, there are spiritual dimensions too. The struggle between good and evil, which is reflected in sickness, came to a climax on the Cross where Jesus crushed the serpent's head. The power of Satan has been broken.

✝ *Dear Lord, help me to recognise that sickness is about more than microbes; teach me to look to You for deliverance. Amen.*

♥ Don't look for magic; look for the miracle of God's healing love.

7th March Illness

2 Chronicles 16 : 12

"In the thirty ninth year of his reign, Asa was afflicted with a disease in

his feet. Though his disease was severe, even in his illness he did not seek help from the Lord, but only from the physicians."

☞ Asa was one of Judah's worst kings. Even after thirty nine years as king he had not learned to depend on God. He plundered the temple of its treasures, introduced the worship of idols and even offered his children in sacrifice. The depth of his depravity is shown in that though he was seriously ill he did not seek help from the Lord.

One of the saddest things in my ministry is to visit someone, who is very ill, yet they have no apparent desire to seek the Lord's help. God wants us to accept all the help modern medicine has to offer. He is the one who has given doctors and nurses their gifts and skill for healing. But God also invites us to call on Him in our time of illness, confident that He will hear our prayers. When we pray we acknowledge our ultimate dependence on our Heavenly Father.

✝ *Heavenly Father, when I am in need, teach me to lean on You, for You never fail those who entrust themselves to You. Amen.*

♥ Challenge and opportunity are two sides of the same coin. The challenge of sickness gives us an opportunity to lean on God.

8th March — Illness

📖 Psalm 38 : 3

" Because of your wrath there is no health in my body; my bones have no soundness because of my sin."

☞ It is a difficult concept for us to think of sickness as a judgement from God and dangerous to pass that sort of judgement on others or ourselves. When Jesus' disciples wanted to point the finger at a man with congenital deformities asking who had sinned, the man or his parents, Jesus rebuke was stern. 'Neither', was His reply, rather it was to reveal the glory of God. Ultimately all suffering is rooted in sin and the fall. We recognise that sinful lifestyles lead to painful consequences. The person who does not respect the body God has given is likely to abuse and harm it. On occasions there may be a more direct link between sin and sickness, but that adjudication is best left to God. What we need is God's forgiveness, for this is the foundation of the wholeness of life Jesus offers to those who trust Him.

✝ *Lord, we cannot unravel the mystery of how sickness and sin interrelate, but we can be confident that Your forgiveness is freely offered in Jesus. Amen.*

♥ Forgiveness is the answer to the child's dream of a miracle by which what is broken is made whole again, what is soiled is again made clean. (Dag Hammarskjold)

9th March — Illness

📖 Psalm 41 : 3

"The Lord will sustain them on their sick-bed and restore them from their bed of illness."

☞ In Chantilly, just north of Paris there is the residue of a large population of English folk. They had settled there before the First World War because it was a horse-racing centre. I went to visit a very old lady who lived in a ramshackle apartment at the top of several flights of stairs. It was a long time before she opened the door. She was a pitiful sight, obviously very ill having just dragged herself from bed. Yet there was a smile on Mrs. Morell's face. "Thank you for coming" she said, " I've just been praying the Lord would send me someone to light my fire".

It is true that the Lord sustains His children through times of need. His promise is not that we will avoid sickness, that is an inevitable part of our human existence, but that He will sustain us and restore us. Let Mrs. Morell's faith inspire us to trust the Lord to provide for us whatever our need.

✝ *Father at times I am afraid of how I could cope through a period of illness. Help me be confident*
in Your ability to sustain me whatever the future may hold. Amen.

♥ The darker the night the brighter the star

10th March **Illness**

📖 Isaiah 53 : 4 – 5
"*Surely He took up our infirmities and carried our sorrows, yet we considered Him stricken by God, smitten by Him, and afflicted. But He was pierced for our transgressions, He was crushed for our iniquities; the punishment that brought us peace was upon Him, and by His wounds we are healed.*"

☞ Here in this Old Testament prophecy we have a vivid insight into the meaning of Jesus' death on the cross. Suffering and illness is a puzzling mystery, but God enters our pain and shares in our suffering.

There is no torment, no anguish, and no pain – physical, psychological or spiritual that our Lord has not experienced for Himself, Satan has been disarmed and his evil plans thwarted. Sin, which perniciously seeps into everything we do, has been dealt with once and for all. Suffering has been faced down and conquered by the Risen Christ.

Jesus shares our pain, defeats our enemies and heals all our diseases. Wholeness of life begins here and now when we accept Jesus Christ as our Saviour and Lord. It develops as we grow in grace and will find its fullness when we stand in God's presence, perfect and complete in Christ. 'By His wounds we are healed'.

✝ *Lord, we pray for all who are weighed down by the mystery of suffering. Reveal yourself as the God of love who bore all our suffering and offers us in Christ Jesus wholeness of life. Amen*

♥ There is no commentary that opens up the Bible so much as sickness and sorrow. (Bishop J C Ryle)

Willis Cordner

11th March — Listening

📖 1 Samuel 3 : 9

"So Eli told Samuel; 'Go and lie down, and if He calls you, say, 'Speak, Lord for your servant is listening'. So Samuel went and lay down in his place."

☞ Eli had not a good relationship with his sons. They disobeyed God's laws and took for themselves the gifts intended for God. God was very angry with their behaviour and with Eli.

On the other hand, as Samuel's guardian from the time he was a little lad, Eli taught Samuel to tend to Gods temple and learn Gods ways. Through Eli, Samuel learnt how to hear the voice of God. As Samuel grew up, God often spoke to him, giving messages for all the people of Israel. But the place where he first discerned what God was saying, was under Eli's instruction.

As parents or teachers, what could be more important than teaching our children not all the right answers, but how to ask the right questions; to hear the voice of God, and to obey.

✝ *O Lord, in spite of my many failings, help me see how to train young people in my care to listen when you are speaking, and so to respond, for Jesus Sake. Amen.*

♥ To err is human but to really foul things up requires a computer.

Helen Geoghegan

12th March Giving

📖 Exodus 4 : 2

"Then the Lord said to him, "What is that in your hand?"

☞ Just as Moses took up his staff, obeyed and saw a miracle take place (Exodus 4 : 20), may we take whatever little we have to offer and use it with courage and faith to the glory of God.

Just as David took up five smooth stones and approached the

Philistine, Goliath, with a sling in his hand (1 Samuel 17 : 40), may we be equipped to slay the giants of fear, poverty and oppression.

Just as the widow's flour and oil did not run out (1 Kings 17 : 12 – 16), may those working in relief and missionary programmes around the world have the supplies and equipment they need.

Just as the young boy gave Jesus his five small barley loaves and two small fish (John 6 : 9), we give you whatever **we** have today, Lord – our money, our time, our skills, our energies, our prayers. (With acknowledgement to TEAR FUND)

✝ *Forgive me when I seek to hold on to what I have for fear that I will have nothing for myself. Help me discover it is in giving that I receive, more than I can know. Amen.*

♥ A language instructor explained to her class that French nouns unlike English counterparts are masculine or feminine eg. 'chalk' or 'pencil'; though in English these words are neutral. One student asked, "What gender is a computer?" The teacher divided the students into 2 groups, men and women and asked them to decide, and why! (What would you say?)

13th March — Trust

📖 Hebrews 13 : 5

"God has said; never will I leave; never will I forsake you."

☞ A man once experienced a terrible personal tragedy. "Does that now ruin your faith?" asked a friend. "No" came the reply, "It has given me the opportunity for my faith to be put into practice".

The Bible tells us that God **knows** our circumstances, 'O Lord, you have searched me out and you know me. You know when I sit and when I rise; you perceive my thoughts from afar. You discuss my going out and my lying down; you are familiar with all my ways'. (Psalm 139 : 1 – 3) more; He **understands** our feelings; 'The Lord is close to the broken-hearted and saves those who are crushed in Spirit'. (Psalm 34 : 18)

Therefore 'Cast all your anxiety on him, because he cares for you'. (1 Peter 5 : 7)

Faith is not faith until it is put to the test.

† *Help me Lord not just to trust You when everything is going well in my life, but all the time to believe in Your Sovereign care, for Jesus sake. Amen.*

♥ The women concluded computers were male, because;

1. In order to get their attention, you have to turn them on.
2. They have a lot of data, but are still clueless.
3. They are supposed to help you solve your problems, but half the time they **are** the problem.
4. As soon as you commit to one, you realise that, if you had waited a little longer, you could have had a better model.

14th March — Suffering

Philippians 2 : 5 – 8

"Take heart among yourselves what you find in Christ Jesus: He was in the form of God; yet He laid no claim to equality with God, but made Himself nothing, assuming the form of a slave. Bearing the human

likeness, sharing the human lot, he humbled himself, and was obedient, even to the point of death."

☞ Jesus…the man for all seasons;

To those who are illegitimate – *people supposed Jesus was too.*
To those who had a rough childhood – *Herod tried to murder Jesus as a baby.*
To those who have no home – *Jesus was a refugee.*
To those whose friends let them down – *Jesus was denied…and betrayed by His.*
To those who are laughed at – *so was Jesus…and spat upon.*
To those who are lonely – *Jesus was deserted.*
To those who have lost a child – *God lost His one and only Son.*

So then

To the confused – *Jesus is the way.*
To the confounded – *He is the truth.*
To the dying – *He is the life.*
To the one who needs a friend – *He is our High Priest.*
To the hungry – *He is the bread of life.*
To the wounded – *He is the healer.*
To the heart-broken – *He is the Good Shepherd who lays down His life for the sheep.*

† *Thank You that in Jesus we find a merciful, gracious friend who understands our heartfelt needs. Amen.*

♥ The men decided computers however were female, because;

1. No one but their creator understands their internal logic.
2. The native language they use to communicate with other computers is incomprehensible to everyone else.
3. Even your smallest mistakes are stored in long-term memory for later retrieval.

4. As soon as you make a commitment to one, you find yourself spending half your paycheque on accessories for it.

15th March God's Presence

📖 Ezekiel 1 : 25 - 28

"There came a voice from above the expanse over the heads of the four living creatures as they stood with lowered wings. Above the expanse was what looked like a throne of sapphire, and high above on the throne was a figure like that of a man. This was the appearance of the likeness of the glory of the Lord. When I saw it, I fell face down."

☞ It must have been an awesome sight. Not everyday you get a vision of the Glory of God! Ezekiel, note, didn't actually see God..... "No one can see God and live". .. but he saw the appearance of the likeness of the glory of the Lord. That was enough to cause him to fall face down in worship.

100 years earlier, Isaiah had also had a vision of the glory of God (Isaiah 6). It too had struck him with awe; but while the vision was similar, the location and the context of the vision couldn't have been more different! In Isaiah chapter 6, King Uzziah had died after a 50 year reign, and Isaiah still needed to know that God would remain with him. The vision showed that he would.

In Ezekiel chapter 1 however the context was that hundreds of Jews had now been exiled from Jerusalem, away from the Temple, the place where God was located; and forcibly transported to pagan, wicked Babylon! But there God made Himself known to His servant as well...not this time in the Temple, but rather on a mobile throne; a heavenly chariot, demonstrating that God was able to be in all places at all times.

In Psalm 139, David asks this rhetorical question; "Where can I go from your Spirit? Where can I flee from your presence? If I go to the heavens, you are there; If I make my bed in Shoel, you are there." God is not confined to the Temple...He can be in every situation where His servant may be.
In Babylon as well! God is not limited in any way... and according to our specific needs, He reveals His presence in the person of His Son, our Saviour. Surely that is enough to cause us to fall down in adoration, love and praise.

✝ *We praise You, Heavenly Father that Jesus is the radiance of the glory of God, and the exact representation of His being. We worship You, Dear Lord that You are not restricted in where You can be, but by Your Holy Spirit dwell within our hearts. We fall down in adoration for your glory in Jesus, the image of the invisible God. Amen.*

♥ Other men decided that;

a) Computers are most certainly male;
They do what they are told.
They are logical and obedient.

b) Printers on the other hand are definitely female!
Unpredictable.
Hard to manage.
Do the opposite of what you tell them, and
tell you the opposite of what they mean!

Frank Sellar

16th March — The Trinity

📖 Matthew 3 : 16 – 17

"As soon as Jesus was baptized, heaven was opened and he saw the

Spirit of God descending like a dove and lighting on him. And a voice from heaven said, "This is my Son whom I love; with him I am well pleased."

☞ Jesus did not need to be baptized since He had never sinned, but He underwent baptism in solidarity with us. After His baptism the Heavens opened and The Holy Spirit descended. For the Jews of the first century this would have been very significant. They believed that the coming of the Holy Spirit would signify the beginning of the Last Days when God would intervene finally in world history to bring His Kingdom. In this event, therefore, and in the era which it brings in, all three persons of the Trinity are involved: God the Father who declares Himself well pleased with His Son; the Holy Spirit who descends on Jesus; and the Son Himself who submits to His Father's will, a submission which we know from the Gospels leads to His death for the sins of the world. This is a picture of our relationship to God in the present. God the Father wishes to take delight in us; the Holy Spirit is available to help us; the Son has fulfilled the Father's will and through Him we have access to the Father.

✝ *Father we give You thanks that in Your mercy You have given us all that is needful for our Salvation. May we express our gratitude to You in the lives that we lead. Amen.*

♥ Mark Twain once remarked to an American bishop that he had read every word of his sermon before! The bishop protested it was quite original. Twain replied he had read every word in his dictionary.

17th March *St.Patrick's Day* The Trinity

📖 Matthew 28 : 19 - 20

"Go and make disciples of all nations, baptizing them in the name of the Father and of the Son and of the Holy Spirit, teaching them to obey everything I have commanded you. And surely I am with you always. To the very end of the age."

☞ If God has given us all that is needful for our Salvation, then He also wishes that all men and women throughout the world should know it. That is the significance of the Great Commission given in today's passage. The main thrust of the commission is in the command to 'make disciples' of all nations. The task, therefore, involves not just preaching the Gospel to all the world but the much more demanding and arduous task of nurturing those brought to faith. Hence we have the extra clauses involved - not just 'baptizing them in the name of the Father, Son and Holy Spirit' but also 'teaching them to observe all that I have commanded'. As in all the Scriptures, however, God never gives His disciples a task without the means with which to carry it out. He has given His Son full authority over the whole universe and in turn His Son sends us out with full authority to preach and teach. But he does not leave it at that...He promises that He, through the Holy Spirit, will be with us at all times. With this authority and these resources, is it any wonder that early Christians like Paul spend their lives taking the Gospel to the ends of the earth?

✝ *Our Father, who has commissioned us to make disciples of all nations, help us to love others as You have loved them and to use the time and talents You have given us to serve all people in Your name. Amen.*

♥ May your blessings outnumber the shamrocks that grow. And may trouble avoid you wherever you go. (Old Irish proverb.)

18th March — The Trinity

1st Peter 1 : 1 - 2

"Peter, an apostle of Jesus Christ, To God's elect, strangers in the world…who have been chosen according to the foreknowledge of God the Father, through the sanctifying work of the Spirit, for obedience to Jesus Christ and sprinkling by his blood; Grace and peace be yours in abundance."

☞ The people Peter is addressing are undergoing persecution and difficulty and this has caused deep perplexion in the minds of some. Why should they have to suffer in this way? Peter answers that in this Epistle. He begins by giving his credentials as a delegate or representative of Jesus Christ. He then describes his hearers. They are exiles, not from some earthly land, but from Heaven. But they are not miserable exiles with no hope of return, but victorious ones looking forward to going back to Heaven. They have this hope because they have been chosen by God the Father, consecrated (or set apart) by the Holy Spirit and dedicated to obeying Jesus Christ the Son. Again, the Trinity is involved in the whole process of Salvation. God the Father has chosen them; the Holy Spirit is consecrating them; Jesus Christ the Son shows them the way to be followed and obeyed. The sprinkling refers to Exodus 24 : 7 where the blood of the sacrifice is sprinkled on the people as a sign of their undertaking to be obedient. It is, thus, from God the Father, Jesus the Son and the Holy Spirit that grace (God's unmerited favour leading to our acceptance by Him) and peace (a wholeness of life which comes from God's favour) flow in abundance.

✝ *As this broken bread (in Communion) was scattered upon the hills and collected to become one, so may your church be collected from the ends of the earth into your kingdom. Amen.*

♥ Vicar: "I've just preached today to a congregation of asses." Friend: " Indeed, I noted you addressed them as "Dearly Beloved Brethren."

19th March — The Trinity

Ephesians 4 : 4 - 6

"There is one body and one Spirit- just as you were called to one hope when you were called – one Lord, one Faith, one Baptism, one God and Father of all, who is overall and through all and in all."

In Ephesians 4 the hearers are being encouraged to live Christian lives and to live in unity. They are to 'maintain the unity of the Spirit in the bond of peace'. The reason they are to live as one is because of the unity of the divine order. Seven aspects of this divine order are listed – one body (referring to the church), one Spirit (referring to the Holy Spirit, the Third Person in the Trinity), one hope, one Lord (referring, as always in Ephesians, to the Lord Jesus Christ), one faith, one baptism, one God and Father of us all. Two aspects of the Father are then emphasized...His sovereignty over the world...'He is above all'...and His presence in the world...He is 'through all and in all'. In view of this, how can we tolerate divisions amongst ourselves? It is easy to live in our own groups, ignoring or even despising others, but Ephesians reminds us that we are all one body, called to one faith by one God, Father Son and Holy Spirit and that this reality must affect our behaviour as people and as congregations.

O God, who has called us into Your church, help us to maintain the unity of the Spirit in the bond of peace. Amen.

May you always have these blessings: A soft breeze when summer comes, a warm fireside in the winter and always the warm, soft smile of a friend. (Irish saying)

20th March — The Trinity

2 Corinthians 13 : 14

"May the grace of the Lord Jesus Christ and the love of God, and the Fellowship of the Holy Spirit be with you all."

These are among the best known (and most popular?) words in the Bible as they are used at the end of most services of public worship. No matter how long or short the sermon, how exciting or boring the service, this short sentence tells us all that we can go home! Because of that, we don't pay too much attention to the actual words. They come at the end of a letter to a church with which Paul is in profound disagreement. He is going to come to them and the seriousness of the problems between him and certain people in the church is illustrated by his statement in Ch. 13 : 1; that 'any charge must be sustained by the evidence of two or three witnesses'. He finishes the epistle by appealing to them to mend their ways, heed his appeal, live in peace and greet each other with a holy kiss (a symbol of reconciliation). An impossible request? Humanly speaking yes. But then he adds his benediction. It is of course Trinitarian, referring to the Father, Son and Holy Spirit, but the order in which the three Persons occur is determined by their role in our Salvation. First comes the grace of Jesus Christ, without which we could not have Salvation; it is through Him, incarnate, crucified and triumphant that we come to know the Father's love; finally the work of the Holy Spirit is to promote a true fellowship of believers to share in that work, which in turn is a sign of the New Age which has dawned. This is the solution to the impossible request that Paul puts to the church in Corinth in v. 11 to aim for perfection and it is the answer to the problems arising in our present day churches.

✝ *O God, who has called us to be witnesses to You, both by our words and actions, help us, through the grace of our Lord Jesus Christ, to know Your love and to live in the fellowship of the Holy Spirit with one another. Amen.*

♥ During a children's sermon, Rev. Larry Eisenberg asked the children what 'Amen' means. A little boy raised his hand and said, "Tha – tha – tha-; that's all folks!"

Cecil McCullough

21st March — Faith

Hebrews 11 : 3

"By faith we understand that the universe was formed at God's command, so that what is seen was not made out of what was visible."

☞ "Believing what you know is not true," replied a schoolboy to the question: "What is faith?" He expressed a commonly held view that the church deals in wishful thinking while science teaches facts and certainties.

Like the elderly lady who on first hearing of the theory of evolution, prayed: "Lord please may it not be true, and if it is true, please may it not become widely known!"

'We have not lost faith,' George Bernard Shaw wrote: 'We have transferred it to the medical profession.' He was right. For we all have faith…in something.

A young man said to me recently: "I am an atheist." I could not resist the answer: "What incredible faith!" He evidently believed that this complex, orderly and beautiful universe resulted from a mindless explosion and that our lives, which laugh and love, think and reason, worry and reflect came out of nothing by chance. C S Lewis wrote: 'When you argue against God, you are arguing against the very power that makes you able to argue at all.'

✝ *'Bless the Lord O my soul, and all that is within me, bless His holy name!' Amen.*

♥ When we stop believing in God, we do not believe in nothing … we begin to believe in anything. (G.K. Chesterton)

22nd March Faith

📖 John 3 : 16

"For God so loved the world that he gave his one and only Son, that whoever believes in him shall not perish but have everlasting life."

☞ This is probably the best known verse in the Bible. What does it mean to 'believe in' Jesus? Everyone believes that He lived on this earth. But such belief is not 'saving faith'. John's words in Greek could be translated: 'believing on' or 'trusting in' Jesus. When John Paton brought the Gospel to the cannibals of the New Hebrides he had great difficulty translating this phrase into the local language. The islanders had no word for 'trust'. By trusting others you might literally end up in the soup! At last Paton hit on an idea. He sat down at his desk, raised his feet off the floor and leaned back. "What am I doing now?" he asked his native helper. In reply the servant used a word which means ' lean your whole weight upon'. That was the word which was used in Paton's translation of John's Gospel. 'That whoever leans their whole weight upon Him, shall not perish but have everlasting life'.

Saving faith is the trust, which leans entirely on Jesus and His saving work accomplished for us.

✝ *'I am trusting You Lord Jesus, trusting only You, trusting You for full salvation, rich and free'. Amen.*

♥ Weak faith in a strong object is better than strong faith in a weak object.

23rd March **Faith**

📖 John 20 : 29

"Then Jesus told him, "Because you have seen me, you have believed; blessed are those who have not seen and yet have believed."

☞ 'Seeing is believing' is a familiar half-truth. Sometimes we must trust first if we are to see. One can never know the taste of an apple through lectures on horticulture or the recommendation of a friend. 'Taste and see' that is the correct order. Or take the Kerryman who refused to enter water until he learned to swim!

Thomas is rebuked for his refusal to trust the Lord's promises and the testimony of his fellow disciples. 'Unless I see ... I will not believe' John 20 : 24.

Sheldon Vanauken wrote, 'I wanted proof, to see Him eat a bit of fish, letters of fire across the sky...I got none of these. I hung on the edge of a gap. I looked back and knew I could not reject Jesus. I looked round and there was only one thing to do, I flung myself across the gap to Jesus Christ.' He wrote later to a friend: 'On a cold October morning I chose to trust...in Jesus Christ as my Lord and God...and ever since, Christianity has had for me the feel of the ring of truth.'

If we do not take a step of faith in Him, we will never 'see'.

✝ *Just as I am, though tossed about, with many a conflict, many a doubt. Fighting and fears within, without, O Lamb of God, I come. Amen.*

♥ Only believe and you will see, that Christ is all in all to thee.

24th March **Faith**

Romans 10 : 17

"Consequently, faith comes from hearing the message, and the message is heard through the word of Christ."

☞ "I wish my plants were as strong and healthy as yours," said a man as he contrasted his neighbour's healthy blossoms with the pale wizened specimens in his own garden. "Did you ever try feeding them?" his neighbour asked. "Oh I never thought of that". He said.

So people often say: "I wish I had your faith" as though some were fortunate enough to be born with it and others not. But faith is not hereditary. It does not grow in a vacuum, nor is it worked up from within. It is given by God and it needs feed. God's normal channel of granting and sustaining faith is through the Word of God nourished, (1Peter 2 : 2), the soil in which it is rooted and the foundation on which it stands firm (Colossians 2 : 7)

✝ *Beyond the sacred page, I seek You Lord, My spirit longs for You, living Word! Amen.*

♥ If your faith is weak, try feeding it.

25th March Faith

Luke 8 : 25

"Where is your faith?" he asked his disciples. In fear and amazement they asked one another, "Who is this? He commands even the winds and the water, and they obey him."

☞ A man was seen walking through heavy rain carrying an umbrella. He was getting very wet. It was not that the umbrella was defective. While it remained neatly folded under his arm, it did no good whatsoever. I wanted to shout: "Why don't you put up your umbrella?"

The disciples had already got a real faith in Jesus. They had watched Him heal the sick, give sight to the blind and raise the dead. Now faced with a tremendous storm at sea, they panicked. Their faith did them no good whatsoever! Our Lord rebukes them: "Where is your faith?" He was saying in effect: "You have faith in me...Why don't you use it?" Faith is not like an automatic heating system, which switches on by itself. It must be exercised in each situation. So in the storms of life, faith is not only a refusal to panic but also the affirmation that Jesus Christ is in control. That was why Paul in the midst of trying circumstances could write: 'I have learned in whatever circumstances I am in, to be content'.

What is Jesus saying to us about our present circumstances? "Where is your faith?"

✝ *'Oh for a faith that will not shrink, though pressed by many a foe. That will not tremble on the brink, of poverty or woe'. Amen.*

♥ A man complained to his minister about the troubles that had befallen him and added. "It's enough to make a man lose his faith." "Seems to me, Jim" said the minister, "It's enough to make a man use his faith."

John Woodside

26th March — Husbands

Genesis 2 : 24

"For this reason a man will leave his father and mother and be united to his wife, and they will become one flesh."

Have you heard of the three-legged marriage? **The Leaving, The Cleaving and The One Flesh.**

The Leaving is the answer to "Why bother with a little piece of paper?" It signifies the beginning of a new family unit. The new marriage is established in a publically known way. There can be no question that this man is married to this woman and no other. There is a public accountability.

The Cleaving is what Shakespeare would have called 'Either was the other's Mine'. It points to the covenant, the promise that is entered. It speaks of faithfulness and fidelity. Whatever the future holds the couple face it as a pair.

The One Flesh refers to the union of man with woman at all levels of their lives. It refers to sexual union, but also to the growth of the relationship in steadfast love, faithfulness, forgiveness, sacrifice, patience, blessing and healing, leading to maturity.

✝ *Father, make my marriage stand strong in steadfast love, faithfulness, forgiveness, sacrifice, patience, blessing and healing to maturity. Amen.*

♥ Successful marriage is always a triangle, a man, a woman and God.

27th March Husbands

Genesis 5 : 1 - 2

"When God created man, he made him in the likeness of God. He created them male and female and blessed them. And when they were created, he called them "man".

☞ It is a very simple principle. If you want to build something, make something or operate something, the best thing to do is follow the manufacturer's instructions. Whatever it is: a wardrobe, a shelf, a washing machine, or a marriage, the best thing to do is to refer to the manual the manufacturer has included. For a marriage, our creator has provided the Bible. It is a wonderful treasure trove of insights into making relationships work as they are supposed to. It shows us how first we can be in a right relationship with God through His Son Jesus. Then it shows us how that relationship affects all our other relationships. If we want our marriages to be the best they can be, then refer to the Creator's manual. 'As God by creation made two of one, so again by marriage He made one of two'.

† *Father, Your Word is a lamp to my feet and a light for my path, help me to obey it. Amen.*

♥ Put God first if you want your marriage to last.

28th March Husbands

Proverbs 31 : 10

"A wife of noble character who can find? She is worth far more than rubies."

☞ A man once wrote the account of his day with the children. "Opened the door for the children 106 times, shouted "Stop that noise" 172 times, settled 17 quarrels, wiped 19 noses, answered 145 questions, lost my temper 57 times, tied shoelaces 16 times, changed nappies 6 times, felt like spanking them ? times... Was I happy to see her back !!"

It is only when someone is not there we really appreciate his or her worth. How much is your wife worth? Why not show her?

'The woman was made of a rib out of the side of Adam; not made out of his head to rule over him, nor out of his feet to be trampled on by him, but out of his side to be equal to him, under his arm to be protected, and near his heart to be loved'. (Matthew Henry)

✝ *Father thank You for my wife, help me to show how much I love her and appreciate her. Amen.*

♥

A man who finds a godly wife
is rich beyond compare.
She is his greatest prize of life
A treasure rich and rare.

29th March — Husbands

📖 Ephesians 5 : 21 – 25, 28

"Submit to one another out of reverence for Christ. Wives, submit to your husbands as to the Lord. For the husband is the head of the wife as Christ is the head of the church, his body, of which he is the Saviour. Now as the church submits to Christ, so also wives should submit to their husbands in everything. Husbands, love your wives, just as Christ loved the church and gave himself up for her. In this same way,

husbands, ought to have their wives as their own bodies. He who loves his wife loves himself."

☞ Did you know that 'I do', really means, 'I will, daily, lay down my life for this woman?' From the time we're born, we're instinctively 'me' people. As babies we want my food, my comfort, and my nap. When we grow up, we get our wants in slightly more sophisticated ways, but we still expect to be the sun and everyone else to be the planets around us.

Jesus said that marriage for men is the moving of someone else, the wife, to the centre position – and we will revolve our life around her needs, not her life around ours! Marriage is listening to your wife's heart being poured out even when you're dead tired or ready to watch a sporting event. It is putting her fulfillment ahead of yours in sexual love, unloading your day's burdens on the way home so you can focus on her when you get there. It's changing nappies, taking out the rubbish, doing dishes – caring about her world, not just yours. Probably more than anything else 'I do' means the sacrifice of TIME, of taking time to listen to her heart. She needs your attention – and you promised her she would have it. You find your own life by giving your life away to your lifetime love and that is the radically beautiful side of 'I do'.

✝ *Father, help me to love my wife the way You have loved me. Amen.*

♥ Beautiful women grow in the garden of a man's selfless love.

30th March Husbands

1 Peter 3 : 3 - 4

"Your beauty should not come from outward adornment, such as braided hair and the wearing of gold jewelry and fine clothes. Instead, it should be that of your inner self, the unfading beauty of a gentle and quiet spirit, which is of great worth in God's sight."

☞ John was only three years old, but his Dad had already taught him to fish! The first time they went fishing together Dad gave him a little worm to use as bait – John caught himself a little fish.

Then just for fun, Dad decided to let his boy try some serious bait. Wouldn't you know it! Little John reeled in a whopper! When Dad tried to get him to go back to the worm bait – no way, Dad! He had discovered what kind of bait attracts the big ones!

Men are turned on by physical appearance. This fragility is no excuse for lust, and inappropriate attitudes towards women. Females can frankly wear things that are too tight, too low, too high or not enough. That is the tragedy of our superficial, mostly physical, usually sinful, mostly doomed relationships. God describes the package that a truly beautiful woman offers. He says, "Your beauty should not come from outward adornment. Instead it should be that of your inner self, the unfading beauty." Those who carry the radiance and the innocence of an inner Jesus glow, offer the beauty that Hollywood can never match.

If you want the best, seek the unfading beauty of a gentle and quiet spirit, which is of great worth in God's sight.

✝ *Father help me to have that 'Inner Jesus Glow' a beauty that will never fade. Amen.*

♥ 'Charm is deceptive and beauty is fleeting, but a woman who fears the Lord is to be praised'.

James Hyndman

31st March — Comfort When Afraid

Psalm 34: 3

The Lord is my light and my salvation - whom shall I fear? The Lord is the stronghold of my life - of whom shall I be afraid?

From childhood, fear is common to most of us. Darkness, noises and unknown places all make us afraid. It is uncertainty that takes hold of us, and we have all sorts of images of people and situations. Charles Spurgeon, the great preacher of the 19th Century, stood on a London street corner afraid to cross the road. There was a bustle of horses, carts and carriages with their drivers urging the animals on as fast as they could. No rules for road control were in operation at that time. Only when a blind man came along and asked Spurgeon to help him to cross, did he move and the two went together in safety.

Fear can be a powerfu l paralysing emotion. It can make adult people seem like frightened children. But all such experiences God understands, for He is in us and with us through Jesus Christ. He fully knows all we go through. In our darkest moments He is our light to comfort and guide us. He develops in us a faith to learn to trust His care and His goodness. That is what the Psalmist meant when he said, "The Lord is the stronghold of my life." In Him we find perfection and strength. Through every changing and terrifying experience, 'I will never leave you', is His promise. Fear knocked at the door. Faith opened it, and there was no one there.

† *Lord, through all my experiences give me the assurance that You are with me, and will keep me in Your safety. Amen.*

APRIL

The drawing that preceded this 6″ square linocut was quickly sketched with a broad-pointed felt-tip.

It represents the artist's visual response to his reading of John 1 verses 1-5 and 9-14.

Although stated in strong black-and-white terms, this work is but a suggestion of the mind's feeling promoted by the absorbing of the reading.

1st April — Comfort When Afraid

Psalm 34 : 4

"I sought the Lord. He answered me.He delivered me from all my fears."

Think of all the research that goes on for the relief of stress through spas, massage, pills, exercise tapes and consultation with trained people. This craving to end or ease tension and fears has spawned into a whole industry. Sometimes it looks as if folk are willing to pay to fix stress, but have never thought of changing the lifestyle that causes it. It is more than the treatment of the symptoms that is necessary. With God's help and our willingness to change, we can eliminate the root problems. Not that Christ takes away experiences of sickness, unemployment or local turmoil, but He gives us the power and strength to go through them without fear and stress.

I remember a 'good woman' telling me about her fear of heights. She was climbing Mount Errigal in Co. Donegal. She was all right while looking towards the summit. On the last 10 yards she saw the deep slope on both sides. Disaster! All she could think of was the descent. "It was only the confidence of my husband holding me from behind, and telling me to watch my footing that gave me the courage to go down," she said later on. That is the confidence we have in the Lord. He watches us. He holds us. His grip is firm. Trust Him.

Lord, may we know Your Presence and Power through all the dangerous paths of life. Hold us in a firm grip. Amen.

♥ In a country house the front door had sunk, and in order to open it, a hatchet was needed to ease it up. The new minister from their church was visiting, and the little daughter happened to be looking out and saw him coming. The minister heard her voice inside the house. "Ma, get the hatchet, there's the new minister."

2nd April Comfort When Afraid

📖 Matthew 14 : 25 – 27

"During the fourth watch of the night (that is about 4 o'clock in the morning) Jesus went out to them, walking on the lake. When the disciples saw him walking on the lake, they were terrified. "It's a ghost," they said and cried out in fear. But Jesus immediately said to them: "Take courage, it is I- don't be afraid."

☞ It is amazing the frightening power we have in our imaginations and dreams. The disciples here were terrified when they saw this figure walking on the stormy waters of the lake. "It's a ghost," they thought, and were terrified. I knew a little girl who was always in fear when her mother turned out the bedroom light at night and left the room in darkness. She even thought a lion was ready to come in. Once a figure covered with a brown garment came bouncing in. "A lion," she screamed and the beast went under the other bed. Her mother rushed in and scolded her for making such a noise. "Mummy, it's a lion" – "Where?" – "Under the bed." Mother looked, and out crawled her sister covered with a brown coat.

In life we have experiences like serious and heavy times. There is the hatred of bitter hearts, the worries of family, and our own health. We are thrown about, up and down, and it seems that we are going to be lost. But there is Jesus on top of all the waves. Not a strange figure – like a ghost – but our Friend. He is able to control all, and will give us peace and confidence in our living experience. "Don't be afraid," He says. He is able to control and get us to the shore. No one or nothing can take us out of His hold.

✝ *Lord, may we know that because You live in and with us we can face tomorrow and that all our fears are gone. Also that You hold the future and so life is worth living. Amen.*

♥ The farmer was not pleased with what he saw the first time he threw the food to ducks on the ground. He so disliked what he saw he determined to do something about it and went out and bought a file. When he got home he carefully filed to a point the bills of his ducks, and when his task was ended he stood upright and addressed the ducks. "I'm sorry if I've hurt you" he said, "but in future we're going to have fair dos here. It's going to be peck for peck and none of your shoveling."

3rd April — Comfort When Afraid

📖 John 14 : 27

"Peace I leave with you: my peace I give you. I do not give to you as the world gives. Do not let your hearts be troubled and do not be afraid."

☞ Peace – that's what the world longs for and every individual desires not only in the world outside, but also in our own hearts and minds. To be able to rest and relax – without tension – is the great longing of all of us. The problems which we have to face never seem to leave us. What's to become?

Some of us come to that stage in life when we like to make a Will. What's to be done with our property and possessions when we are gone? Now, our Lord had little of this world's goods, but He could leave and give 'that which is priceless'. "Peace I leave with you," He said, "my peace I give to you." Has anyone gone through the turmoil Christ experienced? Criticised, disowned, betrayed, beaten, stripped and crucified. Yet through it all there was that calm and peace in the words He spoke and the tranquillity in the behaviour He displayed . As we trust in Him we discover that peace. We may not be delivered from our sufferings (whatever their nature) but He will give us that inner calm as we rest only upon Him.

Hudson Taylor – a missionary in China – was a man with countless cares but a heart at rest. Once he wrote that in a thousand troubles and worries that beset his life, 999 worked together for good to them that love God – and one more - all things work together for good. The one more makes all the difference in quietening our way and relieving our anxiety.

✝ *Lord give us such strength and protection that will support us in all trials and carry us through all tribulations. Amen.*

♥ A candidate at a local election called at a house. The housewife opened the door "What party does your husband belong to?" he asked. "Take a look at me – I'm the party he belongs to."

4th April — Comfort When Afraid

📖 Hebrews 2 : 14 –15

"Since the children have flesh and blood, Christ too shared in their humanity so that by his death he might destroy him who holds the power of death – that is, the devil – and free those who all their lives were held in slavery by their fear of death."

☞ Yes, the fear of death! It is so uncertain in many respects. When will we die, how, and where will we go? Uncertainty gives us fear. Then the devil held the power of death in every aspect, but Christ destroyed that power. Jesus rose from the dead, and defeated all the powers of hell that tried to hold Him, so that, as we put our lives into His hands, neither life nor death can separate us from His love. (Romans 8 : 38)

Now ,a companion can make all the difference to a journey. Someone with whom we can talk and share all our thoughts, and can be our help in every difficulty. That's what Christ wants to be - our Friend - who will walk with us, support and defend us until we get Home. "I will never leave you nor forsake you," is His promise. We cannot see or feel Him, but we know that He is there at our side, and will hold us as we take that last step – death – and then rest.

✝ *Dear Lord, I expect to pass through this world but once, and any good thing, therefore, that I can do or any kindness that I can show to any fellow creature let me do it now: let me not neglect it, for I shall not pass this way again. Amen.* (Stephen Gilbert 1773 –1855)

♥ "Mummy, did God really make people from the dust?" "Yes dear." "And do they go back to the dust when they die?" "Yes dear." " Well mummy, you go and look. There's somebody coming or going under the spare room bed."

David Burke

5th April — Obedience

📖 Deuteronomy 28 : 2

"All these blessings will come upon you and accompany you if you obey the Lord your God."

☞ As he approached the end of his life on this earth, Moses reminded the Chosen People of their miraculous deliverance from slavery in Egypt and spelled out in detail the law of the Lord. Much of that law seems alien to the industrialised world in which we now live, though the heart of the law, summed up in the Ten Commandments, is as relevant to us today as it was when it was first inscribed on tablets of stone. Law can appear restrictive at first sight, but the goal, and indeed the fruit of law is freedom – freedom from selfish passions, which so easily enslave us, and freedom for women and men to live together in harmony. But as the apostle Paul would grasp so clearly, obedience to the law is only a stepping stone to a much deeper obedience, a personal and harmonious relationship with our loving heavenly Father – therein lies the source of every blessing.

✝ *Father, help us to hear Your voice above the distractions of our daily lives, so that hearing You we may obey you and walk joyfully with You. Amen.*

♥ If we seek that harmonious, personal relationship with God simply by obeying the law we shall fail miserably and indeed find ourselves under a curse, as Moses himself pointed out (Deuteronomy 27:26). But thanks be to God, through His death on the cross Jesus bore that curse for us and set us free. We have only to put our faith in Him!

6th April — Obedience

📖 1 Samuel 15 : 22

"But Samuel replied: "Does the Lord delight in burnt offerings and sacrifices as much as in obeying the voice of the Lord? To obey is better than sacrifice, and to heed is better than the fat of rams".

☞ The prophet Samuel spoke those words to Saul the king when the latter had failed to destroy, in accordance with the Lord's instructions, all the plunder of war in a battle against the Amalekites. His motivation seemed pure enough: he had kept back the best sheep and cattle to offer in sacrifice to the Lord at some later stage.

The story is a good illustration of how we can so easily deceive ourselves, offering the Lord what *we* want to offer, rather than what He is asking for. Such self-deception can creep subtly into the area of public worship, whenever we substitute our own innovations for the approved forms and rubrics. It can creep into our homes, whenever those called to marriage and parenthood give time which should be dedicated to the family to the pursuit of other activities, however good and noble those other things may be; and of course it can creep into our places of work, whenever we channel our energies into projects which are really peripheral to what we are meant to be doing.

✝ *Lord, help us to offer You the sacrifices You are asking of us, rather than those of our own choice. Amen.*

♥ I shall never forget the joyless face of a wealthy woman I once met – and even more her comment: "If only my husband would give me less of his money and more of his time!"

7th April — Obedience

📖 Matthew 7 : 21

"Not everyone who says to me, 'Lord, Lord,' will enter the kingdom of heaven, but only he who does the will of my Father who is in heaven."

☞ I once asked a group of sixth form boys in the school where I am chaplain what they understood by obedience to God. There was a long silence and a lot of scratching of heads. Eventually a boy tentatively suggested "Not to sin". After a bit more probing I got an equally tentative: "Doing people a good turn". Sadly, no amount of probing managed to reach the answer I was looking for, so I prompted; "discerning and doing God's will". A boy responded immediately, hitting the bull's eye! "Reading God's word", he said with some confidence. God does speak directly to us through the scriptures. He also speaks to us through the fellowship of the Church and, in discerning God's personal will for us, we need to listen both to the scriptures and to God's people, if we are to avoid the deceits of the enemy, who is an old hand at disguising himself as an angel of light (2 Corinthians 11:14)!

✝ *Loving Father, we thank You for Your living, life-giving word in the scriptures and for the fellowship of the Church: help us truly to listen to You and do Your will. Amen.*

♥ The great scripture scholar, Jerome, who died in Bethlehem in the year 420AD taught that 'ignorance of the scriptures is ignorance of Christ': we cannot separate God's Eternal Word from the Word made flesh or the written word in the scriptures, – for that matter, from the Body of Christ.

8th April — Obedience

📖 Hebrews 5 : 8

"Although he was a son, he learned obedience from what he suffered."

☞ Although He was the eternal Son of God, it was necessary for Jesus as the incarnate Son to learn obedience -- not that He was ever disobedient, but the temptations He faced were real and the battle for victory was difficult. Where Adam failed and fell, Jesus resisted and prevailed. In that way His humanity was *made perfect*, and on the basis of this perfection He could become *the source of eternal salvation for all who obey Him* (v. 9).

A number of years ago I was privileged to meet and befriend a paralyzed man who radiated the love of Christ. His wife, in comparison, always seemed cold and distant. Then, one day she suffered a stroke, following a minor operation. She became even more physically incapacitated than her husband. But as a person she was transformed, becoming warm and loving. She learned obedience by what she suffered and her humanity was made perfect through her faith in Christ.

✝ *Lord, in all sufferings may we know the fellowship of sharing in Your sufferings, that we may experience the power of Your resurrection. Amen.*

♥ Shortly before her death after a long illness patiently borne over a number of years, a woman was asked the secret of her peace: "Well," she replied, " we can't all be the good Samaritan – someone has to be the wounded Jew."

9th April — Obedience

📖 1 John 5 : 2

"This is how we know that we love the children of God: by loving God and carrying out his commands."

☞ In his first letter, John stresses the initiative of God in reaching out to us in love and the test of authentic faith in God, which is mutual love one for another. How can we claim to love God, whom we have never seen, he argues, if we refuse to love the sister or brother whom we do see? In answer to the question: *What must we do to do the works God requires?* John, in his gospel records Jesus' reply, *"The works of God is this: to believe in the one He has sent"* (6: 28 – 29). In other words, the only 'work' which leads to salvation is faith. Now, in his letter, John sums up the commandments in a single commandment: *that we should believe in the name of his Son Jesus Christ and love one another* (3 : 23). If that one commandment is the motivation of our life, then we do not need to worry or be anxious about details – we are necessarily instruments of God's love in the world.

✝ *Lord, thank You for reaching out to us in love: help us to grasp Your unseen hand, trust in Your love and spread that love around us. Amen.*

♥ 'If you look for the bad in mankind expecting to find it, you surely will.' There is an antidote to that stark message of Abraham Lincoln and that is to look for the good, touchingly illustrated in the film Pollyanna, with its concluding line: We looked for the good - and we found it.

Paul Symonds

10th April — The Goodness of God

📖 Psalm 34 : 8

"Taste and see that the Lord is good; blessed are those who take refuge in him."

☞ Being a Christian does not save anyone from trouble and sometimes our troubles are brought about by our own sin.

Traditionally, in this Psalm, David was looking back at a time when he went over to the Philistines, the enemy camp, and then faked madness to escape (1 Samuel 21 : 10 – 15). Whatever the circumstances, David came so low he felt 'afflicted' (v 2), filled with fear (v 4) and 'poor' (v 6) in the sense of feeling there was nothing left. Perhaps you have been there. Maybe you still are, for even the greatest saints do not escape life's tensions, difficulties and troubles. Think of John the Baptist (Matthew 11 : 2) whose faith was stretched to breaking point.

Always remember that God delivers from all their fears those who seek Him and their mouths are opened in praise so that others are encouraged (v 2). Even more, those who have personally proved God, encourage others to 'taste and see that God is good'.

✝ *Lord help me to taste by trusting You so that others want to taste and see that You are good. Amen.*

♥ Against my will but in order to please my mother I once gave up part of a holiday to visit an old friend of her family. I had met him before and knew his body was twisted with arthritis. His walking was painfully slow and his wife told me he had constant pain and never got anything like a night's sleep.

When he asked if I could play his favourite hymn I wondered what it would be. He chose –

How good is the God we adore,
Our faithful unchangeable friend,
Whose love is as great as His power,
And knows neither measure nor end.

11th April — The Goodness of God

Psalm 136 : 1

"Give thanks to the Lord, for he is good. His love endures forever."

One of the greatest words in the Old Testament is 'chesedh'. It has no equivalent in English. The nearest we can come in translation is 'loving kindness' or the one I prefer, 'steadfast love'.

God's steadfast love was the basis of His relationship with His people Israel. As a nation, they had not been faithful to God. Rather, they had turned away like an unfaithful spouse and rebelled many times like disobedient children against the Father to whom they owed everything. But their God was faithful, not because they deserved it but because of His steadfast love.

This Psalm was written to be used in Church. It celebrates God's love. Read it prayerfully and trace in it God's love and care for you as your Creator (v 4 – 9), Saviour (v 10). Provider (v. 23 – 25).

Although He is 'the God in Heaven' He is not remote from our circumstances and He loves us with an everlasting love.

Lord, I am Your child, help me know I can never stray beyond Your love. Amen.

A book with the title, 'Your God is too small' was published years ago. True? We can get so caught up in ourselves that we miss the majestic power of God. I suggest you walk a cliff path, or imagine doing so. Look at the height, listen to the waves and remember that 'the sea is His and He made it' and 'the strength of the hills is His also'. Then stand in your mind's eye before the Cross and remember that the God of Heaven and the universe loved you there with steadfast love. He still does!

12th April — The Goodness of God

Romans 2 : 4

"Or do you show contempt for the riches of his kindness, tolerance and patience, not realising that God's kindness leads you towards repentance?"

It is strange that a belief in God's love can be made a refuge by those who are unwilling to see and face their personal need for repentance. In the words of Dr. John Stott, "It is not that people are right with God, but that they think they are." They may not claim to be perfect, but they distance themselves from the dreadful sins listed in Romans 1 and, feeling that they are not guilty of such things or the sins which hit the media headlines, they claim the love of God as a cover for their lesser offences. A favourite hymn is, 'For the love of God is broader than the measure's of man's mind and the heart of the Eternal is most wonderfully kind'.

But Paul will not allow us to escape so easily. Greater or lesser though our sins may be, there is no evading the fact that 'all have sinned and fall short of the glory of God' (Romans 3 : 23). God's 'kindness' or love is designed to give us time for repentance.

✝ *Help me, Oh Lord, to see myself as You see me and to ask for Your forgiveness for the sins, which Jesus paid for when He died in my place. Amen.*

♥ God moves in a mysterious way, His wonders to perform.

13th April — The Goodness of God

Romans 8 : 28

"And we know that in all things God works for the good of those who love him, who have been called according to his purpose."

☞ I was a student when the song 'Whatever will be, will be' was at the height of its popularity. My landlady sang it morning, noon and night. It combines a tragic heresy which has been embraced by thousands with the absolute truth that 'the future's not ours to see'. So many accept that, in some fantastic way, our lives are swept along by an impersonal fate which we will never know, and there is nothing we can do about it anyway. Christians, on the other hand, know with the certainty of faith that we step each day into a future under God's control. God has a purpose in life for those He has called which, Paul uncompromisingly affirms, God is working out in all things. You can't have it both ways. Either it is blind Fate or God in control for the good of those who love Him.

✝ *Enough, this covers all my need and so I rest,*
For what I cannot, He can see,
And in His care I safe shall be,
Forever blest. Amen.

♥ Joseph Scriven of Banbridge, Co. Down watched as his fiancée was swept to her death as she tried to cross the river to meet him. After immigrating to Canada, at about thirty–six years of age, he fell in love again and married Eliza Roche in 1854. She took ill and died within three weeks of their wedding. Yet Scriven is best known as the author of 'What a friend we have in Jesus' – Fate or Faith?

14th April — The Goodness of God

Romans 8 : 38 - 39

"For I am convinced that neither death nor life, neither angels nor demons, neither the present nor the future, nor any powers, neither height nor depth, nor anything else in all creation, will be able to separate us from the love of God that is in Christ Jesus our Lord".

☞ In the new millennium there is a sense of euphoria. The truth is that nothing will change as far as the coming of some 'brave new world' is concerned. In an increasingly secular age, the Church may face new difficulties – famine, peril or sword. How then can we face such a possibility, or the lesser pressures of normal life, convinced, as Paul was, that nothing could separate us from the love of God? The answer is not in reserving our feelings when we feel down, but in reviewing what God has done for us. Trace each step in Romans 8 : 31 – 39. How do we know God is for us? He gave His Son up for us all, He chose us in electing grace and supremely in Christ we not only have a Saviour who died for our sins, but a risen and exalted Saviour who pleads our cause at the Father's right hand.

✝ *Help us, oh God not to see things through the window of circumstances but with eyes of faith. Amen.*

♥ Meditate on these words of Bishop J.C.Ryle, "We can never make too much of Christ. We can never have too high thoughts about Him, never love Him too much, trust Him too implicitly, lay too much weight upon Him and speak too highly in His praise. He is worthy of all the honour that we can give Him. He will be all in heaven. Let us see to it that He is all in our hearts on earth."

Derek Poots

15th April — Freedom

📖 Isaiah 61 : 1

"The Spirit of the Sovereign Lord is on me, because the Lord has anointed me to preach good news to the poor. He has sent me to bind up the broken-hearted, to proclaim freedom for the captives and release from darkness for the prisoners."

☞ News programmes are of consuming interest for very many people. Radio news on the hour – every hour and complete TV channels devoted to the latest news, and often bringing it live from distant parts of the world.

What do we do with the news once we have heard it or seen it? Usually very little. We show temporary interest, and only transient sorrow or joy at even the most momentous events, for another big story is always about to break.

We need to take great care not to treat the good news that Christ brings with the same almost dismissive interest. In Luke 4 : 18 – 20 Jesus applies today's words from Isaiah to Himself. This utterly enraged the 'churchgoing' people of His day. Not only were they unable to recognise really good news, but they wanted to kill the messenger there and then. (Luke 4 : 28 – 30) He offered God's gift of freedom from all sorts of devastating illnesses of the soul, but they preferred to remain impoverished, wretched, and enslaved.

✝ *Lord, help me to have a greater interest today and every day in what You want me to hear, than in what I hear from all other sources put together. Amen.*

♥ Instead of being arrested, as we stated, for kicking his wife down a flight of stairs and hurling a lighted kerosene lamp after her, the Rev James P Wellman died unmarried four years ago. (Anonymous, from an English newspaper, quoted by Sir Edward Burne-Jones in a letter.)

16th April — Freedom

📖 John 8 : 34 - 36

"I tell you the truth, everyone who sins is a slave to sin. Now a slave has no permanent place in the family, but a son belongs to it forever. So if the Son set you free, you will be free indeed."

☞ Freedom to choose what we want is often portrayed as a basic human right, whether it be our own political destiny or what to do with our bodies. The important thing is to be able to make the choice and then make it happen.

The teaching of Christ is politically incorrect in today's world. He tells us moral choices are to be made in the basis of what is true - not on the basis of arbitrary personal choice. (John 8 : 34 – 36) This 'frees up' our conscience, and our ability to make God honouring choices. Politically incorrect – maybe; life changing and life enhancing – certainly.

✝ *Lord, please deliver me from making life up as I go along. Deliver me from my sin, so that I may make truly good choices and good decisions each and every day. Amen.*

♥ Mothers all want their sons to grow up to be President, but they don't want them to become politicians in the process. (Attributed to John F Kennedy)

17th April — Freedom

Romans 6 : 22

"Now that you have been set free from sin and have become slaves to God, the benefit you reap leads to holiness, and the result is eternal life."

☞ We regard slavery as evil, and rightly so. Anything that demeans other people, or treats them as objects to be used, or as things of no importance is utterly abhorrent.

The trouble is that slavery is all around us, and we seem to love it! We secretly envy, or even publicly praise those who are slaves to ambition, or image building, or to a life of affluence and indulgence. We are rarely outraged at those things which bring such great pain and deep unhappiness to so many. We may regret them, but we are not moved to much action about them.

The apostle Paul challenges us to be freed from such a life and such desires, and to show such commitment and dedication to serving the Lord that he describes it as 'slavery'. (Romans 6 :22) A life lived like this will be beautiful, holy and eternally worthwhile. 'Slavery' to Jesus Christ enhances our life. He cannot, and will not, demean us or abuse us.

✝ *Lord, help me to offer this and every day to You, so that my life is thoroughly honouring to You, and deeply satisfying to me. Amen.*

♥ Any stigma is good enough to beat a dogma with! (Attributed to Philip Guedalla)

18th April — Freedom

Galatians 5 : 1

"It is for freedom that Christ has set us free. Stand firm, then, and do not let yourselves be burdened again by a yoke of slavery."

☞ A friend asked me recently "Why is church so often such hard work?" This is a good question with no easy answer! Part of the answer may lie in our common practice of reducing Christian faith and Christian living to a series of duties, demands, responsibilities, expectations and rules. This leads to a modern day version of the legalism for which Christ condemned the Pharisees so strongly. (Matthew 23 : 1 – 4)

Not all that enslaves us is poor, shoddy, second rate or, of itself, sinful. Even good things, good practices, good activities can be such a burden to us, that they enslave us in practice and prevent us from delighting in the freedom that Christ bought for us and offers to us.

God's people have been freed in Christ to do what is right! Let's enjoy life lived that way!

✝ *Lord, free me up to see service to You as a delight rather than as a burden; as ministry rather than duty; as a privilege as well as a responsibility. Amen*

♥ Every day people are straying away from the church and going back to God! (Attributed to the comedian Lenny Bruce in 1972)

19th April — Freedom

Galatians 5 : 13

"You, my brothers, were called to be free. But do not use your Freedom to indulge the sinful nature; rather, serve one another in love."

There is both wonderful balance and wonderful wisdom in the teaching of the Scriptures. The exercise of our freedom in Christ (like the exercise of our rights) brings real responsibilities. These are not to restrict or pull back on our level of freedom, but they are God's way of ensuring that we do not slide back into licence or renewed slavery to sin. There is always the hidden danger of self and sin creeping up on us, even unawares, and our freedom in Christ being spoiled.

In Galatians 5 : 19 Paul describes the four main ways in which we can compromise our freedom in Christ and so gratify the sinful nature mentioned in verse 13. These are sexual impurity, idolatry, poor relationships and excess behaviour. How common these are both within the church and outside it!

Perhaps we could take time now to consider which, if any, of these may be creeping up on us and eroding our freedom in Christ.

Lord, thank You for my freedom so dearly bought by Christ at Calvary. Make me watchful, aware and repentant for all that compromises my life and witness to You today. Amen.

♥

To all things cleric
I appear to be allergic.
(Attributed to Alexander Woollcott)

Norman Hamilton

20th April — Easter Joy

📖 Matthew 21 : 9

"The crowds that went ahead of him and those that followed shouted, "Hosanna" to the Son of David! Blessed is he who comes in the name of the Lord!" "Hosanna" in the highest!"

☞ Picture the scene. The crowd of people who had followed Jesus from Bethany, joining the crowd coming out from Jerusalem to meet them. The excitement mounts as they walk back down the Mount of Olives into Jerusalem. What a welcome He received from all those who walked or watched. Two thousand years later I wonder would He even be noticed? How will we welcome Jesus today? What a change He can make to the way that we do things, the people we will meet, the tasks that we have set ourselves. Why not pray that we can begin to do that from now on in some area of our life, where up until now Jesus has not felt welcome.

✝ *Dear Lord I welcome You into every area of my life this day. Help me by the Holy Spirit to show what that means in all I do and say. Amen.*

♥ If you are a Christian full of love, joy and peace why don't you tell your face about it?

21st April — Easter Joy

📖 Matthew 26 : 42

"He went away a second time and prayed, "My Father, if it is not possible for this cup to be taken away unless I drink it, may your will

be done."

☞ There have been times for all of us when we have walked away from situations and responsibilities. Maybe it was due to enormous pressure, limited time, the inability to persevere or sheer fear! However there have been and will be other situations when we have no control and we can't just get rid of them. Here ‚Jesus is not wrestling with God's will or resisting it, but rather He is yielding Himself to it, for He knew that this was His mission in the world. Whatever we have to face today or in the days to come, it will be made easier if we can pray as Jesus did, 'if it is not possible then Your will be done.' He knew that whatever was to happen He was in His Father's hands, and that was enough for Him.

✝ *Lord let Your will be done in my life and give me the peace and assurance that Your grace is sufficient for all that might mean to me today. Amen.*

♥ A great oak is only a little nut that has held its ground.

22nd April — Easter Joy

📖 Acts 2 : 23

"This man was handed over to you by God's set purpose and foreknowledge; and you, with the help of wicked men, put him to death by nailing him to the cross."

☞ The cross was no mistake; it wasn't God's Plan B in case things did not work out. It was to be the ultimate example of His love for His creation. However, that does not excuse the hatred and the wickedness of the people who put Him on the cross. Neither should it make us think, "My sin doesn't matter either. What is it compared to that which nailed Him to the cross?" But then we are looking at it through our own eyes not God's? What a sacrifice God had to make so that our sins could be forgiven forever. What a price Jesus had to pay so that we might see the cross in the glorious light of forgiveness and hope and not the darkness of sin and despair.

✝ *Heavenly Father, thank You for the freedom and forgiveness, which Jesus has bought by His death on the cross. Help me to understand and appreciate it and live in the truth of it today and every day. Amen.*

♥ The Cross is the cost of my forgiveness.

23rd April — Easter Joy

📖 Luke 24 : 1 - 3

"On the first day of the week, very early in the morning, the women took the spices they had prepared and went to the tomb. They found the stone rolled away from the tomb, but when they entered, they did not find the body of the Lord Jesus."

☞ If no other day inspires and encourages us for the future, then let today be that day. The pain of Friday watching Jesus die and the fear of the uncertainty of their future on Saturday was replaced by the confusion and then the joy of Sunday when the disciples realised that Jesus was alive. The women came expecting to find a body, but all they found was an empty tomb. Now 2000 years on from that incredible event, our joy should be none the less triumphant because Jesus is alive!

As we meet to give thanks for the greatest day in the year, let us never forget what the empty tomb means. Jesus has risen. He is alive. Death is not the end. Satan did not win. Life is stronger than death. What else can we say? 'Hallelujah, what a Saviour!'

✝ *Lord Jesus, thank You for what this day means and that because You are alive, death can never be the end for those who walk in faith with You. Amen.*

♥ The best news the world ever heard came from a graveyard.

24th April — Easter Joy

📖 John 11 : 25 - 26

"Jesus said to her, "I am the resurrection and the life. He who believes in me will live, even though he dies; and whoever lives and believes in me will never die. Do you believe this?"

☞ The present St. Paul's Cathedral stands on the site of the old cathedral that perished in the Great Fire of London in 1666. After the fire Christopher Wren spent the next 35 years of his life designing and building the new one. The first stone Wren picked up from the ruins of the old building bore a Latin inscription whose meaning was 'I shall rise again.'

This is great Christian hope. Dying may be difficult, painful, confusing, sudden, but for those who trust in Jesus, it is a doorway to eternal peace with Him. It assures us of a reunion one-day when the new will replace the old and we shall live with Him forever and ever. To live we have to die. Do you believe this?

✝ *Lord, thank You for the assurance of Your presence through the difficult times I have to face in my life. Thank You that one-day I too through faith will live with You in Heaven. Amen.*

♥ 'Do not enter the box, unless your exit road is clear.' (The Highway code).

Robert McMullen

25th April — Depression

📖 Job 3 : 2 - 3

"He said, "May the day of my birth perish, and the night it was said, A boy is born!"

☞ For many people these words are the reality of how they felt or do feel now. For those of us who have felt this, it is wonderful to find such words on the lips of a man of whom God said, "There is no one on earth like him; he is blameless and upright, a man who fears God and shuns evil." (Job 1 : 8) Job's suffering was awful. He cried out in anguish, but when his wife urged him to curse God and die (Job 2 : 9) he wouldn't do it. The book of Job is helpful to read in depression or in trying to understand this difficult subject. It is so honest about pain and suffering and the questions it raises about the point of remaining alive. Job came to a point later where he was able to say, "I know that my Redeemer lives." (Job 19 : 25). Some of his doubts and questions still remained, but he had a solid foundation of trust in God.

✝ *Lord God please help me to hold on to the fact that You made me as a special and unique person and I am of immense value to You. Amen.*

♥ When you are at rock bottom, the only way to go is up.

26th April — Depression

📖 Psalm 6 : 6 - 7

"I am worn out from groaning; all night long I flood my bed with weeping and drench my couch with tears. My eyes grow weak with sorrow; they fail because of all my foes."

☞ Yes, God understands the depth of our despair. This is His inspired word. We are not alone in those black hours. In the night hours, when we don't even have the relief of sleep, God, who never sleeps, is there. When we are emotionally drained, it can seem that we are alone. Others do care but often have difficulty communicating that care in a helpful way. God cares and understands more than we can ever comprehend. In the following verse the writer goes on to say that the Lord has heard his weeping. The God who knows how many hairs are on our heads sees every tear. God the Father who watched His Son die in agony on the Cross knows what pain and suffering are.

✝ *Lord God, thank You that I am never alone. Please help me to grasp something of the measure of Your care for me. Amen.*

♥ "I'm not a pair of curtains," I sometimes felt like saying when someone would say to me, "Pull yourself together."

27th April — Depression

Psalm 13 : 1 - 2

"How long, O Lord? Will you forget me forever? How long will you hide your face from me? How long must I wrestle with my thoughts and every day have sorrow in my heart? How long will my enemy triumph over me?"

☞ We can react to depression and difficulties of any kind in one of two opposing ways. We can either turn from God and then wonder why He seems so far away or we can turn to God. Our pain may obscure our view of God but God has not moved or changed. He is the best one to cope with our anguish and our questions. In my experience of depression it often seemed that God was not there, but looking back now I can see so many ways in which He cared and protected me. God cannot forget us as it says in Isaiah 49 : 15 – 16. 'Can a mother forget the baby at her breast and have no compassion on the child she has borne? Though she may forget, I will not forget you! See, I have engraved you on the palms of my hands...' God wants us to come to Him at all times even with our complaints. Do you see the hope in these verses? The 'How Long' suggests that an end will come. The writer expects the Lord to act.

✝ *Lord, I am so grateful for the way that You listen to my grief and despair. Help me always to turn towards You and not away. Amen.*

♥ Depression is not necessarily a sign of spiritual weakness. It can be an opportunity for extraordinary spiritual growth.

28th April Depression

Psalm 42 : 3,5

"My tears have been my food day and night, while men say to me all day long, "Where is your God?" Why are you downcast, O my soul? Why so disturbed within me? Put your hope in God for I will yet praise him, my Saviour and my God."

Sometimes you may feel that you can't cry any more – then you do! David's enemies mocked him. Sometimes even the well-meant words of others, 'Trust God' can be just the same in the midst of the darkness. We feel we are not being a 'good witness' because we believe in God and yet are so miserable. Here there is hope. How can the writer say that he will yet praise God? Look how he puts it, 'My Saviour'. God is not an impersonal force or even a God in whom he has some belief but someone with whom he has had a personal life-changing encounter. On that basis and also on the basis of what He has known of God, both personally and in the life of Israel ,he knows that he can trust the God who is his Saviour.

There is hope for the future. Circumstances may change or they may not, but in them we can know God. We may feel we have no person in whom to place our hopes but with God there is always hope, not to mention the ultimate hope of being with Him in heaven where there is no sorrow or weeping.

✝ *Father I praise You that with You there is salvation and true hope for the future. Amen.*

♥ A poster I saw said, 'All I have seen helps me to trust God for all I have not seen.'

29th April — Depression

Lamentations 3 : 17, 19 - 24

"I have been deprived of peace; I have forgotten what prosperity is. I remember my affliction and my wandering, the bitterness and the gall. I well remember them, and my soul is downcast within me. Yet this I call to mind and therefore I have hope. Because of the Lord's great love we are not consumed, for his compassions never fail. They are new every morning; great is your faithfulness. I say to myself, 'The Lord is my portion; therefore I will wait for him."

Jeremiah saw the destruction of his country and he felt pain. When everything in life seems to go wrong what do we remember; what do we focus on? That is crucial in depression and suffering. It takes great effort to call to mind the Lord's great love in midst of blackness. Gently we can help each other with this. I think we can cling to this fact even when we have no feeling of it. It is not hypocritical to act on what we know and not on what we feel, i.e. to be in fellowship, to listen to God's word being taught even when we don't feel so inclined. However to do that we need understanding from fellow worshipers.

If the Lord is 'our portion' – we belong to Him and have committed all our life to Him for better or worse, we can wait for Him. The road through depression is by the stepping stones of truth, especially the truth about God – 'his compassions never fail,' ' great is your faithfulness.'

✝ *Father help me to hold on to You when I feel that there is nothing else to hold on to. Father create in me a willingness to show Your love to others when they are suffering.*

♥ Maybe sometimes our prayer is, 'Lord, give me patience and give it to me now!'

Joan Singleton

30th April — Confessing of Sin

📖 Psalm 32 : 2 – 5

"Blessed is the man whose sin the Lord does not count against him and in whose spirit is no deceit. When I kept silent, my bones wasted away through my groaning all day long. For day and night your hand was heavy upon me; my strength was sapped as in the heat of summer. Then I acknowledged my sin to you and did not cover up my iniquity. I said, "I will confess my transgressions to the Lord"– and you forgave the guilt of my sin."

☞ My daughters recently planted sunflower seeds as part of a school project. Once they were established, they were given the plants to take home and told to take care of them. They did that very well until they put the plants by the window in my study in order to provide them with more light. Under my care they flourished for a while until I forgot to water them and I found two droopy and weary plants one morning. Their 'strength was sapped' by the heat of the sun, and lack of water, and very sad they looked.

The girls' sunflowers looked like how David felt on account of his sin and his failure to acknowledge it to God. He had kept quiet and had then to carry around the guilt and the burden of all those wrong actions, words and thoughts by himself. Just like many people today who are very unhappy with how they are living and the sort of person that they are, but who will not turn to God, through Jesus Christ His Son, for His forgiveness.

✝ *Merciful Father, help me to turn to You for the forgiveness I desperately need and which You are so ready to give. Amen.*

♥ The sunflowers have survived – despite my neglect!

MAY

This 5″ square reproduction of the Bullfinch linocut is only a little reduced from the 6′ square of the originally carved linoblock

Most of the black ink prints in its edition are watercoloured in grey, pink and in greens, The colours of the cock bird and his surroundings - but this illustration is taken from on that is monochrome tinted.

1st May Confessing of Sin

Psalm 51 : 7

"Cleanse me with hyssop, and I will be clean; wash me and I shall be whiter than snow."

☞ It is a good job, from David's point of view, that there was no tabloid press in his time, no journalist rummaging in his private life, because had there been they would have found lust, adultery, conspiracy and murder, amongst other things. And all of these lie behind what he writes here in Psalm 51 (you can read about it in 2 Samuel 11+12). David had gone badly wrong, but, at least in relation to how to deal with his sin, David got it right. In contrast to his approach in Psalm 32, here he realises that his greatest need is to have God 'cleanse' him, or literally 'un-sin' him. He knows that only God can make him clean. There is nothing that he can do for himself in this regard, no sacrifice can make up for what he has done, neither can any experience that he could go through, nor any effort that he could make on his own behalf. Only God could deal with this for him and make him as 'white as snow.'

It is the same for each of us as it was for him. We cannot make up for what we have done, even if it is not on the same scale as David, but God can, and has, in the death of His Son on the cross.

✝ *Heavenly Father, Thank You for Jesus' death on the cross where He gave His life to cleanse me from my sin. Amen.*

♥ T T I C D N A B G C isn't a typing error – it stands for 'Things that I can do nothing about but God can.' Our sin is one of those T T I C D N A B G C.

2nd May — Confessing of Sin

Proverbs 28 : 13

"He who conceals his sins does not prosper, but whoever confesses and renounces them finds mercy."

☞ What was the first thing that Adam and Eve did when they realised their mistake in taking the fruit? They tried to cover it up. Both verbally and literally, they tried to hide their mistake and to cover it up. Mankind has been at the same thing ever since. Some try to deny their guilt outright – " *I haven't done anything wrong – I'm a pretty good person*!" Others will admit that they have done something but deny that there is anything wrong with it – *"I did it, but, why shouldn't I do something if it feels good to me?"* Still more, will admit that they have done something, agree that it is wrong, but try to excuse themselves on account of certain circumstances. – *"I know that I shouldn't have done it but I couldn't help myself*!"

Why do we persist in attempting to cover things up when honestly confessing them to God would bring forgiveness?

✝ *Heavenly Father, You know All things and You know my wrong doing better than I even do myself. Help me not to try to cover it up but to confess it to You. Amen.*

♥ Barbara Johnston has some good advice for us, 'if you want God's fire to burn brightly in your heart, rake out yesterday's ashes.'

3rd May — Confessing of Sin

James 5 : 16

"Therefore confess your sins to each other and pray for each other so that you may be healed. The prayer of a righteous man is powerful and effective."

☞ When we see 'therefore' in the Bible then we always need to ask what it is there for. And, what it is there for here is to link this verse with what has gone before. James has just been writing about how wonderful prayer is, and how we can bring those who are sick to God, he is now telling us to be enthusiastic about praying in all situations, and perhaps, especially when it comes to sin. When we are aware of our sin and want to get rid of it, what are we to do? We are to pray. James says, there will be situations when we feel so burdened and threatened by our sin that the best thing to do is to get together with others and pray with them. It is a step that we all find hard to take – admitting our faults and failings to others and asking them to pray with us and for us – but it can be an invaluable one.

✝ *Lord God, Help me to appreciate how valuable prayer is and be ready to pray with others – even about my sin. Amen.*

♥ There is a tradition that James was nicknames 'Camel Knees' because his knees were so callused and hardened through the time he spent on them praying to God. None of us would like to known as 'Camel knees", but, wouldn't being known as a man or woman of prayer be a marvellous thing?

4th May — Confessing of Sin

1 John 1 : 9

"If we confess our sins, he is faithful and just ,and will forgive us our sins and purify us from all unrighteousness."

In the previous verse John has written of those who try to deny that they do wrong and says that they are fooling themselves. That has to be right, doesn't it? We either have to be extremely self–deluded or incredibly conceited to believe that we are living the perfect life. What, then can we do about our sins? Nothing, except confess them. John tells us. Admit our wrongdoing to God, and throw ourselves on His mercy by asking Him to save us. Which is exactly what He will do because He is faithful and just. All who confess their sin to Him and trust in Christ are forgiven and have their sin forgotten. God promises to do that and He keeps His promises.

Heavenly Father, Help us to be realistic about ourselves, and do the only thing that we can do – confess our sins to You. Amen

Psychologists tell us that the only way to deal with things that trouble us is to bring them out into the open and face them. In doing so they are doing something that would surprise many of them – following God's instructions here!

Tom Conway

5th May — The Obedience of Christ

📖 Psalm 40 : 6,8

"Sacrifice and offering you did not desire, but my ears you have opened...I desire to do your will, O my God; your law is within my heart."

☞ Practicing medicine in a language not your own has it's problems! My Tumbuka accent is so poor that I get answers to questions I didn't ask! My patients answer the questions they *think* a doctor should ask. Question: "Are you eating well?" Answer "I'm 52." I have asked them to "Jurani makutu" – 'listen carefully.' Literally, means 'Open your ears!'

Our theme for the next few days is the obedience of Christ. At the heart of much of our *disobedience* is our failure to 'open our ears.' We do what we *think* God expects of us, without really listening to His voice.

The psalmist makes it clear that God desires obedience in everyday affairs, rather than observance of empty rituals. Even today, obedience is sometimes limited to a list of religious activity e.g. church attendance or regular giving. Don't get me wrong. These things are good, but God wants us to get beyond ritual. He wants us to open our ears, and obey Him as He speaks to every aspect of our lives.

Listen carefully! What is God asking you to do today?

✝ *Lord, in every part of this day, open my ears to Your voice, and help me to obey You with a willing heart, as Jesus did. Amen.*

♥ Junior Missionary Language Blunder No. 1 "I went to the post office to collect my urine." (Katundu = package, kutunda = urine)

6th May — The Obedience of Christ

Isaiah 53 : 10

"Yet it was the Lord's will to crush him and cause him to suffer, and though the Lord makes his life a guilt offering he will see his offspring and prolong his days, and the will of the Lord will prosper in his hand."

☞ Obedience can get you in trouble! Isaiah's 'suffering servant' will be 'crushed' as a result of obeying the Lord's will. Of course, he was prophesying about Jesus, who was obedient 'even to death on a cross.' (Philippians 2 : 8)

In many parts of the world today, obeying God's command to stand up for the poor or oppressed may result in torture or death. In the West, we may not risk physical suffering for the sake of Christ, but genuine Christian living always challenges the thinking and actions of spirit of the age.

To obey God is to swim against the tide of cynicism, materialism, pluralism and hedonism that blights our world. It isn't easy! For all the talk of tolerance, the world hates those who rejects its values.

Think about our values, our lifestyles and our goals. Are they really all that different from those around us who do not know Christ?

✝ *Lord Jesus, You had the courage to be different - to obey even when it got You into trouble. Lord grant me the same courage to follow You in radical obedience. Amen.*

♥ Junior Missionary Language Blunder No 2: "I've lost my pet lion." (chona winu = cat, chona chinu = lion).

7th May — The Obedience of Christ

Matthew 26 : 42

"He went away a second time and prayed, "My Father, if it is not possible for this cup to be taken away unless I drink it, may your will be done."

☞ It's difficult to find words that are adequate for this verse. The emotions, the inner struggle, the quiet resolve that lie behind Christ's words are well beyond my understanding.

He was obedient, even to the point of drinking from *this cup* of suffering. He knew what was expected of Him, and He didn't shrink from it.

My 'cups' pale into insignificance. For me to obey may mean giving up some time, or money. I may have to say sorry and lose some pride. I may have to stop watching a film on TV, or discipline myself to pray. Not much really, yet all too often I leave my cup full. I hand it back to God, unwilling to drink it.

When I think of Gethsemane and Golgotha, all I can do is be thankful that Jesus drained His cup, for me.

✝ *Lord, thank You that You didn't shrink from paying the price for my disobedience. Amen*

♥ Junior Missionary Language Blunder No. 3: "I'd like some marijuana." (Chambo = fish, chamba = marijuana).

8th May The Obedience of Christ

📖 John 8 : 29

"The one who sent me is with me; he has not left me alone, for I always do what pleases him."

☞ I'm sure that most of us welcome the promise of God's presence. Working overseas for the first time in a new culture, any new experience or time of stress, often prompts us to turn afresh to God and ask Him to stay close. It was important for Jesus – He mentions it several times in John's Gospel (8 : 16,29; 16 : 32).

But today's verse reminds us that God's presence in our lives is *conditional* – conditional on our obedience. 'He has not left me alone, **for** I always do what pleases Him.' It makes sense. Our obedience (or lack of it) reflects our desire (or lack of it) to be close to God. Willful disobedience shuts the Lord out of our lives. He cannot reside where He is not welcome. Christ's obedience was both the precondition and the evidence of His Father's presence.

Too often, I have driven Him away. Thankfully, He is ever ready to be welcomed back in. (Revelation 3 : 20) .

When or where do you need God to be with you today? Is disobedience keeping Him away?

✝ *Lord Jesus, help me to do what pleases You, and do not leave me alone. Amen*

♥ Junior Missionary language Blunder No 4. "Before St. Patrick came we used to go to the toilet." (I was attempting to say we worshipped spirits – vimbuza = spirit, vimbuzi = toilet)

9th May — The Obedience of Christ

Hebrews 5 : 8

"Although he was a Son, he learned obedience from what he suffered."

Obedience doesn't follow automatically when you become a Christian (you may have noticed!). It needs to be *learned*. As we read today, even Jesus had to learn obedience.

What does this mean – that He was imperfect in some way? No. But in Jesus' life we can see a series of events that increasingly tested His obedience. The temptations in the desert, the rebuke of Peter, the threats of the priests and Pilate are all steps climbing higher and higher towards the ultimate test of His obedience – the cross.

It was in suffering, in overcoming the temptation to give up when things were tough, that Jesus learnt obedience. The Lord's teaching methods have not changed. Here in Malawi, people face material and physical challenges that would overwhelm my faith. They face them daily, with acceptance of God's will, and trust for His provision. It's no surprise, then, that their Christian maturity and love surpasses mine.

Jesus knows how hard it can be to obey, even in the midst of suffering. In the areas of our lives that are difficult right now lets ask for His help to keep listening to God, and doing what He says.

✝ *Lord Jesus, You experienced suffering first hand, and, through it, grew in obedience. Help us keep obeying even when life is hard. Amen.*

♥ Junior Missionary Language Blunder No. 5: "Your leg's broken – you need a sin doctor." (chiwangwa = bone, zakwanganga = sin) Perhaps we all need a 'sin' doctor!

Neil Kennedy

10th May — A Call to Social Action

Matthew 25 : 34 - 40

"Then the King will say to those on his right, 'Come, you who are blessed by my Father; take your inheritance, the kingdom prepared for you since the creation of the world. For I was hungry and you gave me something to eat, I was thirsty and you gave me something to drink, I was a stranger and you invited me in, I needed clothes and you clothed me, I was sick and you looked after me, I was in prison and you came to visit me.

Then the righteous will answer him, 'Lord, when did we see you hungry and feed you, or thirsty and give you something to drink? When did we see you a stranger and invite you in or needing clothes and clothe you? When did we see you sick or in prison and go to visit you? The King will reply, 'I tell you the truth, whatever you did for one of the least of these brothers of mine, you did for me.'"

Surprise!

Whoa!! What's all this? Justification by works? A social gospel? **I DON'T THINK SO!!** Clearly, evangelism and social action were two sides of the same coin in Jesus' ministry, which gives me a nagging feeling that our lives shouldn't be any different from His.

What's more, this is the acid test. Jesus is going to gauge the extent of our love for Him by our reaction to the poor. To borrow a famous phrase, "He hasn't gone away, you know." Jesus is still here, working undercover, giving us opportunities to demonstrate to others the grace which He has shown to us.

Day-by-day He challenges us through the poor. Those who rise to the challenge and give themselves to others with that same self-sacrificing love are confirming their reservation for a place in the Kingdom. Those who have it in their power to relieve the suffering of others but neglect to do so, deny any knowledge of Christ and are destined for hell. As

Jesus said on another occasion, "You can't serve God and Mammon." He also told us that the last day is going to spring a few surprises!

✝ *Lord, thank You for your amazing grace to me. Help me to set aside self-interest and pass on a little of that grace to those less fortunate than myself. Amen.*

♥ Aw, man! This is getting heavy. I thought all I had to do was pray that "sinner's prayer", I didn't know it was going to cost me!

11th May A Call to Social Action

📖 Zechariah 7 : 5, 9 - 10.

"Ask all the people of the land and the priests, 'When you fasted and mourned in the fifth and seventh months for the past seventy years, was it really for me that you fasted?... This is what the Lord Almighty says: 'Administer true justice; show mercy and compassion to one another. Do not oppress the widow or the fatherless, the alien or the poor. In your hearts do not think evil of each other."

☞ **Going through the motions**

Seventy years of piety disappear down the loo with one simple question, "Was it really for Me?" They wanted to know if it was God's will that they fast as they had done all these years but God wanted a different kind of fast, not just a fast from food for a period of time but a fast that spilled over into everything they did. He wanted real self-denial, not just avoiding the meat, potatoes and two veg. but actually putting others first!

God's vision of a successful society is not measured in the number of millionaires but rather on the value placed on the "little ones", the disenfranchised, the marginalised, those not in control of their own destiny. He wants to see a society that reflects His character. When we demonstrate His compassion in our lives we are truly "evangelical" because we make Him manifest (II Corinthians 4 : 10).

✝ *Lord, keep me from mistaking piety for real Christianity and help me to remember that people don't care how much I know, until they know how much I care! Amen.*

♥ We might attend church twice every Sunday and always show up at the mid-week, but if our lives don't reflect the character of God we might as well be at home, with our feet up, in front of the box!

12th May — A Call to Social Action

📖 James 5 : 4 - 5.

"Look! The wages you failed to pay the workmen who mowed your fields are crying out against you. The cries of the harvesters have reached the ears of the Lord Almighty. You have lived on earth in luxury and self-indulgence. You have fattened yourselves in the day of slaughter."

☞ **Putting our money where our mouth is.**

Though we may not see ourselves as such, in a world-wide context, we are the wealthy. Unfair! I hear you cry, we work hard for our money and gain it by honest means. We don't defraud anyone out of their wages! This scripture doesn't apply to us! Or does it?

We, in the West, have tremendous economic power. Our collective buying power can very easily be abused on our behalf, if not with our consent. We live in a complex, urban society where we are so far removed from the production of the goods we consume that we have no idea if they were produced in oppressive working conditions, or manufactured using child labour. Our main concern is price, and if the price is right we are reluctant to examine the means of production too closely. Maybe we should pause and consider whether the lifestyle that we enjoy is made possible through the exploitation of others.

✝ *Lord, protect me from the danger of letting my self-interest get the upper hand when I'm choosing which product to buy. Amen.*

♥ Maybe we can't all be Billy Grahams, but if our friends see us paying over the odds for "fair trade" goods it should at least give them "food for thought."

13th May — A Call to Social Action

📖 Luke 5 : 12 - 13.

"While Jesus was in one of the towns a man came along who was covered with leprosy. When he saw Jesus he fell with his face to the ground and begged him, "Lord, if you are willing you can make me clean." Jesus reached out his hand and touched the man. "I am willing," he said. "Be clean!" And immediately the leprosy left him."

☞ **Touching the "Untouchables"**

Leprosy was a death sentence, and not just for the fact that it was a disease for which there was no cure. In Jesus' time it also meant exile from human society. The law required them to keep at least six feet away from healthy people or 150 feet if they were standing upwind, and most people applied their own rules which went far beyond the law. Lepers soon learned to stay clear of other people, if they knew what was good for them!

Strange then, that this guy sought out Jesus. It says a lot about his perception of Jesus. Stranger still, at least to the onlookers, that Jesus actually touched him. Jesus' action says a lot about Him. He could have kept His distance and healed this man but He "touched" Him. He didn't just heal the disease, He healed the hurt of rejection and isolation.

Our society also has its "untouchables", the AIDS victims, homosexual men and women, the down-and-outs. Do they see us as a source of help? Do we reach out to them and try to heal the hurt, even if we can't heal the "disease?"

✝ *Lord, take away my heart of stone and give me Your heart of compassion that others may see a little of You in me. Bring this story to my mind the next time I try to stay "upwind" of a down-and-out. Amen.*

♥ God is not against trying and failing, but He is against us failing to try. Trying and failing, and trying again is called learning.

14th May — A Call to Social Action

📖 Luke 16 : 19 - 21.

"There was a rich man who was dressed in purple and fine linen and lived in luxury every day. At his gate was laid a beggar named Lazarus,

covered with sores and longing to eat what fell from the rich man's table. Even the dogs came and licked his sores."

☞ None so blind .....

We tend to think that spirituality and money are incompatible, yet in Jesus' teaching it's quite clear that there are few things more spiritual than the way we use our money. What we have been given is never just for ourselves alone, it is also to enable us to bless others. In fact, Austin Farrer believed that, 'what we have done with our money is what we have done with our lives'.

That was very true in the case of this rich man, he kept his wealth exclusively for his own use. In fact, he was so absorbed in the enjoyment of his wealth that he didn't even **see** poor Lazarus lying at his gate. This self-serving attitude was the distinguishing characteristic of his life. Throughout my life I have often been struck by the ready generosity of people who didn't have very much to begin with, and by the meanness of some people for whom financial worry was an unknown. It seems that the more we have the less inclined we are to share.

✝ *Lord, open my eyes to those in need and protect me from my greedy, selfish nature. Help me to spend my time and my resources for the benefit of others and not just for my own self-gratification. Amen.*

♥ If scripture doesn't convince us of the need for social action, Abraham tells us that not even seeing a ghost will do it (v.31). Now, how scary is that!

David Boyd

15th May — Children

Deuteronomy 6 : 6 - 7

"These commandments that I give you today are to be upon your hearts. Impress them on your children. Talk about them when you sit at home and when you walk along the road, when you lie down and when you get up."

Modern life is so crazy. Parents feel they have little time and even less energy to have deep spiritual discussions with children who appear much more interested in TV or computer games anyway.

Deuteronomy suggests two daily opportunities to talk to our families about God in a natural way.

1. '**When you sit at home.'** In our house we try at least once a day to all sit down and share a meal together and at that meal we say, sing or sometimes 'rap' a grace. Simple. Fun. But still daily acknowledging God as Creator, Sustainer and Lord.

2. '**When you walk along the road'** or ' when you drive your children to school' or ' when you take your children for a bike ride in the countryside.' As you admire nature and growl at the litterlouts, talk about our Creator's creativity and power and our selfishness and carelessness, which threaten to spoil everything. Get the idea?

Watch out, children soon get wise to the empty words. God's ways must be 'upon our hearts'. Our lessons will only be natural if they are from the heart and lived out in practice.

Heavenly Father, thank You that You are our Creator, Sustainer and Lord. Amen.

The try-angle will take you round the hardest of corners.

16th May **Children**

Joshua 24 : 15

"But if serving the Lord seems undesirable to you, then choose for yourselves this day whom you will serve, whether the gods your forefathers served beyond the River, or the gods of the Amorites, in whose land you are living. But as for me and my household, we will serve the Lord".

☞ We parents must be prepared to take a stand for what is right. If our children are ever going to handle peer pressure they need strong role models in us, even if at times they resent us.

I suppose the bottom line is we all follow someone or something, be it a team, a trend, a celebrity or a friend. We base a lot of our lives on what others do or think.

Joshua had decided the best option for him and his family was to serve the God who had rescued them from slavery in Egypt. It's ironic but true that the first step towards living a truly 'free', strong, independent life is to willingly surrender our lives to someone else, that someone being God. Jesus echoed this idea when He declared 'If you hold to (obey) my teaching you are really my disciples. Then you will know the truth and the truth will set you free.' (John 8 : 31 – 32)

In a society where moral and spiritual foundations are largely collapsing, our children need parents who will demonstrate the truth of the hymn:

'Your bondage is freedom, Your service is song
And, held in Your keeping, my weakness is strong.'

✝ *Heavenly Father, I willingly surrender my Life to You. Amen.*

♥ Children disgrace us in public by behaving just like we do at home.

17th May Children

📖 Proverbs 22 : 6

"Train a child in the way he should go, and when he is old he will not turn from it."

☞ You never forget how to ride a bike. After years without practice your feet still find the pedals and away you go, whistling down the lane.

The lessons we learn as children stay with us for life, often becoming part of who we are as adults. This is true negatively and we hear a lot nowadays of adults struggling to come to terms with childhood trauma such as abuse or their parents' divorce. Thankfully it can also be true positively and children raised in God–honouring, loving, people–friendly homes often grow to share their parents' values.

So if, as part of our covenant relationship with our Father in Heaven, we teach our children by word and example to have reverence for God, to love their neighbour and care for the environment we do not only do them, but their future world, a big favour.

✝ *Heavenly Father, help me teach my children by word and example to love You as I do. Amen*

♥ Parents of brilliant children are great believers in heredity!

18th May — Children

📖 Ephesians 6 : 1 - 2

"Children obey your parents in the Lord, for this is right. "Honour you father and mother"...

☞ If it used to be the case that children were 'seen and not heard' the pendulum has well and truly swung in the opposite direction. These days youth is worshipped and young people indulged or feared. Respect for age and the wisdom of gathered experience has been turned upside down.

Ever notice how commandment number 5 above is like a bridge between 1 - 4 (which are to do with our relationship with God) and 6 – 10 (which are to do with everybody else)? That suggests to me that if we want to have a safe, healthy, law–abiding society we need to work on our relationship with God and those closest to us, i.e. our family. Reverence for God + families = positive society, in that order.

So children should be encouraged to respect their parents, teachers, elders and so on. Anarchy is corrosive but obedience to God and our parents make for stability.

Of course the sting in the tail here is really for parents. The challenge for us is to live lives worthy of respect and give instructions worthy to be obeyed!

✝ *Heavenly Father, help me live my life worthy of Your love. Amen.*

♥ To really know a man, observe his behaviour with a woman, a flat tyre and a child.

19th May

Children

Ephesians 6 : 4

"Fathers, do not exasperate your children; instead bring them up in the training and instruction of the Lord."

☞ It's so easy by careless sarcasm, or failure to hold our own tongues, to frustrate or knock the heart out of our children. A hundred and one things are weighing on our minds and nerves, and the dam bursts somewhat unfairly when one of our children is unfortunate enough to be naughty just then.

By contrast Rob Parsons speaks of 'catching children doing something right' and really praising them. Parents need to be positive and affectionate, with the patience of Job, the Wisdom of Solomon and more negotiating skills than the United Nations put together!

We parents know all that, but it's tough. This is the only chance we get at this and we've never done it before.

Thankfully, we have an example to follow and a helping hand from our Loving Father in Heaven, His patient correction, His willingness to forgive, His love which never ends. Those who, by His grace in Christ ,share membership of His family can benefit from His wise and powerful help with their own.

✝ *Heavenly Father, help me be patient, affectionate, quick with praise, slow to anger and encourage my children in all things. Amen*

♥ Silence is a friend that will never betray.

Andrew Watson

20th May **Bereavement**

Psalm 23 : 4 - 6

"Even though I walk through the valley of the shadow of death I will fear no evil, for you are with me; your rod and your staff they comfort me. You prepare a table before me in the presence of my enemies. You anoint my head with oil; my cup overflows. Surely goodness and love will follow me all the days of my life, and I will dwell in the house of the Lord forever."

☞ The late Mother Teresa of Calcutta said that the greatest disease in the modern world was loneliness. For those recently bereaved this may be the most acute pain. In this most beloved of Psalms, David remembers that the Lord as his Shepherd will be his companion by his side in every situation and at all times providing all that he needs.

When the valley of death casts its shadow, the Lord's rod and staff are there – these were used for counting, guiding, protecting, rescuing and supporting the sheep. They are symbols of the Shepherd's love. We are guests at His feast in v 5; His steadfast love and goodness will literally 'pursue' us all our days; and our destiny is to dwell in His house forever. Though sometimes lonely, we'll never walk alone. 'The valley may be dark, the shadows deep. But oh the Shepherd guards His lonely sheep. And through the gloom He'll lead me home. My Heavenly Father watches over me.'

✝ *Lord, thank You that You will never leave me, nor forsake me. Help me to feel Your presence with me today. Amen.*

♥ He who runs from God in the morning will scarcely find Him the rest of the day.

21st May **Bereavement**

John 14 : 3

"If I go and prepare a place for you, I will come back and take you to be with me that you also may be where I am."

Jesus here makes a promise and, as we try to find a firm place for our foot when walking on marshy ground, we should jump on this as a firm place to stand. And what a promise! He is coming back to take us to be with Him.

A missionary returned home after 40 years service in Africa; no one was there to meet him. On the same boat was the President of America returning after 4 weeks big game hunting and the bands were there to greet him. The missionary arrived in his lonely room. Gutted, he got down on his knees and cried out "Lord, why no welcome for me when I come home?" The Lord whispered in his heart "You are not home yet". When you feel as low as that man, just remember, Jesus is getting your room and your welcome ready; you're not home yet; but He is coming to take you home. Lift up your head; your redemption is closer now than when you first believed. And what a glorious day that will be when we see Jesus face to face!

✝ *Lord, if today I feel so weary or low I think I cannot go on, help me to remember there's a wonderful homecoming waiting for me some day. Amen*

♥ The Lord sometimes takes us into troubled waters, not to drown us but to cleanse us.

22nd May — Bereavement

📖 Romans 12 : 15

"Rejoice with those who rejoice; mourn with those who mourn."

☞ Paul Tournier, who wrote many books on the subject of counselling, said that "What we say to people matters less than the attitude of mind they see we have towards them." Often when we want to reach out to those in distress or mourning we wonder what we can say. If Tournier is right it is not our words that matter most, but our attitude. We can be sure that where there is genuine love and compassion, where there is real listening, where there is a real desire to understand and to draw alongside, there will be a healing work done. Those who mourn often feel like lepers because people avoid them out of embarrassment. Jesus reached out and touched the leper who felt so unwanted and rejected. In Jesus' Name reach out with hand and heart to the hurting and grieving; let them know you care; and when their mourning turns to rejoicing, you will share their joy too.

✝ *Lord, don't let me run away from anyone who needs me today, but instead help me move towards them with Your love. Amen.*

♥ The thing most often opened by mistake is the mouth.

23rd May — Bereavement

📖 2 Corinthians 1 : 3 - 4

"Praise be to the God and Father of our Lord Jesus Christ, the Father of compassion and the God of all comfort, who comforts us in all our troubles, so that we can comfort those in any trouble with the comfort

we ourselves have received from God."

☞ There is nothing quite so hollow as the person who shakes your hand and says "I know how you must be feeling," when that cannot possibly be the case. In contrast when someone who has been through what you are going through comes alongside and is simply there, their presence, even with few words spoken, will breathe strength and hope into your aching heart.

This verse helps us see our sufferings as a pathway to ministry. What we have received we can give to others. This is how God works. 'Freely you have received, freely give.' What hard times have you been through? Did you or do you think you are the only one? No, there are many, many others, and if you received the Lord's grace and comfort, it was so that in turn you might be a channel of it to these others. Your suffering is not a stumbling block to faith but a stepping stone to ministry. You have something real and precious to give to others. Ask God to send them across your path.

✝ *Lord, I now believe I have something from You I can give to others. Give me the courage to do that today. Amen.*

♥ Don't be a stagnant pond that takes but never gives; be a reservoir which receives and then gives out life-giving water.

24th May — Bereavement

📖 Hebrews 4 : 15 – 16

"We do not have a high priest who is unable to sympathise with our weakness, but we have one who has been tested in every way, just as

we are – yet was without sin. Let us then approach the throne of grace with confidence, so that we may receive mercy and find grace to help us in our time of need."

☞ I well remember a friend saying how he had unburdened himself one day to his minister. It was not a time of bereavement, but rather of many burdens and a sense of failure. His pastor just put a hand on his shoulder and said, "Jesus understands." The burden was lifted. Our loving Lord Jesus is such a gentle and merciful Saviour because He knows the struggles and trials of this earthly life. He too cried out with tears and pleaded that the cup might pass from Him. So when He sees the buckled reed He does not break it, and the smoldering flax He does not snuff it out, but instead He repairs and builds up. Some feel under the burden of bereavement and loss that they will never truly live again. But Jesus as with those on the Emmaus road can put hope in our hearts again. 'In every pang that rends the heart, The Man of Sorrows has a part. He sympathises with our grief, and to the sufferer send relief. Though now ascended up on high, He bends on earth a brother's eye. Partaker of the human name. He knows the reality of our frame.'

✝ *Thank You, Lord Jesus, that there is nothing I will pass through this day that You haven't met and don't understand. Amen.*

♥ There are two ways to remove a burden: one is to banish the load, and the other is to double the strength.

David Cupples

25th May Failure

📖 Daniel 5 : 27

"You have been weighed on the scales and found wanting."

☞ Poor old Belshazzar should have known better. He had seen his father, Nebuchadnezzar, learn at the hands of God just who was boss. The most powerful of all Babylon's rulers, Nebuchadnezzar had been reduced to running around like a wild animal by the sovereign God. From stealing articles from the temple in a devastated Jerusalem to saying of God, "Then I praised the Most High; I honoured and glorified Him who lives forever."

Belshazzar had failed to learn from that lesson – that man's chief end is to glorify God and enjoy Him forever. He had gone after his own glory and had failed life's ultimate test. By taking his eyes off the Lord he was bound to fall short of God's standards. That is why it is so important to walk with God **EVERY** day – **in** His word and **by** His word. Don't be found wanting today.

✝ *O God, help me to learn from You every day, so that by Your strength and guidance I may never be found wanting in Your eyes. Amen.*

♥ We all may diet, but be careful, don't lose weight in God's eyes!

26th May Failure

📖 Mark 14 : 37

"Then he returned to his disciples and found them sleeping. "Simon," he said to Peter, "are you asleep? Could you not keep watch for one hour?"

☞ The disciples had been through an extremely busy few days – the triumphal entry, clearing the temple, final encounters with the religious leaders, the Last Supper, trying to understand what Jesus was saying in His conversations with them. No wonder when they went out into the quietness of Gethsemane after a good meal that they dozed off, while waiting for Jesus.

When busy and tired, we can be susceptible to failure. Jesus saw this in His disciples, 'The spirit is willing, but the body is weak'. Sometimes it is good to take time to re-sharpen our spiritual sword. Jesus encouraged the disciples to pray for themselves that they may be protected from temptation. In our busy world we must guard our time with God and our time for rest so that we are fit and ready for service whenever God's call comes.

✝ *Heavenly Father, help me to prioritize this day in such a way that I am ready to answer Your call to serve at any moment. Amen.*

♥ Don't get so earthly tired that you are of no heavenly use!

27th May — Failure

📖 Luke 22 : 31 – 32

"Simon, Simon, Satan has asked to sift you as wheat. But I have prayed for you, Simon, that your faith may not fail. And when you have turned back, strengthen your brothers."

☞ In one sense we can take comfort from this – that even the great men of the Bible failed the Lord at times. Recently, I helped a couple from Taiwan with a problem. Afterwards as we chatted, Mike said to me – "Peter was the disciple who denied Jesus." Peter's failure to stand up for Jesus is one of the famous parts of the Bible and yet it is only half the story.

In his shame Peter knew what he had done, but Jesus forgave him. His faith was renewed, out of repentance came growth and Peter went on to be instrumental in the development of the infant Christian church. Isn't it good to know that God does not discard us like rubbish when we fail Him? If you are dealing with spiritual failure today – remember Peter and what God was able to do with someone who let Him down but was determined to keep striving.

✝ *Father, I thank You that, like Peter, You are willing to help get me get up, dust myself down, and give me a new start. Amen.*

♥ Through God, your cloud can have a silver lining.

28th May — Failure

📖 Hebrews 10 : 21 - 22

"Since we have a great priest over the house of God, let us draw near to God with a sincere heart in full assurance of faith, having our hearts sprinkled to cleanse us from a guilty conscience."

☞ It is often said that a game of football involves 22 professionals running around a pitch with 40,000 amateurs screaming at them how it should be done! Of course unless you have played to that standard it is unfair to criticize. I can remember once, watching a game at Wembley and being amazed at how hard the ball was kicked not only in shots on goal but also in passing movements.

The same could never be said of Jesus. He watches over us and, rather than shouting at us in frustration, He pleads for us to the Father who is able to help. Is that not amazing that YOU are top of Jesus prayer topics? The reason why He prays is because He has been through this life and knows what we have to face, so rather than criticize He would rather support and encourage us.

✝ *Father, I thank You that Jesus loves me so much that not only did He die for me, but He also continually prays for me. Amen.*

♥ Your greatest supporter is cheering you on today to win your life's match.

29th May — Failure

📖 James 3 : 2

"We all stumble in many ways. If anyone is never at fault in what he says, he is a perfect man, able to keep his whole body in check."

☞ My niece has just started to walk. Her home has not yet adapted to a 'toddler' staggering and slipping and tripping her way around the house. So it plays havoc with the nerves, watching her stand near to the hearth or the coffee table rocking backwards and forwards.

Inevitably, she stumbles and falls.

Like children, we too stumble in our spiritual walk. When we stumble we fail. And failure can rob us of our confidence – it leaves us feeling foolish and discouraged. We must remember this – EVERYONE fails. NO–ONE is perfect except Jesus Himself.

The challenge for us today is how well are we walking with God. Are we getting stronger and swifter – or still toddling around and meeting with failure regularly? We can move on, for God supplies the strength we need to grow and to make failure something that we meet with less and less.

✝ *O God, today help me to take strong, bold steps for You that help me to grow up in You and make failure something I have to deal with less frequently. Amen.*

♥ Time to remove those 'Beware! Toddler on Board' Stickers over your life?

Peter Lyle

30th May — The Holy Spirit

📖 Genesis 1: 2

"Now the earth was formless and empty, darkness was over the surface of the deep, and the Spirit of God was hovering over the waters."

☞ Have you seen any of those TV programmes where people have their rooms changed (restyled completely) or their gardens transformed?

What a tremendous change God's Spirit brings about as He 'broods' over the early earth and 'hatches' new life. From a dark, watery, mucky mess, God's Spirit totally transforms the whole landscape…from empty to full…from darkness to light…from chaos to order.

That is so typical of the creative Holy Spirit of God. Whether it's the whole Universe or a tiny life of one individual person like you or me, when God's Spirit gets to work, the changes are truly 'awesome'.

Sometimes things in our lives can seem so empty and bleak that we lose all hope of change. We begin to despair that...real...permanent...life-transforming **change** is beyond us.

Maybe it is **beyond us**...but it's certainly not beyond the scope, the love or the power of God's Spirit.

As we are **willing**, God's Spirit is **able** to bring about life transforming change in us today. Why not open ourselves up to all that God's Spirit would want to do in us right now?

✝ *I want to co-operate with Your Spirit in all the changes, which You wish to bring about in me. Have Your way fully in me. Amen.*

♥ Here is a weather forecast: If to-day is starting off bleak and dark...Think how bright it could be by the end if God's Spirit gets to work...There is hope!

31st May — The Holy Spirit

📖 Exodus 31 : 3

"The Lord said, "I have filled him with the Spirit of God, with skill, ability and knowledge in all kinds of crafts."

☞ In my house...there are always jobs to be done...and it's often me who hasn't done them! In this story there is a job to be done - A TENT

OF MEETING (a kind of mobile Church building) to be made. When God commands something to be done, He also provides the people with the skills and abilities to do it. So the Holy Spirit, who is so creative and imaginative Himself, fills Bezalel with the skills and abilities to get the job done.

There are many jobs to be done today...God given tasks. Many of them are very small, some much larger. As God fills and controls our lives by His Holy Spirit, so He equips and empowers us **to be** what He wants us to be and **to do** what He wants us to do.

Satan whispers in our ears and we say to ourselves, "I have no skills or abilities, which God could use, I am so ordinary, so useless, I would never be able to..."

But there is a job to be done, a job, which **you** and only **you** can do today. If **you** don't do it then nobody else can. Listen to God's commands; use the skills, which He gives to you. Ask Him to fill you with His Holy Spirit and step out in faith to serve Him.

✝ *Father, here I am, wholly available. I would love You to use me today. Amen.*

♥ Little is much if God is in it.

JUNE

The "Bannside Home" shown here can be seen across the Bann by one who travels by train from Coleraine to Castlerock on the Derry line.

The linocut from which this is reduced is 8.7" wide.

It was commissioned by The Royal Ulster Academy of Arts in 1999, who own half of the edition of 50 prints and what remains of the handcut block from which it was printed.

1st June — The Holy Spirit

📖 John 14 : 16 – 17

"I will ask the Father, and he will give you another Counselor to be with you forever – the Spirit of truth."

☞ Do you remember any time in your childhood when you were left all on your **own** in the house? I do! Part of me liked it and another part of me didn't. (Ok, I admit it; I was scared, especially if it was dark). The disciples felt a bit like that too. All this talk of Jesus leaving made them feel very fearful and insecure. Who could ever take His place in their lives? It seemed as if He was abandoning them. They didn't like the idea of being left all alone while Jesus went off somewhere else…(and neither do we).

But He is not abandoning either **them** or **us**. He promises to send 'another Counselor'…the Holy Spirit, who will be with us forever. Here is a great promise. We are not, and we never will be, **alone** in this world. Not for one minute. All that Jesus was to those first disciples; the Holy Spirit is to us today!

Jesus is closer to us now than He was to those first disciples. He was with them, but by His Holy Spirit He now lives right inside us…That's as close as He gets!

✝ *Father God, it's wonderful to know that Jesus lives in me, by His Holy Spirit…May He shine from my life today. Amen.*

♥ Living for Jesus will be easier today when the Spirit of Jesus lives in me.

2nd June — The Holy Spirit

Romans 8 : 26

"The Spirit helps us in our weakness. We do not know what we ought to pray for, but the Spirit himself intercedes for us with groans that words cannot express."

☞ I watched a goalkeeper in a boys football match let in a really 'soft' goal recently. He didn't say a thing. He didn't need to. The groans from his lips and his head in his hands said it all powerfully.

Sometimes when we are struggling, when we are feeling something deeply and intensely. We just can't find the words...but the groans say it all.

In some of the weakest, most difficult and most pain-filled times in our lives, our Friend the Holy Spirit, comes right along side us. With inexpressible groans He brings our heart cries before the Father in Heaven.

Are you in a situation today where you want God's will, but are very unsure and confused about what He wants and wills for you right now? Are you praying about something that is really troubling you but you don't know **how** to pray?

Do you feel very alone and on your own in a particular situation? You are not on your own. God has given us His very own Holy Spirit as our Friend. He is right here with you. When we don't know **what** to say or **how** to pray...He does. He will bring our 'heart' cries before the Father in Heaven. What a wonderful helper the Holy Spirit is. What a brilliant Friend!

✝ *O Father in Heaven, hear my cries and the Holy Spirit's 'sighs' and let Your will be done in my life. Amen.*

♥ God's way is the best way for my life right now!

3rd June — The Holy Spirit

📖 Ephesians 5 : 18

"Do not get drunk on wine, which leads to debauchery. Instead be filled with the Spirit."

☞ Isn't it amazing that when people get drunk that they often want to sing! Surely it isn't amazing then that when Christians are filled with the Holy Spirit, with His Presence, love and power, that one of the most natural overflows is a whole new desire to worship, praise and bless God, together with other Christians. God's command to us is to 'go on and on being filled with the Holy Spirit.' That seems to point to an ongoing, regular occurrence in our lives.

I recently read of a petrol tanker that had come to a halt at the side of the road. The reason...**it was out of fuel!** Imagine that! Think of all the endless resources available to that driver, millions and millions of litres, back at the depot. Yet it was all no use because the driver had neglected to 're-fill'. How like our lives? How often we are dry and empty as Christians. Not because God isn't faithful, not because God can't supply...but simply because we haven't obeyed His command to come back to the depot and re-fill with His Holy Spirit.

Are you slowing down spiritually? Are you running on empty?

Take some time to come back to God and in His Presence ask to be re-filled with His Holy Spirit...Today!

✝ *Heavenly Father, I want to empty my life of myself...so that You might fill me afresh with Your Holy Spirit so that I might live to praise You. Amen.*

♥ I haven't stopped drinking; I've just changed 'Spirit'.

Alvin Little

4th June Heaven

📖 John 17 : 24

"Father, I want those you have given me to be with me where I am, and to see my glory, the glory you have given me because you loved me before the creation of the world."

☞ There are those who criticise Christians and say we are always talking about the **next** world. They say, "Why don't you learn to enjoy the world you are living in now instead of looking for some 'pie in the sky?'

Well, bless them, we do enjoy this wonderful world. God has given us all things richly to enjoy. (I Timothy 6 : 17). The true Christian is not a killjoy or a spoilsport – he loves life and fun, but he is not so big a fool as to think he is here forever. The old poems says:

'As the leaves must fall
So will we all
And this world's blooms
Will be over soon.'

Christians think about Heaven because those who trust in Jesus are surely going there. What could be more wonderful than being where Jesus is …and seeing His glory!

✝ *Thank You Father that Heaven is where Jesus is. Increase my desire to be with Him. Amen.*

♥ Teacher:"All the children who want to go to Heaven please stand up." Everybody stood up, except one wee lad. Teacher: "And don't you want to go to Heaven?" Little boy, "I do...but not just yet!"

5th June — Heaven

📖 John 14 : 2 – 3

"In my Father's house are many rooms; if it were not so, I would have told you. I am going there to prepare a place for you. And if I go and prepare a place for you, I will come back and take you to be with me that you also may be where I am."

☞ I like to know where I am going ... don't you? Would you set off to another country without knowing about the conditions, or start on a long journey without consulting a map? Oh, but you say ... we cannot know Heaven. Didn't the Apostle Paul quote Isaiah when he said, "No eye has seen, no ear has heard, no mind has conceived what God has prepared for those who love him." There ... you cannot know about Heaven! Never quote half a text! Paul goes on to say, "But God has revealed it to us by His Spirit." (1Corinthians 2 : 9 – 10)

The Bible has shown us wonderful things about Heaven. It's our travel guide...more, Jesus is the one who will come back and actually accompany us there, so that along with Him we may also be in His wonderful home, forever!

✝ *Thank You Father that knowing Your Son as our personal Saviour is Heaven on the way to Heaven. Amen.*

♥ In the film 'Chariots of Fire', Eric Liddell said, "When I run, I feel His pleasure." In Heaven we'll never get cramp!

6th June Heaven

📖 2 Corinthians 5 : 1

Now we know that if the earthly tent we live in is destroyed, we have a building from God, an eternal house in heaven, not built by human hands.

☞ St. Paul was certain of Heaven... "Now we **know**..." Elsewhere, in 2 Corinthians 12 : 1 – 5, he tells us of his glimpse of Heaven. The vision was so wonderful that he longed to be there. "For me to live is Christ and to die is gain...what shall I choose? I do not know! I desire to depart and be with Christ, which is better by far, but it is more necessary for you that I remain in the body." (Philippians 1 : 21 – 24)

St. Peter was also certain of Heaven "Praise be to the God and Father of our Lord Jesus Christ! In His great mercy He has given us new birth into a living hope through the resurrection of Jesus Christ from the dead, and into an inheritance that can never perish, spoil or fade – kept in Heaven for you."

Thank God for the certainty of Heaven for all who trust in Jesus. Peter exhorts us. "Therefore my friends, be all the more eager to make your calling and election sure."

St. Paul and St. Peter both want us to be sure of Heaven. We can be certain too by trusting the Saviour who calls us to come to Him.

✝ *Dear Father, take away my fear of the unknown. Help me to see that Heaven, not earth is what is truly real. Amen.*

♥ A children's song says;

Heaven is a wonderful place
Filled with glory and grace
I want to see my Saviour's face
For Heaven is a wonderful place.

Sam Workman

7th June Compassion

📖 Psalm 145 : 17 – 20

"The Lord is righteous in all his ways and loving towards all he has made. The Lord is near to all who call on Him, to all who call on Him in truth. He fulfills the desires of those who fear him; he hears their cry and saves them. The Lord watches over all who love him, but all the wicked he will destroy. "

☞ The more comfortable we become in the West, the less we think about Heaven. (For this world has become my home.) The better off we are, the less we show compassion for the poor! (For in our comfort we forget others who are in need.)

Today approximately 35,000 children will die of malnutrition, and 100 million street children will go to bed without a roof over their heads. God have mercy on us!

In Psalm 145 we see the contrast between our world which is consumer-driven, individualistic, busy and stressed, and God's world which is full of Shalom (completeness) community dependent and unhurried contentment.

Why are our lifestyles so dominated by **our** world rather than **God's** world as seen in the Bible? Perhaps we have fallen for the lie that the more we have, the better off we are. Maybe we could afford to shed much of the 'things' that dominate our lives; regularly give away money and share with the vast numbers of starving and homeless people in the two-thirds world resources that we would scarcely miss, and discover perhaps for the first time, the wellbeing that comes from dependence upon others, and most of all dependence upon God.

✝ *Forgive me for storing up treasures on earth, rather than treasures in Heaven. May You not regard me as wicked, neglecting the cries of those who are most vulnerable, but rather grant me a heart of compassion for the poor. Amen.*

♥ Which is more important? To give charity or do justice?

8th June Mercy

📖 Micah 6 : 8

"He has showed you, O man, what is good. And what does the Lord require of you? To act justly and to love mercy and to walk humbly with your God."

☞ "Everything I have I've earned with the sweat of my brow. I owe no man anything, and what I have I deserve." Ever heard that kind of comment? It's far from being honest, not very merciful, and hardly humble! Or try and fool ourselves that we are not well off, and we have become deluded! In a world where millions of children are starving, where tens of thousands of adults are crippled by civil wars and violence, and unspeakably vast numbers of elderly people die of neglect and poverty, we must not put our heads in the sand and pretend that these problems will simply go away. God calls us to 'act justly, to love mercy and to walk humbly' with Him. That will mean learning His priorities, thinking His thoughts and living out His compassion. Jesus put it this way; 'Woe to you who are rich, for you have already received your comfort. Woe to you who are well fed now, for you will go hungry; Give to everyone who asks you and do to others as you would have them do to you. Be merciful, just as your Father is merciful. For with the measure you use, it will be measured to you.' (Luke 6 : 24 – 38)

How might I therefore act justly, love mercy and walk humbly with God today?

✝ *Dear God, strengthen, encourage and bless the work of Christian Organisations that try to put Jesus' words into action in our needy world, and help me see how I might be part of that too, for His names sake. Amen.*

♥ **Question:** Lord, why don't you do something about all the poverty in our world? **Answer**: Well, what's stopping you?

Frank Sellar

9th June Marriage

Genesis 2 : 18

"The Lord God said, "It is not good for the man to be alone. I will make a helper suitable for him."

Near the end of the eighteenth century a young boy was apparently abandoned by his parents in the forest of Lacaune, France. He was left to fend for himself. Years later the boy was found. He resembled an animal more than a human being. His speech consisted of grunts.

"It is not good for man to be alone." We were made for relationship. It is through contact with others that we come to know who we are. It is in our fellowship with others that we grow and mature.

The expression rendered 'a helper suitable for him' literally means ' one who co-responds to him'. Men and women were created to complement, supplement and complete each other. True Christian marriage reveals and illustrates this more fully than any other relationship.

✝ *Thank You that You saw the necessity for people not to be alone. Thank You for my friends, relations and all I meet in my daily life. I pray that they too will benefit from meeting me. Amen*

♥ In all the wedding cake, hope is the sweetest plum.

10th June Marriage

📖 Genesis 2 : 24

"For this reason a man will leave his father and mother and be united to his wife and they will become one flesh."

☞ My best man offered the following words of wisdom on our wedding day which we have found to be true: "A wedding is not a marriage. A wedding in an event which may or may not someday become a marriage. What you have on your wedding day is not a beautiful garden. Simply a vacant plot of land and some gardening tools."

The tools are things such as Time, Love and Commitment. For a relationship to grow and become beautiful requires that we have time for each other (physically, emotionally and spiritually), that we express and demonstrate love and that we remain committed to each other through thick and thin.

As a couple work in the garden of their marriage they become one and are beautiful to behold and model a relationship to be desired.

✝ *Please Lord, do not let me take my marriage or my relationships for granted. Help me give time to build up these relationships and my relationship with You. Amen*

♥ Happiness grows at our own fireside and not to be picked in a stranger's garden.

11th June Marriage

📖 Matthew 19 : 6

"So they are no longer two, but one. Therefore what God has joined together, let man not separate."

☞ The question was about divorce. Jesus chooses to focus His answer on marriage. He invites His listeners to consider a long lost kind of marital commitment: for better or for worse, until death. It was a promise of fidelity free from any reasons for withdrawal. It was the ground for both a more demanding love and a more secure trust. His followers found it a crazy sort of commitment and He admitted it was, but said that the Father made it possible.

In a wedding song, Don Francisco says, "I could never promise you in just my strength alone, that all my life I'd care for you and love you as my own."

Thankfully God knows our weaknesses and makes some allowance for us, yet He also offers us much more. He offers us the presence and power of the Holy Spirit so that our promises are made in His strength and can last all of our lives.

✝ *Heavenly Father, I am so grateful that You know my every weakness and You are there to help and guide me day by day. Amen*

♥ Before we set our hearts upon anything, let us examine how happy those are who already possess it.

12th June — Marriage

📖 Ephesians 5 : 25

"Husbands love your wives, just as Christ loved the church and gave himself up for her."

☞ Although the admonition to love as Christ loved is addressed directly to husbands, this applies equally to wives who are to similarly love their husbands with the same quality of love.

Wives tend to be much better than husbands at this, therefore these words are more directed towards men. I remember seeing a letter which read, 'Dearest Ruth, I would climb the highest mountain for you. I would swim the widest ocean for you. I would cross the hottest desert and blaze a trail through the deepest jungle. Love Ross. PS I'll be over on Saturday night if it doesn't rain'.

There's a ring of truth in those words. I can promise to be there in the crucial times, but it's often in the everyday give and take of life at home that I fail to deliver. Yet it is in those very settings that the greater challenges of living and loving are met.

Husbands especially, what can you do today to express your love in a sacrificial way?

✝ *Loving Father, what can I do today that will help others? Thank You that You are there for me not only in times of great difficulty but also during my routine day. Amen.*

♥ Want of care does us more damage than want of knowledge.

13th June Marriage

Hebrews 13 : 4

"Marriage should be honoured by all, and the marriage bed kept pure, for God will judge the adulterer and all the sexually immoral."

☞ One of the biggest challenges facing the church today is to honour the covenant of marriage. The rate of breakdown is the same inside the church as it is outside. Society is increasingly self-centred and unwilling to permanently commit to anything. Sex is all about self-gratification.

Yet Christian marriage is about a covenant relationship which is faithful rather than fickle, permanent as opposed to transitory, serving and giving to one another rather than self-seeking.

Our ability to keep these covenant relationships is directly related to our dependence upon the Spirit of God to give us the ability to love our spouses as Jesus loves us. To love in the way described by Paul in 1 Corinthians 13. The support marriages receive from within our local faith communities is also crucial as we seek to honour a covenant which mirrors our relationship to the coming bridegroom.

✝ *Lord, I want to support people in their relationships and marriages. Please give me the wisdom to be a supporter and not a meddler. Amen.*

♥ Kindle not a fire that you cannot extinguish.

Mairisine & David Stanfield

14th June Doubt

📖 Genesis 18 : 10,12.

"The Lord said, "I will surely return to you about this time next year, and Sarah your wife will have a son." Sarah laughed to herself as she thought. "After I am worn out and my master is old, will I now have this pleasure?"

☞ For the next few days we will consider the subject 'doubt'. The dictionary defines doubt as - Feeling of uncertainty, undecided frame of mind, inclination to disbelieve.

It is this third definition which applies to Sarah, she could not believe or accept what the Lord had promised. Of course it was going to require a miracle for Sarah to have a son. Sarah failed to see or understand that it was God who had spoken, who said she would have a child.

Think of the great and glorious promises there are in the Word of God and yet at times we are inclined to doubt them and hesitate to place our trust in them. God made a promise to Sarah and fulfilled it.

✝ *Dear Lord help my unbelief. Amen.*

♥ Got any rivers you think uncrossable?
Got any mountains you cannot tunnel through?
God specialises in things thought impossible,
He can do what no other can do.

15th June — Doubt

Matthew 11: 2 – 3

"When John heard in prison what Christ was doing, he sent his disciples to ask him, "Are you the one who was to come, or should we expect someone else?"

☞ The circumstances or situation we find ourselves in can colour our outlook on life. If we are in a beautiful or pleasant environment it is easy for us to experience joy and happiness. On the other hand if we are surrounded by dark and bleakness it is natural for us to feel depressed or uncertain.

John was in prison, in a dank and dismal cell; undoubtedly this coloured his thinking.

And the one who had confidently said out in the beautiful countryside beside the river Jordan "Look, here comes the Lamb of God," was now asking, "Is Jesus really the Messiah, or should we expect someone else?"

We all experience doubt and uncertainty in the days of difficulty and darkness.

But even in the darkest night, as we stretch out our hand, we will be able to touch the hem of our Master's garment and be at peace.

✝ *Dear Lord we are so grateful, that no matter how dark the night, You are there. Amen.*

♥ Some go through a forest and see no firewood.

16th June Doubt

📖 Matthew 14 : 31

"Immediately Jesus reached out his hand and caught him. " You of little faith," he said, "why did you doubt?"

☞ The ship the disciples were in on Gennesareth was being tossed around in the fury of the midnight storm. For the disciples the worst thing was that Jesus was not with them.

In the storms of life how important it is for us, to have Jesus with us.

When Payne the atheist was dying, a friend standing at his bedside said, "hold on." The despairing reply from the bed was, " but I have nothing to hold unto."

Contrast that with the words of Paul "I know whom I have believed, and am persuaded that He is able to keep that which I have committed to Him, against that day".

Peter seeing Jesus walking on the water, with his usual impulsiveness, thought if Jesus can do that, why can't I. 'Lord bid me 'come'. And Jesus said come. And Peter stepped out of the boat.'
We prefer to stay in the security of the old boat, it's safer there, but we will never know the adventure and thrill of walking on the water with Jesus, attempting new things.

How easy to doubt or to become discouraged, when we step out of the old boat and launch into the deep. That is what happened to Peter.

✝ *Dear Lord, having stepped out of the old boat, save me from doubting, from taking my eyes off You. Amen.*

♥ People may doubt what you say, but they will always believe what you do.

17th June — Doubt

📖 John 20 : 25

"The other disciples told him. "We have seen the Lord." But he said to them, "Unless I see the nail marks in his hands and put my finger where the nails were, and put my hand into his side, I will not believe."

☞ Thomas was not with them when Jesus came. Think of what Thomas missed because he failed to join with the others in the Upper Room.

We too can miss something vital, when we fail to meet with others in God's house.

Thomas had difficulty in believing that Jesus had actually appeared to those who gathered in the Upper Room.
Martin Luther said, "The art of doubting is easy for it is an ability that is born within us."

Thomas's nature was to question, to doubt.

Os Guinness believes in doubt – "as a path towards mature faith." The difference between doubt and unbelief is crucial. Unbelief is a willful refusal to believe. Doubt is the question, to seek the truth through reasoning. We should not feel guilty because we are unsure. When in doubt we should pray for wisdom to discover and know the truth.

✝ *Dear Lord deliver me from a closed mind, and led me into truth and genuine faith. Amen.*

♥ Do something. Either lead, follow or get out of the way!

18th June — Doubt

James 1: 6

"But when he asks, he must believe and not doubt, because he who doubts is like a wave of the sea. Blown and tossed by the wind."

☞ What is doubt? It is to be torn between two, between faith and unbelief. To be in doubt is to be of two minds.

We see this very clearly illustrated in Mark 9 where the father brings his son to be healed. He says to Jesus, "If you can do anything take pity on us and help us." Jesus replied, "all things are possible to those who believe." To which the father cried out; "Then I believe. Help me with my doubts." (Eugene Peterson's translation) His doubts were not unbelief, because Jesus never responded to real unbelief. He was unsure, uncertain, if Jesus would heal his son, but he was hoping and praying that he would.

When we come to God in prayer, asking, as James puts it here, we must leave the outcome to a loving God, who will not cause his child needless tears, otherwise it may led to unbelief or despair.

✝ *Dear Lord, deliver us from doubt and despair, and help us to know that one day when the mists have rolled away, we will understand. Amen.*

♥ When you try to prove to someone that a machine won't work, it will.

Jim Hagan

19th June — Forgiveness

Psalm 32 : 1 - 2

"Blessed is he whose transgressions are forgiven, whose sins are covered. Blessed is the man whose sin the Lord does not count against him and in whose spirit is no deceit."

☞ In an increasingly complicated world – where most of us are deluged with information and opinions – it's difficult to know which choices and options are best. The above verses are from a 'Wisdom' Psalm; such Psalms are concerned with how to live our lives so that we do make the right decisions. Excellent! Much needed. Until we actually look at the advice given. Then it becomes more puzzling (often, even to the minority who still go to Church).

This language is unfamiliar to many modern people, archaic, and even offensive! The way to live a sensible happy life? Recover a close friendship with God. St. Augustine said to God: "You have made us, and our hearts are restless until we find you." Profound words. However, the Psalmist insists that to get to that stage we must allow God to deal with the root of our unhappiness: we need honesty ('no deceit') to admit our sins against God and our neighbour. To swallow our pride and say: "Lord, sorry!" And the result? The start of a friendship, which will lead to a life, blessed by God. We have His promise for that.

✝ *Heavenly Father, sorry! Forgive me and change me. But Heavenly Father, bring me closer to You, so that I know I am forgiven. Amen.*

♥ The man who thinks he has no faults has at least one.

20th June Forgiveness

📖 Psalm 103 : 12

"As far as the East is from the West, so far has he removed our transgressions from us."

☞ Do you want a sobering thought? No? Here it is anyway: God holds us accountable for the things we do due to our weaknesses. This is a shock! The living God is fully aware of the reasons for our particular sins. Many of these are not of our making (whether inherited or the result of our upbringing), and, even harder, may be really beyond our control.

Here is a more encouraging thought, it is given to us in this Psalm: the Lord knows how we are made- all our weaknesses- and He takes it into account. He will be compassionate.

How can both be true? God is holy, He cannot, and will not, ignore our sin. God is love; it is against His nature not to show mercy. God is perfect. All His attributes are perfect. This means He will not ignore one of them. Reconciling these has been costly for God. How costly takes us beyond this Psalm and to the cross of Jesus: to 'remove transgressions' showed – as Charles Wesley put it – "Amazing love! That you my God should die for me."

✝ *Heavenly Father, thank You for who You are: holy and loving, loving and holy. May I find both at the cross of Jesus. Amen.*

♥ Look for a person's motives before you judge his actions.

21st June Forgiveness

Matthew 6 : 14 – 15

"For if you forgive men when they sin against you, your Heavenly Father will also forgive you. But if you do not forgive men their sins, your Father will not forgive your sins."

The disconcerting thought occurs that perhaps Jesus actually meant this! Matthew puts this saying of Jesus after the 'Lord's prayer'. Think of the opening words: 'Our Father in Heaven'. St. John said in his first letter; "How great is the love that the Father has lavished on us, that we should be called children of God!" Jesus came to bring us into this relationship. At His cross we are not only forgiven, but His Father becomes our Father. Such is His love.

However, our natural earthly fathers are like us, a mixture of good and evil. We inherit both aspects; our genetic inheritance from them helps shape our nature. But what do we inherit from our Heavenly Father? Jesus says that one such distinctive mark is the willingness to forgive those who have hurt us. Indeed, that extraordinary willingness to forgive MUST be present. Disconcerting, isn't it?

✝ *Heavenly Father, help me forgive other people in exactly the same way that You have forgiven me. Amen.*

♥ To err is human
To forgive takes restraint;
To forget you forgave
Is the mark of a saint.
(Suzanne Douglas)

22nd June Forgiveness

Matthew 12 : 31

"And so I tell you, every sin and blasphemy will be forgiven men, but the blasphemy against the Spirit will not be forgiven."

☞ One of the most difficult and intimidating sayings of Jesus! This sin will not be forgiven, in this world or the life to come. Ironically, it is often genuine Christians who are fearful of having unwittingly committed this sin. Such people need have no fear: anyone who genuinely loves Jesus cannot simultaneously love Him and reject the Spirit of God who delights in bringing glory to Jesus. We can also rule out cases where we are uncertain if the Spirit is at work in particular instances. Our Lord will not hold genuine blunders against us.

The key to understanding lies in the background to this verse. In response to a miracle by Jesus, the Pharisees accused the Lord of working by the power of Satan. It seems that they really did recognise the presence of the Sovereign Creator Spirit of God in Jesus, and deliberately and knowingly rejected Him. And, as it is God the Spirit who brings us to Jesus the Son of God for forgiveness, they were refusing the Divine mercy. How can we avoid this fearful pitfall? Love Jesus! Simply love Jesus. We are safe with Him. And, in Him, we discover that it is the gracious Holy Spirit who has brought us to Jesus.

✝ *Gracious Holy Spirit, bring me to Jesus, and, through His cross, bring me to the Father. Amen.*

♥ Man is the only animal that blushes - or needs to. (Mark Twain)

23rd June — Forgiveness

Ephesians 4: 32

"Be kind and compassionate to one another, forgiving each other, just as in Christ, God forgave you."

☞ Those of us who are Christians aren't generally noted for being kind and compassionate. Nor, unfortunately, are we especially noteworthy for forgiving each other (or, our neighbour, come to think of it). Why not? Because we remain sinful! Christians really need to remember this; the combined effect of our natural self-deception, and the breezy humanism, which is the Spirit of the age, militates against so doing.

However much it irks the ego, we must keep reminding ourselves that this is why Jesus died. Firstly, there really are aspects of our lives, which are deeply unlovely. Secondly, and equally important, meditating on the Father's love in the cross there is real healing and forgiveness. If we are going to forgive, we need to remember again and again, that, in Christ, God forgave us.

✝ *Heavenly Father, by Your Spirit help me to so know Your forgiveness in Jesus that I too can forgive. Amen.*

♥ You can try to teach a pig to sing, but it's a waste of time, and only annoys the pig.

Stephen Rea

24th June — Jesus - Prophet, Priest and King

Luke 24 : 19

"...Jesus Christ was a prophet, powerful in word and deed before God and all the people."

Christ as Prophet. The title 'prophet' that is used of Jesus in this verse literally means 'someone who speaks out publicly'. These sad disciples, who didn't realise that they were now talking to Jesus who was alive after His crucifixion, had often been deeply challenged by His words, and had often recognised that He spoke with an authority that the religious leaders of the day simply didn't possess. By calling Jesus a prophet, they were recognising the very special role He had come to fulfil as a Teacher. Tragically, however, at this point their understanding of Jesus fell far short of what it should have been, for they couldn't see that Jesus had come, not only to be a Prophet but also to be a Saviour. It is essential to hear what Jesus says to us as we read Scripture, but it is more essential still to be related to Him as our risen Lord.

Lord, let me today hear and understand Your teaching as a Prophet but also let me know Your love as my Saviour. Amen.

There is no profit for us if Jesus is only a prophet to us!

25th June Jesus - Prophet, Priest and King

Hebrews 5 : 5 - 7

"Christ did not take upon himself the glory of becoming a high priest, but God said to Him, "You are my son, today I have become your Father." During the days of Jesus' life on earth, he offered up prayers and petitions with loud cries and tears to the one who could save..."

Christ as Priest. Since the appointment of the very first priests early in human history, priests have needed two things ... a meaningful contact with God and a deep and genuine understanding of people. Without these two characteristics, no priest could possibly intercede on anyone else's behalf. Jesus possesses both to the full! First, He not only knows God intimately, He is the very Son of God, and is in a unique position to present our needs to God;

and second, because He has lived and died in this sinful world, there is no experience we can ever face that Jesus has not faced Himself. What a reassuring thought it is, that today there is Someone in Heaven who knows us so well and who knows God so well, that He is able to be our Mediator with God Himself.

✝ *Father, thank You for bringing Your Son Jesus down to earth to understand my needs, and back to Heaven to speak to You about those needs. Amen.*

♥ At one time the Priests went through the Temple curtain to speak to God on our behalf. When Jesus died, God tore that curtain for certain.

26th June — Jesus - Prophet, Priest and King

John 18 : 36

"Jesus said, "My kingdom is not of this world. If it were, my servants would fight to prevent my arrest by the Jews. But now my kingdom is from another place."

☞ **Christ as King**. In this verse Jesus is speaking both negatively and positively. Negatively, He is telling Pilate that the kingdom He has come to establish poses no threat to the rule of the Romans, and that any charges of treason against Him are groundless. Positively, Jesus is telling us that His kingdom is not found within geographical and physical boundaries, but is a kingdom established within the hearts and minds of those who will crown Him King. There is perhaps no better illustration of the type of relationship we are expected to have with Him. We are to respect, honour and revere Him as a loved Lord, and we are to serve and submit to Him, and do all in our power to promote His cause, as the One who reigns over us. What do we know of such a relationship? Can I honestly say today that Jesus the King has total control over every aspect of my life?

✝ *Lord, give me the Grace I need today to allow Jesus to reign over me. Amen.*

♥ The kingdom of Jesus is not maintained by arms but is manifested by hands and feet to do His will.

27th June Jesus - Prophet, Priest and King

📖 Matthew 16 : 16

"Simon Peter answered, "You are the Christ, the Son of the Living God.""

☞ **Christ as Son of God**. Jesus has been discussing His identity; the Disciples report that there is a wide range of public opinion about who He really is, but Peter hits the nail on the head as he shares his own conviction that Jesus is the Son of God. The title 'Son of God' is to be understood in three ways.

First, that Jesus is the second Person in the Trinitarian Godhead along with the Father and the Holy Spirit.

Second, that He is subject to the Father's will. We are taught in Scripture, for example, that even Jesus does not know when He shall return to earth, for only the Father possesses that information.

Third, that His birth in Bethlehem was through the supernatural activity of the Holy Spirit.

While all this might seem to be meaty theology, what is very simply understood is that Jesus the Son has come from the Father to save us and to bring us to the Father for all eternity. What wonderful good news.

✝ *Father, thank You for Your Son. I want to understand more and more why He has that Title, but more than that, I want to love Him as my Saviour and Friend. Amen.*

♥ If you love the Son, shine for Him today.

28th June Jesus - Prophet, Priest and King

📖 John 20 : 28

"Thomas said to Him, "My lord and my God!""

☞ **Jesus as God.** Thomas had spent a sad week in disbelief about the Resurrection of Jesus. He had been absent on the previous Sunday when Jesus had appeared to the Disciples, and he refused to believe them when they told him what had happened. This time when Jesus appears, Thomas is present and he responds to Jesus in this wonderfully simple but definite statement of faith. The notable thing is that Thomas is clear in his belief that Jesus is God. If we are looking for a Scripture passage that we can quote to affirm Christ's Divinity, there is none simpler than this. 'Jesus is God'. Notice also that Thomas makes this a personal matter. He uses the word 'my'. He declares his submission to and love for Jesus as his personal God and Lord. Belief that Jesus is God is one thing ... commitment and obedience to Him as God is quite another.

✝ *Lord Jesus, give to me that unshakable belief in Your Divinity and that unwavering commitment to Your rule in my life. Amen.*

♥ Doubt that leads to belief is better than belief that leads to doubt.

Howard Lewis

29th June Eternal Life

📖 Luke 18 : 18

"A certain ruler asked Jesus, "Good teacher, what must I do to inherit eternal life?""

☞ This incident is recorded in Matthew, Mark and Luke. It is the story of the 'Rich Young Ruler'. The man wanted to know about Eternal Life. And his question is being asked by many today. 'Eternal Life' is not just a quantity of life; it is also a quality of life. Eternal life is the type of life a person receives whenever they trust in Jesus Christ as their personal Saviour and Lord. However, like many today, this Rich Young Ruler had an inadequate view of Jesus. Notice that he called Jesus 'Good Teacher' when in fact He was the Son of God. He also had an overly optimistic view of his own abilities to please God, for he claimed in Luke 18 to have kept all the Commandments of God. He thought he could by his own efforts inherit Eternal Life. The Gospel of the Lord Jesus Christ asserts that Eternal Life is a gift. It is the 'Gift of God' (Romans 6 : 23). Today God offers us Eternal Life. It is received by His Grace and through faith in the Son of God. The Rich Young Ruler did not receive Eternal Life. He did not want it enough.

✝ *Lord I'm fed up with my life as it is. Give me help to receive Eternal Life as a gift from You. Help me to worship no other gods and to know that You are the living and True God. In Jesus name. Amen.*

♥ Today may be your Birthday. If it is Many Happy Returns. "Happy Birthday to you." It could be the first day of your spiritual life if you ask God the correct question and obey His word. If it is may God bless you. "Happy Birthday to you."

30th June — Eternal Life

📖 John 3 : 36

"Whoever believes in the Son has eternal life, but whoever rejects the Son will not see life, for God's wrath remains in him."

☞ The Apostolic Gospel simply states that Eternal Life is connected to belief in Jesus Christ. The New Testament is clear: Eternal Life is received through belief in Jesus. It is equally clear that those who do not obey the teaching of Jesus Christ will not have Eternal Life, in fact they are under the judgement of God. Do you see how central to Christianity the Person of Jesus is? Without Jesus there can be no saving relationship with God. The 'wrath of God' is as great a reality as the 'love of God'. Without faith in the Lord Jesus Christ divine chastisement rests upon us. In John 3 : 35 we are told that the Father has given all things into the hand of His Son. Jesus can give us Eternal Life. That's the point. It's a question of life or death. So let's be sure to ask God to help us make the correct choice.

Eternal Life is a life lived by faith in God's word. It is a life of forgiveness, purpose and peace. It goes on after the body dies.

✝ *I need to be forgiven. I have made a mess of my life and I realise that I am under the judgement of God. Help me now to turn to You. Thank You that Jesus died for me. I want to believe in Him. I understand that this means that I must obey His word. Give me Grace and Power today. In the name of the One who gives life to all who trust Him in saving faith. Amen.*

♥ Try to lift yourself up by your own shoelaces? You cannot do it. You cannot earn eternal Life. It is received by believing the Lord Jesus Christ. It may be raining today. If it is and you have to go outside you will take your umbrella! Belief and action go together.

JULY

"Crown Imperial" is a 19" x 8" cut made in linoleum in the manner of the early European printed herbals.
The bee and the slug are included as reminders of environmental relationships among flowers and their animal surroundings.

1st July

Eternal Life

📖 John 10 : 27 - 28

"My sheep listen to my voice; I know them, and they follow me and I give them eternal life, and they shall never perish; no one can snatch them out of my hand."

☞ In these verses the word 'and' is used five times. There are six fantastic points made in these two verses. Look at it for yourself. It is easy to get the six points. I love these verses. They are so reassuring. The people who love Jesus, the Good Shepherd hear His voice and obey it. They follow Him and He gives them Eternal Life. That's great. But there is more. They will never perish and they are safe forever in the mighty hand of God. This is like a waterfall. There is so much here for us today. The greatest thing about these verses however is that Jesus Christ knows His people. He knows how we feel. He knows what gets us down and what makes us happy. He knows us in an intimate way. The Bible tells us elsewhere (Psalm 8) that the moon and the stars are the work of God's finger. That being the case then all who have Eternal Life are totally secure for time and for eternity.

✝ *Lord I thank You that You know Your people. I praise You for the gift of Eternal Life. It is great to know no matter what happens, and should the very worse happen, that I am safe in the hands of Almighty God. Help me to follow You today. Amen.*

♥ Years ago a College friend of mine worked during the Summer holidays for a Security Company in London. The firm moved money and other valuables around the City. He explained to me one day, that if they were ever held up they would not be heroes but that they would hand it over. God can never hand His people over. No threat can force His hand. No enemy can make Him release His hold on His people.

2nd July — Eternal Life

1 Corinthians 15 : 51 - 52

"Listen, I tell you a mystery; we will not all sleep, but we will be changed – in a flash, in the twinkling of an eye, at the last trumpet. For the trumpet shall sound, the dead will be raised imperishable, and we will be changed."

☞ Heaven is a great reality. It is where God has His throne. The first Coming of Jesus was marked by great humility, the Son of God was born of a woman; born under the Law and He became obedient unto death 'even death on a cross'. (Philippians 2) The Second Coming of Jesus will be marked by great Power. This power will be displayed in public as God vindicates Himself and His people. His Second Coming will be sudden. The dead will rise up from their graves. 'Cemetery' means the place of the sleeping. They are raised and then all who love the Saviour will be 'caught up together with them, to be forever with the Lord'. Christians will be changed. They will be given a new body. A body like His. We make arrangements for most things. Holidays, the celebration of Christmas, education etc., are usually all well planned . We need to make arrangements for the great and sudden conclusion of History. On that day 'every knee will bow and every tongue will confess that He is Lord'. Be assured Jesus is coming again and His Lordship over everything will be acknowledged by all.

✝ *Thank You, Dear Lord, for the assurance of final victory over temptation and sin. Lord Jesus, I want to serve You as Lord for that is what You are. Let me live this day as if it was the last day in the course of History. For Christ's sake. Amen.*

♥ A very keen young minister wanted to have a really Biblical Church even down to having a suitable text in each room of the Church complex. In the Choir Room he had 'O sing a new song to the Lord'.

In the Committee Room he had the text 'Now concerning the offering'. Every room was suitably decked out with a text. All that is but one … the crèche. He thought long and hard about it. Then he had a bright idea. He had '"We shall not all sleep, but we shall all be changed', fixed to the wall."

3rd July — Eternal Life

📖 1 John 5 : 11 - 12

"And this is the testimony; God has given us eternal life and this life is in his Son. He who has the Son has life; he who does not have the Son of God does not have life."

☞ John is affirming that God is the giver of Eternal Life. God Himself is Eternal and He gives Eternal Life 'in His Son'. The 'testimony' of God is about Salvation. Salvation is the essential content of God's revelation in the Scriptures. The central Truth about Salvation is that it is only to be found in Jesus. Eternal Life is the essence of Salvation and it is the very life of God in all that have Jesus as Saviour. Everyone does not enjoy this life for 'it is as impossible to have Eternal Life without having Christ as it is impossible to have Christ without at the same time possessing Eternal Life.' (J.M. Boice)

✝ *Thank You Gracious God that You give Your people Eternal Life. I want to express my love for You and I know that my love will always be imperfect. You have given the world Your perfect Gift, the Lord Jesus Christ. May my life today glorify Your Name and Your Son. Equip all that will speak Your word today and grant that many people may believe and live. In Jesus Name. Amen.*

♥ A wee boy was coming home from Sunday school on a cold and windy Sunday morning. His Teacher had given him a Bible text on a little colourful card. It read 'Have faith in God'. As he made his way along the footpath with his Dad, he dropped his Bible; the text fell out and was blown away on the wind. He was heard to call out to his Dad "I've lost my faith in God." It is good to know that if we lose our faith in Him, He never leaves the people to whom He gives Eternal Life.

Joe Fell

4th July — Christlikeness

📖 Matthew 20 : 27 - 28

"...and whoever wants to be the first must be your slave – just as the Son of Man did not come to be served, but to serve, and to give his life as a ransom for many."

☞ At the end of June 1999, just before the Orange march at Drumcree, a group of Christians from England came to Portadown to fast and pray for a week for a breakthrough in the political situation, and in the sectarian logjam which had developed. I had the privilege of attending a Day of Fasting and Praying on Saturday 3rd July, along with some 150 Christians from around Ireland. During the worship time the pastor from England, Paul White, came over to me with a basin of water and a towel and asked if he could wash my feet. (I was so relieved I had worn clean socks that morning!) As he did so it portrayed something of the attitude of these English Christians towards the Irish, that, not only would they take a week off work to come to pray and fast in Portadown, but that their attitude was one of servanthood and of humility. This is the practical demonstration of the verse, where Jesus tells us He did not come to be served, but to serve. He washed His disciples' feet. He continued to reach out to a world He knew would reject Him. He came to lay down His life out of love. He did not just tell us that He loved us from the beautiful surroundings of heaven, but demonstrated it by becoming one of us. This gives me great hope. Isn't He wonderful? Don't you want to emulate Him?

✝ *Lord, thank You that You didn't just speak words of love, but You demonstrated it for us. Thank You that it is in dying that we live. That it is in giving that we receive, that it is in serving that You exalt us. Help us to pour ourselves out for those around us, for our family, for our fellowship, prayer group or church, for our community. Lord help us to truly know that, with You, we can make a difference. Amen.*

♥ Keep your ideals high enough to inspire you, and low enough to encourage you.

5th July — Christlikeness

📖 Lamentations 3 : 22 – 23

"His compassions fail not. They are new every morning: great is Your Faithfulness".

☞ My mum died at the beginning of December 1998. My father had died in 1969. The funeral service for my mum really uplifted the Lord and I had the privilege of giving the appreciation message at her funeral. For the rest of December I felt quite down, lacking motivation, but the compassions of the Lord do not fail. Truly they are new every morning and great is His faithfulness. As the song, based on the Scripture verse, goes on to say we have 'Strength for today and bright hope for tomorrow.'

Sometimes I have come into the office feeling depressed, lacking the motivation to work, but as I read my daily devotional and meditated on the Scripture passage, believing that God is speaking to me through it, then my spirit would lift and that day would become meaningful and not 'just another day'. Truly there is power in the Word of God. Truly His Holy Spirit takes His Word and writes it on my heart. He will write it on your heart also. If you are feeling down, if you are feeling without hope, know that the Lord's compassion is there for you. His hands are outstretched, waiting for you to come to Him. He is a faithful God. We let Him down. I let Him down often, but He will never abandon us, because He is a faithful God.

✝ *Lord, thank You for who You are. That You are a God of compassion. That Your mercies and Your compassions never fail. Thank You that You give each of us who trust in You strength for today and bright hope for tomorrow. We Love You Lord, we love You. Amen.*

♥ ' This is a day that the Lord has made. Rejoice!'

6th July — Christlikeness

📖 Colossians 3 : 13

"Bear with each other and forgive whatever grievances you may have against one another. Forgive as the Lord forgave you."

☞ Michael McGoldrick is an Evangelical Catholic who lives just outside Portadown. As a result of the stand–off at Drumcree, in July 1996, his son (Michael) was murdered by the L.V.F. gang. Michael and his wife, Bridie, were on holidays in Warrenpoint at the time when they heard the news on the radio. They were devastated. They contemplated suicide – Michael was their only son. They thought they had nothing to live for. But God's grace came into this situation, Michael and Bridie both came into a wonderful, living, personal relationship with Jesus Christ and Michael was able to express his forgiveness of the LVF murderers of his son, both before and during the funeral. The media relayed this all over the world. In the last few years, Michael has shown that this forgiveness was real. He started an interdenominational ministry, bringing relief to orphanages in Romania and his warehouse is now located in a Loyalist section of Portadown. He has reached out and built bridges of friendship with many Christians in the Protestant community. Some people get really angry when they hear Michael speak out such forgiveness, because they think that in some way it's minimising the crime of the murder of his son. However, Michael knows that his son's murderers need to come to repentance themselves individually. Jesus forgave unconditionally while dying on the cross, saying "Father, forgive them for they know not what they do." Michael too has received the grace from God to forgive with all his heart.

✝ *Lord, thank You that You are such a wonderful model of forgiveness to me. Thank You for showing me how to live in this area. Please give me Your grace, Your compassion, Your strength to be able to forgive unconditionally as You did. Amen.*

♥ Life is made up of getting and giving, forgetting and forgiving.

7th July

Christlikeness

1 John 3 : 2

"Dear friends, now we are children of God, and what we will be has not yet been made known. But we know that when he appears, we shall be like him, for we shall see him as he is."

☞ It was a real privilege to attend the United Prayer Breakfast, November 1998, in the Stormont Hotel, Belfast. Sixteen politicians from the Dail/ Senate in Dublin and sixteen politicians from Northern Ireland (including ten Unionist members of Westminster and the new Assembly) sponsored this annual Prayer Breakfast. The guest speaker at this function, (attended by over 300 leaders from political, church, business and community life North and South of Ireland) was Senator Connie Mack, a senior Republican Senator from Florida. He could well have spoken about international relationships, etc, but he chose to speak about how he came into personal faith in Jesus Christ through the bi-weekly Senate Prayer Breakfasts. It was through fellow Senators befriending him and inviting him along, that he finally attended and accepted Jesus in his life. True friendship was the key. It is vital that we build friendships with people around us. Value those cups of coffee. Value those walks. It was through friendship that Senator Mack became a child of God. There is this misconception that everyone is a child of God. In fact everyone is created in God's wonderful image and likeness and so deserves dignity and respect, irrespective of their beliefs. As John chapter 1 says, "It is those who receive Jesus, who believe in His name, that in truth become real children of the Living God." But Christians let us value our status, that we are truly children of our God. God is our Father. It gives me real hope to know that Jesus is coming back. At the celebration of the Eucharist, we often say, 'Christ has died, Christ has risen, Christ will come again.' Jesus said to His disciples that He would return to the earth in the same manner as they saw Him ascend to heaven from the Mount of Olives. Sometimes when I feel down, it gives me great hope to know that Jesus is coming back to bring me and other believers in Him, home to heaven. It doesn't matter what our bodies look like. Whether they are diseased or are old or young, wretched or not - when He comes back, Scripture says, 'We will be like Him' and our bodies will be changed, 'in the twinkling of an eye', into glorious bodies, and we will rule and reign with Him for ever. What a wonderful hope!

✝ *Lord, thank You for the fact that You will come back and take us, who believe in You, home. Lord, let this hope truly inspire us. Thank You Jesus, that You are my friend. Help us to value friendship. Help us to take the space to reach out and be a friend to others, just as You are a friend to us. Amen.*

♥ If you are idle, be not solitary, if you are solitary, be not idle.

8th July **Christlikeness**

📖 1 John 3 : 16

"This is how we know what love is: Jesus Christ laid down His life for us. And we ought to lay down our lives for our brothers."

☞ As an eighteen year old from Kells in County Meath, I drifted into university, very insecure and knowing that I didn't really trust people. Through a girlfriend, I came to know love, which radically changed my life. From an introverted person I became secure, developed confidence and trust in people and became quite outgoing. Some two years later both of us came into personal faith in Jesus Christ through a Charismatic Prayer Meeting in University College, Dublin. I am sure that if we hadn't come to know the love of God in Christ Jesus that our love for one another would have become introverted and self-centred. But we came to know truly the Source of Love, our Father God, who sent His only Son that we might have a real relationship with Him, and eternal life both now and forever.

I remember that morning, in February 1973, waking up in my bed–sit in Rathmines and taking up the Bible to read. Now it was no longer just the inspired, authoritative Word of God, it was His love letter to me. I couldn't leave it down. The words, as it were, 'leapt out of the pages'. I had fallen in love with the King of the Universe. I realised how incredibly and passionately He loved me. I remember cycling into University that morning, singing His praises. I met a university porter on the way in and he said, "Good morning, Paddy, you look so happy, you must be in love." I said "Yes," without bothering to explain that my love was not for a woman as he assumed, but for the Living God.

Because Jesus laid down His life for me, I certainly want, with His help and grace, to lay down my life for others. I know in certain Arab countries, in Ethiopia, in China, many believers in Jesus have literally suffered martyrdom for their faith in Jesus. In our modern 'Celtic Tiger' economy, the challenge for Christians is to take up our cross daily and follow Him. To reach out to our fellow believers, particularly those who are carrying a lot of pain, and also to manifest His compassion to the poor around us.

✝ *Lord, thank You for Your incredible love for me. Thank You, Jesus, that You just didn't talk about Your love, but that You demonstrated it by laying Your life down for me. Help me to give myself for others. Help me to love believers is Jesus, irrespective of what church they are in, to build bridges of friendship with them and make manifest Your compassion to a lost and dying world. Amen*

♥ Some dream of worthy accomplishments, while others stay awake and do them.

Paddy Monaghan

9th July

Humility

Zechariah 9 : 9

"Rejoice greatly, O Daughter of Zion! Shout, Daughter of Jerusalem! See your king comes to you, righteous and having salvation, gentle and riding on a donkey, on a colt, the foal of a donkey."

Television schedules are discarded so that we can be there when he steps out of Airforce One. Limousines are imported. Hundreds of security staff have invaded. Every manhole is checked. Trees are cut down so that he will never be out of sight. Motorways come to a standstill. Do not drive unless it is necessary. The President of the USA has entered our world. It is hard to miss it.

When the President of Presidents entered our world it was very different. Apart from an advance angel and a live choir of angels, there was little hoopla or fuss. And as far as security was concerned it was as dangerous and vulnerable as could be. A carpenter midwife. Rampant filth.

Like a King on a donkey, it seems a crazy way to arrive. Yet, it was a parable about all that He would teach. A new Kingdom. A radical alternative. Some seemingly crazy stuff like, 'Blessed are the meek; if someone wants to save his life he must lose it'; and 'love your enemies' Different? 'Follow me'.

✝ *Lord, help me see through the seeming importance of riches, fame and power in this world to live by the upside down values of Your Kingdom. Amen.*

♥ If Jesus said these things today, would they lock Him up as insane?

10th July — Humility

John 13 : 5

"After that he poured water into a basin and began to wash his disciples' feet, drying them with the towel that was wrapped around him."

It seems so logical. The first are first. What do we expect? A nerd at Top of the Pops! Two left feet replacing Michael Owen in the England attack! A failure at GCSE or Leaving Cert - getting accepted for a post -graduate course in nuclear physics! Come on! No, it is a world where the first are first and the last are last. Such a world, however, leads to inferiority complexes, insecurities and a sense of alienation. It increases the stress of trying in vain to impress, and a falseness and shallowness that is keen not to let people know what we are really like. So logic leads to many illogical acts in everyone's constant struggle to be the first and avoid being the last.

Into the midst of this graceless world comes an irrational idea, a revolutionary concept, a scandalous possibility. Grace. Unnatural and certainly not of this world. God treats us like Jesus treated His disciples. The first becomes last in order that the last might be first.

✝ *Lord, may I wash the feet of those with whom I live and work and socialise. Help me smash the graceless world that leaves us all something less than who we really are. Amen.*

♥ Manchester City in the Champions League. Crazy stuff this Kingdom of God.

11th July — Humility

📖 John 13 : 14 - 15

"Now that I, your Lord and Teacher, have washed your feet, you also should wash one another's feet. I have set you an example that you should do as I have done for you."

☞ A few years ago I watched one of the worst choirs I'd ever seen. I was sitting beside the late Rich Mullins, one of the top names in Christian music. I suggested that they weren't that good and Rich agreed and then he added that he was going to sing with them, unrehearsed. Fifteen minutes later he was doing just that. As I listened, it had to be the most beautiful noise that I'd ever heard. You see, for this big star it wasn't important that he got bigger and sounded great. The children from this school on an Indian Reservation in New Mexico were more important. To sing with them was not for his good, but for theirs. The Kingdom of God on stage. A pop star singing with an out of tune choir. Suddenly the world is different. Radically changed.

✝ *Lord, help us not just to know the story of Your example to us. Help us to live it in everyday, ordinary ways. Amen.*

♥ Where in the day ahead is your out of tune choir? (Hope you're not reading this on a Saturday night or Sunday morning!!!)

12th July — Humility

📖 Philippians 2 : 6 - 8

Who, being in very nature God, did not consider equality with God something to be grasped but made himself nothing, taking the very nature of a servant, being made in human likeness. And being found in appearance as a man, he humbled himself and became obedient to death - even death on a cross.

☞ Wouldn't it have been great if Jesus had said to Peter, "Peter, I'd like you to go to Church, Peter, I'd like you to pray this prayer? Peter, I'd like you to agree to this confession of faith. Peter, I'd like you to put your hand up at a Gospel meeting." It would make faith so much easier.

He didn't. He said, "Peter, follow me." That is so unnatural for us. It seems that the natural drive within me is to make myself into God. I want to have my way in everything. I want my rights. Surely I have rights. The Jesus who asked us to follow gives up His rights to die for those who have made themselves His enemies. Being meek, He inherits heaven and earth. 'Follow me'.

✝ *Lord, forgive my pride. Give me humility, that I may follow Jesus. Amen.*

♥ The more you know you're being humble, the less humble you are - T BONE BURNETTE

13th July Humility

📖 2 Corinthians 8 : 9

"For you know the grace of our Lord Jesus Christ, that though he was rich yet for your sakes he became poor, so that you through his poverty might become rich."

☞ The first becomes last, that the last might come first. What Jesus said, He lived. In His death these words become incarnate. As Jesus hung on that cross He was the cursed of the world. One moment suffocating, the next moment pushing Himself up on those nails to breathe. Nowhere there the glory of heaven. He who was from Heaven, who was sinless and was Lord over all, became the very last person on earth. Why? So that we who were last, might become first. Me. Deserving of a hellish death for my rebellion, selfishness and contribution to this world's sinful disaster. Me. The last person on earth who should be an heir to God. Me. First, because He became last for me.

✝ *Lord Jesus, thank You for Your sacrifice. Thank You for becoming cursed that I might be blessed. Amen.*

♥ Is there a last out there, in my world, that I can make first?

Steve Stockman

14th July — Grace

📖 Galatians 1 : 3 - 5

"Grace and peace to you from God our Father and the Lord Jesus Christ, who gave himself for our sins to rescue us from the present evil age, according to the will of our God and Father, to whom be glory forever and ever. Amen"

☞ As Christians we are familiar with the good news that Jesus has died or given Himself for our sins. Here, in his opening greetings to the churches in Galatia, Paul wants to emphasise its practical implications. It is to rescue us from this present evil age.

Drawing upon the book of Daniel and of Ezekiel, Paul sees the world divided into two periods. This present age with its alienation and death and the new age, inaugurated by the Messiah, which brings resurrection life, unity and peace. Jesus, as our Messiah has already established the new age through his death and resurrection. Everything broken and made faulty through sin has now been restored and brought into harmony through Jesus Christ. The point is that, already, we are the children of the age which is to be. In Christ we are a new creation, the old has gone and the new has come.

✝ *Father, enable us this day to live as those who have been set free from all those things which would separate us from yourself and from each other. Help us to live as the children of a new day. Amen.*

♥ The Kerry atheists society have started a 'Dial a Prayer' service. When you phone.....nobody answers.

15th July — Grace

📖 Galatians 1 : 11 - 12

"I want you to know, brothers, that the gospel I preached is not something that man made. I did not receive it from any man, nor was I taught it; rather, I received it by revelation from Jesus Christ."

☞ The source of the gospel which Paul preached was and is important. He set aside two possible origins. It was not something which he made up himself. This reminds us of Peter's amazing statement at Ceasarea Phillipi, where he confesses that Jesus is the Christ, the Son of the living God and Jesus says, "Peter, this is not something which you made up yourself, that is, flesh and blood did not reveal it to you." The second origin, would have been common among the Rabbi's during catechetical instruction. They would seek to demonstrate the truthfulness of what they were saying by piling up venerable sources and footnotes from one eminent scholar or another. Paul says, "I did not receive this gospel from any man, nor was I taught it." Paul's claim is that he received the gospel by revelation from Jesus Christ himself . The Christian gospel is a revealed religion. Its authority resides in itself and it authenticates itself as credible. The gospel is a gift of grace.

✝ *Thank You Father, that You did not leave us in ignorance concerning Yourself and what You have done for us. We receive with joy the knowledge of our salvation which You have revealed to us through Jesus Christ our Lord. Amen*

♥ A Jewish Rabbi, a Roman Catholic priest and a Liberal Protestant minister were wrestling with a serious moral issue. The Rabbi argued. 'The Torah says...' The priest contended. 'The Church says.......' The minister commented. 'Well, it seems to me.....'

16th July — Grace

📖 Galatians 2 : 15-16

"We who are Jews by birth and not 'Gentile Sinners', know that a person is not justified by observing the law, but by faith in Jesus Christ. So we, too, have put on faith in Christ Jesus that we may be justified by faith in Christ and not by observing the law no-one will be justified."

☞ The simplest definition of 'justification', I know, is that of Tom

Wright, which is "to be declared in the right." It's what the BBC programme 'Rough Justice' seeks for the innocent who have been declared guilty and are suffering imprisonment. It is obviously difficult to be declared in the right if you are in the right, it is apparently impossible for those, like us who are sinners before God, who are seeking to do what is right, that is by keeping the law. Our only hope for being justified is what Jesus Christ has done for us. His perfect life and substitutionary death are the sole grounds of our justification. This we receive by faith alone. Paul is exasperated by some Jewish Christians who were demanding that Gentiles be circumcised, eat only kosher food and keep the special Jewish festivals in order to be justified before God. Jews know, he argues, that no one can be justified by the keeping of the law alone and so do we. Jesus Christ has done everything necessary for us, so that by faith alone in Christ alone, everything will be all right even though we know that as sinners, everything is all wrong.

✝ *Lord, today, we want to celebrate with joy this amazing love which has secured the salvation of people like us. 'Amazing love, how can it be, that you my God should die for me!' Amen.*

♥ Worry is like a rocking chair, it gives you something to do, but it doesn't get you anywhere.

17th July — Grace

📖 Galatians 3 : 26

"You are all Sons of God through faith in Christ Jesus."

☞ This is the primary identity of those who have believed in Jesus Christ. They are the Sons of God. We have been given the full legal status of adopted sons with all the rights and privileges. In Roman law adoption was widely practised. Several Emperors had adopted men not related to them in order to grant them their office and authority. An adopted son was in all legal respects equal with those born into the family. They were given the same name, the same inheritance, the same position and the same rights as the natural born son.

God sent his Son, who by his divine nature was the Son of God, in order that we, who are not his children by nature, might be his children by adoption. As the sons of God, we have the same name, the same inheritance, the same position and the same rights as the one who is Son of God by virtue of his divine nature!

✝ *Gracious God, we ask again for the witness of Your Spirit with our spirit to assure us that we are the sons of God. Help us to express to you, the Holy One of Israel, our love and worship with the intimacy of a child as we call you 'Abba' – Father.*

♥ The phone rang in the hospital: Murphy: "How is my wife?" Nurse: "She is in labour. Is this her first baby?" Murphy: "No, this is her husband."

18th July — Grace

📖 Galatians 3 : 28

"There is neither Jew nor Greek, slave nor free, male nor female, for you are all one in Jesus Christ."

☞ In the ancient world, like today, identity produced patterns of privileged status and self -assertive prejudice. They were expressed according to the fundamental cleavages of human existence, namely: ethnicity, economics and sexuality. Our world is still divided according to these primal elements of race, money and sex. The Balkan crises or the Troubles of Ulster are about ethnicity. The social divisions of India into various castes are mirrored in the tensions between middle and working classes or our society. The gender wars over the roles, status and position of men and women is a continuation of the tensions of the past.

Paul's understanding of the gospel is breathtaking and radical in its claims. Here he is his most magisterial. In Christ, Jew and Gentile, slave and free, male and female are one. He is affirming a radical equality in Christ with those who are different from us. Paul remains a man, a freeman and a Jew yet, he sees himself at one with women, slaves and Gentiles.

The implications of this for Ireland and every other divided society is nothing less than revolutionary.

✝ *Our Father, we are privileged to be part of such a radical movement. Release us from our prejudices so that we might live in unity and equality with those who are in Christ but are different from us. Amen.*

♥ Life is like a shower. One wrong turn and you're in hot water.

Trevor Morrow

19th July — God is Loving

Deuteronomy 7 : 7 - 9

"The Lord did not set his affection on you and choose you because you were more numerous than other peoples, for you were the fewest of all peoples. But it was because the Lord loved you and kept the oath he swore to your forefathers that he brought you out with a mighty hand and redeemed you from the land of slavery, from the power of Pharaoh king of Egypt. Know therefore that the Lord your God is God, he is the faithful God, keeping his covenant of love to a thousand generations of those who love him and keep his commands."

☞ Who could have imagined that an extended family unit of 70 people (Deuteronomy 10 : 22) would have become the great nation that Moses is talking about.

God is God! A statement of fact, we are left to ponder the mystery of God, His will and decisions. This often leaves us spiralling into vast eternity, sensing our own smallness and inability to explain.

God is Love! He set His affection on you, Moses tells the Israelites. We might love a nation that was strong, but God chooses to love the fewest of all peoples. God did not love them because of their achievements but He chooses to love them despite themselves. Again the mystery of Love, it originates from within the character of God and we cannot fathom it. However, we can appreciate and respond to it. Love is not only expressed in words but in action. 'He brought you out with a mighty hand and redeemed you from the land of slavery'. (v. 8).

God is Faithful! By doing exactly as He said He would, God has proven His faithfulness and this He has been doing for thousands of generations. As for the Israelites, so for God's people today, in giving Jesus for our redemption He has lavished us with love and proven His faithfulness.

✝ *Praise be to the Lord, the God of Israel, because He has come and redeemed His people. (Luke 1 : 68) Amen*

♥ Judge each day, not by the harvest, but by the seeds you plant.

20th July — God is Loving

📖 Deuteronomy 32 : 10 - 12

"In a desert land he found him, in a barren and howling waste. He shielded him and cared for him; he guarded him as the apple of his eye, like an eagle that stirs up its nest and hovers over its young, that spreads its wings to catch them and carries them on its pinions. The Lord alone led him..."

☞ Today's passage is part of the Song of Moses sung to the people of Israel on the eve of their crossing into the land God promised to their forefather Abraham.

The Apple of His eye. Although God is forming a nation of people, this speaks singularly of Jacob, highlighting the personal aspect of God's love. In the crowd, we are the apple of His eye; we may not even love ourselves yet ,when God sets His love on us, we become the centre of His focus.

The Eagle and its Young. The pinion of a wing is its tip, and here we have a beautiful picture of an eagle concerned that her young should fly and grow up to be like the parent. Carrying on the tips mimics the flight, they learn from her; she stirs them from the nest so they will learn, yet she watches carefully so that none can be hurt. A picture of parenthood and of the love of God as our parent.

As God's children we are the apple of His eye and we are lovingly parented so that we might be like Him. God has only our well–being in His heart.

✝ *Lord God, help me to appreciate the fact that I am the apple of Your eye . All the lessons You are teaching me are because Your desire is that I would be as You are. Amen.*

♥ Greatness does not depend on size.

21st July God is Loving

📖 John 3 : 16

"For God so loved the world that He gave his one and only Son, that whoever believes in Him shall not perish but have eternal life."

☞ This is of course the best known of all Bible verses, and it is no surprise that it tells us positively and clearly the good news of God's salvation.

God's motivation for giving His Son is 'love'. We can only begin to understand the cost of God's giving when we ,who are parents , sense that our little loved ones might possibly die, due to sickness or some other enormous tragedy. It is right to say **so loved** because God's love is enormous. Love never takes; it always gives and the action of God's love is to give His only Son, the most precious of all gifts.

We wouldn't give at such cost for a trivial thing, and neither did God. The purpose of His loving gift was the salvation of who ever would believe in Him. The whosoever are you and I. Let us today contemplate again such love that God has acted in this costly way for our eternal salvation from sin and death. Let us take time to say 'thank you' in our praise.

✝ *Thank You, God, for the tremendous value You have placed on my life shown by the tremendous sacrifice you personally suffered for my salvation. Amen.*

♥ True love is never being apart, but suffering while you are.

22nd July — God is Loving

📖 Romans 8 : 35

"Who shall separate us from the love of Christ? Shall trouble or hardship or persecution or famine or nakedness or danger or sword?"

☞ **The answer is NO!** Paul in this section of Romans chapter 8 explains why the love of God is like superglue: it never lets go. God's love for us began in eternity. He has always loved those He has purposed to love and, because God is God, His purpose is always completed. If God's eternal purpose was to love us, then whatever happens to us in this life by way of opposition doesn't really count. This gives us tremendous security. Our security is grounded in the love of God, begun in eternity and taking us into eternity.

The answer is YES! *If God is for us, who can be against us*. For those who are God's children and facing difficulty of any description today, we need to know the security of God's eternal love. If the difficulty is very strong, God's love is infinity more powerful. If the difficulty is incredibly intense, then the love of God is infinitely more deep.

✝ *Thank You, God, that all Your promises are' yes' in Jesus Christ. Help us have a right and eternal perspective on Your love for us. Amen.*

♥ My barn having burnt to the ground, I can see the moon. (Chinese Proverb)

23rd July — God is Loving

📖 1 John 4 : 10

"This is love: not that we loved God, but that He loved us and sent His son as an atoning sacrifice for our sins."

☞ **We didn't love God, we loved ourselves**. John defines love alone from God's perspective. We tend to reverse this and think of love in terms of how we feel about God at any particular moment. Thinking like this will always be dependent on how we feel. John's starting point is our sinfulness, our deviation from the will of God and our rebellion against Him .Therefore Scripture is so true when it says we did not love God.

We must therefore love others (1 John 4 : 7) Again our motivation to love is not found within ourselves or even within others, but only because God first loved us and we follow His example. Considering what God has done for us leaves us no alternative but to love others!

✝ *Lord, we are so grateful that You decided to love us and we thank You for the salvation given to us. Help us today to love others as You have loved us. Amen.*

♥ If you have a pleasant neighbour, it is likely that he does too.

Samuel Mawhinney

24th July Guidance

📖 Psalm 37 : 3 - 5

"Trust in the Lord and do good; dwell in the land and enjoy safe pasture. Delight yourself in the Lord and he will give you the desires of your heart. Commit your way to the Lord; trust in him and he will do this."

☞ These are the words of a King. King David was not a perfect human being, although he was a great man who followed God. At the start of verse 3 he says it is important to have faith in God, but this must be wedded to a good lifestyle. That's a good place to start when thinking about what God might want us to do in our lives. He won't want us deliberately to break His commands. We need to believe in God, and also to obey God. When He says (for example) 'You shall not covet' we can take this as guidance. In fact, we should delight to live this way because in doing so we will discover who we truly are as people, and what we really want from life (v 4). Do you know what the desire of your heart is? God knows, and He knows best.

✝ *Lord, guide me through Your Word which gives clear advice and commands on the most important things in life. Thank You for it. Amen.*

♥ A slap on the back often pushes out the chest.

25th July — Guidance

📖 John 16 : 13

"But when he, the Spirit of truth comes, he will guide you into all truth. He will not speak on his own; he will speak only what he hears, and he will tell you what is yet to come."

☞ What is the Holy Spirit? That was a question which puzzled the early followers of Jesus, just as it confuses many people today. Jesus explains that the Holy Spirit is a Person who speaks the truth, which He hears from God the Father. Elsewhere in the Bible, there are stories of how the Spirit told people to do certain things – always in line with God's truth, or to help explain the truth more persuasively. Today, Christians will speak of being led by God to particular courses of action, and we understand that the Holy Spirit does this in our lives. As we read, so the Spirit leads us deeper into God's truth, helping us to understand its message. It's a supernatural relationship, and a gift to all followers of Jesus. He will lead us when we ask Him.

✝ *Holy Spirit, lead me today in everything. Prompt me to live according to Your will and purpose. Help me to trust You for guidance in everything. Amen*

♥ Lord God of Hosts, be with us yet. Lest we forget – lest we forget!

(Kipling)

26th July **Guidance**

📖 Acts 15 : 22

"Then the apostles and elders, with the whole church, decided to choose some of their own men and send them to Antioch with Paul and Barnabas. They chose Judas (called Barsabbas) and Silas, two men who were leaders among the brothers."

☞ The first Christians struggled with many issues, which would not concern the Christian Church today. One of these issues was whether Gentile believers could be welcomed unconditionally into the Christian Church, which began as a Jewish movement. The issue threatened to divide the Church, and wise guidance was needed to prevent it. The leaders of the Church met at Jerusalem to consider the issue and came to their conclusions. This is the story told in Acts 15. The Authority of the leaders (called apostles and elders) was recognised, because it was understood that these were people who walked closely with God and who would want the very best for the Church at large. The Church was prepared to accept that God was guiding them through their leaders. Today, many Churches function in similar ways, with elders or bishops who are trusted to pray and consider God's plan for the Church at large.

✝ *Lord, guide those who have been identified and called as leaders in the Church. Keep them faithful and prayerful as they seek to lead the people of God on earth. Amen.*

♥ When happiness gets into your system, it is bound to break out on your face.

27th July Guidance

Romans 12 : 2

"Do not conform any longer to the pattern of this world, but be transformed by the renewing of your mind. Then you will be able to test and approve what God's will is – his good, pleasing and perfect will."

☞ I remember learning about the litmus test in chemistry class at school. It seemed amazing that a simple piece of coloured paper could indicate whether a substance was acid, neutral or alkaline. God has given us a litmus test to use when testing whether something is His will or not. At first sight, it may seem risky simply to use our minds for this task. What influences the way we think most of all? TV and the media? Music? The opinion of your friends? Your partner? For each of us it will differ, but for all of us the influences are there. If we are to be guided safely and reliably by our minds, then they need to be transformed and renewed by God. He needs to be the main influence, through His Spirit, the Bible and other Christians who will help discover His will.

✝ *Remind me today, Lord, that the way I think will determine the way I behave. Help me to measure and assess the influences upon my mind, and to cut out the harmful things, which serve only to cloud my judgement. Amen.*

♥ Most folk are as happy as they make up their minds to be.

28th July — Guidance

📖 James 1 : 5

"If any of you lacks wisdom, he should ask God, who gives generously to all without finding fault, and will be given to him."

☞ If you could ask for anything in the world and know that it would be given to you without limit, what would it be? Wealth? Influence? Power? Happiness? Wisdom may not sound the most exciting lottery win, but it is undoubtedly the best. God is ready to give wisdom to His children, because He Himself is wise. This might be wisdom for a particular situation. 'O God, what do I do next?' Or it might be wisdom in general: 'Lord, I am constantly being asked for my opinion and advice. Help me to get it right'. Solomon was a very wise King in Old Testament times, and he wrote down a summary of his thinking on all kinds of issues in the Proverbs. Try reading six proverbs a day for a month, asking God to gift you with wisdom. He is a God who gives generously.

✝ *Lord, there are times when I need the kind of wisdom which reaches beyond mere common sense. Help me to recognise those times, and to come straight to You for help when they arise. Amen.*

♥ The man who knows he has enough is rich indeed.

David Bruce

29th July Unity

Psalm 133 : 1 – 2

"How good and pleasant it is when brothers live together in unity! It is like precious oil poured on the head, running down on the beard, running down on Aaron's beard, down upon the collar of his robes."

☞ My teenage son has introduced me to the delights of hair gel. Fashions move round; I had always associated Brylcreem with World War 2 fighter pilots. People have always used oils and ointments on their heads, not just to keep unruly hair in order but to indicate something special. Olive oil for anointing is still used in some church traditions as a symbol of the blessing of the Holy Spirit. What Psalm 133 is saying is that when we get together and agree - God is pleased. Have you ever felt something a bit special and better when you went to a service or meeting which was not just for your own denomination but embraced others? That something extra could be the blessing of God on His people in unity.

✝ *The Lord bless you and keep you: The Lord make His face to shine upon you, and be gracious to you: The lord lift up His countenance upon you, and give you peace. Amen.*

♥ Whatever did Aaron's wife say to him about all that oil over his collar, so hard to remove?

30th July — Unity

Malachi 3 : 16

"Then those who feared the Lord talked with each other, and the Lord listened and heard. A scroll of remembrance was written in his presence concerning those who feared the Lord and honoured his name."

☞ Think of the people you worship with each Sunday? How many of them do you know by name? How many do you pray for regularly? Do you know anything of their real concerns? I wonder if our fear of awkwardness with each other drives out the proper fear or reverence for the Lord of which Malachi speaks.

Methodist churches used to have 'class meetings'; small groups where the members got to know each other and were accountable to each other. Many churches are recovering the joy and the challenge of getting to know each other in small groups. There is a special joy when we meet face to face with Christians from other backgrounds. Set yourself a target to pray for and get to know perhaps two people from your own church and someone in your district from another church.

✝ *Lord, when I go to church next, help me to see people's faces and not just the backs of their heads. Lead us into a quality of fellowship that is more than a smile and a greeting; as we talk with each other may You listen and hear, in Your mercy. Amen.*

♥ What kind of Christian am I? A hermit crab scuttling back into my shell, or a butterfly fluttering around but never landing, a jelly fish drifting with the tide or perhaps a salmon swimming against the stream with a single purpose.

31st July Unity

📖 Ephesians 4 : 4 – 6

" There is one body and one Spirit – just as you were called to one hope when you were called – one Lord, one faith, one baptism, one God and Father of all who is over all and through all and in all."

☞ 'Why is it that, when two Christians meet perhaps for the first time, within five minutes they are chatting to each other as if they have been friends for years? It is because they have certain things in common. They share the same Father. They share the same Saviour. They share the same Holy Spirit. They share the same Book. They share the same Future'. (Rev. Russell Birney.)

What do you do when you visit a strange place, say on holiday, and are dismayed there is no church there of your particular 'brand'. Don't settle for a walk in the woods or a quiet time in your hotel room. Seek out people who love Jesus and find out how much and Who you have in common.

✝ *Lord, when I think I'm all on my own lead me to Your people, and help me to overcome the differences of culture and language. Amen.*

♥ A Presbyterian was stranded on a desert island, so he began to build different buildings to meet the needs of life. When he was rescued they asked him, "why two places of worship?" He replied, " In order that I have a church that I don't go to."

AUGUST

During his Youth Hostelling days Robert Sellar and two of his friends met with a shepherd man atop Garron Head, Co. Antrim.

As his friends and the old man got into conversation, R.G. laid back and made the pencil sketch on which this woodcut is based.

The cut is made from plywood and is 7″ x 9.5″.

1st August Unity

Ephesians 4 : 15 – 16

"...speaking the truth in love we will in all things grow up into Him who is the Head, that is Christ. From Him the whole body, joined and held together by every supporting ligament, grows and builds itself up in love as each part does its work."

☞ Samuel Hebich gives this very simple insight to Ephesians 4: "You and I cannot make a tub. It requires a good carpenter to make a tub, or it will hold no water, because it is not made of one piece of wood."

There are 4 things to make a good tub:

1. It must have a good bottom.
2. Each of the pieces must be fitly joined to the bottom.
3. Each one must be fitly joined to his fellow.
4. Each one shall be kept close by the bands outside.

One piece may be narrow and the next piece wide, yet it shall be a good tub, but if a little stone or a bit of a stick come between the pieces it will not do at all. What is the small stick or stone between the pieces of wood? It is a little quarrel, the hard word, and the dirty bit of money that keeps brother from being fitly joined to brother. What is the piece of wood that falls out of the circle? It is the proud unforgiving spirit that every one can feel is in the meeting and which causes the heavenly peace to run out. Oh beloved, be fitly joined together.

✝ *Lord, show me the little things I do or say or think which cause the heavenly peace to run out. Amen.*

♥ A rector wrote to his bishop (so they say). 'Dear Bishop, Under no circumstances will I leave this parish to undertake the duties you ask of me. I remain your humble and obedient servant.'

2nd August Unity

📖 1 Corinthians 1: 22 – 24

"Jews demand miraculous signs and Greeks look for wisdom but we preach Christ crucified, a stumbling block to Jews and foolishness to Gentiles, but to those whom God has called, both Jews and Greeks, Christ the power of God and the wisdom of God."

☞ A vision for Ireland (shared at Christian Renewal Centre, Rostrevor). Someone saw in a dream the island of Ireland covered in flagpoles with different churches and parties. Somewhere in the middle was the cross of Christ, but small and obscured by the flagpoles. Gradually, people began to haul their flags down and to turn to join each other at poles. The flagpoles grew smaller and the cross grew larger. Human beings have always wanted to obscure the cross and assert their own 'flag' whether it is pride in a country or a church or even an individual personality. The simple truth is, while we fly these flags we cannot affirm Christ crucified and we are divided from each other. But where Christians gather at the foot of the cross, there is great hope.

Lift high the cross, the love of Christ proclaim
till all the world adores his sacred name!
O Lord, once lifted on the tree of pain.
Draw all the world to seek you once again.
(G.W Kitchen and M.R Newbolt)

✝ *Lord, please let our flagpoles grow smaller and the cross grow larger. Amen*

♥ Speak when you are angry and you will make the best speech you will ever regret.

John Faris

3rd August — Faithfulness

Deuteronomy 7 : 9

"Know therefore that the Lord your God is God; He is the faithful God, keeping His covenant of love to a thousand generations of those who love Him and keep His commands.""

☞ Temperamental people are hard to live with, whether in the home or in the work place. The trouble is, you never know where you stand – one day you can do nothing wrong, the next you can do nothing right. It all depends which side of the bed they got out of that morning!

Wouldn't it be awful if God were like that? But we need have no such fear, for He is the faithful God – He is reliable and trustworthy, He keeps His promises. When people enter into a relationship of love with God, that is perhaps one of the most startling discoveries they make. "Though the mountains be shaken and the hills be removed, yet my unfailing love for you will not be shaken, nor my covenant of peace be removed," says the Lord, who has compassion on you. (Isaiah 54 : 10)

Quite simply, God is saying to His children, "I love you, and nothing will ever happen to make me change my mind." Why don't you take Him at His word?

✝ *Father, remind me today that, even if my circumstances have changed, You have not. Amen.*

♥ There are no changes in God's love, though there may be changes in the way of showing it. (C.H. Spurgeon)

4th August — Faithfulness

📖 Lamentations 3 : 22 - 23

"Because of the Lord's great love we are not consumed, for His compassions never fail. They are new every morning; great is your faithfulness."

☞ Not to put too fine a point on it, Jeremiah, the writer of these words, had been going through the mill. His city was in ruins, his people had been scattered and he himself was broken – hearted. His tears had flowed freely, his prayers had gone unanswered and his suffering seemed endless. When you stand in Jeremiah's shoes, it hurts:– a serious illness, the death of a loved one, a wayward teenager … the shoes come in many styles.

Yet when things were at their blackest and Jeremiah was in the depth of despair, he began to see glimmers of light. What had preserved his life in spite of the pressures? Simply this: God had not abandoned either him or his people. The river of God's goodness might have run low, but it had by no means dried up. Every morning brought fresh signs of God's continuing love. What a great theme that has been for God's people in every generation.

Great is Your faithfulness!
Great is Your faithfulness!
Morning by morning new mercies I see;
All I have needed Your hand has provided –
Great is Your faithfulness, Lord unto me!

✝ *Lord, I thank You that we can face each new day together, and that today You will provide all that I need. Amen.*

♥ Who knows where you will discover God's kindness today- keep your eyes open!

5th August **Faithfulness**

📖 Luke 16 : 10

"Whoever can be trusted with very little can also be trusted with much, and whoever is dishonest with very little will also be dishonest with much."

☞ Periodically, I am asked to supply a reference for someone applying for a new job. Employers considering potential candidates want to know something of their track record. How do they get on with people? What about time keeping? Are they reliable? Past performance is a good indicator of future potential.

Jesus, in Luke 16 : 10, reminds us that in spiritual matters our track record is also an important spiritual indicator. What a person does with the small things of life, they also do with the big things. Their faithfulness or dishonesty with material riches is an indicator of how they deal with spiritual issues. In other words, it is not possible, as some imagine, to divide our lives into material and spiritual compartments, as though one has no bearing on the other. When God reviews our lives, He takes in the whole picture and He assures us that faithfulness in the present will lead to reward in the future. No task God entrusts to us today is trivial, but is an opportunity to serve Him faithfully. Happy indeed are those to whom God can entrust the small things in life.

✝ *Gracious God, help me so to live and work today that, at its end, You might readily say, "Well done, good and faithful servant".*

♥ Faithfulness in little things is a big thing. (Chrysostom)

6th August — Faithfulness

📖 2 Timothy 2 : 2

"The things you have heard me say in the presence of many witnesses, entrust to reliable men who will also be qualified to teach others."

☞ If you have ever played 'Chinese Whispers', where a message is relayed from person to person around a circle, you will know how easily the message can be distorted. What is received at the end, often bears no relation to the original. Of course, party games are harmless fun, but what if the message is an accident report to a 999 operator? In a matter of life and death, faithful transmission is all-important.

For Paul, the Christian message has life or death importance – hence his concern that it should not be distorted or corrupted. Those who teach others should be faithful, reliable, and trustworthy. Nearing the end of his life, Paul hands the gospel torch to Timothy, who in turn must pass it on to others.

That's how you and I came to hear about Jesus. Faithful people sharing what they themselves had learned. We, in turn, have a responsibility to invest the truth of the scriptures in the lives of others, with our children, in our youth group, with our neighbour, in our congregation. Take in as much as we can, and pass on as much as we can.

✝ *Lord, today, as I thank You for those who helped me to know You, please use me to help others. Amen.*

♥ The real mark of a saint is that he makes it easier for others to believe in God. (Anon.)

7th August **Faithfulness**

📖 2 Timothy 2 : 13

"If we are faithless, He will remain faithful, for He cannot disown himself."

☞ A good father, who keeps his word to his children, is a great blessing. When a reward or treat is promised, they know that they can count on him to come up with the goods. When it comes to misbehaviour, they also know where they stand – certain actions will have inevitable consequences. But when fathers make promises which are not honoured, or issue warnings which are never acted on, children take their words with a large pinch of salt.

In verses 11 –13 of 2 Timothy 2, we find what Paul calls 'a trustworthy saying', with promises both for blessing and for judgement. Those who suffer for their faith, even to the point of death, or who patiently persevere in the face of difficulties, will experience reward. Equally, those who turn away from Christ will find that He turns from them. Be assured that God is faithful to all His promises. None of His words are empty; none of His promises are false. That way, you and I are left in no doubt about where we stand. He will remain faithful.

✝ *Father, thank You that You are trustworthy and utterly faithful to Your word. Help me likewise to be faithful, both to You, and in every aspect of my life. Amen.*

♥ Though men are false, God is faithful. (Matthew Henry)

Mervyn Burnside

8th August Money

📖 Ecclesiastes 5 : 10

"Whoever loves money never has money enough; whoever loves wealth never is satisfied with his income. This too is meaningless."

☞ One morning I was driving through Dublin with some business colleagues. A top of the range Mercedes pulled up alongside us at the traffic lights. Envious glances were exchanged. Then one colleague remarked "While we're stressed out trying to get one of those that man is worrying about how to hold unto his".

The words in the Bible verse above imply a great fondness for money and wealth. Love, which should be directed towards God and other people, is focused somewhere else. Money (cash, bank balances, credit cards) and wealth (property, land, shares etc.) can become a primary driving force in our lives.

This is dangerous ground and the warning here is stark. Such a passion will not bring long term happiness. Ultimately it will lead to a disappointment and discontent, with or without a Mercedes!

✝ *Lord, thank You for reminding me that money and wealth never fully satisfy. Amen.*

♥ A budget is a way of worrying about our expenditure before we spend rather than afterwards.

9th August — Money

📖 Matthew 6 : 19

"Do not store up for yourselves treasures on earth, where moth and rust destroy, and where thieves break in and steal".

☞ Jesus is speaking here to His disciples. This is an extract from what is often called the 'Sermon on the Mount'.

Later Jesus talks about how we can trust God to provide food, clothes and other necessities each day. However, we often look for security in accumulating various forms of wealth for our families and ourselves. 'Store up' suggests piling up in excess of our needs, rather than merely being prudent.

In times past, stocks of silver or gold could rust or be stolen. Nowadays our earthly wealth can be devastated by currency devaluation, fraud, fluctuations in stock market or property values and so on. No investment is completely secure.

Jesus' comments are a reminder to invest for heavenly values as a priority rather than short term earthbound security.

✝ *Father, I am sorry that so often I find it easier to look for security in my possessions rather than You. Amen.*

♥ An economist is a person who can't see something working in practice without asking whether it would also work in theory.

10th August — Money

📖 Matthew 6 : 24

"No one can serve two masters. Either he will hate the one and serve the other, or he will be devoted to the one and despise the other. You cannot serve both God and money".

☞ I was reading recently about the background of a murder victim. The unfortunate man had been a drug dealer, a para military and a police informer on both sides of the Irish border. Inevitably his double (or treble) life led to a sudden and horrible death.

Sometimes we might be tempted to think we are clever enough to manage dual loyalties.

But Jesus is clear, both generally and specifically, in relation to money. Dual sovereignty doesn't work. At first, choices may be made deep down inside without full awareness even to us. Eventually, however, if we are devoted to something else we will come to despise Jesus.

He who wants the best for each of us cares enough to speak openly and uncomfortably about the facts of life.

✝ *Lord Jesus, today and for the rest of my life I choose You. Amen.*

♥ There is no limit to what you can achieve if you don't mind who gets the credit.

11th August Money

📖 1 Timothy 6 : 6-7

"But godliness with contentment is great gain. For we brought nothing into this world and we can take nothing out of it".

☞ To understand fully today's verses, we must realise that previously the writer has referred to people who think being devoted to God leads to financial gain. Not so. The way to achieve life- enhancing super profits is devotion mixed with contentment.

Contentment without godliness could mean a passive acceptance of life. But Jesus didn't always accept things as they were. So Paul here is not encouraging merely being passive.

Our relationship with God and our inner attitude can give a satisfaction that is not based on favourable circumstances, though we are not immune from life's ups and downs. Sometimes this may mean accepting our situations or letting go of ambitions and desires, which are not part of God's agenda for our lives – this can be painful.

But always remember the promise of great gain. Sounds like a super investment considering that someday we will have to leave behind all of what we've accumulated anyway.

✝ *Dear Lord, I believe in Your great gain and want to follow You, even when acceptance brings temporary pain. Amen.*

♥ Ohno second- that minuscule fraction of time it takes to realise that you have just made a really big mistake.

12th August **Money**

📖 Hebrews 13 : 5

"Keep your lives free from the love of money and be content with what you have, because God has said, "Never will I leave you; never will I forsake you".

☞ In an industralised world money is necessary as a unit of exchange and measure of value. But if we allow ourselves to grow too fond of money it may become a controlling force, which can never be satisfied.

God wants us to be free from that sort of bondage. The antidote is a decision to adopt a positive attitude of contentment and acceptance in our present circumstances.

The strong promise of God's company helps us do this even when others seem to be passing us out. The quotation here comes from a time when God's people were facing frightening challenges under a new leader. See Deuteronomy 31 : 6. Now the promise is applied to us as individuals.

The basis of contentment and acceptance is trusting God. All too easily and quickly money and possessions can be taken from us. But, with God, 'never' means 'never ever'. What a deal!

✝ *Thank You, God, for having Your promise written down and that Your 'never' means 'not ever, no matter what'. Amen.*

♥ Blame Storming – sitting around trying to decide why a project failed or a deadline was missed and who was responsible.

John Thompson

13th August — God is Just

📖 Genesis 18 : 25

"Far be it from you to do such a thing – to kill the righteous with the wicked, treating the wicked and the righteous alike. Far be it from you! Will not the judge of all the earth do right?"

☞ Abraham's anguished cry comes in response to the revelation that the Lord has given him concerning the destruction of the cities of Sodom and Gomorrah. Their wickedness was already well –known (Genesis

13 : 13) and would later become proverbial. Yet to Abraham, Sodom and Gomorrah were more than names on a map. For him these cities meant living people. It was in Sodom that his nephew, Lot, lived together with his wife and daughter. It was the king of Sodom whom Abraham had helped following his defeat in battle. (Genesis 14). Thus when God proposes judgment, Abraham is flooded with dismay and the result is one of the boldest and most earnest intercessory prayers in all Scripture.

In his prayers Abraham was not bargaining with God as is sometimes thought. For Abraham knew God to be a just and righteous God. He knew, too, that he himself was but dust and ashes (Genesis 18 : 27) and he knew how important it was to be humble in the presence of a sovereign God. Yet he persevered in his plea so that, when God said He would spare the city for the sake of 50 righteous, if that number could be found, Abraham asked if he would do so for 45, then 40, then 30, then 20 and finally 10. Why did Abraham stop at 10? We may never know. Yet one thing is certain. Abraham was reassured. He did not need to drop his figure any lower. Whether Sodom was consumed or not, the universe was on a solid footing. The Judge of all the earth will do what is right.

This is a Bible truth that comforts and disturbs. It is comforting, because God's justice is the guarantee that one day all the wrongs that characterise what the Bible calls 'this present evil age' will be put to right. It is disturbing because God's justice means that each of us comes under His just judgment since we must all appear before the judgment seat of Christ. (2 Corinthians 5 : 10). A man once said to Dr. Billy Graham, "When I get to heaven all I will ask for is justice" to which Billy Graham replied, "My friend, if all you get is justice then you will go to hell." In every case, including our own, the judge of all the earth will do what is right. There is but one way to avoid what is our just desert and that is to call on the coming Judge to be our present Saviour. Then we can look forward to that future meeting with joy, knowing that, since on the cross God has judged our sins righteously, there is now no condemnation for those who are in Christ Jesus.

✝ *Gracious Father, Thank You that Your Son, the Lord Jesus, loved us and gave Himself for us on the cross so that we might be rescued from this present evil age, and be delivered from the wrath that is to come. Amen.*

♥ I've no idea when Jesus is coming back. I'm on the Welcoming Committee, not the Planning Committee! (Tony Campolo).

14th August — God is Just

📖 Deuteronomy 32 : 4

"He is the Rock, his works are perfect, and all his ways are just. A faithful God who does no wrong, upright and just is he."

☞ One of the things that we mere mortals often have the audacity to do is to place God in the dock. We then assume the role of the prosecuting barrister by asking God to explain why He did this or why He did that. If He fails to do so to our satisfaction, we refuse to believe Him or trust Him. But the Bible knows nothing of any man or woman who has God in the dock. The Bible knows only of a God who has us in the dock. For it is we, and not God, who are 'the guilty party'.

The Song of Moses, which makes up Deuteronomy 32 recognises this fact. Israel was forever putting God in the dock and they frequently murmured against God and against Moses. There was even a point where their complaining was so great that Moses cried to the Lord that he might die, such was the burden of responsibility that God was asking him to shoulder. (Numbers 11: 14) But while Moses found himself wearied by the people whom God had called him to lead, he never joined them in their complaining. Because it is never God who is guilty, only us.

Our adversary, the devil, will try to make us believe otherwise, especially when life is painful and the way ahead seems fraught with difficulties. It is in such times that we need to proclaim, with Moses, the name of the Lord, praising His greatness and rejoicing in His goodness. A young Scottish covenanter by the name of Richard Cameron lost his life when he was just thirty–two years old. His enemies cut off his head and his hands and they took them to the young man's father who was being held prisoner in the Tolbooth jail. As they showed him the head and hands they asked him, "Do you know them?" He took them on his knee, bent over them and kissed them. "I know them!" he said, "I know them. They are my son's, my dear son's." And then, weeping and yet praising he went on, "It is the Lord! Good is the will of the Lord who cannot wrong me nor mine but has made goodness and mercy follow us all our days."

What of us? Shall we murmur and complain against God when things don't appear to be going our way or shall we remember that His works are perfect, that His ways are just, that He does no wrong and that in all things He works for the good of those who Love Him?

✝ *Lord, be gracious to me, for I long for you; be my strength in the morning and my help in time of trouble. Amen.*

♥ Custard Christians: those who get upset over trifles. Yogurt Christians: those who sour everything they mix with. Cream Christians: those who make you go "MMMMM".

15th August God is Just

📖 Isaiah 1 : 17

"Seek Justice, encourage the oppressed. Defend the cause of the fatherless, plead the case of the widow."

☞ A minister and his family went to see Andrew Lloyd–Weber's production of 'The Phantom of the Opera'. They found the show impressive with its magnificent costumes, brilliant acting, spellbinding music and stunning stage sets. From their front row seats they could almost reach out and touch the Phantom's mask and they just about had their heads taken off by the chandelier as it came crashing onto the stage. The whole thing was just fantastic. But from the same vantage point they were also able to look at the orchestra pit. There the scene was very different. The flautist, in every playing pause, was reading a gardening magazine, the bass guitarist would slide out a sports magazine every chance he had and the drummers were busy doing crossword puzzles!

It seemed a strange thing that people who were so close to the action as to be part of the drama itself could be so indifferent to what was taking place in their midst. Yet that was precisely the position into which Judah had drifted in the time of the prophet Isaiah. They were God's people caught up in His redemptive purposes for the world. But like the musicians in 'The Phantom of the Opera', they had long since lost their sense of awe and had become dull to the immense privilege they had as God's chosen people. It wasn't that they had stopped believing in God or that they had ceased to practice their religion, for they still observed the religious festivals, (v 13–14), offered the prescribed sacrifices (v11) and engaged in corporate prayer (v15). Yet the prophet had only words of rebuke and condemnation for them because they had forgotten the moral and social dimensions of living as the people of God.

It is not enough to participate in worship. It is not enough to enjoy singing hymns. It is not enough to have our emotions stirred and our hearts warmed. “Religion that God our Father accepts as pure and faultless,” says James, “is this; to look after orphans and widows in their distress and to keep oneself from being polluted by the world.” (James 1 : 27) The Bible nowhere teaches that we can earn eternal life by our good deeds and our social concerns but it does teach that it is impossible to receive the gift of salvation without being changed by it. It is like a new suit of clothes. God expects us not only to own it but also to wear it and only by wearing it daily in practical, righteous living can we be sure that we have got it.

✝ *Lord God, show me the way I should walk , teach me to do the things that pleases you and lead me into the place of righteousness, for Your name's sake. Amen.*

♥ I am extraordinarily patient, provided I get my own way in the end. (Margaret Thatcher.)

16th August God is Just

📖 Isaiah 61 : 8

“For I, the Lord, love justice; I hate robbery and iniquity. In my faithfulness I will reward them and make an everlasting covenant with them.”

☞ These words are set in the broader context of Israel's return from exile in Babylon where they had experienced the loss of their rights as a people in what was literally ‘robbery with iniquity’. But because

God loves justice and remains faithful to His covenant with them He will bring about their restoration so that all will see that they are a people whom God has blessed. (v 9) The corollary of this is that what characterises the Lord should also characterise His people. Those who live their lives under His rule are to be holy as He is holy. They are to act justly and to love mercy. (Micah 6 : 6) They are to seek first His kingdom and His righteousness. (Matthew 6 : 33)

The late TS Mooney, a Presbyterian elder from the city of Londonderry once wrote an article for a church magazine entitled 'What sort of society do we want?' He wrote, 'I want to see a church that will send out into the world of business and economics a stream of men, whether employers or employees whose hearts the Lord has touched and who in their daily work will remember that they have a Master in heaven. I want to see a Church enthusiastically preaching that Gospel that was reputed to have turned the world upside down. To see that Gospel by the power of the Spirit producing church members who will take its message to their fellows and whose lives will be a convincing testimony to its power. That would be a religious revival and such a movement would leave its mark on every part of our social, political and business life.' Our daily prayer, ought to be that of the hymn writer who wrote,

Breathe on me breath of God;
Fill me with life anew,
That as You love, so I may love,
And do what You would do.

✝ *Make me sensitive to Your Spirit and Your will, O God that I may faithfully and lovingly represent and reflect You in my daily life. For the glory of Jesus Christ. Amen.*

♥ What is morally wrong can never be politically right.

(Abraham Lincoln)

17th August — God is Just

1 John 1 : 9

"If we confess our sins He is faithful and just and will forgive us our sins and purify us from all unrighteousness."

There is a story told of a servant who stole one of his master's chickens. He thought he had got away with it but the next day one of his work mates came up and said that he had seen him steal the chicken and started to blackmail him. From that day on the servant's life was riddled with problems. He had the difficulty of finding the money to pay his mate. "It is no good," he said, "I shall have to do something about it." So he went to the master and said, "You know that chicken you lost the other week. I stole it." "I know you did," replied his master. "You know?" "Oh yes," said the master, "I saw you do it and I've been waiting all this time for you to come and tell me."

We cannot tell God anything about ourselves that He does not already know and that includes our sins. For He knows the very worst about us. But there can never be a proper relationship between us until we are happy that He knows and until we have opened our lives up to the gaze of Him whose eyes we cannot evade anyway! The only valid response to sin that the Bible knows, therefore, is confession. It is to say, "I did it." Yet confession doesn't come easily to us and we often fight shy of it. John says that if we would have fellowship with God we must accept responsibility for our actions. When we do, He is 'faithful and just and will forgive us our sins'. Not just by glossing over them or pretending they're not there, but He does it righteously, through the death of Jesus His Son, who scrubs away the stain, who soaks up the punishment and who speaks to the Father in our defense. For He is the atoning sacrifice for our sins, and not only for ours but also for the sins of the whole world. (1 John 2 : 2)

✝ *Lord God, have mercy upon me. Cleanse me from my sin, create in me a clean heart and continually renew a right spirit within me. Amen.*

♥ Give us clear vision that we may know where to stand and what to stand for, because unless we stand for something we shall fall for anything. (Peter Marshall.)

David Johnston

18th August — Encouragement

📖 Acts 4 : 36

"Joseph, was a Levite from Cyprus, whom the apostles called Barnabas (which means Son of Encouragement)"

☞ I was nervous, apprehensive and feeling very inadequate. It was the first night of preaching a series of sermons at a large Convention. A man approached me just before the service and said, "I don't wish to sound critical but we've never had a good preacher at this Convention". What an encouraging comment to a nervous visiting preacher! I turned to him and said, "Thank you, Barnabas!"

The Barnabas we read of here was a genuine encourager. He is known primarily for his ministry of encouragement. What a reputation to have! It was based on reality. He really did encourage other people. What are we well known for? Our gossiping? Our critical spirit? Our negativity? Our 'gift' of dividing churches and causing quarrels?

Every Christian needs encouragement. Every church needs encouragers. You can be one!

✝ *Lord, help me today to encourage someone. Amen*

♥ A faith-lift is a Barny-gift!

19th August Encouragement

📖 Acts 11: 23

"When he arrived and saw the grace of God, he was glad and encouraged them all to remain true to the Lord with all their hearts".

☞ Barnabas travelled to Antioch to find out what was going on. Reports of God doing great things had filtered back to the church in Jerusalem. Both Jews and Gentiles were being touched by the Lord. For some in Jerusalem it was acceptable, even expected, that God would bless Jews. If the Gentiles were also being blessed by God then this was worth investigating. Barnabas was sent and quickly discovered the clear evidence of the wonderful work of God.

His reaction is worthy of imitation. He wasn't jealous, dismissive or opposed to Gentiles coming into the church. He encouraged, affirmed and taught them. Indeed he stayed for a whole year. How do we react when God really blesses other people not like us and other congregations?

✝ *Lord, when You do new things help me to be an encourager. Amen.*

♥ Rejoice with those who rejoice!

20th August — Encouragement

Acts 14 : 22

"They returned...strengthening the disciples and encouraging them to remain true to the faith. "We must go through many hardships to enter the kingdom of God," they said."

☞ The person who helped me to become a Christian nearly 40 years ago still prays for me every week and keeps in touch with me. I am so thankful to the Lord for his interest, prayers and constant encouragement. His encouragement has been ongoing like that of Barnabas. In our verse today we read of Paul and Barnabas returning to Antioch to appoint elders, renew friendships, and encourage the new Christians. Encouragement is an essential ingredient of discipleship. It fosters and facilitates growth.

Also note that flattery is not encouragement. Barnabas encouraged people with the truth. He spoke with realism about hardships. Growth pains are part and parcel of the normal Christian life. Biblical encouragement is all about truth.

✝ *Lord, please help all who are going through hardship. Amen.*

♥ Praise and pray and peg away!

21st August — Encouragement

2 Timothy 4 : 2

"Preach the Word; be prepared in season and out of season; correct,

rebuke and encourage – with great patience and careful instruction."

☞ An experienced preacher was giving advice to a young preacher just beginning his ministry. He said, "Always remember that Jesus said, 'Feed the sheep don't fleece them'!"

A wise preacher is one who heeds these words of Paul to Timothy in our verse today. They speak of a faithful preaching and teaching ministry, thorough preparation, patient perseverance, and a balance of correction, rebuke and encouragement. The word, encouragement, has the idea of urging a person to pursue a particular course of conduct. It is exhorting rather than comforting. The church today needs the teaching of God's Word rather than the opinions of people. Christians are to live life-styles which are deliciously, delightfully and distinctively different. That kind of living has an impact on others.

✝ *Lord, help those in our congregation who preach and teach to be faithful to You and help me to encourage them. Amen.*

♥ Are we feeding the sheep or amusing the goats?

22nd August — Encouragement

📖 Hebrews 10 : 24 - 25

"And let us consider how we may spur one another on towards love and good deeds. Let us not give up meeting together, as some are in the habit of doing, but let us encourage one another – and all the more as you see the Day approaching".

☞ " Oh no! Not Sunday morning! I won't bother going to-day". Ever thought like that? Most people have at times. Isn't it interesting that the writer's call to encourage one another is in the context of meeting together?

One of the most dominant attitudes in society today and in the church today is "What's in it for me?" It is essentially a spirit of selfishness. Jesus calls us to a spirit of service. The writer of Hebrews does the same. He asks us to think in ways in which we can really help each other to grow as Christians, spurring each other on to love and good deeds. An important part of preparing for the Return of Jesus is to prioritize meeting together…it is a means of giving encouragement.

✝ *Forgive me Lord for too often thinking only of my own needs and not thinking of others. Amen.*

♥ Giving up and giving out or meeting up and looking out.

Ken Clarke

23rd August — Youth

📖 Psalm 86 : 11

"Teach me your way, O Lord, and I will walk in your truth, give me an undivided heart, that I may fear your name."

☞ David, the author of this Psalm, has to be one of the most accessible people in the Bible. In one breath he reaches great heights of worship and adoration of God and then sinks to almost total despair about his own circumstances. He is just so downright human, so like us.

But look closer. He has an incredible confidence in the one he both complains to and worships. The one whose truth he wants to walk in. You see David has a long memory. He has not forgotten the early confidence that he placed in God, as a teenager, when he was rewarded with great and easy success. Nor has he forgotten the lonely years of alienation when a promise of what he was to become seemed totally ridiculous. Most of all, he has not forgotten that it was in what seemed crazy that the treasure of intimacy with God his Lord was found. Out of this place of knowing, and being known, he now longs for the security of a heart that will never turn away from such a rare and special relationship. What Psalm 86 tells us, is that for David's God to fail to keep him, or us for that matter, is simply impossible. To know God and to trust Him is to know that whatever, yes, whatever life is chucking at us, God is for us.

✝ *Lord, it gets really tough at times, and that is when I don't know if You really are there or if there is any sense in life at all. Give me David's longing for an undivided heart and the ability to trust You no matter what. Amen.*

♥ Take time to write a journal of your relationship with God. It will amaze you how consistently He works things out for your good.

24th August — Youth

📖 Psalm 119 : 9

"How can a young man keep his way pure? By living according to your word."

☞ Perhaps one of the most sought after conditions today is a sense of wellbeing. Vast sums of money change hands in the pursuit of inner peace and self–knowledge. In another time, a different age, there was no such expectation that personal, inner equilibrium was even obtainable, never mind one's right. Today any sense of being told how to live, or what set of values to embrace is rejected as an immature and somewhat old-fashioned mindset.

What is so fascinating about Psalm 119 is the energy and determination with which the writer searches after God's word. He longs for a knowledge of it as if his life depends on it. Perhaps it does! When he finds God's word he meditates on it and is overjoyed by what it tells him! Who in the world would want to be so totally controlled by someone else's world, view and dictates? Answer: Someone who knows the person behind the dictates!

It is impossible to trust someone we do not know. It is even more unlikely that we will declare our own wisdom to be inferior to that of someone we have no history with.

Psalm 119 calls us to get right into God through His Word: to encounter Him. Not to read it and meditate on it and submit to it as and end in itself! But to meet Him, and ourselves through it. A sense of wellbeing! That will be found through the mysterious process that takes place between mind and spirit as 'the Word' is devoured!

✝ *Lord, come and fill Your Word with that mysterious insight that only You can give. Give me the gift of understanding and the insight that leads to a relationship with you. Amen.*

♥ An acquaintance can take place in a moment. Relationships take a lifetime.

25th August Youth

Isaiah 40 : 30 - 31

"Even youths grow tired and weary, and young men stumble and fall; but those who hope in the Lord will renew their strength. They will soar on wings like eagles; they will run and not grow weary, they will walk and not be faint."

☞ The more we progress as a human race the less it seems we need the crutch of religion and a belief in a superior being. We can explain most things scientifically and those we can't, we soon will have an explanation for them. We have thrown off the restraint of right and wrong, truth and falsehood. Truth is found in a moment, when what feels right is a sound enough basis for action. The freedom to **be** has become so good. Well for the moment at any rate.

Yet the soul, the inner me, the core person has never been more lonely, more confused, less certain of the future and more aware of being finite. Where is hope to spring from? Where is it found and what is its gift to us?

Hope is in the Lord! It does not need hopeful circumstances to raise a vision of a better tomorrow. Hope is the one thing that brings order to chaos, and meaning to despair. Hope is in the Lord!

All our self–knowledge is worthless and will ultimately disappoint us if the source of that knowledge is not God Himself. Young people, who have so much energy and ability to grab life by the throat, even they will run out of steam and become exhausted. But when they focus on, and draw wisdom and meaning from God, they will soar!

What is interesting is God's patience with us. Despite His vantage point above the universe from where He watches our antics, as one would observe grasshoppers, He waits. Waits for us to realise that He alone is the source of freedom, significance, meaning and hope.

✝ *Lord, we do not naturally turn to You. We want to prove we can do it all by ourselves! Help me to see that turning to you is not weakness. Rather it is the source of real freedom and wholeness. Amen.*

♥ When we come to our senses and risk the reasoned leap of faith, we can't believe our foolishness. However, the one must come before the other.

26th August Youth

📖 Matthew 19 : 21

"Jesus said to the rich young man, "If you want to be perfect, go, sell your possessions and give to the poor, and you will have treasure in heaven. Then come, follow me".

☞ How is it that for generations our worth has been defined by what we own and possess and not by who we are? This has never been more the case than for the current generation of teenagers. Designer clothes, designer families, designer food! Then there is the now. "I want it now, in fact I must have it now", and the makers of movies, advertisements and TV soaps tell us this is the route to happiness and fulfillment.

It seems though that in one form or another, this way of thinking has been around for 2000 years!

Jesus was strangely free of it. Well He was God you say, He didn't need to worry. One click of His fingers and He would have what He liked. Yes, He was God, but by a clear choice He had temporarily set

His majesty aside and entered our world, taking on **all** the limitations of being a man. It is from that vantage point that He calls us to free ourselves from the burden of possessions. In so doing we look forward to something much more worthwhile.

Jesus knew how to enjoy Himself, sure He did. He also had real human needs for food, friendship and family. He also knew that to have either possessions or personal needs as the first priority was pure folly! To live in plenty, while others lacked the basics for life was intolerable to God, His Father, who created us for community and equality. "Come, follow me," means embracing a worldview that swims against the tide, but actually it is where life is really at.

✝ *Lord, I find it so hard to believe that embracing Your way of living is better than what I see others all around me doing. Give me the ability to see things from Your perspective and the courage to follow You. Amen.*

♥ Consider how quickly you lose interest in that thing that you thought you couldn't live without. Perhaps Jesus wasn't so far out after all.

27th August — Youth

📖 Luke 24 : 25 - 27

"Jesus said to them; "How foolish you are, and how slow of heart to believe all that the prophets have spoken! Did not the Christ have to suffer these things and then enter His glory?" And beginning with Moses and all the Prophets, he explained to them what was said in all

the Scriptures concerning himself."

☞ Have you ever lost a friend? Someone who meant so much to you that you feel you will now suffocate with despair. How can life ever have meaning again? All the things you were going to do together. The expectations of how he would make a difference in your life and the life of others. The fun it was to be with them; the security they brought to your life just by their existence. Now it is gone!

It is both amazing and indeed a mystery how we often must go through the darkest times just so we can understand something or someone so much better. This was the experience of these disciples. Their hopes were in tatters. Their hero was dead – killed in disgrace. Now these wild stories about His body having vanished. It was all so unbearable. Now this stranger wants to know all about it. Actually it was good to talk about it!

As they walked from Jerusalem to Emmaus, they talked, and He listened. That was what was so good. He listened. Even though it was all so confusing, and the pain, oh the desperate pain of grief. How can anyone understand that? But He did.

Jesus was the best really when it came to inter-personal skills. He knew instinctively how to reach the depth of need before Him. He still does. These poor, disillusioned disciples needed so badly to pour out their hearts to someone who could help them make sense of this senseless moment in their lives. But look, once Jesus has listened carefully, He explains. He brings the scriptures to life for them. But, then He was, and is, the Incarnate Word. He's still in the same business today.

✝ *Lord, when it seems impossible to believe there is any hope, You are the source of hope. Help me to understand that and to run to You when these dark floods threaten to drown me. Thank You that You always bring meaning into the worst of moments. Amen.*

♥ The scriptures only make sense from the perspective of a relationship with their author.

Roz Stirling

28th August Grief

📖 Psalm 51 : 17

"The sacrifices of God are a broken spirit; a broken and contrite heart, O God, you will not despise."

☞ Often we think that God comes to us and asks for our time and more often for our money. These things, yes occasionally but only afterwards. First He asks for our heart.. If we say 'yes' we bring to Him different kinds of hearts, happy hearts, sad hearts, divided hearts, lonely hearts.

The Bible has scores of different kinds of hearts but the one He asks for is a broken and contrite one. Why a broken heart above all others? Maybe there is a clue in the alabaster box that contained exquisite fragrance. It was perfectly sealed and only as it was broken could the perfume be poured out. So too with our hearts. Often like the alabaster box they too are sealed, not letting others in and especially not letting the heart behind the universe in. What then are we to do with the wounds, the pain, the traumas and the tragedies of life? We can bring them to Him and surely there will be an unsettling at first, painful emotions, maybe even fear. He has promised as we give Him our broken hearts He will mend them and make them like fragrant, well watered gardens, tending and caring for them with delicacy and love.

✝ *Lord we come to You in our brokeness and admit that sin and being sinned against has broken our hearts as it has Yours. Our hearts are divided and unsure, come, through Your Holy Spirit and give us a new heart that can draw life from You. Amen.*

♥ So long as we imagine it is we who have to look for God, we must often lose heart, but it is the other way about - He is looking for us. (Simon Tugwell)

29th August Grief

📖 Ecclesiastes 3:4

"A time to weep and a time to laugh, a time to mourn and a time to dance."

☞ I remember the devastating yet wondrous time when my mother died. I saw momentarily through the visible into the invisible. I began to understand and experience that the polarity and complementarity of life and death were intricately woven together. As I looked through the visible, the invisible opened up. As my mother left time for eternity immanence and transcendence touched. So too I discovered in the midst of my tears that this was not just a time for weeping but sometimes in the midst of weeping there was laughter. Mourning mixed with laughter! What a complex tapestry of experience! Humour was somehow deeper and stranger than tears.

God who is outside of time, and to whom all things are present, can come into time, any time, past present or future and turn our mourning into dancing, our fears into laughter and somehow, someway in His presence and in His time our grief can become with Him a beautiful thing.

✝ *Lord Jesus, teach us how to weep and laugh, mourn and dance in the right proportions. Amen.*

♥ I am reminded of part of a poem ' Pasture by Robert Frost:

I'm going out to clean the pasture spring;
I'll only stop to rake the leaves away
(And wait to watch the water clear, I may):
I shan't be gone long -You come too.

30th August Grief

📖 Isaiah 53 : 3

"He was despised and rejected by men, a man of sorrows, and familiar with suffering. Like one from whom men hide their faces He was despised, and we esteemed him not."

☞ The grief Jesus carried was primarily the grief and sorrow of the bearer of sin, yet He carried our loss and our pain as well.

In His dying and death He identifies with our rejections, abandonment and pain. His disciples one by one left Him. Pilate condemned Him, His Father turned His face from Him, and by cruel hands He was crucified.

Many have had much to bear, on every side, and have been carrying burdens for a lifetime. Our lives have been a soaking sadness and sorrow. These sadnesses will affect us for a very long time and in various ways until we uncover them, mourn the loss and feel our sorrow in His presence for 'there is no sorrow like unto His sorrow'. Grief becomes the door to our healing, our freeing, and to the grace of God.

✝ *As You, Lord, identify with us in our grief and sorrow help us with You, to enter into the pain, the deep hole inside and to work through it tentatively and eventually to move ahead. Amen.*

♥ God is not a symbol of goodness, goodness is a symbol of God. (G K Chesterton)

31st August — Grief

📖 Jeremiah 8 : 22

"Is there no balm in Gilead? Is there no physician there? Why then is there no healing for the wound of my people?"

☞ Why? Why? Why? The question most asked in trauma, grief, loss, abandonment and sorrow. Why? Why? Why?

Grief and our grievous reactions to death, loss, rejection, being sinned against and exposure, and the concomitant feeling of inadequacy, inferiority that accompany the deep losses and unmet longings often cause us to cry out Why? Why? Why? Why is there no one there for me? Why is there no balm in Gilead, why is there no healing process? We believe that the answer to our questions will bring relief, but answers can at best bring slight ease. Healing will only come as we allow another, Jesus, into the wounds and then they will loose their power to hurt, to damage. He is the balm of Gilead, who wants to attend to the wounds of His people, to meet us in the depth of our sorrow, in our deep places, with His comforting grace and His embracing love. What does He promise, what is this balm? It is His presence...

✝ *Establish us in your steadfast presence, hold us in your radiant love, for your heart is greater than my wounds. Amen.*

♥ Your inadequacy is your first qualification (John Gaynor Banks)

SEPTEMBER

Here is a 4″ x 5″ cut-out, an actual size detail from the 8.8″ x 10.8″ linocut of a Goldcrest in a Scots Pine″

About 1987 a study had been made in crayons of a branch of a pinetree in the garden: it had no "centre of interest" in it and so was left in store as a sketch that might prove of use some day.

About 1993 a goldcrest came to a shrub close by to the house window, and the quick bird drawing that resulted from that snatch of a few minutes was exactly what was needed to impose in the twig study and complete the composition of the final print.

1st September — Grief

John 11 : 35

"Jesus wept."

This, the shortest verse in the Bible, is no ordinary statement about no ordinary man. These words about Jesus let me know in my heart that poignantly and empathetically, Jesus has been where I have been in tears, grief and mourning, only more so. But also He, the most masculine of all men- evidenced as we watch Him clear the temple, deal with the Pharisees, is here weeping (the word originally means, 'snorting' or 'crying copiously').

He lived in a compatible world of men. If Jesus can weep, then He has modelled the way for all other men (and women), not to be afraid to weep too, but to weep at times both publicly and without shame.

✝ *Lord shed Your light on the areas of our grief and woundings. Be present to our pain, as we come weeping, to the cross, the place of our healing. Amen.*

♥ Aslan is not a tame Lion ! (CS Lewis – Aslan is the Lion in the Narnian Series who is a type of Christ).

Vivienne Murtagh

2nd September — Prayer

Isaiah 65 : 24

"Before they call I will answer; while they are still speaking I will hear."

Here's an oft-quoted verse that is misleading out of context! It is doubtless true God knows our unspoken prayers and the longings of our hearts before we are capable of addressing them to Him. But Isaiah is referring to the future believers, (v 25), when Eden is restored, old enmities are gone (the wolf), fear is removed (the lamb) and natures are changed (the lion, the carnivore, will become a herbivore!). Such will be the unity and oneness in the world to come, that God will act for our good without us having to say a word. The picture is one of contentment, peace and utter wellbeing! And for today? Yes, it is true the Lord, the Spirit, transmits our prayers, even our inarticulate groaning, through to HQ with precision and clarity (Romans 8:26 – 27). This is an interim provision till we reach the 'holy mountain' (v.25) where the Lord dwells in the midst of His people, and the Spirit's role as a communications satellite will then be redundant!

✝ *Lord, I appreciate so much the help your Holy Spirit gives as I pray, so please help me maximise the benefit I can get from this privilege today. Amen.*

♥ When we work, we work…when we pray, God works!

3rd September Prayer

Psalm 66 : 18

"If I had cherished sin in my heart, The Lord would not have listened."

C.S.Lewis wrote, "Praise is the appointed consummation of our enjoyment of God" so it should be a regular and meaningful part of every Christian's life. 'Praise the Lord!' or 'Hallelujah!' is a scriptural command, not a noisy, unwelcome instruction or a fatuous remark as it has become in some of our meetings together. This psalm is a two-part hymn of gratitude by Israel in witness to the nations (vs. 1 – 12) and by an individual believer communicating his appreciation of the Lord to all who understands God's ways (vs. 13 –20). The writer cannot contain himself, so great is his own sense of gratitude for a relationship with the God who heard and answered his own prayers. He recognises (v. 18) that if there had been any hypocrisy in his approach to God, then the line would have gone dead (Luke 18 : 9 – 14) and prayer would have remained unanswered.

The New Testament control of this verse should spring to mind easily, 'If we confess our sins, he is faithful and just and will forgive us our sins and purify us from all unrighteousness.' (1 John 1 : 5 – 7). Transparency before God is one of our greatest, and always pressing, needs and if we've gone off–the-boil spiritually, here's the first place to look for the reason.

✝ *Lord, take away my inhibitions and self-centredness and help me to verbalise the great things you have done; but also deliver me from double standards and hypocrisy which could compromise my witness before others. Amen*

♥ The Christian disciple can never take the 'L' plate off his life, and risk travelling on his own.

4th September — Prayer

Matthew 7 : 7 - 8

"Ask and it will be given to you; seek and you will find; knock and the door will be opened to you. For everyone who asks receives; he who seeks finds; and to him who knocks, the door will be opened."

Very humbling, these verses. They predicate that we are beggars before God, spiritually shortsighted and undiscerning. Here we have what has been called 'beggars logic.' We are to persist in asking for God's grace like beggars (spiritually, this will always be our state) and to be confident that the one who responds to our asking, who reveals Himself to our seeking, who is committed to be a Father, knows what good gifts His children need…and supremely, as Luke's account vitally adds, the gift of the Holy Spirit. Don Carson reminds us this is 'not prayer envisaged as an occasional pious request for some isolated blessing, but prayer that is a burning pursuit of God…a divinely empowered response to God's open invitation, 'You will seek me and you will find me when you search for me with all your hearts.' (Jeremiah 29 : 13)

Lord, I'm such a stop-start kind of Christian; so please give me persistence in this 'burning pursuit' of you that should be the goal of my prayer life. Amen.

Ask =

Ask
Seek
Knock

5th September — Prayer

📖 Romans 8 : 26

"The Spirit helps us in our weakness. We do not know what we ought to pray for, but the Spirit himself intercedes for us with groans that words cannot express."

☞ What about those times we cannot pray? When the children are so ill, when work problems pulverise us, when something has been said that hurt us so much, when we lie in hospital draped with catheters and IV drips, and at best our prayers amount to a few inarticulate words. Then 'the Spirit Himself intercedes for us with groans that words cannot express.' That is, the Spirit says those things we want to say but cannot mouth. He doesn't give armchair advice but rolls up His sleeves and helps us in our weakness. That's top-grade help! So we have two intercessors: one in heaven, our Lord Jesus who intercedes about our sin problem (8 : 34) and one in our hearts, the Holy Spirit in person. No wonder the theme of the chapter is how greatly God loves us, and yet we've possibly only experienced perhaps 5% yet of all that lies in store for the Christian believer!

✝ *Lord, help me keep going at the coal face today, even if the situation is unpromising and my* resources are few, because it's *Your Holy Spirit's help I'm counting on. Amen.*

♥ Seven prayerless days make one weak!

6th September — Prayer

James 5 : 14 - 16

"Is any one of you sick? He should call the elders of the church to pray over him and anoint him with oil in the name of the Lord. And the prayer offered in faith will make the sick person well; the Lord will raise him up. If he has sinned, he will be forgiven. Therefore confess your sins to each other and pray for each other so that you may be healed. The prayer of a righteous man is powerful and effective."

☞ This promise does not apply to a backsliding Christian, a wayward Christian or a doubting Christian. James defines it as applicable to the righteous Christian who is able to pray both effectively and fervently. "Count me out" we say, "I'm not going to be able to pray boldly. I doubt my righteousness, I know I'm not sinless – I sin daily in thought, word and deed – I hardly know how to pray. This must be a promise for other people." Wrong! James anticipates our objection with the example of Elijah, who had the same human weaknesses as we have but God worked through him. Yes, we can be men and women of prayer and James ends by suggesting we start by praying for those who need the Gospel. As God hears our prayer and saves those members of our family, our friends, colleagues, they will be rescued from hell and many sins they would have plunged into will be averted.

✝ *Lord, I'd really prefer to pray for someone terminally ill and see them instantly healed but help me to pray today, in faith, for someone I know who needs rescue from the worst fate of all. Amen.*

♥ C.H. Spurgeon took some visitors to see 'the healing apparatus' in his church and opened the door on a room full of people at prayer!

Gordon Fyles

7th September — God's Glory

📖 Exodus 33 : 18

"Then Moses said, "Now show me your glory".

☞ As he led the slaves God had rescued from Egypt through Sinai towards the Promised Land, Moses found the task God had given him too heavy a burden to carry. Sometimes the people turned against him, and at times they even forsook the One who had redeemed them. God was not going to abandon his servant, and assured Moses of his continuing help and presence. But Moses wanted more: "Show me your glory", he prayed. Our trials may not be nearly as difficult as those Moses faced. Nevertheless, life can be hard, and we can at times feel our load is more than we can bear. God assures all who trust Him, of His help and constant presence. But more, He offers to show us His glory too. It is seen in the face and smile of His beloved Son. The apostle, John, wrote of Jesus: 'We have seen His glory!'

✝ *Lord, as I face today's responsibilities, may I keep before me the vision of Your glory which shines from the face of the crucified and risen Saviour and may I know that You will never leave me nor forsake me. Amen.*

♥ Often God's glory is seen in the most unexpected people in the most unlikely places. Try looking today for a face or word or action which reflects Christ!

8th September — God's Glory

📖 1 Samuel 4 : 22

"The glory has departed from Israel for the ark of God has been captured.":

☞ Greedy, rapacious priests had led the people of God astray. God was grieved that the worship of His great name had been corrupted. When His people were attacked by the Philistines, they went to defend themselves, foolishly thinking that if they carried the holy ark of the covenant with them into battle, all would be well. But the enemy captured the ark and the priests themselves were killed. God had withdrawn His glory for a time.

It is a subtle temptation to imagine that if we carry with us some charm or a holy object such as a Bible, it will guarantee us success and the blessing of God. Such thinking is seriously in error. God demands clean hands and a pure heart. Only Christ can give us that. When He is with us, and we follow Him obediently in faith, His glory will stay with us right to the end.

✝ *Lord, forgive me that I sometimes try to manipulate You for my own ends, and remind me throughout this day that Your blessing is given to those who love and obey You for Jesus sake. Amen.*

♥ A Chinese girl was looking after her little brother in fields which were skirted by steep cliffs. Suddenly, the little boy ran from her towards the cliffs. In desperation she prayed to luck charms she wore, but he ran even faster. Suddenly, she remembered a 'god' she had heard about. 'Please help me, Jesus', she cried. At that moment, a butterfly flew near the boy and he stopped to watch it long enough for his sister to catch up with him and take his hand again.

9th September God's Glory

Matthew 17 : 2

"There he was transfigured before them. His face shone like the sun, and his clothes became white as the light."

When the Son of God laid aside His glory and entered Mary's womb, He truly became a man, though He remained truly Very God. His divine glory was veiled by His human form. At times, as when He stilled the storm on Galilee, his disciples caught glimpses of that hidden glory. But here, on the mountain of transfiguration, his God-head was allowed to shine forth in radiant splendour. The strangest aspect of this experience given to Peter, James and John, was that he discussed with Moses and Elijah His impending death! That was because it was to be in His sacrifice for sin and subsequent resurrection, His glory would shine brightest.

The effects of His Passion can always be with us. The glory of the cross is that it brings us into the loving embrace of the Father, as our sins are cleansed and we are welcomed into His family.

✝ *Glorious Saviour, once crucified for my sins and now risen and exalted to be my Lord, give me the assurance today that I am truly Your child and that one day I too will see You face to face in Your heavenly glory. Amen.*

♥ A friend told me of her godly father's dramatic passing from this scene of time. For days, the old man had lain unconscious in a deep coma. The family were gathered, waiting for him to die. Suddenly, he opened his eyes and sat upright in bed, his face shining, gazing – not at them but into the far distance. As they watched him in amazement, he called out in clear, ringing tones, 'Yes, Lord, I come!' and fell back on the bed, asleep in Jesus.

10th September — God's Glory

📖 John 2 : 11

"This, the first of his miraculous signs, Jesus performed in Cana of Galilee. He thus revealed his glory, and his disciples put their faith in him."

☞ The Gospels speak often about 'miraculous signs' but unexpectedly usually the writers are saying no sign will ever be given to unbelieving people. Only occasionally are miraculous signs spoken of positively, as in this text. Jesus had just rescued a wedding from disaster and saved the reputation of the bride's father (v9) whose provisions had run out, by turning water into wine. His disciples who had already believed in Him now had their faith confirmed. This person who they were sure was the chosen Christ of God had power even over nature!

We are wrong if we think miracles will convince unbelievers. It doesn't work that way. The signs performed by Jesus Christ bear witness to His glory, but only those who are already looking to Him see His glory in them. God wants us to put our faith, not in the signs, but in the Saviour.

✝ *Lord Jesus Christ, Creator and Sustainer of all You have made. Your glory fills the heavens and the earth; help me today to truly trust You, and in Your own special way confirm my feeble faith, helping me to know most certainly that You are the Son of the living God. Amen.*

♥ History tells us that the Apostle Thomas founded the Christian Church in India. He travelled there, not by jumbo jet from Tel Aviv airport, but on foot, across Arabia, into Afghanistan, through the Khyber Pass, travelling on until he reached South India. There he was martyred for his faith, but not before many had believed in Christ. Thomas' faith was confirmed when he saw the risen glory of Jesus who said, "Put your finger in the nail print in my hands – be not faithless, but believe!" Jesus went on to say, "Blessed are those who have not seen me as you have done, but yet believe!"

11th September God's Glory

2 Corinthians 3 : 18

"We, who with unveiled faces, all reflect the Lord's glory, are being transformed into his likeness with ever-lasting glory, which comes from the Lord, who is the Spirit."

☞ The Apostle Paul has been writing about Moses who veiled his face after he had communed with God because the people could not stand the reflected glory of God shining from him. He goes on to say that those who have not received the grace of God in Christ have a kind of veil over their minds and are unable to see the grace of God in the face of Jesus. But those who have found that Christ is the Saviour of the world, have had such a veil of unknowing taken away. Now they see his glory.

This new relationship of openness between them and God, is having the ongoing effect of making them like the Lord Jesus, for they love what He loves, do what He does, and think as He thinks. The steady, daily transformation in their lives happens as the Spirit teaches them ever more the truth of Christ.

✝ *Lord Jesus Christ, often I am ashamed that I fail to reflect Your glory, for I do not think, act and speak as You would. Forgive my shortcomings and help me to apply the truth of the Saviour to my living that I may reflect just a little of His glory. Amen.*

♥ Duncan Matheson who became a great evangelist, as a young man went to hear Robert Murray McCheyne preach at an open–air communion service in the grounds of Elgin Abbey in Northern Scotland. He couldn't remember much of the sermon, but what impressed him was that McCheyne preached with 'a seraphic fire on his face and eternity stamped on his brow'.

David Searle

12th September Joy

1 Corinthians 12 : 26

"If one part of the body suffers, every part suffers with it; if one part is honoured, every part rejoices with it."

☞ 'There's not much to sing about in my life, not much colour.' Perhaps this describes someone you know.

I have always admired those gardeners who have the ability to provide colour at all times of the year. For every season they have a different set of plants that add beauty and joy to their garden. Even in the dead of winter they can produce trees with stunning bark or leaves to brighten the drabness. A walk in such a place is a reason for constant appreciation. So too in life God is always working, and somewhere in the Kingdom of God there is reason for praise and gladness. While in your part of the 'garden' it may be quiet and colourless, in other parts there may be a bursting of some new blessing, a brilliance of activity of new life, of answered prayers and a cause for rejoicing.

Too often we have such a narrow field of vision, perhaps extending to just our own church fellowship or maybe even a few people within it.

If however, we could lift our eyes and see what God is doing in another fellowship, in another part of the world, we too could share their joy.

Perhaps the challenge today is to make contact with a missionary society, to receive their news-sheet or to subscribe to a Christian publication that opens us to the wider world of the church. By the way, we mustn't forget to share our blessings too, that others will have reason also for joy because of us.

✝ *Dear God, help me to learn how to rejoice with those who rejoice, and not to retreat into dullness. Amen.*

♥ No doubt there is truth in the saying that a burden shared is halved, while a joy shared is doubled.

13th September — Joy

📖 Deuteronomy 6 : 4 - 5

"Hear O Israel; The Lord our God the Lord is One. Love the Lord our God with all your heart and with all your soul and with all your strength."

☞ May I quote from an unknown source: 'I would like to buy $3 worth of God please. I would like just a little. Not enough to explode my soul or to disturb my sleep. Not enough to take control of my life. I'd like just enough to equal a cup of warm milk, just to ease some of the pain of guilt.'

Does this describe your life? One of the reasons why some people do not have joy in their Christian experience is because they do not want to be fully committed. There is a 'but' in their life. As Jesus said of the church in Revelation 3 : 14 – 22, they were neither hot nor cold and as a result they were repulsive to Him. Joy is the experience of those who do not hold back in giving their all to Jesus.

Perhaps it is the fear of losing control, or being asked to go somewhere or do something, or the thought of giving up the comfort zone we enjoy. Yet can there be any wisdom in holding back and losing the prize of the joy of the Lord?

Ponder the following:

But we never can prove
The delights of His love,
Until all on the altar we lay;
For the favour He shows,
And the joy He bestows
Are for them who will trust and obey.
John Henry Sammis

✝ *Heavenly Father, as I seek to put you first today with every part of my being, may I experience again the joy of full surrender. Amen.*

♥ A short time ago someone sent a letter to a national newspaper, 'I have attended church now for 30 years. That means I have listened to approximately 1560 sermons. I can remember very few of them. What does that say about sermons as a form of communication?'

Various people sent in replies, until this letter ended the correspondence.

'I have been married for 30 years. During that time I calculate my wife has made, and served up approximately 10950 breakfasts, dinners and teas. I can remember very few of them, but what I know is that I have been well nourished every week.'

14th September Joy

📖 Psalm 51 : 11 – 12

"Do not cast me from your presence or take your Holy Spirit from me. Restore to me the joy of your Salvation and grant me a willing spirit, to sustain me."

☞ In the lost property department of our church you are sure to find an array of things. Umbrellas are possibly top of the list, followed by Bibles and hymnbooks, coats and some toys. But would you believe that one of the very common things is 'joy.' Yes many people have lost joy; not I hasten to add in the church, but in their lives. There are different reasons for this today. I would like to consider just one.

In Psalm 51, the psalmist, David prays, "restore unto me the joy of my salvation." Obviously he has not lost his salvation but he has lost the joy and enjoyment of it. We need to look at the background of this Psalm to discover the reason. This psalm flows out of the tragic events in David's life when he yielded to the temptation to commit adultery and the subsequent murder of a man.(2 Samuel 11). Sin has made him miserable and has brought a barrier into his relationship with God. Psalm 51 is the way to mend this and is David's honest prayer of repentance. Perhaps you think you have not sinned as much as David did, after all you may not have murdered or been unfaithful in marriage. However, it is not the greatness of the sin but the fact of sin that has this effect.

Perhaps you need to name your sin and repent of it as David did, then joy will return. You could use the words of this Psalm as your own prayer.

✝ *Have mercy on me O God, according to Your unfailing love; blot out my transgressions. Wash away all my iniquity And cleanse me from my sin. Amen.*

♥ 'May your neighbours respect you. Trouble neglect you. The angels protect you and heaven accept you.' Irish Blessing.

15th September — Joy

📖 Hebrews 12 : 2

"Let us fix our eyes on Jesus, the author and perfector of our faith, who for the joy set before him endured the cross, scorning its shame, and sat down at the right hand of the throne of God."

☞ Each year during the dark winter days there is a strange attraction of the travel agent. Those glossy brochures with pictures of sun, sand and blue skies are very appealing. It only takes a two inch square photograph to encourage us to part with our money and invest in the long-range joy. Although the holiday may not be for many months it has given us something to hope for in the cold and dark days of winter.

As believers we have a much better two by two picture, in fact we have many pictures of the hope we have ahead of us. Although words often fail, scripture gives many reasons to look to the future. Here in Hebrews it tells of the Saviour looking forward and seeing 'the joy set before Him'. He was prepared to pass through many difficulties including the cross because of the long-range hope and joy.

Consider the following passages prayerfully; 'In this you greatly rejoice (hope) though now for a while you may have had to suffer grief in all kinds of trials.' (1 Peter 1 : 6) 'We rejoice in the hope of the glory of God.' (Romans 5 : 2) 'So fix your eyes not on what is seen, but on what is unseen.' (2 Corinthians 4 : 18).

Whatever your experience today, remember the best is yet to come!

✝ *Gracious Lord, enable me to fix my eyes not on the pain, but on the glory; not on the dark days, but the bright skies. Amen.*

♥ Honolulu – it's got everything, sand for the children, sun for the wife, sharks for the wife's mother. (Ken Dodd)

16th September — Joy

📖 Romans 14 : 17 – 18

"The Kingdom of God is not a matter of eating and drinking, but of righteousness, peace and joy in the Holy Spirit, because anyone who serves Christ in this way is pleasing to God and approved by men."

☞ I wonder if I asked you to name the most important commands for the Christian, what would you come up with? Take a moment and try it. I suppose you had things like to be humble, to follow the 10 commandments, to witness for Christ, to live peacefully with others. What place did Joy have in your list of expectations? I suspect for most of us it was either very low on our list or not at all.

Here in Romans 14 : 17 – 18 we see how the kingdom of God is a matter of righteousness, peace and joy. These we are told please God. To seek after right-living according to God's standard we affirm; to be at peace with, and know the peace of God we agree; but joy? Yet here we have the expectation that joy should be as important. To neglect this it would seem is displeasing to God.

To pursue joy and to be joyful is an act of the will. No command would be given in scripture if it were not possible and also beneficial. So even in the difficult situations of life as we are to pursue righteousness and peace, so too we are encouraged to serve Christ with joy in the Holy Spirit.

Such a thought as this has the ability to change many a person's thinking and living!

'Let us rejoice and be glad.' Revelation 19 : 7

✝ *The fruit of the Spirit is love, joy, peace; patience, kindness, goodness; faithfulness, gentleness and self-control.' Grow Your fruit in me. Amen.*

♥ Joy = **J**esus first
Others second
Yourself last.

John Kirkpatrick

17th September — Neighbourliness

📖 Exodus 20 : 16 - 17

"You shall not give false testimony against your neighbour." You shall

not covet your neighbour's house. You shall not covet your neighbour's wife, or his manservant or maidservant, his ox or donkey, or anything that belongs to your neighbour."

☞ The Ten Commandments conclude with two, which specifically mention our duty to our neighbour. In reality the last six have to do with our treatment of other people, but these two tie in with two of the earlier God-oriented commandments. The first commandment prohibits any god-worship other that of the true God. The tenth shows what happens when we substitute other people for God and see them as the purveyors of all things: we try to get those things by any means possible. Covetousness is a form of idolatry.

The third commandment forbids abusing the name of God, while the ninth forbids abusing the name or reputation, or character of our neighbour. Here we see the profound inter-relation between living rightly in relation to God, and living in right relationships with other people. Disobeying these commandments violates two precious gifts. Bearing false-witness misuses the gift of words and communication; coveting abuses the gift of trust in relationships, as people become protective and cautious rather than open and vulnerable.

In Ireland we can see the effects of such disobedience on a large scale. Covetousness has resulted in an idolatry of land and territory, of power and influence. Bearing false witness about the other community has been in pulpits and in theological seminaries and textbooks. The detachment from mammon and commitment to truth-telling which God requires in these final commandments will require all of us who claim the name of Christ not to envy but appreciate and respect our neighbour's space, and not to bear false witness but communicate honestly with our neighbour.

✝ *Lord, forgive us for the times we have found it easier to believe the worst about others, and when we have been guilty of spreading half-truths rather than risking open communication and dialogue. Save us from lying tongues and covetous hearts, in Jesus' name we pray. Amen.*

♥ Blurting out the complete truth is considered adorable in the young, right smack up to the moment that your child says "Mummy, is this the fat lady you can't stand?"

18th September Neighbourliness

📖 Leviticus 19 : 18

"Do not seek revenge or bear a grudge against one of your people, but love your neighbour as yourself. I am the Lord."

☞ Right in the middle of the books of the Law, in a chapter dealing with regulations on such diverse subjects as vineyard harvesting, fair pay, treatment of the disabled, dress codes and tattoos, we find a statement which Jesus says sums up the law: 'Love your neighbour as yourself.'

The regulations that from this command may seem a little time-bound and irrelevant today. (although the worlds of modern business and ecology could be significantly enhanced if some of the principles were taken seriously.) Nevertheless, what these chapters in Leviticus show is the all-embracing nature of holiness. Christ's commentary on this verse (Mark 12 : 31) makes it clear that the rationale behind even the most obscure laws was a desire to honour the Creator and respect the neighbour.

For God's Covenant people, every area of life was God's. There was no dichotomy between sacred and secular. How they treated their neighbour betrayed whose they were. For us the context is different.

Holiness comes not from the Law, but from the Spirit. But the extent of that holiness is still all embracing.

In Ireland we have struggled to live in holiness. Sometimes we see the law without seeing the reason behind it. As a result we slip into unloving burdensome requirements on 'their' shoulders as prerequisites for our acceptance. Sometimes we even use 'holiness' as an excuse to withhold love. Scripture is clear we cannot claim to be holy unless we love our neighbours as we love ourselves; unless the concern we have for their well-being matches the concern we claim to have to our own 'holiness.'

✝ *Lord, help me not to bear grudges or seek revenge. Enable me to see that the depth of my love for You will be shown in the depth of my love for others. In Jesus' name. Amen.*

♥ Revenge is counter-productive: A couple were regularly kept awake at night by their neighbour's dog barking. One night the annoyed young man got up and went outside for a few minutes. On arriving back his wife asked him where he had been. "I've put the dog into our garden," he replied, "Let's see how they like it!"

19th September — Neighbourliness

📖 Matthew 5 : 44 - 46

"But I tell you: Love your enemies and pray for those who persecute you, that you may be sons of your Father in heaven. He causes his sun to rise on the evil and the good, and sends rain on the righteous and the unrighteous. If you love those who love you, what reward will you get? Are not even the tax collectors doing that?"

☞ Often retaliation, bitter attitudes, and lack of forgiveness are excused on the grounds that 'it's understandable...you can't expect love and forgiveness.' Well, Jesus **does** expect it, and although, yes, humanly speaking it is understandable, such understandable behaviour gets us nowhere in bringing in the kingdom of God.

Here Jesus undermines the natural tendency to fight back, to defend our reputations, and to harbour resentment towards those who have wronged us. Is this not a blueprint for getting walked on? No, it is actually incredibly liberating. Jesus is effectively saying that in our personal relationships, there is actually nothing to distinguish us from those we call our enemies. We're all just ordinary 'sinners', as bad as each other, imprisoned by our natural tendencies.

The 'spiritual tendencies' come only through new birth. Religious cliches are cheap and empty. Many talk of being born again. But if we are born again, we have our father's nature, and the love He had for His enemies is well demonstrated from the stable to the cross. Here Jesus places the reality of the new birth, our becoming 'children of God', firmly in the context of our attitude towards our enemies.

✝ *Father, I am Your obedient child. May Your nature permeate my life so that, like Christ, I can love my enemies and pray for those who persecute me. Forgive me for failing so often in this regard, release me from my natural tendencies and empower me by Your Spirit to live the life of love. Amen.*

♥ It takes your enemy and your friend working together to hurt you to the heart; the one to slander you and the other to get the news to you. (M. Twain.)

20th September Neighbourliness

📖 1 Corinthians 13 : 1

"If I speak in the tongues of men and of angels, but have not love, I am only a resounding gong or a clanging cymbal."

☞ In the middle of several chapters regarding spiritual gifts, Paul puts everything in perspective. The Corinthian problem, still current today, was their tendency to return to a self-oriented way of living.

Even the things which God was giving specifically for the benefits of others (spiritual gifts), and in particular the most outwardly spectacular of those (tongues, miracles etc.) were being used by the Corinthians in a selfish and proud way, as an excuse for self-indulgence and spiritual 'one-upmanship'. They were regarding their newfound faith and the accompanying charismata as toys to be played with. They had started to live for themselves again.

This of course was a blasphemous misuse of the holy and divine. As Christians we live first for God, then for our neighbours, and lastly for ourselves. John Stott has said that when we reverse this and live for ourselves first and God last, then it is the ones in the middle – other people who suffer.

Tongues without love, is only one example of how our religious activity can actually harm people rather than help them, hinder the kingdom rather than extend it. In Ireland we often excuse a variety of dubious religious and pseudo-religious activities on the grounds that at least 'the word' is being preached. But is it? In what ways have the unloving actions and attitudes, or the exclusivist structures and paraphernalia that have accompanied 'the word', actually negated it, and made it as incomprehensible to our neighbour as self-indulgent glossolalia?

✝ *Lord, I ask not for spectacular gifts nor spiritual ecstasies, for You know my heart better than I, and You will give them to me if I need them, and when I will not be tempted to abuse them. Rather, I ask for a loving spirit, so that not only the words I speak but also the way I speak them will bless the heart of my neighbour. In Jesus' name. Amen.*

♥ On 'empty vessels': Disraeli once referred to a political opponent as 'a self –made' man who worshipped his maker!

21st September Neighbourliness

📖 Galatians 5 : 14

"(For) The entire law is summed up (fulfilled) in a single command: "Love your neighbour as yourself."

☞ The NIV has left out the little Greek word *gar*, 'for', which begins this verse and links it with the previous command in verse 13. There Paul says 'serve one another in love', something which is only possible if, in Jesus, we have entered a whole new way of living. As Paul says in verse 16 we are now to 'live by the Spirit'. Paul is not introducing a new legalism here. He never asks the Christian to live a certain way because of a particular law. He knows himself such a lifestyle brings death. Rather he motivates us to Christian holiness by showing us a better way.

We are to serve one another not out of adherence to a law, but out of a spirit of love. Love, he says, is the underlying motivation for the whole law. A law kept lovelessly is actually a law transgressed. Love is a fruit of the Spirit (v.22)- therefore we do not love by obeying a law, but through 'living by the Spirit' (v.16). The law is not 'fulfilled' (NIV has 'summed up') by new laws, or better laws, but by an entirely new paradigm. The external rulebook is replaced by an internal power. In the Spirit we are free (v23) to love. And if the Spirit is guiding us, we need not worry about sinning or breaking the law. If we are truly keeping in step with the Spirit (v.25) reverting to legalism, or abusing our freedom by sinning will not be options.

Paul's message is stark. In all your religious activity, don't miss the obvious. Everything in the law is fulfilled in this one command: "Love your neighbour as yourself'. In Ireland where the threats of life-quenching legalism, and love-quenching amorality, are present in equal measure in our churches, we would do well not to miss the obvious.

✝ *Lord, save us from the oppression of legalism, and the sensual selfishness of libertarianism. Help us to walk with You, keeping in step with Your Spirit, so that, after loving You, our greatest desire may be to love and serve our neighbour. In Jesus' name. Amen.*

♥ Don't miss the obvious. Holmes and Watson were camping. "Watson, looking up, what can you deduce?" said Holmes. Watson proceeded to tell the time by the stars, the weather forecast by the wind direction, and the season of year by the constellations. "Don't be so stupid," said Holmes, "someone has stolen our tent."

David Montgomery

22nd September — Tiredness

📖 Ecclesiastes 12 : 12

"Be warned, my son. Of making many books there is no end, and much

study wearies the body."

☞ This is the verse we used to quote as students to try to keep our studies under control! And it was written in the days of clay tablets and papyrus. If there were a lot books then what about now with the Internet! So if you're a student reading this at the start of term then remember to keep your studies in perspective and put God and His wisdom first. If you study non-stop you'll be exhausted and ineffective.

But it's not just for students. The book of Ecclesiastes teaches us that life without God is meaningless. And there's nothing more wearying than living a meaningless life. It leaves us tired in a way that a good night's sleep won't remedy. If you are immersed in the things of this life, whether academic achievement, career, family or home, without submitting it all to God, then you'll end up very weary. To understand life, we need to remember our Creator and find out about Him and His ways through His number one Book, the Bible.

✝ *Father God, please help me to put You first in my life. Please refresh me as I acknowledge You as my Lord, the Creator of the universe. Amen.*

♥ When I first went to university I was in awe of the learned professors. But as I went on with my studies I began to realise that they only knew a great deal about very limited areas. They might know a lot about the transmitters in a human brain but wouldn't have a clue about why a baby cries. The only one who understands our world and us inside-out is our God. He's the One to be in awe of.

23rd September — Tiredness

📖 Isaiah 40 :28

"Do you not know? Have you not heard? The Lord is the everlasting God, the Creator of the ends of the earth. He will not grow tired or weary, and His understanding no one can fathom."

☞ God's people were complaining that God didn't seem to care about them. Isaiah reminds them of two really important things.

1. God is all-powerful. He created everything. So there's no point turning to man-made idols rather than our Creator God. Think what you are tempted to trust in, perhaps your own abilities, physical fitness, the value of your home. Compare that to trusting in God who never gets tired and understands everything.

2. God cares for each of us. That is the most amazing thing. The God who created the universe cares about each of us. We only disqualify ourselves from receiving His help if we think we can manage alone and consider ourselves strong and powerful. So if we're tired and not coping, that's a great start! We can then turn to our Lord God and He will give us strength.

✝ *Creator God, I am tired and I cannot cope alone. Please renew my strength as I put my hope in You. Amen.*

♥ Isaiah 40 : 31 But those who hope in the Lord will renew their strength. They will soar on wings like eagles; they will run and not grow weary, they will walk and not be faint.

24th September — Tiredness

Matthew 11: 28

"Come to me, all who are weary and burdened, and I will give you rest."

☞ What wonderful words the Lord Jesus spoke to a crowd of people in Galilee. They come after serious warnings to those who refused to respond to Jesus.

To whom does Jesus offer His rest? All who are weary and burdened. These people would have been burdened with lots of religious rules by which they tried to make themselves good enough for God. They were probably weary of the struggle of day to day living. It's so easy for us, even if we're Christians, to burden ourselves with guilt, and forget that we really are forgiven.

What is the 'rest' Jesus promises? It is clearly not a life of ease and relaxation, because he says we should take on his 'yoke'. This word was used to speak of taking a course taught by a particular teacher. You 'put on their yoke'. But with Jesus as our teacher, it's not a heavy burden of rules that we'll never be able to keep, but a wonderful relationship with Him. It's fascinating that God offers rest in the Old Testament and Jesus tells us that it is He who can give us this rest in the New Testament.

✝ *Thank You Lord Jesus for the rest of knowing You and please help us as we serve You as Your disciples. Amen.*

♥ I have to confess the idea of a life of endless leisure is appealing at times and I felt a twinge of disappointment when I realised that a sunbed by the swimming pool, finishing off my partially read Maeve Binchy, wasn't what Jesus meant by 'rest'.

But endless leisure is actually very weary and a life of purpose serving our Servant King, Jesus, is the start of our rest, with eternity to look forward to.

25th September — Tiredness

📖 2 Corinthians 4 : 16

"Therefore we do not lose heart. Though outwardly we are wasting away, yet inwardly we are being renewed day by day."

☞ Does ill health, aches and pains and tiredness surprise you? If we are Christians, we shouldn't be surprised, because we're part of a fallen world. The world seems to play a great game of pretend in relation to health, especially to getting old. As Christians we can be completely honest. Yes, we face the aging process like everyone else, but inwardly we can already experience the resurrection power of Jesus each day. So don't despair. However weak and tired you feel, Jesus in His resurrection power can renew you inwardly.

How can we be renewed daily? The writer goes on to tell us to fix our eyes on the unseen but permanent things. If we fix our eyes on 'body beautiful', or physical fitness, or anything else in this world, we'll be disappointed. The outward signs of aging remind us that we are getting closer to eternal glory. If we're Christians we're heading for an eternity with the risen Lord Jesus. So as we fix our eyes on our risen Lord Jesus he will renew us for the struggles of each day.

✝ *Loving Father, please help me not to despair when I feel worn out, but to fix my eyes on the Risen Lord Jesus and be given resurrection energy. Amen.*

♥ Grow old along with me. The best is yet to be. (Browning)

26th September — Tiredness

Galatians 6 : 9

"Let us not become weary in doing good, for at the proper time we will reap a harvest if we do not give up."

☞ It is easy to become weary of doing good both in the church and in the wider community. However, our churches would be transformed if all of us put this verse into practice. Not 'This church is really letting me down and not caring for me' but 'God has put me in this church family to serve Him – what can I do?'

Yet it's hard to keep at it year after year! It's tempting to think of retirement at some point, but retirement doesn't seem to get a mention in the Bible! Our area of service may change but our attitude should be the same.

The verse says to do good, but to whom? The answer is in the next verse. Our first responsibility is to our church family – other Christians. But we should also seek to do good in the wider community.

Don't give up, says Paul the writer. There will be a harvest; but harvests are not immediate things, so keep at it.

✝ *Dear Lord Jesus please help me to follow Your example and give myself for others. Amen.*

♥ Remember good works cannot earn us a place in heaven – they're not a 'please am I good enough?' but they're a 'thank you' to our Lord who died so that we know we're going to heaven.

Joanna Samuel

27th September Sex

📖 Genesis 2 : 24 – 25

"That is why a man leaves his father and mother and is united with his wife, and they become one. The man and the woman were both naked, but they were not embarrassed."

☞ For a man and a woman to experience a nurturing and fulfilling companionship with one another, means cutting ties of dependence from their parents so that they can enjoy mutual acceptance and enjoyment with one another. They are free to take their own decisions without asking permission or checking it out elsewhere even in their heads. God has given us bodies and sexuality. Both a gift of God and a powerful driving force in all of us. Each couple brings their whole selves to a marriage; whatever it is to be a man and whatever it is to be a woman, and that includes sexuality. This is offered freely to the other.

Since most people have some hang–ups about the beauty or otherwise of their bodies or their sexual competence, mutual acceptance, patience and encouragement are required so that sensuality can be explored and enjoyed.

✝ *O God, in whose image we are made, may we enjoy You and know more of the pleasure of love and commitment in marriage. We are mindful of those whose relationship is far from one of equality and of those for whom close companionship is either a memory or, as yet, an unfulfilled longing. Amen.*

♥ The two become one. Which one? Neither. It's a new one.

28th September Sex

1 Corinthians 7 : 3 – 5

"The husband should fulfill his marital duty to his wife, and likewise the wife to her husband. The wife's body does not belong to her alone but also to her husband. In the same way, the husband's body does not belong to him alone but also to his wife. Do not deprive each other except by mutual consent and for a time, so that you may devote yourselves to prayer. Then come together again so that Satan will not tempt you because of your lack of self-control."

☞ Here is explicit recognition of the powerful drive of sexuality and the way it is to be enjoyed within a marriage relationship. God has given us bodies and sexuality is the gift of a good and loving creator and not an invention of the devil. It may be the case that there is too much exploitation of sex, but the denial of sexuality or smothering it under spirituality is not the Christian way. In a marriage the man and the woman should bring to each other what is likely to be their only intimate experience of physical sexuality with another person. Neither the man nor the woman ought to leave the other short–changed. If sexuality is a gift form God, it is a gift we give to each other. Any abstinence for prayer is by mutual agreement and is temporary and is not to be a religious excuse to avoid sex.

✝ *Lord, help me learn the body language and the sexual needs of my spouse. Amen.*

♥ Real happiness can only be obtained by unselfishness.

29th September — Sex

Genesis 39 : 6 - 9

"Joseph was well-built and good–looking, and after a while his master's wife began to desire Joseph and asked him to go to bed with her. He refused and said to her, "Look, my master does not have to concern himself with anything in the house, because I am here. He has put me in charge of everything. I have as much authority in this house as he has, and he has not kept anything back from me except you. How then could I do such an immoral thing and sin against God?"

☞ Women can be predators as well as men! Men can be physically attractive to women and sexually desirable. Joseph's refusal of Potiphar's wife's advances are based on two things. Firstly, on the obvious trust which Potiphar has placed in him and the privileges which went with it, all of which would be subverted and betrayed if he gave in to these advances. Secondly, Joseph understood that to do such a thing would be a sin against God, who was with him.

Joseph knew where the boundaries were and he was determined to live within them. We know from the story that this involved some considerable risk. Here was a powerful woman filled with sexual desire.

Then, as now, marriage relationships are not always respected, either by those within them or those outside them. Temptation can come from unexpected quarters. When temptation comes we need to be aware of others and our own marriage vows.

✝ *Lord, help people who may be sexually frustrated. Help me to recognise a predator when I see one. May I never exploit people. Give strength to those who are vulnerable. Amen.*

♥ Compliments can be the wrapping paper for trouble.

30th September Sex

Song of Songs 2 : 1

"Kiss me – full on the mouth! Yes! For your love is better than wine."

Here is passion. Here, cautious reserve has gone. Here is the excitement of touch. Not a handshake! Not a peck on the cheek! But lips on lips in passion, full on the mouth! Wow! Do religious people get up to this kind of thing? If they do, do they ever say so? Not so as you could notice. But here it is in the Bible. God doesn't seem to be ashamed of it. Buttoned up people cannot do justice to a passionate God.

Here also is responsive passion, not something taken for granted, but something enjoyed and acknowledged as such. 'Your love is better than wine'. Are we freed up for passion? Are we freed up to be positive about the one who is loved, to use words of appreciation so that the other knows how we feel and knows that what goes on is more than physical excitement?

Lord I thank You for lips to kiss and love that is better than wine. Be kind, O God, to those who long for love. Amen.

♥ A dry stick may once have been a young sapling.

OCTOBER

In the 1970's the artist designed his first stained glass work as a memorial installed in Ballycastle Presbyterian Church: this linoprint 13" x 6.7" is based upon it, and its text is Mt 28 vv 19-20. It is full of Christian Symbolism.

1st October Sex

1 Corinthians 6 : 9 - 11

"Unjust people who don't care about God will not be joining his kingdom. Those who use and abuse each other, use and abuse sex, use and abuse the earth and everything in it, don't qualify as citizens in God's kingdom. A number of you know from experience what I'm talking about, for not so long ago you were on that list. Since then, you've been cleaned up and given a fresh start by Jesus, our master, our Messiah, and by our God present in us, the Spirit." (Peterson: The Message)

☞ Here is the negative side of what is so positive about the kingdom of God. There are many ways of living which are inconsistent with the kingdom; the use and abuse of people made in God's image; of God's good gift of sex; of God's good earth.

Injustice is a serious matter, a form of social vandalism. To live unjustly with one another is a sign that we do not care about God.

If life is a journey, it is important to know the Highway Code of God's kingdom. Stay on the straight and narrow. Avoid the verges and soft shoulders. Since we have been restored to a right relationship with God and cleaned up and since God lives in us, we ought to know better than to live in the old ways. People, sex and the earth are to be treated with respect. Live out what we are. Live up to new standards.

✝ *Lord, let me not be a vandal in Your good creation. May Your people be signs of Your kingdom. Comfort those who are being shown little respect in their relationships. Amen.*

♥ Sexual exploiters and fat cats can be a menace in God's good earth.

Rosemary & John Dunlop

2nd October Praise

📖 Psalm 34:1

"I will extol the Lord at all times; His praise will always be on my lips."

☞ These are difficult words to face up to with honesty and to live out with integrity. When all is well, we are tempted to enjoy the moment and forget about God, and when life is hard, coldness and resentment toward God can easily set in.

So what are we to do? Go with the flow of our mood or swim against that particular tide? Wisdom and truth call us to choose the latter and to remember three things.

First of all, remember that our faith is not based upon a set of rules, but upon an intimate relationship with God himself. God loves us deeply and we must allow this relationship to develop, so that whatever circumstances we move through we automatically know Him as we would a trusted friend.

Secondly, be open to the grace; the gifts which God gives us, so that we may know His love more and more and be challenged and strengthened as we walk life with Him.

Finally, remember peace is deeper than feelings and circumstances. Do not let busyness, sorrow or happiness blind us to this.

✝ *Father, afresh I open my life to Your love and peace. Give me the humility, wisdom and courage to receive these gifts. Amen.*

♥ Be sure and praise your wife, even if it shocks her!

3rd October Praise

Psalm 100 : 3

"Know that the Lord is God. It is He who made us, and we are His."

☞ On a clear night, leave the lights of town and city and look up. Star upon star and galaxy upon galaxy stretch out to unfathomable depths. Look in a mirror and see that familiar face. Look at the eyes and think of the private world that spins behind them. Take out a photograph of family or friends and give thanks for the intricate threads that bind you together.

The Lord is God and He has made a world of great majesty, mystery and love; a world which, albeit palely, reflects His glory. And this great God calls us to know Him and be loved by Him; a ragged people raised to honour; a captive people freed to praise; a scattered people brought together.

✝ *Father open my eyes to see Your majesty, open my eyes to hear Your voice and open my heart to give You praise. Amen.*

♥ May the saddest day of your future be no worse than the happiest day of your past.

4th October Praise

Isaiah 61 : 1 & 3

"The Spirit of the Sovereign Lord is on me because the Lord has anointed me to preach good news to the poor…to bestow on them a crown of

beauty instead of ashes, the oil of gladness instead of mourning, and a garment of praise instead of a spirit of despair. "

☞ There is no use pretending that life is all sunshine, at times it can be awful. There is no virtue in running away from the reality of suffering, either others or ours.

Isaiah, writing many hundreds of years before Jesus was born, knew that there was poverty, pain, hurt, slavery and darkness in the world. Yet he also knew that God would not leave us chained to these things.

Jesus, early on in his preaching read from these words in Isaiah. He was in the synagogue in Nazareth at the time and when he had spoken the words of the prophet, every eye was fixed upon Him. Very deliberately, He then proclaimed these words of liberty. "Today the scripture is fulfilled in your hearing". The one who would bring forgiveness and freedom had come, and mourning and despair could be replaced by gladness and praise.

✝ *Father, help me to bring my guilt and pain to You, so that I may know the freedom and strength which You give through your Son. Amen.*

♥ Grace makes you gracious. The Giver makes you give. (E. Stanley Jones).

5th October — Praise

📖 Acts 2 : 46 – 47

"Every day they continued to meet together in the temple courts. They broke bread in their homes and ate together with glad and sincere hearts,

praising God and enjoying the favour of all the people, and the Lord added to their number daily those who were being saved."

☞ Sometimes, when life crowds in on us, we long to be alone, up a mountain, on a quiet beach, or if things are really bad, a desert island. And yet deep down, we know we wouldn't want to live isolated lives. The fact that solitary confinement is often used as a punishment, reminds us that it isn't only fictional Robinson Crusoes that seek the companionship of others.

This shouldn't surprise us. As people we are made in God's image and God is Trinity: one God yet an eternal relationship between the Father, the Son and the Holy Spirit. We, made in the image of God, are created for relationships, a relationship with God and with others. It is from relationships that our witness to Christ is strengthened, the sharing of lives and praise and the wonder of being united around bread and wine.

✝ *Father, thank You for my brothers and sisters in Christ. Help me never to disown them but in love receive them as part of Your family. Amen.*

♥ Do all the good you can,
By all the means you can,
In all the ways you can,
In all the places you can.
At all the times you can,
To all the people you can,
as long as you ever can.'
(John Wesley)

6th October Praise

Ephesians 5 : 19

"Speak to one another with Psalms, Hymns and Spiritual songs, sing and make music in your heart to the Lord."

☞ Too often, Christians are seen as those who cannot enjoy life and who do their best to ensure that others join them in their dullness. To be fair, this is sometimes our own fault. We forget what joy and life really mean and end up only being able to point out the bad in our society and unable to show people the good.

Paul calls us to be filled with the Spirit of God and to vibrantly celebrate our faith together. From this vantage-point, life and wholeness can flow into all our relationships. When this joy and vitality is seen in our life together, when there is a need to criticise, people will know that we do this, not to impoverish them, but because we are pointing them to someone and something better.

✝ *Father, may Your Holy Spirit make us sensitive people who live life to the full and may this be seen and lived out in our lives together. Amen.*

♥ Little Johnny's new baby brother was screaming up a storm. He asked his mom, "Where'd we get him?" His mother replied, "He came from heaven, Johnny." Johnny says, "WOW! I can see why they threw him out!"

David McCarthy

7th October Honesty

📖 Proverbs 11:1

"The Lord abhors dishonest scales, but accurate weights are his delight."

☞ "No one ever got rich being honest," said Mr. Wormwood, the car dealer. "Customers are there to be diddled".

Poor Matilda in Roald Dahl's story was horrified at her father's secret of mixing sawdust with the oil in second-hand car gearboxes, so that they wouldn't rattle; but that's how he had become rich. Mr. Wormwood was hardly an attractive character for all his ill-gotten wealth; and for all their outward appearance of success, business people who cheat customers today are no better.

As a child, we used to watch carefully the points of the scales when the confectioner weighed out a quarter of sweets on the weighing machine. Some assistants were mean, others generous, and an extra sweet could make all the difference to ones day. According to the book of Proverbs, it is not only children who get upset by meanness and dishonesty, but God too, whereas integrity is his great delight.

Even if no one else notices...God sees and He takes note!

✝ *Heavenly Father. It's so tempting to cheat, especially when we think nobody notices. Help me to be transparently honest all the time. Amen.*

♥ A person involved in a shady business never has a sunny life.

8th October — Honesty

Exodus 20:16

"You shall not give false testimony against your neighbour."

It's amazing how ordinary, decent, upright people who would never dream of cheating someone else of a penny, have no difficulty writing off someone else's character. The 9th commandment is a demand for honesty, not only in actions but in speech as well.

Just because someone comes from a different family background, race, political party or denomination does not mean to say we are at liberty to speak disparagingly about them or dismiss their integrity. It only takes one remark to destroy a reputation. We must be especially careful that what we say or claim or pass on to others about them is true, otherwise we are guilty of dishonesty…theft of their good name. When we give false testimony we not only degrade others, but we demean ourselves and devalue the faith in God that we profess.

✝ *Dear Lord, let no unloving thought find birth here to-day*
Nor let any influence pass out into the world from here
Save that which will promote
Peace, happiness, Hope and Love.
Make us one at heart that through our unity of purpose
And desire
We may become a single spiritual force, against all evil.
Strengthen in each of us the Power of Love.
Teach us to forbear and to forgive.
Grant us serenity and
Let our hearts be filled with warm good will towards all mankind.
So that we may stand before the world as a pattern of humility
And of service to our fellow men and God.
Through Jesus Christ our Lord. Amen

(Written and distributed in Enniskillen in 1987 after the bombing at the Cenotaph)

♥ Muddled prayer "Let my friends be all forgiven. Bless the sins I love so well"

9th October — Honesty

📖 2 Corinthians 4:2

"We have renounced secret and shameful ways; we do not use deception, nor do we distort the word of God. On the contrary, by setting forth the truth plainly we commend ourselves to everyone's conscience in the sight of God."

☞ What a terrible thing when people aim to achieve the right thing but in an underhand way. The gospel of Jesus Christ is not only the truth, but it is only commended when it is presented truthfully.

It is liberating for any Christian to realise that as they seek to win others to a living faith in Jesus Christ, they do not have to hide their doubts or difficulties from anyone else or pretend that everything is easy or trouble free when it's not. The word of God does not need us to 'massage the truth'. It is well able to stand on its own merits, and as we seek to live obediently under its authority, even in the midst of our own personal struggles, others will come to realise that here is someone who can be trusted, not avoided, has integrity, not pretence and is real, not plastic veneer.

✝ *Dear Lord, enable me today to live honestly, truthfully and openly, so that the Word of God is commended and not distorted, for Jesus Sake. Amen.*

♥ A lady at the end of a mission service once commended the Rev.

Mr. Burke, a famous Irish preacher, "Thank you! We knew nothing about sin until you came amongst us".

10th October — Honesty

📖 Ephesians 4:28

"He who has been stealing must steal no longer, but must work, doing something useful with his own hands, that he may have something to share with those in need."

☞ Last week, our neighbours had their car broken into and their radio stolen. The week before a mother had her handbag pick-pocketed as she stood in the supermarket queue waiting to pay for her groceries. Not long before that, I chased a man from our kitchen who had broken into the house while the children were being tucked up in bed. He made off with our money and the TEAR Fund box. All these incidents make us angry, upset and annoyed. Instead of using our hands for evil, the Bible urges us to put them to good use. Instead of stealing we must use them for work. That way, instead of taking from other people, causing anxiety, trouble and pain, we will be able to **give** to them instead. How much more fulfilling to be able to share resources with others rather than stealing from them! Jesus can enable this transformation to take place in me.

✝ H*elp me O God to be a giver rather than a taker. Amen.*

♥ A bishop once asked a school class if someone could tell him who he was? Remembering a previous instruction, a small girl replied, "Yes Sir…a miserable sinner".

11th October Honesty

Luke 19 : 8 - 9

"Look Lord! Here and now I give half of my possessions to the poor, and if I have cheated anybody out of anything, I will pay back four times the amount". Jesus said to him, "Today salvation has come to this house."

☞ Zacchaeus lived on **Quality Street** the best road in Jericho. His house was beautiful, and Zacchaeus had earned the right to live there...by demanding more taxes from his fellow Jews than the Romans required...and keeping the change! He lived in **Darkness** alienated from his friends and ill at ease with himself. Then one day he heard Jesus was passing by. This was something he didn't want to miss, even if he was so small! "Zacchaeus, come down immediately," said Jesus. "I must stay at your house today". Out of the sycamore tree he leapt. **Good news** at long last! Jesus prepared to spend time with him and the **Contrast** between Jesus' purity and Zacchaeus' dishonesty was so great, he just had to make amends. He put right all that was wrong in his life, so that there were great **Celebrations** in Jericho that day....and in Heaven too!

Jesus never passed that way again, but Zacchaeus took the opportunity to get his life sorted out when he had the chance.

✝ *Lord, if I cheated anybody out of anything, give me the courage to pay back what I owe today and maybe even more. Amen*

♥ Zacchaeus' chocolates ended up making it a sweet day!

Frank Sellar

12th October Greed

Psalm 119 : 36 –37

"Turn my heart towards Your statutes and not towards selfish gain. Turn my eyes away from worthless things, preserve my life according to Your word."

The world of the 21st Century is a vastly different place from the world in which the Psalmist wrote hundreds of years before the time of Christ. And yet, while much has changed outwardly, we human beings are much the same inwardly. The problems that afflict our societies are less to do with what's on the outside and more to do with what's on the inside. As the old dictum says, "The heart of the human problem is the problem of the human heart." Our self–centred hearts are constantly being drawn away from God with the promise of personal gain and the like. It was just the same in the Psalmist's day. How can we be delivered from these things? The answer is, when our hearts are turned to God, to His ways and to His Word. When we have Christ, the living Word, these other things will be seen for what the really are – worthless vanities!

Lord, turn my heart away from empty ways and increasingly towards You and Your ways. For Christ's sake. Amen.

Ten years from today, what will you wish you had done now?

13th October Greed

📖 Proverbs 15 : 27

"A greedy man brings trouble to his family, but he who hates bribes will live."

☞ Bribery, corruption, shady deals – it's an almost weekly occurrence for details of these things to be carried in our newspapers and featured on our news bulletins. It was the same when the book of Proverbs was written. But the writer of that book warns against these things and against this way of life. The person who wants to honour God will not seek after unjust gain. The Christian who wants to please the Lord will have nothing to do with bribes. Not only do these things displease our Saviour, they bring trouble on our families. There's a solemn warning in this verse that at the end of the day, a life given over to greed and self-gain will reap a sad harvest. But there is also a wonderful promise of blessing for those who walk the way of Christ. Thomas Watson (a Christian from an earlier generation) once made the observation, "Most men pray more for full purses than for pure hearts". Let's endeavour, by God's grace, to be men and women who see that it's those with pure hearts are richer than those with full purses.

✝ *Lord, help me not to be greedy and to say 'no' to unjust gain. For Christ's glory and honour. Amen.*

♥ Our incomes are like shoes; if too small they pinch; if too large, we stumble. (Colton)

14th October Greed

Luke 12 : 15

"Then he (Jesus) said to them "Watch out! Be on your guard against all kinds of greed: a man's life does not consist in the abundance of his possessions".

☞ We live in an increasingly materialistic age where the acquiring of possessions is of great importance to a great number of people. We are bombarded from without by many reasons as to why we ought to have that latest item on the shop-shelf. We are bombarded from within by strong desires to have and to get more…and more. We covet. When Jesus warned against "all kinds of greed", he was really speaking against covetousness. An illustration of this is the rich person who had abundance of possessions but didn't possess the one thing that really counted, the knowledge of God. So let's take heed, let's be warned and let's be wise.

✝ *God, I confess my covetousness. Teach me and help me to see what's really important in life.*

♥ Money never made a man happy yet, nor will it.

15th October Greed

Ephesians 5:5

"For of this you can be sure: No immoral, impure or greedy person – such a man is an idolater- has any inheritance in the kingdom of Christ and of God."

☞ I once heard of a child who was causing quite a stir because he had pushed his hand into the opening of a very expensive vase and couldn't pull it out again. Parents and others came to help, but to no avail. They couldn't get his hand out. Finally, there was nothing left to do but to break the beautiful, expensive vase. In the midst of the broken pieces of vase, it became clear to everyone why the child had been so stuck. He had spotted a penny in the vase, had reached in for it but then found he couldn't get his clenched fist out of the vase. He refused to let go of the penny and ended up giving himself and others a lot of grief.

The verse before us today teaches in a very straightforward and solemn manner the consequences of not letting go of certain things. A life given over to immorality, impurity and even greed will bring far more serious (and eternal) consequences than a broken vase!

✝ *Lord, deliver me from these things, and help me to let go and prepare me for Your heavenly Kingdom. I ask these things for Jesus' sake. Amen.*

♥ If your riches are yours, why don't you take them with you t'other world? (Benjamin Franklin)

16th October Greed

📖 1 Timothy 6:9

"People who want to get rich fall into temptation and a trap and into many foolish and harmful desires that plunge men into ruin and destruction."

☞ It isn't money that is the root of all evil, but rather, the 'love of money'. That's what this verse (and the next) teaches. Money isn't the problem, it's the constant desire and longing to get more and more money that is the problem. This verse says that such a desire for more, put people on a slippery slope that turns out to be downright dangerous. The desire to get rich continues to ensnare, and will destroy many. Ultimately, this is true in a spiritual sense and Jesus taught the same thing in the parable of the Sower (Mark 4). He spoke of how "the deceitfulness of wealth and the desire for other things come in and choke the word, making it unfruitful". In an increasingly materialistic society which is out to 'get rich', let us demonstrate a different way...a better way...God's way.

✝ *Father in Heaven, deliver me from being trapped and ruined by greed and help me in the power of the Holy Spirit to show that Your way is best. For Jesus' sake. Amen.*

♥ Don't fear tomorrow. God is already there.

Stephen Johnston

17th October Healing

📖 2 Kings 5:14

"So he went down and dipped himself in the Jordan seven times, as the man of God had told him, and his flesh was restored and became clean like that of a young boy."

☞ Namaan was not impressed by the Jordan. It seemed a poor substitute for the rivers of the Lebanon where he came from. In fact it took some clever persuasion from his servant to get him to take the plunge, even though Elisha had told him that that was what he had to do to have his leprosy healed. But once he overcame his pride and his resistance to such a passive task, he found that the outcome was restoration, a healing which didn't just remove the signs of his physically and socially disabling disease but which remade him with all the vigour of youth. Often God also has to tackle our sense of pride and self-sufficiency before he can deal with the other problems we bring to Him, but still He offers us new life as we're willing to accept it on His terms rather than our own.

✝ *Open my heart, Lord, to see how pride has damaged my spirit and limited the effects of Your healing power in my life. Amen.*

♥ There's no problem in life, no matter how complex, which if looked at in the proper way, doesn't get more complicated still!

18th October — Healing

📖 Psalm 103 : 2 - 3

"Praise the Lord, O my soul; and forget not all His benefits – who forgives all your sins and heals all your diseases..."

☞ In these short phrases there are at least four main themes: praise, memory, forgiveness and healing. One thing worth noticing is the sequence of ideas; the spiritual pattern of cause effect. Unless you are very different from me, then I imagine any illnesses you may experience would be top of your list. Sometimes, I might want forgiveness from God or others so that relationships can be fixed up and I can feel comfortable again. Always, I am placed firmly at the centre of my agenda. But the Psalmist's starting point is a Lord so wonderful that He demands our praises. This praise is accompanied by active remembering in which we recall all the good things God has done, and so drag our minds away from their natural focus on our own difficulties. It is when we come with this attitude, recognising God's greatness and goodness that we can easily experience the forgiveness and healing we want and need.

✝ *Dear Lord, help me to recognise the signs of Your majesty and love when You seem far away and my problems blot out everything else from view. Amen.*

♥ You can't change the past, but you can ruin a perfectly good present by worrying about the future. (Murray Watts in 'Rolling In The Aisles').

19th October — Healing

📖 Matthew 4 : 23

"Jesus went throughout Galilee, teaching in their synagogues, preaching the good news of the kingdom, and healing every disease and sickness among the people."

☞ Like Father, like Son. Here Jesus is doing exactly the same sort of thing that the Psalmist got excited about in yesterday's reading. Jesus actions were an important part of his credentials, and many people believed in Him because of His miracles and healings. This is a sort of 'News Headline' verse setting out the big themes of Jesus' ministry. He taught churchgoers to get His message across to those with no particular religious connections that He cared for the physical needs of those He met. As the body of Christ here on earth, these themes should also characterise the life of the church today. God promises that if Christians unite in using their Spirit–given gifts and abilities, then together we can take on the task. We are called to be a people obedient to God's word, who explain Jesus' message in language and style that others can understand, and demonstrate God's love for them in practical ways. Like Father, like Son.

✝ *Dear Jesus, show me what gifts You have given me and help me to get involved in Your work here and now. Amen.*

♥ God so loved the world that he did not send a committee.

20th October **Healing**

📖 Acts 3 : 6-7

"Then Peter said, "Silver or gold I do not have, but what I have I give you. In the name of Jesus Christ of Nazareth, walk". Taking him by the right hand, he helped him up, and instantly the man's feet and ankles became strong."

☞ Passages like yesterday's and today's always make me feel uncomfortable. My situation seems to be the reverse of Peter's. He was asked for money but didn't have any. Instead he gave healing from Christ, and the life of the crippled beggar was transformed. In one miraculous moment he was given the ability to run and jump, the opportunity to earn his own living without ever having to beg again and possibly, even the chance to become a husband and father. When I am faced with similar tragedies, however, it sometimes seems that all I can give is my money. Many Christians today have seen miraculous physical healings in the biblical pattern. That has not been my experience so far. Perhaps my faith is too small, my mind too conditioned to scepticism. Whatever of that, I can still give what I have where it is needed, and I can reach out a hand of support to other damaged pilgrims. And always, I must be willing to let God do the unexpected.

✝ *Dear Jesus, give me Your strength so that I can be strong when others need to lean on me. Amen.*

♥ Most people are bothered by those passages of Scripture they don't understand - but I have always noticed that the passages that bother me the most are the ones I do understand. (Mark Twain)

21st October Healing

📖 James 5 : 14 –16

"Is any of you sick? He should call the elders of the church to pray over him and anoint him with oil in the name of the Lord. And the prayer offered in faith will make the sick person well; the Lord will raise him up. If he has sinned, he will be forgiven."

☞ When thinking about healing in the church today, this reading offers a pattern worth considering. It presents what health care workers would call a protocol for dealing with sickness. The onus for initiating action is placed on the sufferer, no one has the right to barge in where they're not wanted. The responsibility for responding lies with church leaders, who are called to pray with the person, and to anoint them with oil. This may seem odd, but the symbolism for God's healing Spirit would have been obvious to the early church. Perhaps we need to reclaim this symbol in the age of aromatherapy! A crucial element is the call for all involved, not just the sufferer, to confess their sins openly to each other (see v16). If illness is linked to sin in some way, James reassures us that God will deal with that too. When faced by ill health, I wonder whether we're ready to try God's prescription as well as following doctor's orders.

✝ *Dear Father, help me to be open and obedient to Your word, even when the consequences make me uncomfortable or afraid. Amen.*

♥ A poor life this if, full of care. We have no time to stand and stare. (Leisure' by William Henry Davies.)

Graham McGeown

22nd October — Temptation

📖 Matthew 26 : 41

"Watch and pray so that you will not fall into temptation. The spirit is willing, but the body is weak."

☞ In a 'Dirty Harry' movie, where motor–bike cops break the law to rid the city of criminals, Clint Eastwood's last line is a speech: 'A man's gotta know his limitations.' Temptation dares us beyond God's limitations for our lives, but knowing these limitations is not enough, we need to know our personal limitations or weaknesses too!

Joseph is a good example. He knows adultery is wrong, so when Potiphar's wife tries to seduce him, he gets out of there fast! Peter, however, says "I will never do this. I will never deny You Jesus!"; and then ignores Jesus' advice to 'watch and pray' as well as his own weaknesses. He's snoring in minutes and denying Jesus three times in an hour!

The point: Jesus doesn't want us to be spiritually naïve – 'I will never do this' often does! Our bodies are weak; our wills – not that strong! Watch and pray because a person's gotta know **all** their limitations. Do you?

✝ *Father, You and I both know my weaknesses; keep me watchful, keep me prayerful, keep me from falling, because one day with You is worth a thousand elsewhere. Amen.*

♥ Imagine a Clint Eastwood Version (CEV) of the Bible to sit alongside the KJV or the NIV; "You've gotta ask yourself a question, Philistine," said King David: "Did I fire five stones or was it six! Do you feel lucky? Well, do ya, Punk?!" Perhaps we should know our limitations for Clint's bible applications!

23rd October — Temptation

📖 2 Corinthians 11 : 3

"But I am afraid that just as Eve was deceived by the serpent's cunning, your minds may somehow be led astray from your sincere and pure devotions to Christ."

☞ Remember starting out with Christ? How close we were? How pure it was? How, then, can we be deceived?

It probably begins with a question: 'Did God really say…?' Soon we jazz up our faith and down-play God's foolish love. The devil coaches pride to disbelieve God and sets for us a new task…to believe in ourselves! So we enter Eden, sitting there in the grass, making idols to our own greatness, and the devil smile on!

Dietrich Bonheoffer, a brilliant young Christian executed in Flossenburg Concentration Camp for opposing Hitler, found this way out of Eden: "When a man really gives up trying to make something out of himself...then he wakes with Christ in Gethsemane."

If we are approaching an 'Eden-experience' we must ask God to take us to another garden, Gethsemane, where Jesus accepts His mission – the Cross: 'Not my will but Yours be done!' Gethsemane replaces Eden for the Christian. Can we kneel beside Jesus here?

The key: It's the kneeling beside Jesus that keeps us from being deceived.

✝ *Father, keep me resting on my knees and not on my laurels that I may believe in You, Lord, and be faithful to Jesus my friend. Amen.*

♥ Apparently in older times doctors had a lot of cases of ministers with knee problems due to prayer, similar to cleaners who used to kneel to clean old marble steps. Today, both professions no longer suffer from bad knees. The cleaners because of 'The Hoover', the ministers...?

24th October — Temptation

📖 Galatians 6 : 1

"Brothers, if someone is caught in a sin, you who are spiritual should restore him gently. But watch yourself, or you also may be tempted."

☞ The Tetsi fly is a furry elephant of a bug. Those who know what it is are petrified by it. I watched a programme once about a coach-load of Europeans on safari. In one scene, a Tetsi fly gets into the coach through a window. The Europeans panic and scream and some people dive over and under seats, while others form a swot-team. Eventually the brute is dead.

What's so bad about the Tetsi fly? It carries a horrible disease the local call, 'The Sleeping Illness', which, with enough bites, leaves its victims entranced, unaware of the world around them. Not very pleasant!

When sinful thoughts enter our minds and we stop swotting them like dangerous bugs, they bite, and with enough bites, our consciences' don't work! Sin has us.

The task: Jesus doesn't ask us to condemn sin-bitten Christians, He asks us to restore them – gently! But be careful too, because the bug that bit your friend is close by and knows why you are here. It wants to bite; watch it doesn't.

✝ *Lord, give me the determination to swot sin; the self-giving love to restore a friend; and the maturity in Christ to protect my own vulnerability from the sin that caught and floored my friend. In Jesus. Amen*

♥ I bet you never thought you would see the day when you would give thanks to God for midges. Now, I believe, this day has come; don't you?

25th October — Temptation

📖 James 1 : 14

"When tempted, no-one should say, 'God is tempting me.' For God cannot be tempted by evil, nor does He tempt anyone."

☞ Teenagers break down a fence and climb a steep bank to where a huge tree stands. They throw a rope up over a branch like Wild West cowboys making a swing. But the branch is old... the strain too much! It cracks. There's a fall. A boy gets hurt.

Who's to blame? The court says the landowner; the mother of the boy, God! Like the mother, we can blame God because bad things happen. Like the Court, we can blame the Landowner whenever we break fences and get hurt. But the truth is, God is not to blame! He is neither attracted to evil nor does He attract us to do evil.

So when we break down God's fences, ignore His warnings and fall, who is to blame? Answer: we are!

The Fact: taking blame allows us to take responsibility for our own sin and evil desires. Then we repent – Lord! It was I! Then we can walk with God again on His narrow path, between the hedges! There is no better place to walk.

✝ *Father, I blame so many people or things for the wrongs I do, but in the end, I did them because I wanted to. The Desire was mine. Forgive me, Lord, and may I, as the deer pants for water, long after You instead. Amen.*

♥ In an old joke a mother leaves a boy at home to look after a newly made bowl a trifle: "not even a lick!" the boy promises. The mother comes home and half the trifle is gone! "Who did this!" "I don't know," the boy said, "it must have been the cat!" "Really, I didn't know cats could use spoons!!"

26th October — Temptation

1 Corinthians 10 : 13

"No temptation has seized you except what is common to man. And God is faithful; He will not let you be tempted beyond what you can bear. But when you are tempted, He will also provide a way out so that you can stand up under it."

☞ In Tom and Jerry, Tom chases Jerry into a dimly lit room where instead of a squeaking mouse, the shadow of a lion opens a wide mouth. Roar! Tom's eyes pong out, his feet brake, he U turns and skedaddles. As for Jerry, well, he stops making hand-shadows behind his torch and eats the cheese!

Sometimes sin seems invincible. "What's the point," we say, "We can't win!" Christian morale dips low. But Paul says "No temptation has seized you except what is common to man!"

And as for God? He makes sure we're on a level playing field, that temptation is never too great for us and there's always a way out.

So when tempted, ask God to switch on His light in the darkness – the shadows will shrink and our opponents, well, they'll seem less formidable! From here we can walk into victory.

Wise Christians: don't listen to temptation's looney tunes; instead embrace (and memorise!) God's Promises – like this one! 'When you are tempted, He will also provide a way out so that you can stand up under it.'

✝ *Lord my morale is low – I keep falling for the same sin. Help me to stand up to my temptations no matter how big they make themselves. And may I keep to Your promises and use the exits provided. In Jesus' name. Amen.*

♥ We started the week with television, and so we finish in the immortal words of another cartoon character, "That's all folks!" at least from me, anyway. Thanks.

James Burnett

27th October — Holiness

📖 Leviticus 11 : 44a

"I am the Lord your God; consecrate yourselves and be holy, because I am holy".

☞ Who has had the greatest influence on your Christian discipleship? I am grateful that as a young believer I was taught that the Christian must live a distinctive life, and the mark of the difference can be summarised by the word 'Holiness'. But what was the reason? It was because God was now my Heavenly Father that I had to bear the family likeness, to grow more like Him. Of course it would be the height of arrogance to suggest that a human being could become holy as God. However, He encourages us to set our sights on that goal through this verse from Leviticus. More than this, he has planted His Holy Spirit in us to transform us, and thereby gives us an aspiration to inspire each of us throughout our whole lives, to seek holiness of life that increasingly becomes more like His.

✝ *Lord, make me more like You every day that I live. Amen.*

♥ Two Kerrymen were talking. "Sean", said Mick "Did you know we only use a third of our brains?" "No", said Sean "What happens to the other third?".

28th October Holiness

Exodus 20 : 8

"Remember the Sabbath day by keeping it holy."

Yesterday we said that at the heart of what it means to be holy is to be distinctive. The nation of Israel was commanded by God to hold the Sabbath as special, a sign not only of its holiness, but of theirs, as God's chosen people. Sadly, it can be all too easy to keep special religious days in the calendar and yet for our hearts to be far from the Lord, something demonstrated frequently in Israel's history. Yet what an opportunity the rest of 'once a week' gives us to proclaim the holiness of God in a world quite literally working itself to death, around the clock, throughout the year! God's wise and gracious command to His people is "Remember the Sabbath Day by keeping it holy", set **apart** from common use, set aside, **for** the worship of God and **to** declare a distinct and different set of values to the world around us.

Lord thank You for the gift of Your day, may I use it as You intended for Your glory, the good of others and my own blessing. Amen.

"All out attack mixed with caution" (Jim Mc Laughlin, Shamrock Rovers Manager on his tactics for a 1985 European match).

29th October Holiness

1Thessalonians 4:7

"For God did not call us to be impure, but to live a holy life."

☞ God calls each of His children to live a life marked by holiness. We may have a view of holy living that is passive, even inactive. But the holiness God wishes to see in our lives is that which is modeled on His own character. It has its negatives, but even these are positive, for to say that God is completely without sin is to say something wholesome and attractive, the same should be said of us. Impurity and holiness do not mix, the former will ruin the latter. Our hearts instead should be set on 'the striving after' a positively holy life, a life that rejoices in discovering the way God would have us live, the attitudes He would have us form, the desires He would have us seek. Such a life is not only most honouring to our Heavenly Father and most satisfying for us, His children, but has the most profound impact as a witness for Him.

✝ *Lord forgive the impurity in my life and help me seek holiness of thought, word and deed to which You have called me. Amen.*

♥ Never in history of the FAI cup had a team wearing hooped jerseys lost a final in a year ending in 5. (Home Farm FC programme notes 1985)

30th October — Holiness

📖 1 Peter 2 : 9

"But you are a chosen people, a royal priesthood, a holy nation, a people belonging to God, that you may declare the praises of Him who called you out of darkness into His wonderful light".

☞ One of the quests of postmodern culture is for significance. To ask, 'what on earth am I here for?' leads many only to despair, because there are no answers except meaningless ones. But if you know God made you in His image, and that, despite all the ravages of sin in you He has not given up on you; If you know He has forgiven your sin by the blood of Christ and has begun to recreate His holy likeness in you, then you can see your life in an entirely different context! Peter uses beautiful terms here to describe Christians, 'chosen people, a royal priesthood, a holy nation, a people belonging to God'. People with a purpose and a meaning, "that you may declare the praises of Him who called you out of the darkness into His wonderful light". Talk about significance! Doesn't it make all the struggles for holiness worthwhile?

✝ *Father I thank You that in You I have meaning and the greatest reason in all creation for my existence, make me faithful to You. Amen.*

♥ A sweater is a garment worn by a child when his mother feels cold.

31st October — Holiness

📖 1 Peter 2 : 22 – 23

"He committed no sin, and no deceit was found in his mouth'. When they hurled their insults at Him, He did not retaliate; when He suffered, He made no threats. Instead He entrusted himself to Him who judges justly ."

☞ Living a distinctive, holy life for God is not easy. It goes against our natural sinful grain; it brings us into conflict with the values of our society, which does not honour the Lord. It can be a struggle. If ever there was someone whose life brought Him into direct opposition to the accepted customs and beliefs of His day it was the Lord Jesus. His gracious words, loving deeds and life of obedience to His heavenly

Father so infuriated Israel's leaders that they conspired to have Him executed, and even then His holy character was demonstrated in the nature of His death, even to those who nailed Him on to the Cross! Are you prepared for such a reaction? You may think that you will be loved for living a holy rather than an impure life, quite the reverse. At times it may seem like more than you can bear. At such a time remember the Cross. Remember that the One who hung there called on you to carry your own cross too. But also that He is now the Risen One, who promises that same joyous Resurrection to all who follow Him whatever the cost.

✝ *Lord I thank You for Your holy life and death for me. Give me grace to live a holy life for You, whatever it costs. Amen.*

♥ The older you get, the further you had to walk to school as a child.

David Moore

NOVEMBER

The linocut "Draughts in Comfort", 7.5" x 9.5", is based on a pencil drawing of a brother and sister acting as models in a figure-drawing art class.

1st November Repentance

2 Chronicles 7 : 14

" ...If my people who are called by my name humble themselves, and pray and seek my face, and turn from their wicked ways, then I will hear from heaven, and will forgive their sin and heal their land."

☞ God made this promise to King Solomon. It has been used often as a challenge to the Churches in Ireland. Christians have been called upon to 'humble themselves and pray and turn...' so that peace may come. What does it mean? When Rehoboam, Solomon's son became king, he abandoned the ways of his father and became over-confident in his own strength. However, the mighty army of Egypt attacked Jerusalem and Rehoboam was told that God was abandoning him because of his unfaithfulness. 2 Chronicles 12 tells how Rehoboam repented as he and his leaders humbled themselves and said, "The Lord is just".

By acknowledging that they had acted wrongfully and that God had a right to punish them, the rulers of the land accepted the Lord's justice and were in turn accepted by Him. In the days, which followed, God allowed Jerusalem to fall, but brought good to the whole country through its converted king.

✝ *Lord, You are the Judge of all the earth, help us to be humble before You that we may trust You to do right for all people and us. Amen.*

♥ The sole survivor of a shipwreck shouted to the heavens from his storm tossed lifeboat, "What have I done to deserve this?" A voice boomed across the darkened firmament, "Do you want a list?"

2nd November Repentance

📖 Isaiah 55 : 7

"Give up your crooked ways and your evil thoughts. Return to the Lord our God. He will be merciful and forgive your sins."

☞ In this chapter of Isaiah we are invited to experience and enjoy what God alone provides – nourishment for the hunger in our hearts, an understanding of His purposes and the joy of seeing His presence in the world.

However, the passage also makes it clear that if we do not give up our expectation to have things our own way, or stop feeding our minds with the hopes and dreams the world offers, then there is no chance of finding God's ways or walking in His will.

The problem with having a mind of your own is that it doesn't leave room for the better wisdom, which comes from the Spirit of Christ.

The 'evil thoughts' in the verse are not debased or particularly wicked schemes, but rather the self–opinionated attitude which insists on having things our own way regardless of the feelings or ideas of others.

✝ *May the mind of Christ my Saviour live in me from day to day; by His love and power controlling, all I do or say". Amen.*

♥ Never get rid of something, until you have something better to put in its place.

3rd November Repentance

Luke 5 : 32

"I have not come to call the righteous, but sinners to repentance."

☞ Jesus had just invited a most unusual person to join His group. Matthew was a despised taxman whose only friends were those of his own kind. That night Matthew threw a party attended by Jesus. The politically correct and the religious people questioned the propriety and example Jesus was setting as He associated with these social outcasts.

"Only those who know themselves to be sick will call a doctor", said Jesus. "I have come to invite such people to a new life".

Loss of appetite is usually a sign of sickness in our bodies, so if we have no hunger for more of God's influence in our lives then we must be spiritually sick. Unhappily those who are, usually don't know it. Therefore, they don't call on the name of the Lord to be saved.

✝ *Lord, fill us with a hunger for You and Your word. Then, by Your Spirit satisfy us with good things and send us about our business. In the Name of Jesus. Amen.*

♥ Jesus accepted Matthew just as he was. That made others mad because they worked hard at making themselves acceptable!

4th November

Repentance

Luke 15 : 17 – 18

"When he came to his senses he said, "How many of my father's hired servants have bread enough and to spare, but I perish here with hunger! I will rise and go to my father, and I will say to him, Father, I have sinned against heaven and before you."

☞ When this 'prodigal son' went to seek employment on the farm and with the family he had deserted, it is told that he arrived back at the house to find the doors locked and the windows shuttered. They had seen him coming and no matter how hard he knocked there was no reply.

Eventually an upstairs shutter opened and his only brother stuck his head out, swore at him and then made room for his father to shout, "So you've come back; spent up no doubt! What do you think you're playing at, turning up here without so much as a letter? Don't you realise your poor mother is heartbroken and we have had an uphill struggle to get the business back on its feet after you took half the assets?" He slammed the window.

Shortly the door opened. It was his father again. "Okay," he said, "I'll give you a last chance on a three month trial..."

Of course that is not the story we know. But it's more like the one we expect!

✝ *Lord, thank You that knowing us, and knowing all about us, You accept and welcome us home. Lord Jesus, I come. Amen.*

♥ In spite of what you think, God is not annoyed with you.

5th November **Repentance**

Romans 2 : 4

"Are you presuming on the rich kindness, tolerance and patience of God? Do you not know that God's kindness is meant to lead you to repentance?"

☞ Not long ago, Les Miserables by Victor Hugo finished a successful run in Dublin's Point Theatre. At the beginning, Jean Valjean one of the heroes is a thief who has exploited the bishop and stolen his silver. Valjean is caught, the treasure is recognised and he is brought before the surprised cleric. Instead of taking revenge, the bishop announces that the silver was a gift and Valjean has forgotten the candlesticks.

Released, with this wealth, the thief spends the rest of his life making amends by doing good, and being hunted by those who cannot tolerate such mercy being shown. Philip Yancy in his book, "What's so amazing about grace?" offers that story as an illustration of God's free gift of forgiveness to us. Who would be so wicked as to play on this generosity? To act with such thanklessness would be a sign that we have never truly received the wonderful forgiveness He offers in Jesus Christ.

✝ *Lord Jesus, thank You again for dying for me. By this love I see what I am worth to You. Please grant me Your Spirit so that I may show my love for You by loving others. Amen.*

♥ Little children let us not love in word or speech, but in deed and truth. (1 John 3 : 18)

Des Bain

6th November Gossip

Psalm 141: 3

"Set a guard over my mouth, O Lord; keep watch over the door of my lips."

☞ The Old Testament Law was as much concerned with what went into the mouth as with what came out! We too guard our lips from admitting things that are often taboo, such as cigarette smoke or alcohol, things that are unhealthy like cholesterol, things that from time to time are unfashionable like meat or, worst of all, cabbage, sprouts or liver, things we just don't like. How much more important to guard those unseen things that we allow through the doors of our lips in the other direction. Things that will never cause cancer or pickle our liver, they will never make us overweight or induce a heart attack, they may go in and out of fashion but, above all they taste so good. Like chocolate or chips they are a real temptation and we savour every morsel – the juicy, succulent words of 'the gossip'!

✝ *Lord, may the sentry who guards my lips keep out what ought not to come in and keep in what ought not to go out. Amen.*

♥ Gossip is when you hear something you like about someone you don't. (Earl Wilson)

7th November Gossip

Proverbs 11 : 13

"A gossip betrays a confidence, but a trustworthy person keeps a secret."

☞ Can you keep a secret? Really? Are you sure? You don't ever prefix what you say with, "Now, I'm not sure about this but …" or with, "Now, don't tell this to a soul…" You don't sometimes share a morsel or two with a close friend, just for prayer of course? Do you ever hurry somewhere simply because you can't wait to share what you know with the people you are going to meet? Or have you ever been in a conversation where you aren't listening to the person who is talking because you are excitedly poised to tell what you, and only you know?

Have you ever avoided eye contact with a friend because you have betrayed his confidence? Have you ever wished you could take words back, but it's too late? Have you ever blushed when she smiled trustingly at you because she doesn't know that now everybody else knows?

✝ *Lord, help us to bear one another's burdens and to do so with loving discretion. Amen.*

♥ Gossip is a verbal form of the crime of 'receiving stolen goods'.

8th November — Gossip

📖 Matthew 12 : 36 - 37

""I tell you", said Jesus; "people will have to give account on the Day of Judgment for every careless word they have spoken. For by your words you will be acquitted, and by your words you will be condemned."

☞ The scary thing about these verses is that they refer to 'careless' words. These are not the grand speeches that we make or the riotously funny comments we come out with at parties or even the well-tuned insults that cut like a knife. The 'careless' words seem to be those that we never notice as they slip out, those that almost no one else in the group notices. They are words that we never remember saying but they are words that may hurt a bruised spirit, or discourage an already bedraggled struggler.

These words reflect the heart of the speaker because they are spoken instinctively, without preparation. They are so natural that they go unnoticed by him. But they are noticed by the One who sees the depths of our hearts and they are evaluated by the One who understands the effects that they have had on the depths of other hearts.

✝ *Lord, help me to have my heart so in tune with Yours that my careless words will be instinctively loving and gracious, so that they might enrich everyone who hears them. Amen*

♥ If Christians are to be like 'little children' then maybe we should only speak when we are spoken to.

9th November — Gossip

📖 1 Timothy 4 : 7

"Have nothing to do with godless myths and old wives' tales; rather train yourself to be godly."

☞ Some myths and 'old wives tales' contain a lot of truth. Indeed they do, but many of them contain ugly superstition and bigotry among other unsavoury elements. It can be difficult to distinguish the truth from the dross and even when we do, the dross still lingers in our minds, affecting our actions and relationships. So, the next time we find ourselves commenting that a child taken out before being baptized will never thrive or thinking that someone's eyes really are too close together, let us stop. Let us pause to reflect on why we have spoken as we have done. Isn't it better to soak our minds in Scripture so that we think like Jesus rather than like a fairground fortuneteller; we live by faith rather than by fear and we reach out to potential friends rather than reject those who just might turn out to be enemies.

✝ *Lord, help me to listen to You rather than to old wives' tales and to reject godless myths in favour of Your eternally trustworthy word. Amen.*

♥ Go on...look out for a ladder you can walk under today!

10th November **Gossip**

📖 1 Peter 4 : 15

"If you suffer, it should not be as a murderer or thief or any other kind of criminal, or even as a meddler."

☞ It's so much fun to meddle, if not in actions at least in words. It's a pleasure to tinker, without having to take responsibility. It's even better to feel righteous anger when our well-meaning interventions have been rudely snubbed. We poke our noses in where we are not wanted or needed, then glory in being 'persecuted for righteousness sake'. Peter warns us that 'suffering' which comes as a result of our meddling has no spiritual value, in fact it is well deserved. Consistent Christian living may well bring suffering but this is quite different from the self-inflicted wounds of the self-righteous do-gooder. Being rejected for witnessing to Christ is entirely different to being rejected as an interfering busybody. Maybe we need to pause before stepping in with our 'wisdom', pray, ask advice from a wise friend and, unless we have no other option, keep silent.

✝ *Lord, when I'm absolutely convinced that I have all the answers, help me to shut up until I wise up. Amen.*

♥ The things most people want to know about are usually none of their business. (George Bernard Shaw)

Drew Gibson

11th November — Caring

📖 Isaiah 49 : 15 - 16

"Can a mother forget the child at her breast and have no compassion on the child she has borne? Though she may forget, I will not forget you! See, I have engraved you on the palms of my hands; your walls are ever before me."

☞ A student for the ministry, who had conducted worship in a Mid-western town of the U.S.A., was invited for lunch, by members of that congregation, a retired couple who had served as missionaries in China, for forty years. At the moment of introduction, the young visitor failed to pick up the surname of his host and hostess.

The main topic of conversation during the meal was the exploits and achievements of their son, Henry. Slowly the young preacher was getting fed up with these recollections and was about to explode, especially upon hearing this final piece of family history; the returned missionaries told him, they had given Henry all their savings so that he could launch his own magazine. The sum mentioned was $600. Before the young man could speak, the old man cut in; "Haven't you heard of our son ...Henry Luce?"

Of course he had heard of Henry Luce, the Founder Editor of 'Time' and 'Life' and 'Fortune' magazines. He had quoted 'Time' just that morning. The parental investment in Henry had been repaid in affection, appreciation and in kind a thousand times.

God's concern for, investment in and remembrance of His people is expressed by Isaiah. More enduring than human affection, is God's love for us. He constantly reminds Himself of His people. As the ancient traveller tattooed the likeness of his loved ones on his palms, God keeps forever before His vision the names and destiny of His own. The walls of Jerusalem may have been literally broken down, but in God's perception they were standing as a sure defense.

✝ *Oh God, whose purposes for us are wise and kind and life-long, give us the trust which can watch and wait for the outworking of all Your plans. Amen.*

♥ Choose for us, Lord, let not our weak preferring,
Rob us of good, You have for us designed;
Choose for us, Lord, your wisdom is unerring,
And we are weak and blind.

12th November — Caring

📖 Luke 14: 12 –13

"Then Jesus said to his host, "When you give a luncheon or a dinner,

do not invite your friends, your brothers or relatives, or your rich neighbours; if you do, they may invite you back and so you will be repaid. But when you give a banquet, invite the poor, the crippled, the lame, the blind, and you will be blessed."

☞ If the parable in Luke chapter 14 verses 7 – 14 reflected social attitudes in Jesus' day, it would appear, that the love of publicity, a quest for the best seats and the praise of one's fellows are not new phenomena. Against such worldliness Jesus set His face. His followers, humble in spirit, were commissioned to offer the powerless and the forgotten respect, understanding, and a sense of self-worth.

Those who placed significance upon contrived conviviality of boon companions, and were generous to their equals, in the knowledge that they would soon be rewarded, could expect no reward at the resurrection. Those who offered hospitality and a rehabilitating ministry to vulnerable and needy people, as categorized in verse 13, were assured of Christ's approval and God's vindication on That Day.

The servants of Christ are called to serve with compassion, all classes and conditions of people, for many reasons, among them these three;

1. In God's common grace we share a common humanity. Most of us are healthy, prosperous and well adjusted emotionally, but not all are so blessed. Were we in the situation of such people we would look for a caring friend and a helping hand.

2. Our Master's Caring and Saving ministry involved great sacrifice. To be in Luther's phrase. 'Little Christ', cannot be achieved by wishing, or walking in 'golden slippers in the sun', but by sacrifice and self-giving.

3. Generous acts commend our faith, yet, even if belief is not offered in return, we go serving for Jesus sake. Our basic motivation is obedience to our Lord. Duties are ours; results are God's.

✝ *Almighty God, by whose grace we are what and who we are, enable us to fulfil the mission of Christ, in our small corner. As we give thanks that Jesus saved the world through His cross. Help us to recall that He also, fed humanity with bread and served His fellows with a towel. Amen.*

♥ A Christian is a person to whom God has committed other people.

13th November Caring

📖 Philippians 4 : 6

"Do not be anxious about anything, but in everything, by prayer and petition, with thanksgiving, present your requests to God."

☞ "All is lost! To Prayers! To Prayers!" So cried a character in 'The Tempest', when storms overwhelmed them at sea. In many ways such a response is typical of modern man's estimation of prayer ... an activity to be resorted to when human ingenuity has failed. This is, of course, the opposite of Christian perception of prayer. Prayer is an audience with the King, involving reverence; a trustful communication within the Family, marked by acceptance; a helpful exchange among friends, bringing enrichment and the contribution of a fellow labourer, presupposing solidarity and mutual up-building.

1. The Pressures of Life. The Christian has not been promised immunity for the common ills of humanity. The unknown tomorrow and its potential for stress and challenge evoke anxiety and foreboding. Worrying changes nothing and so the apostle warns

against it.

2. The Place of Prayer. The issues and anticipations, which cause us to worry, should bring us to God in prayer. We should use every type of petition, in urgency and confidence.

3. The Peace of God. Every prayer is answered, even though, at times, the answer is 'No'. Whatever the divine answer, the awareness of God's peace standing guard over our hearts prepares us for the journey ahead.

✝ *Aware, Oh God, that acceptance of Your will is our truest devotion, we conclude all our petitions with our Lord's words, "Your will be done". Amen.*

♥ A child's prayer as first quoted in 'Punch'. Oh, God, look after Yourself, for if anything should happen to You, we are all in trouble.

14th November — Caring

📖 1 Peter 5 : 2 - 3

"Be shepherds of God's flock that is under your care, serving as overseers - not because you must, but because you are willing, as God wants you to be; not greedy for money, but eager to serve; not lording it over those entrusted to you, but examples to the flock."

☞ Eric Nash, who trained for the Anglican ministry, joined the staff of Scripture Union, in 1932 with the conviction that his work was to evangelise the great Public Schools of England.

John Richard Bridger, a pupil at Rugby School became a Christian at a Scripture Union Camp and returned to his school planning to set up a Christian Union. This group became known as 'the meeting' and to it Bridger invited John Stott.

At a meeting in the Lent Term, conducted by Eric Nash, John Stott waited behind to ask some questions. Eric Nash discerned that he was dealing with a seeking soul. Later Stott wrote, 'He took me for a drive in his car, answered my questions and explained to me the way of salvation'. In his diary for Monday, February 14, 1938, John Stott wrote, 'Yesterday really was an eventful day'.

Within a few days Eric Nash had sent John Stott a little booklet on Christian growth. A correspondence on essential Christian topics began between the young Stott and his 'pastor'. Eric Nash wrote John Stott a weekly letter of spiritual counsel and encouragement for over five years.

✝ *Lord Jesus Christ, the Shepherd, we are thankful for all those who have helped us along the way to faith. Enable us to serve others in this way, tactfully and faithfully, in Your strength. Amen.*

♥ Only the Christian Church has Pastors. Other creeds have prophets, pundits, gurus, but only the Master commissioned pastors. (Scott Latourette)

15th November — Caring

📖 1 Peter 5 : 7

"Cast all your anxiety on him because he cares for you."

☞ John Williams, a Christian poet, who worked, for a while in London, often helped in a Youth Club, in the evening. One evening after the Club he caught the 11.46pm train from Victoria and as he settled into the compartment and began reading, he was aware that with him were another English man and an American. Suddenly the Englishman collapsed on the floor in a convulsive fit. The American calmly opened his shirt collar and placed his handkerchief in the Englishman's mouth so that he wouldn't bite his tongue. Then just as calmly the American began to talk. "I am sorry about this, but it happens about two or three times every week. You see we were in the Korean War together, and I was wounded and left for dead, in no man's land. This man from England came to carry me back to safety. No sooner had we settled in what we thought was a safe bunker, then a shell exploded and the next thing I knew was that I was in hospital. I was invalided out of the Army back to America, when I learned that the Englishman would never recover. I left my job, broke off my engagement, came here and found him and now I look after him. He did it for me; there is nothing I would not do for him."

The two men, the sick one now recovered, got off at their station and left John Williams to reflect upon an unforgettable story of human caring.

✝ *Oh, God, we give thanks that when the cares of life, trials and 'the tears of things', weigh heavily upon us we can leave all our anxieties upon You. Throughout this day, may Your encircling grace make us equal to life's challenges. Amen*

♥ A Cynic's Proverb; A friend in need, is a friend to avoid.

Arthur Clarke

16th November — Worry

📖 Matthew 6 : 25 , 27

"Therefore I tell you, do not worry about your life, what you will eat or drink, or about your body, what you will wear. Is not life more important than food, and the body more important than clothes? Look at the birds of the air, they do not sow or reap or stow away in barns, and yet your Heavenly Father feeds them. Are you not much more valuable than they?"

☞ Bob Dylan has a great song, one of the lines in it goes like this, "It may be the devil or it may be the Lord, but you have to serve somebody". Even the dogs in the street know that many people serve and love money. Money exerts a tremendous attraction over people. It is so easy to understand why. Money gives a person power, privilege and property. It gives one all sorts of options. The trouble is that money is easily lost and spent. So there is the need to protect your reserves and go on making lots more of it. It is a big trap.

In recent years Ireland has gone from being a poor country to being one of the richest in the world. It seems to be all too much for many people. They don't need Jesus anymore! They remind me of rabbits caught in and bewildered by the headlights of the tractor.

✝ *Lord Jesus help me not be lured by money and material things. Amen.*

♥ A pastor was trying to encourage a good collection for the poor. "Try to give £100. (He looked over his glasses!) Well maybe £50. (They still seemed unmoved) How about £20. (Still not wildly enthusiastic) Well come on at least £5... and if you can't manage £5 this collection is for you!"

17th November — Worry

📖 Matthew 6 : 31 –33

"So do not worry, saying "What shall we eat?" or "what shall we drink?" or "what shall we wear?" The pagans run after all these things, and your Heavenly Father knows that you need them, but seek first His kingdom and His righteousness, and all these things will be given to you as well."

☞ Stop today for two minutes and write down the most important things in your life. Out of all those pick out the three most important of all, according to priority. Try to be ruthlessly honest. Some of them might be family, money, security, fame, fortune, car, health, pleasure, God etc. Your no.1 is your predominant passion – it is your main driving force. If you are seeking fame passionately, that will guide most of your decisions.

Try to be very honest. Just because you are a bishop, an elder of the church or a devout Christian does not necessarily mean you are seeking God first. To be passionately involved with the Father, Son and Holy Spirit is no small achievement. It requires a big effort, a great dying to oneself and much more. It brings such a great reward. Isn't it amazing that when we succeed in 'seeking God first' the most beautiful peace tumbles into our lap?

✝ *Lord, in my life, help me to live passionately with, for and in You. Amen.*

♥ This man was telling a priest that he loved God so much that he never encountered any distractions in prayer. His shepherd was doubtful of this claim. "I bet you a tenner, you cannot say the Our Father without being distracted". "No problem", said the man and off he went. "Our Father who are in Heaven….. was that a tenner or a fiver you said???"

18th November — Worry

John 14 : 1

"Do not let your heart be troubled. Trust in God; trust also in Me."

☞ How many 'born worriers' have I met in my life! How many really good people, are choked by worry? Jesus says, "Do not let your hearts be troubled, trust in me".

For some people it is much easier said than done. Imagine you are at home alone. A terrible character knocks on your door and won't go away. You decide to bring him in, give him some drinks and send him on his way. You do. But when he is finished drinking he starts smashing everything in the house. Eventually he leaves. You promise yourself never to entertain him again! Worry is like that. If you bring it in and entertain it, it destroys you. Promise yourself and Jesus, with the help of His grace never again to give in to worry. Have some line from scripture like this 'I can do all things through Him who strengthens me', and defeat the enemy.

✝ *Dear God, with the help of Your grace I will do all I can not to give in to worry today…or any day. Amen.*

♥ An antique dealer arrived at the pearly gates of heaven. St. Peter asked him to wait there until his return but when the saint came back the gates were gone and so was the dealer.

19th November — Worry

John 14 : 27

"Peace I leave with you; my peace I give you. I do not give to you as the world gives. Do not let your hearts be troubled and do not be afraid."

☞ I don't think many people understand the meaning of the 'peace' that Jesus promises His true followers. For example, most politicians say they want peace but see no problem in waging war on the infant in the womb. Peace is a deep inner 'fullness' that comes from union with God and living out His commandments. Peace flows richly in our lives, when we are obedient to what He commands us to do. Many people never attain peace because they relentlessly pursue their own ways – they (consciously or unconsciously) refuse to do things God's way. Only those who live Spirit-filled lives (as opposed to material-centred lives) grasp that great recipe for peace that Jesus gives us. 'If you lose your life, you will find it'. You have no idea what peace the Lord will give you, if you give your heart to Him.

✝ *Help me Lord to stop being selfish so that in returning love for love, I may experience Your peace that surpasses all understanding. Amen.*

♥ A man saw a wonderful colour in his dream. He searched everywhere to find it. Eventually he gave up saying it was probably only a pigment of his imagination.

20th November — Worry

Philippians 1: 21

"For me to live is Christ and to die is gain."

☞ One of my favourite books (which I would scarcely loan to my best friend) is simply called 'In Christ' by William Grossow. It was first published in 1960. This wondrous expression 'In Christ' occurs over 150 times in St. Pauls letters. After his revelation on the road to Damascus, Paul is taken over by Jesus. His whole life is Jesus – In Jesus. In fact, he says in one of his letters 'Jesus is everything'. The whole secret is get more and more into deep friendship with Jesus, allowing His words to enter deep into our hearts through prayer and reflection. Many fail in this because they allow their hearts to be clogged by silly worldly things. As we live more deeply in Jesus we find love flows more freely in us, in the most practical ways.

✝ *Dear Lord, do not allow me to spoil my short life with silly things. Amen.*

♥ A little Dublin man arrived in heaven – thrilled with himself, "I want to see St. Paul", he said and he insisted until he got his way. "Hey, St. Paul! I always wanted to ask you, did you ever get any reply to all those letters you sent to the Corinthians?"

Aiden Carroll

21st November — Renewal

Psalm 51 : 10

" Create in me a pure heart, O God, and renew a steadfast spirit within me."

☞ I need a renewed heart today. Rubbing shoulders with people can soil my clothes and breathing polluted air can clog up my sinuses. My imagination can also become unclean and absorbing the mores of the TV and the methods of the unbelieving world can corrupt my heart. Pray constantly 'God, cleanse the thoughts of our hearts by the inspiration of Your Holy Spirit'. King David spoke of his heart as the centre of his personality. His was deeply stained and his life was in bits. He coveted the beautiful Bathsheba and he hadn't the strength of character to walk away from temptation. He cries to God for cleansing and pleads for radical renewal. Many today are broken-hearted and all of us know what it is to have a divided and unclean heart. God is the Great Heart-Renewer. Jesus said, "Blest are the pure in heart for they shall see God". No wonder this penitential Psalm is often recited at Holy Communion.

✝ *A heart, in every thought renewed. And full of love divine: Perfect and right and pure and true. A copy, Lord of Thine. Amen*
(C Wesley)

♥ A Sunday school class was studying the 10 Commandments. They were ready to discuss the last one. The teacher asked if anyone could quote it. Susie replied, "Thou shalt not take the covers off the neighbours wife."

22nd November — Renewal

📖 Isaiah 40 : 31

"...but those who hope in the Lord will renew their strength. They will soar on wings like eagles; they will run and not grow weary, they will walk and not faint."

☞ I need renewed energy for today. Waiting upon God is more than passivity or contemplation. Think of waiting for a waiter. Waiting can mean deliberate action. J.H. Newman said, "One secret act of self-denial, one sacrifice of inclination to duty, is worth all the mere good thoughts, warm feelings, passionate prayers in which idle people indulge themselves." The powerful eagle waits on the high crag for the thermal currents and then rises higher and soars without effort. Sometimes God wants us to strive less and soar more so that we get nearer to Him and catch His vision of the world. It's all about timing. There is a wind of the spirit into which we can launch ourselves with courage and in confidence that God's timing is perfect. We can exchange our weakness for God's strength. Yet only sometimes we need to fly and sometimes run but most often we walk. Following Christ is for the long haul and 'follow' is what disciples do. Learn to listen for His follow me' and feel the firm grasp of His loving hand.

✝ *Dear Lord, in the problems of today, help me to wait for Your opportunities and rise to higher heights with You. Dear Lord in the rat race of today, renew my inner and outer life that I will run patiently looking unto Jesus. Dear Lord, in the pilgrimage of today, may I walk hand in hand with you? Amen.*

♥ Six years old Angie and her four-year-old brother Joel were sitting together in church. Joel was restless and talkative. "You're not supposed to talk in church". She said. "Why? Who's going to stop me?" Joel asked. Angie pointed to the back of the church and said. "See those two men standing by the door? They're hushers".

23rd November — Renewal

📖 Ezekiel 37 : 3 - 5

"He asked me, "Son of man, can these bones live?" I said, "O Sovereign Lord, you alone know." Then he said to me, "Prophesy to these bones and say to them, Dry bones hear the word of the Lord! This is what the Sovereign Lord says to these bones: I will make breath enter you, and you will come to life. Then you will know that I am the Lord."

☞ I need spiritual renewal today. Ezekiel was taken to the killing fields and had a vision of resurrection. These bones were all that remained of a defeated army. They were dislocated, desiccated and dead. Churches can be the same with disunity and disobedience. The Destroyer can defeat individual believers. This can happen when we get over-tired or when we neglect the means of grace. My Christian life stands or falls according to my daily obedience to the scriptures. Scripture Union or other daily reading notes are an essential discipline for the army of Christ. Are you defeated? When did you stop praying? In order to resurrect a bad golfer's game the coach suggested that he approach each shot with 'visualise, verbalise and actualise'. God gave the prophet the vision, He spoke the word into the situation and the defeated dead revived and became a mighty army. "Do it again Lord and be glorified in Your church today."

✝ *Show me myself and show me my Saviour and let the Book live to me. Amen.*

♥ At Sunday school John listened intently when they told him how Eve was created out of a bone from Adam's ribs. Later in the week his mother noticed him lying down and asked him what was the matter. John said, "I have a pain in my side. I think I'm going to have a wife".

24th November Renewal

Acts 4 : 31

"After they prayed, the place where they were meeting was shaken. And they were all filled with the Holy Spirit and spoke the word of God boldly."

I need renewed courage today. "God does nothing except by prayer" said John Wesley. Prayer is opening the door of our need to the plentiful grace of the Lord Jesus. Here the persecuted church prayed and there was a general release of unity, generosity and evangelism accompanied by miraculous signs and wonders. Sometimes we all need a good shake and self-emptying so that we can be filled again with the Holy Spirit. Renewal in the Holy Spirit is followed by a renewed desire to share the gospel. "Christians are like Arctic rivers - frozen at the mouth!" (Wilson Carlisle, founder of the Church Army). Fear of reputation, rebuff and our own inadequacy make us clam up. I ask God today to make me an honest Christian because then I will honestly be a witness and my work will not be a denial of my words. We need to pray in the perfect love, which casts out fear and gives us holy boldness.

✝ *Enlarge inflame and fill my heart with boundless charity divine;*
So shall I all my strength exert and love them with a zeal like thine,
And lead them to thy open side, the sheep for whom the Shepherd died.
Amen (C Wesley)

♥ The preacher was wired for sound with a lapel mike as he moved briskly about the platform jerking the mike cord as he went, sometimes almost tripping on it before jerking it again. After several circles and jerks, a little girl in the front pew whispered to her mother, "If he gets loose, will he hurt us?"

25th November — Renewal

Romans 12 : 2

"Do not conform any longer to the pattern of this world, but be transformed by the renewing of your mind. Then you will be able to test and approve what God's will is – His good pleasing and perfect will."

I need renewed thinking today. Our mind matters. We don't leave our brains behind when we come to church! Humans find their true stature when we love God with all our mind. Yet our mind is corrupted by sin and needs 'a dayspring for our dimness'. To repent means to change ones mind. To have a renewed mind does not mean that we only think about Christian things but that we think Christianly about all things. We are called to holy non-conformity and to be a counter–culture, which challenges the godless materialistic presumptions of secular society where God is missing but not, missed. Changed thinking leads to changed behaviour and changed behaviour leads us to changed lives. In this frame of mind we will be able to enter in to God's best will for us.

May the mind of Christ my Saviour live in me from day to day.
By His love and power controlling all I do or say. Amen.
(Kate B Wilkinson)

A six-year-old complained to his father about the long and tedious sermon and asked what the preacher did the rest of the week. "Oh he's a very busy man taking care of church business, visiting the sick, ministering to the poor...and then he needs time to rest. Talking in public is not an easy job, you know". The boy thought about that and then said; "Well, listening isn't easy either".

Ken Todd

26th November — Persecution

Matthew 5 : 10 - 12

"Blessed are those who are persecuted because of righteousness, for theirs is the Kingdom of Heaven. Blessed are you when people insult you, persecute you and falsely say all kinds of evil against you because of me. Rejoice and be glad, because great is your reward in heaven, for in the same way they persecuted the prophets who were before you."

☞ When we look at the life of the early church, it would seem that the church saw her responsibility as that of evangelising the world. On the other hand, her expectation was that she would be persecuted by the world. Should it not be expected then, even in today's world, Christians should be oppressed, insulted and persecuted 'because of righteousness' and 'because of me'. As John Stott has written, ' Persecution is simply the clash between two irreconcilable value systems'.

Pastor Samuel Lamb of China, who was in prison for over twenty years and is still under great pressure from the Chinese authorities, has written, 'Those who are persecuted because of righteousness are blessed. Suffering for righteousness is participating in the sufferings of Christ. Every Christian should participate in this suffering. The greatest help during these times of persecution is to keep looking to Jesus. He is always near. The greater the persecution, the nearer He is. The reward in heaven is only an extra bonus'.

✝ *Lord, may there be such evident righteousness in my life and evidence that I belong to You, that people will be drawn to You, regardless of what they think about me, say to me or do to me. Amen*

♥ There are no great men, only great challenges that ordinary men are forced by circumstances to meet. (Admiral Wm. Halsey)

27th November — Persecution

Luke 6 : 27 – 28

"I tell you, Love your enemies; do good to those who hate you; bless those who curse you, pray for those who mistrust you."

☞ How are we to love our enemies? Jesus says our love will be expressed in our deeds, our words and our prayers.

Constantin Caramen from Romania was in prison three times because of his faith. He writes of these verses. "This is no easy assignment. We are inclined to dislike those who hurt us. The best thing we are able to do is to ignore them. But God requires something totally different. He wants us to bless those who hate us. To pray for those who persecuted us. That seems impossible. Remember that blessing someone does not mean that we approve of their actions. In fact, we disapprove of their behaviour, but they need God. That's why we need to pray for them, and bless them with the love of the Lord."

Jesus even tells us to love them. We could never find it in our hearts to love an enemy. It just goes against our nature. Where in the world will we find people who can? We will only find it in people who are no longer of this world, but now belong to the Kingdom of God. In Christ, who forgave us first, we are able to do the unusual deed of embracing an enemy, of loving those who hate us, of praying for those who persecute us, of blessing those who curse us. Such a prayer may save them but, in any case, it will save us'. And so, through us, Christ can reach that hard heart, so that it may discover Christ's forgiveness and have eternal life.

✝ *Lord, as You loved me when I was not easy to love, give me love for and help me to pray for those in my country who are perceived as 'enemies', even those who have killed people I know. Bless them, Lord. Amen.*

♥ A diamond is a chunk of coal that stayed on the job under pressure.

28th November — Persecution

📖 Luke 22 : 63 - 65

"The men who were guarding Jesus began mocking and beating him. They blindfolded him and demanded, "Prophesy! who hit you?" And they said many other insulting things to him."

☞ Idris Nalos is a Presbyterian minister in Sudan. He studied in Kenya and returned to Juba to start an Arabic-speaking church in an area that is besieged by rebels. Many Christian leaders were arrested or permanently 'disappeared'. His family advised him to flee. In July 1997 the military police came for him in the middle of the night. Idris writes – 'On 26th July, from eight in the morning until midnight, we were forced to stay standing up straight. After that we were blindfolded and taken away to another house where we were kicked and beaten with sticks and whips. This went on for three days and nights. After a few days I was desperate. I told them that they had better kill me straight away. They answered me by saying that they wanted to kill me slowly…' Idris later required surgery for a broken jaw and several teeth missing 'Can he have followed far who has no wound or scar?' (Amy Carmichael)

✝ *Lord, forgive me when I complain about the least little inconvenience or frustration, especially when I know what You, the sinless one went through for me. Amen.*

♥ Closer is He than breathing, and nearer than hands and feet. (Alfred, Lord Tennyson)

29th November — Persecution

📖 Hebrews 11 : 36 – 37

"Some faced jeers and flogging, while still others were chained and put in prison. They were stoned, they were sawed in two; they were put to death by the sword. They went about in sheepskins and goatskins, destitute, persecuted and mistreated - the world was not worthy of them."

☞ When the recipients of the letter to the Hebrews read of some who experienced 'jeers and flogging', they would think of members of their own community who had suffered some of these things in earlier days. If similar experiences awaited them, it might help them to realise that they were not the first to travel this path.

Do such things happen today? Yes. 'On January 20th 1999, in Indonesia, angry Muslim villagers attacked a church youth retreat in the north of an island. In the church group there were 124 Christians, 84 of them children between the ages of 3 and 15 years old. Everyone was marched outside and made stand in three groups – children, teenagers and adults.

Singling out a 15 year old boy, Roy Pontoh the villagers asked him in front of everyone, "Who are you?" He replied, "I am a soldier of Christ". To everyone's horror, they slashed and chopped off his left arm. They asked him again, "Who are you?" Back came the reply, "I am a soldier of Christ". They hacked at his right arm though it did not sever. Among those watching was Roy's nine-year-old brother, Marlan. They tried to make Roy recant, forcing him to say, "Alahu Akbar", but he replied, "As far as I know. Jesus Christ is the only Lord" at that they sliced his stomach, and his intestines gushed out. Still he was conscious. A third time they asked him, "Who are you?" As he gasped his reply, "I am a soldier of Christ," he was beheaded. His body was thrown into the gutter, but his spirit no doubt entered through gates of gold: (from 'Compass Direct" April 23, 1999)

✝ *Lord, we pray for those around the world, in many places, who suffer for the Faith – for those in prison, for those who face death, those who are beaten, expelled from their families and communities, who meet in secret – and all because they love You. Amen.*

♥ I am not worthy of these servants, soldiers of Jesus Christ.

30th November Persecution

2 Timothy 3 : 10 – 12

"You know about my teaching, my way of life, purpose, faith, patience, love, endurance, persecution, sufferings, the persecutions I endured... In fact, everyone who wants to live a godly life in Christ Jesus will be persecuted."

☞ In verses 10 and 11, 2 Timothy 3, Paul has been writing about his way of life, his sufferings and about how the Lord rescued him from them all. However in verse 12 Paul makes it clear that his experience was not unique. He sought to live a godly life in Christ Jesus and suffered as a consequence. Shortly after Paul and Barnabas suffered abuse in the cities mentioned in verse 11 (Antioch, Iconium and Lystra), they returned to instruct the believers there, saying, "We must go through many hardships to enter the Kingdom of God" (Acts 14 : 22). It will be the same for all who seek to live such a life, as Jesus predicted. In Matthew 10 : 22, Jesus told His disciples, "All men will hate you because of me". Jesus said to His disciples in John 15, "If the world hates you, keep in mind that it hated me first. If you belonged to the world, it would love you as its own". It is only for those who are both in the world and in Christ simultaneously that persecution becomes inevitable. Since the perfect man, Christ Jesus, was crucified for His sinless life and candid testimony concerning God His Father, there is surely little possibility that the world will gladly accept those who earnestly pursue a life in conformity to Christ's.

If Christians today are not meeting persecution from our western, comfortable, privileged society, it is not because the world has come to appreciate goodness. Is it because so few believers have determined to live genuinely Christian lives – lives which are 'godly in Christ Jesus?' At the same time, many around the world in many countries know what it is to 'know Christ and the power of His resurrection and the fellowship of sharing in His sufferings'. (Philippians 3 : 10)

✝ *Lord, as a Christian, I do not want or need to suffer because of my sheer stupidity. However, I want to love You and follow You consistently and I am willing to be part of the fellowship of sharing in His sufferings. Amen*

♥ Never, never, never, never give up.

Douglas Mark

DECEMBER

A crayon sketch drawn in unusually cold conditions in situ, the morning after an exceptionally heavy hoarfrost on already-fallen snow was the original on which this 7.7" x 8.5" linocut was based.

It bears the title "Larne and Inver Parish Church - Winter" and it was cut in 1944 or 1945.

This reduced copy is taken from the last print of the edition of 50.

1st December — Self Denial

📖 Mark 12 : 42

"But a poor widow came and put in two very small copper coins, worth only a fraction of a penny."

☞ When the Temple Treasurer came to count the money at the end of the day, those two copper coins weren't going to matter very much – but Jesus recognised that they certainly mattered to the widow who had given them.

Her offering may have been very low in monetary value, but it was very high in faith value. It was an offering, which showed the gratitude of her heart to the one who was worshipped at the Temple and the loyalty of her life for the work done there in His name. It was an offering that came from sacrificial saving and top priority giving.

A Challenge: Measured in the currency of gratitude, loyalty and the overall resources at our disposal, how much are our offerings worth? Do we actually think about what we give? Would we miss it much? Does it represent any kind of self-denial or sacrifice?

✝ *Lord Jesus Christ even though you were rich, you became poor, so that we might become rich. Help me to give back to you in a way that shows my gratitude and expresses my loyalty to your work. Amen.*

♥ A cheerful giver puts a smile on God's face. (2 Corinthians 9 : 7)

2nd December **Self Denial**

📖 Luke 9 : 23 - 24

"Then he said to them all: "If anyone would come after me, he must deny himself, take up his cross daily and follow me. For whoever wants to save his life will lose it, but whoever loses his life for me will save it."

☞ Following your favourite football team is a wonderfully exciting experience when they are winning and the crowds are cheering – it is not much fun when they're losing and the weather is lousy and the crowds are dwindling.

Maybe that was the kind of warning that Jesus was trying to give to Peter, following His exciting, convinced, courageous statement of faith. Peter had got it right, but there would still be many days when life would be neither easy nor exhilarating – there would be lots of difficult times and demanding experiences. Indeed following Jesus with any kind of faithfulness would almost certainly bring some demands and difficulties that would not otherwise have been there at all.

There will be some days when we just have to put our heads down and keep going. We will only be able to do so when we keep our eyes focussed on Jesus, who suffered so many things, was killed and on the third day rose again.

✝ *Lord, Jesus Christ, may the quiet assurance that you are the truth and the way and the hope for my life, always keep me going when I am tempted to feel that following You is too hard. Amen.*

♥ There are sometimes almost more people on the pitch than in the seats when I go to watch my local team – if you ask me I'll tell you who they are!

3rd December

Self Denial

John 3 : 30

"He must become greater; I must become less."

It's not so easy to take second place or to step into the background, especially if we have been used to being at the centre of activity and attention.

It might be all right if it meant being relieved of some of our duties and responsibilities, and taking life a bit easier – but becoming less important without giving up any of the burdens of service, or the destiny of imprisonment and death, could not have been very attractive.

However that was the scenario which John the Baptist was ready and willing to accept – indeed he felt **he must**- because he recognised the supreme importance of who Jesus was, and the vital life of eternity that only Jesus could give.

Perhaps we sometimes foolishly get this verse reversed in our lives – that Jesus sometimes becomes less rather than greater, because our lives grow busy, our plans get bigger, and our preferences become more earthbound.

✝ *Forbid it Lord that I should boast, save in the death of Christ my God;*
All the vain things that charm me most, I sacrifice them to His blood. Amen.

♥ Go on! Put your personal preferences on a diet!

4th December

Self Denial

John 12 : 25

"The man who loves his life will lose it, while the man who hates his life in this world will keep it for eternal life."

Sometimes people get pretty close to hating their lives in this world – life has become dark and burdensome and they feel dejected and defeated in a way that is very hard to overcome. Sometimes our sensitivity and availability may be vital in helping a friend through such an experience.

However in today's verse Jesus is talking about a different kind of hating of life – he means hating the dangers that are lurking in the background when life is sweet and good. He's talking about making a very deliberate decision that we will not fall in love with our own agenda for life, so much so that we miss out on what only Jesus can give us – willingly accepting this constant constraint because we know and believe that only Jesus holds the key of life, both now and into eternity.

This is the only strong foundation for life, both when it is going well, and when it is tough and difficult.

✝ *Lord of eternal life, help me to hate my life when I am in danger of loving it too much – and help me to love others when they are in danger of hating their lives too much. Amen.*

♥ Get a wee bit of hate into your life today!

5th December

Self Denial

Galatians 5 : 22 – 23

"But the fruit of the Spirit is love, joy, peace, patience, kindness, goodness, faithfulness, gentleness and self-control, against such things there is no law."

☞ Today is the anniversary of the opening of the first stretch of motorway in the U.K. – the beginning of a network that was supposed to open up the country, bringing huge travelling benefits. Perhaps if you have ever sat in a motorway queue you might have your doubts.

We need have no such doubts about the positive benefits of opening up our lives to the activity of the Holy Spirit. When the Spirit has unhindered access, He is able to produce very good results, bringing honour to God, help to other people, and harmony to our own living – results which are indisputably good.

No matter how hard we try or how far we travel, by ourselves we cannot really achieve or sustain the lovely qualities listed in today's text. They are the result of a journey begun in faith with Jesus Christ, continued and completed in the fellowship of the Spirit, whom Jesus promised would come to be our Helper.

✝ *Lord help me, today, to clear away some of the obstacles which inhibit Your access to my life and which limit Your opportunities to produce the lovely fruit of the Spirit. Amen.*

♥ There is a big open road ahead of you today and you have power under the bonnet – you can go places with Christ, and for Christ!

Robert Bell

6th December

Stress

📖 Psalm 38 : 8

"I am utterly spent and crushed; I groan because of the tumult of my heart."

☞ In Psalm 38 David describes what it is like to hit rock bottom. Physically, he was suffering extreme pain. Mentally, he was 'utterly spent and crushed', (v 8). Spiritually, he was in 'tumult (v 8 b). Socially, all his friends avoided him 'like the plague' (v 11) while his enemies were 'cock-a-hoop' at his plight (v 12).

Why was he suffering so much? David says, "because of my sin" (v 3). Not only did he recognise that, he was genuinely sorry (v 18) and made no attempt to shift the blame. How difficult it is to admit that we have been at fault, that we have absolutely no excuses and that all we can do is hang our heads in sorrow and say, "My fault; mine alone; to my great shame".

When like David, we have gone wrong and confessed our fault, the Bible has one final word…WAIT! Wait for the Lord (v 15).

Few things benefit the soul so much as waiting in hope for the Lord.

✝ *Lord, when I have been foolish and brought misery upon myself, give me the grace to recognise my sin, to acknowledge it as my very own and to wait upon You alone for mercy through Christ Jesus. Amen.*

♥ A summer assistant was visiting at a particular home. When he rang the doorbell he noticed the shadow of someone moving around inside, but no one answered the door. He decided to leave a note. On it he wrote, "I called to visit … Revelation 3: 20." The reference reads, "Behold I stand at the door and knock. If anyone hears my voice and opens the door, I will come in". The following Sunday morning he was shaking hands at the door after the service and as the lady from the house was coming she slipped him a note. On it was another reference, Genesis 3 : 19, which is ... "I heard you in the garden and I was afraid because I was naked; so I hid".

7th December Stress

Proverbs 12 : 25

"Worry weighs us down; encouragement picks us up".

☞ One cause of anxiety, familiar to some of us, is the experience of having a child leave 'the nest' and go to university. Imagine how the parents felt who received this letter: -

Dear Mum and Dad,

I've fallen in love with a fellow called Pat. We've been going together for 9 weeks and are getting married in the Spring. Meanwhile I have moved into his flat – I think I might be pregnant. I have dropped out of university. Pat says that it's a waste of time.

On the next page she continued-

Mum and Dad, what I have written above is completely ***untrue****. But it* ***is*** *true that I got very disappointing results in my first tests. (*Story adapted from 'Growing strong in the seasons of life' by Charles R. Swindoll)

A bright girl! Even disappointing results can sound like good news from a certain perspective. When we see the things that 'weigh us down' in the perspective of God's unfailing goodness, that is sure to 'pick us up'.

✝ *Thank You Lord that You care about me more than I care about myself. Help me to view all my worries and fears in the light of Your overwhelming grace through Jesus. Amen*

♥ Somebody once said, "You needn't try to tell me that worrying doesn't make any difference, because nothing I worry about ever happens!"

8th December Stress

📖 Jonah 2 : 1-2

"From inside the fish Jonah prayed to the Lord his God. He said: "In my distress I called to the Lord, and He answered me. From the depths of the grave I called for help and You listened to my cry."

☞ As he was sinking in the depths Jonah cried out to the Lord using words from the Psalms (compare the verse above with Ps. 120 : 1 and Ps. 86 : 13). So often in our darkest hours we find the Psalms give expression to the deepest yearnings of our hearts.

It is very striking to notice the change halfway through this verse. When Jonah begins he is speaking **about** the Lord: "He answered me..." but then we find him speaking **to** the Lord: -.. "You listened **to** my cry". There is all the difference in the world between speaking about the Lord and speaking to Him. So often it is when the Lord leads us through dark and difficult days that we pour out our hearts to Him and rediscover an intimacy, which is precious beyond words. Whenever we pass through the depths we can find ourselves drawn closer to the Lord than ever before.

✝ *Lord, whenever my heart grows faint, lead me to the rock that is higher than I. For You have always been my refuge, a strong tower against the enemy of my soul. Search me, O Lord and know my heart; test me and know my anxious thoughts. See if there is any offensive way in me and lead me in the everlasting way, for Jesus' sake. Amen.*

♥ Two little boys met. "How old are you?" "I'm five. How old are you?" "I don't know". "You don't know how old you are?" "No" "Do women bother you?" "No". "You're four".

9th December **Stress**

📖 Matthew 11 : 28

"Jesus said, "Come to me, all you who are weary and burdened, and I will give you rest."

☞ The invitation to come to Christ and find rest for our souls is inseparably connected with the next verse, "Take my yoke upon you and learn from me...and you will find rest for your souls". (Matthew 11 : 29)

At first sight the two statements jar. Why on earth would someone who is 'weary and burdened' volunteer to take on a yoke? When we understand how a yoke works we can see the link.

A good yoke is formed to follow the contours of an individual ox's neck. Otherwise there will be places where the wood presses against the skin causing pressure sores. The animal becomes very restless and cannot work. A good yoke fits snugly around the ox's neck and distributes the stress evenly. He can then comfortably haul heavy loads for years without developing any pressure sores.

People who suffer from excessive stress in some area of life do not find rest for their souls by doing nothing. That leads to total frustration! The pressure needs to be redistributed in a way, which suits that individual, enabling them to achieve without suffering.

To give us inner peace, Jesus calls us to customized workloads.

✝ *Father, You have promised to make me lie down in green pastures and lead me by still waters, restoring my soul. Help me to recognise that if I find myself unable to lie down and relax, because of the flood of responsibilities, which threaten to overwhelm me, then I mustn't be on the right track. Grant that I may learn to know the difference between being driven by personal ambition and being led by You.*

O Lord, lead me in the paths which are right, for Your Name's sake. Amen.

♥ A sign was erected outside a house, which said, **"This house and land will be given to anyone who is truly content."** A wealthy businessman who was passing saw it, and thought, "I am a rich man and have all that I need, so I certainly qualify. I'll claim the land before someone else does".

He went to the door and explained he was there to claim the land "Are you truly content?' the owner asked. "Yes I am. I have everything I need". "Well, if you are truly content, what do you want this house for?"

10th December

Stress

Philippians 4 : 6-7

"Do not be anxious about anything, but in everything, by prayer and petition, with thanksgiving, present your requests to God. And the peace of God, which transcends all understanding, will guard your hearts and your minds in Christ Jesus."

☞ Paul wrote, "Do not be anxious about anything." Was he never anxious? Of course he was. In this same letter he tells the Philippians that he is sending Epaphroditus "so that you may be glad and I may have less anxiety". (Chapter 2 : 28) Paul knew about anxiety.

Is it wrong to be concerned for our loved ones and our churches? Not at all! So what is the difference between concern which is right and good and anxiety which is not? A proper concern is heaven-born, depends on the Lord and resonates with hope, joy and grace. Anxiety is earthbound, totally absorbed with human problems and human solutions and is graceless, joyless, hopeless and debilitating. To transform earthbound anxiety to heaven born concern we must shift the focus from earth to heaven by "prayer and petition with thanksgiving". That is why the Scriptures tell us, "Cast all your anxiety on Him, because He cares for you". (1 Peter 5 : 7).

✝ *Father, as the fog hides the sunlight, so the gloom of circumstance and incident hide the light of Your love. In Your grace take me by the hand. Then I will know that even though I may stumble, You will not fall. Father I cast all my anxiety upon You. In Jesus' Name. Amen.*

♥ A minister was walking down a street when he saw a little boy at one of the doors trying to reach the bell. However, he was just too small, so the minister went over and rang it for him. He turned to the boy with a smile and asked, "What will we do now?" The boy replied, "Run".

Alison McCaughan

11th December — Assurance

1 John 3 : 1

"How great is the love the Father has lavished on us, that we should be called children of God! And that is what we are! The reason the world does not know us is that it did not know him."

☞ How do I know and how can I be sure that I am a true Christian? Is it not a bit arrogant for someone to say of himself that he is a Christian and that he is on his way to heaven? Is it not like saying I'm better than others? Have you ever heard or perhaps even asked questions similar to these?

To say I am a Christian in the New Testament is not a personal commendation of oneself and ones achievement. It is simply a statement of fact about a relationship. It is similar to saying that "I am a son of my father." Now I did nothing to bring that about but I am without doubt a son of my father, it is not a boast, simply a statement of fact.

In the same way when someone says "I am a Christian and I am sure about it" - it is not some boast about a quality he feels he has achieved in his life - it is a statement of fact about what God has done for him. How amazing, as John puts it 'we are the children of God'.

Likewise the New Testament refers to the Christian as one who is united to Christ as in marriage. I have just recently completed a mortgage application form. One of the first questions asked was Are you married? Now it wasn't asking me was I an exemplary husband, I am not, and it would be odd if I answered "not sure". So we are married to Christ when we come to Him in repentance and faith. We are not making claims about our goodness but simply describing a fact.

✝ *Loving Father, thank You that You have lavished Your love on me day after day. Amen.*

♥ Notice outside Kentucky Fried Chicken:- 'Save a cow, eat a chicken instead.'

12th December Assurance

📖 Romans 8 : 16

"The Spirit himself testifies with our spirit that we are God's children."

☞ One of the wards I like to visit in hospital is the maternity ward. It is a great pleasure to be able to share the joy experienced by parents at the arrival of a baby. One of the first questions I am invariably asked is "Who is she/he like?" "Isn't he the picture of his father?" or "She's got her mothers eyes but her fathers temperament don't you think?" and so it goes on. In most families there is a strong family resemblance between parents and children and through time children begin to share not only their parents looks but their parents interests and habits as well : its the sign of being in the family.

The Bible tells us that one of the signs we know we are Christian is that we are becoming more like our Father who is in Heaven. We have new interests: reading the Bible, praying, worshipping God together, sharing the good news, new desires, especially the desire to know God more and more, new joys in seeing people become believers themselves and new tears, tears of sorrow at sin and ungodliness in the world and tears of repentance over our own sin.

Have you noticed your life changing? Has the Holy Spirit begun to reshape and remould your desires so that they are based not upon self but upon God? Give thanks, for this is confirmation of your salvation. This is the spirit bearing witness with our spirit that we are the children of God.

✝ *Gracious God and Loving Heavenly Father help me change my life so that it is not based on me but on You. Amen.*

♥ Bumps make you bitter or better.

13th December — Assurance

📖 Hebrews 10 : 22
"Let us draw near to God with a sincere heart in full assurance of faith, having our hearts sprinkled to cleanse us from a guilty conscience and having our bodies washed with pure water."

☞ It is not an uncommon thing for a Christian from time to time to lack assurance. It happens to far more people than those who would care to admit it, perhaps because they feel, mistakenly, that it is a sin to doubt. Some of the greatest Christians in history went through times of real doubting, not least John Newton who wrote that lovely hymn "Amazing Grace". Do you at times lack assurance? You are not on your own.

This does not however mean that we are to do nothing about it. Sometimes there are hindrances to assurance which with Gods grace and help we can overcome. Let me make a suggestion:

Assurance can be hindered because we do not have a clear understanding in our minds about the truths of Gods word. An understanding of Gods word in our minds is so vitally associated with assurance in our hearts. For example one of the major reasons so many people lack assurance is because they cannot point to a day or date in which they were converted. But the actual date according to scripture has nothing to do with it because salvation is not what 'I' do but what God has done in me. (Hebrews 10 : 22). So the vital issue is not that you know a date, give thanks if you do, but that you have evidence of the new birth in your life. So it is important in our minds to have a clear understanding of the doctrines of the Christian faith. Doctrine is not supplemental, it is fundamental, it is not 'pie in the sky' but liberating and life at its most real.

✝ *Dear Father let me understand clearly the truth of Your word and help me share this joy with others. Amen*

♥ Anti - drink sign: 'Too many cans and you can't.'

14th December — Assurance

📖 Psalm 119 : 11

"I have hidden your word in my heart that I might not sin against you."

☞ One of my great passions in life is football. A few weeks after being installed in my congregations I formed a football team to play in a local league. Our first friendly match was against the local Parachute Regiment, which was based in our village. We were annihilated 8-0 not surprising considering we were inexperienced, totally unco-ordinated, unfit and overweight. We knew why we were sunk without trace so we went on training programmes, lost weight and got some expert help. Six months later we beat the same team 2-1. Obvious obstacles had to be overcome and they were, temporarily at least! Some times Christians are sunk without trace in the Christian life through lack of assurance. More often than not this, assurance is hindered because of our daily living and walking with God, or lack of it. In this there are two clear obstacles to full assurance of faith.

Firstly neglecting the public and private reading of Gods word, worship and prayer. One of the first questions we need to ask ourselves if we have doubts and lack of assurance is this "When was the last time I read my Bible and prayed?" or "How many weeks have I been absent from worship and the prayer meeting?" God has given us His word and the privilege of prayer and worship, neglect these in the modern world and we are sunk.

The second main area in our spiritual life, which hinders assurance is a carelessness with regards to sin. If we are careless about sin, if we are knowingly disobeying God we will never find peace and contentment as a Christian. But if we confess our sins then we are forgiven.

✝ *Dear Father, help me walk with You daily. Help me listen to others about what You mean in their lives. Amen*

♥ Child talking to Mum: "Mum, do you remember that valuable antique vase that you told me had been handed down from generation to generation?" "Yes." "Well, this generation just dropped it."

15th December — Assurance

📖 John 10 : 14

"I am the good shepherd: I tell you the truth, the man who does not enter the sheep pen by the gate, but climbs in by some other way, is a thief and a robber…."

☞ The village of Pomeroy where I live is the highest village in Northern Ireland, situated in the foothills of the Sperrin Mountains. It is sheep breeding country and many in my congregations are Shepherds. For us John chapter 10, the story of the Good Shepherd is particularly meaningful, especially when it comes to the topic of Assurance. Three thoughts from this passage; remember Jesus is the Shepherd, the Christians are the sheep.

(1) THE SHEPHERD OWNS THE SHEEP verses 3,4,12
That is the first thing that may be said about the true shepherd and His sheep. He owns them. The Christian belongs to Jesus because He laid down His life to redeem them, and verse 29 puts it even more profoundly- the Christian belongs to Jesus because God has given us to Him as His love gift, just as a father gives his daughter in marriage to her groom.

(2) JESUS KNOWS THEM verse 14
Just as God knows Jesus so Jesus knows us if we are Christians. This is quite astounding, to think that the Lord Jesus knows us and is related to us in the same sense that is comparable between the Father and the Son. Is that not mind blowing!!!

(3) HE CARES FOR THE SHEEP verse 11
This is a personal care, not a pretended care which is so prevalent in the world. Jesus knows the depth of our character, our personality, our need- there is not a corner of our life that Jesus doesn't know, there is not a sin He is not aware of and not a sorrow that He hasn't entered into with us. The measure of this? He laid down His life for us.

Can we say with faith and confidence "Blessed Assurance this Jesus is MINE"?

✝ *Thank You good Shepherd for taking care of me. Amen.*

♥ Notice in church bulletin: The church flowers are always given to the sick after the service. Next week the Ladies Guild will hold a rubbish sale. Don't forget to bring your husbands!

William Bingham

16th December — God as Reconciler

Isaiah 2 : 4

"He will judge between the nations and will settle disputes for many peoples. They will beat their swords into plowshares and their spears into pruning hooks. Nation will not take up sword against nation nor will they train for war any more."

☞ Swords and spears are sharp instruments. They are crafted to penetrate flesh, precipitate bleeding and cause death. Their use leads to tears, pain and loss. They seek to destroy what God has made and loved. People feel they need swords and spears if they want to defend themselves from other swords and spears, or they are pure instruments of hate.

Plough shares and pruning hooks are also sharp instruments. They are crafted to penetrate the ground, they are useful tools in preparing the ground to receive seeds and nurture further growth. The farmer is using them to work with God's creation to bear fruit.

We need to learn the ways of the Lord so that our grip on swords and spears is loosened; as we learn to love the Lord more, we fear our enemies less. In turn we are set free to tighten our grip on plough shares and pruning hooks, in consequence we work with God rather than against Him.

✝ Lord we confess that we are fascinated by swords and spears, they make us feel safe and secure, yet we know that Your Word offer us a more secure defense. Lord help us to work with You rather than against You in building peace and hope in our land.

♥ An exasperated mother whose son was always getting into mischief finally asked him "How do you expect to get into heaven?" the boy thought it over and said, "Well I'll just run in and out and in and out and keep slamming the door until St. Peter says, "For heaven's sake Jimmy, come in or stay out."

17th December God as Reconciler

📖 Matthew 5 : 23 - 24

"Therefore if you are offering your gift at the altar and there remember that your brother has something against you, leave your gift there in front of the altar. First go and be reconciled to your brother; then come and offer your gift."

☞ Bad relationships and good worship don't mix easily. Tensions between worshippers affect the atmosphere, family members sitting on the opposite side of the church because of some argument a generation ago over a field does not help the whole congregation to worship together in spirit and in truth.

Some people attempt to ignore the conflict in the vain hope that it will go away. God notices when we carry into our worship, hatred, envy or tension. Before He answers our prayers He wants us to go and sort out our relationships. Without that reconciliation, then God says in Amos 5 : 21 ' I hate, I despise your religious feasts; I cannot stand your assemblies'. Who do you need to talk to before Sunday?

✝ *Lord You are a relationship Father, Son and Holy Spirit; You are concerned about the quality of our relationships. You want our relationships to reflect Your justice and mercy. Forgive us if we divorce our worship from our relationships. As You have poured Your grace on us, may we pour out that grace on others. Amen.*

♥ As Bill, a pillar of the community, came out of church he whispered to the minister; "That was wonderful for **them.**"

18th December God as Reconciler

📖 2 Corinthians 5 : 18 – 21

"All this is from God, who reconciled us to Himself through Christ and gave us the ministry of reconciliation: that God was reconciling the world to Himself in Christ. Not counting men's sin against them. And He has committed to us the message of reconciliation. We are therefore Christ's ambassadors as though God was making his appeal through us. We implore you on Christ's behalf: Be reconciled to God. God made Him who had no sin to be sin for us, so that in Him we might become the righteousness of God."

☞ It was a moment of embarrassment. I was introducing to a cross-Community Church Forum two people from the trade union movement who had been asked to give us training on handling our sectarianism. One of them was an atheist. I had to admit that we in the churches had much to learn from people who were working together on the factory floor.

Ironic isn't it! Reconciliation was God's idea. Paul makes it clear. 'All this is from God'. Yet in the churches in parts of Ireland we have marginalised reconciliation to the fringes of church life. Even worse we have often misused theology to make reconciliation more difficult. Words like listening, understanding,forgiving often comes more easily to worldly people than churchy people. Yet if Christians cannot be ambassadors of reconciliation, have we been reconciled to God at all?

✝ *God You are passionate about reconciliation. You just love to see people dwelling together in true unity. You gave up Your own Son to make reconciliation possible. You hurt when Your people despise each other. For when we hate someone else we hate You. Lord teach us to be as passionate about reconciliation as You are. Amen.*

♥ Today is the anniversary of our marriage. Now wasn't that a piece of inspired reconciliation? All this is from God.

19th December — God as Reconciler

📖 Ephesians 2 : 16

"And in this one body to reconcile both of them to God through the Cross, by which he put to death their hostility."

☞ I write this in July 1999 in Co. Armagh. My neighbourhood is filled with images of hostility. You can see them on flagpoles and gable walls. Hostility has become a way of life in Mid Ulster. Paul lived in a similar environment. Gentiles and Jews were two separate tribes. They had a long violent history of hostility. They were divided by religion, culture and language.

Yet Jesus died on the Cross for both Jew and Gentile. God is big enough to love opposites at the same time, Jews and Gentiles, older brother and younger brother, Protestants and Catholics, Residents Groups and Orangemen. In God's sight we are all sinners in need of a Saviour. The Cross cuts right through our ancient hostilities. It removes our pride and give us the courage to be crucified ourselves as we reach out both hands to both tribes in our community.

✝ *Lord You reach out to younger brothers who run away to foreign lands but You also reach out to elder brothers who stay self-righteously at home. Your Father heart is broken by their ancient quarrel. Lord give us Your grace to reach out to elder and younger brothers in our families, congregations and communities. Amen.*

♥ 'Dirty Little Rascals' is a film about boys growing up. One boy is alienated from his friends for the gross sin of liking girls. The film concludes with him telling the other boys, "I want to be friends with you as boys but you must realise I will also be fond of girls". God is big enough to love both friends and enemies simultaneously.

20th December — God as Reconciler

📖 Colossians 1 : 20

"And through Him to reconcile to himself all things whether things on earth or things in Heaven by making peace through His blood shed on the Cross."

☞ Babies make good reconcilers. I wonder why? It is not their grasp of language for they only coo, gurgle and cry. It is not their size for they can be carried in one hand. It is their lack of threat, their powerlessness, and their vulnerability that gives them the power to bring families together around the cot smiling and wondering who he or she looks like. Babies bring perspective to life. Hatred, envy and pride seem inappropriate before this tiny face. In a manger in Bethlehem lay one who was a special baby. The one who was the firstborn of all creation chose to become a helpless vulnerable baby. He later became even more vulnerable shedding His own blood on the Cross. His powerlessness, His vulnerability, His love is the best model for all who seek to be reconcilers in our communities.

✝ *Thank You for Jesus for giving to us a baby. The same one who created the earth also gurgles helplessly in a dirty stable in Bethlehem. Lord teach us to be helpless children before You so that we might be born again into Your family. Amen.*

♥ The mother-in–law looked at the newly born baby and commented to her son–in–law "Lovely child, beautiful, not a bit like you".

Tony Davidson

21st December — Christmas

📖 Micah 5 : 2

"But you, Bethlehem Ephrath, though you are small among the clans of Judah, out of you will come for me one who will be the ruler over Israel, whose origins are from of old, from ancient times."

☞ Bethlehem was a real 'one horse town', small and insignificant. Yet, in the midst of the Assyrian attack on Judah, it was not the strong fortress of Jerusalem that would provide the true deliverer. Bethlehem was where the Messiah would be born. Isn't that often God's way? In fulfilling His promises and building His kingdom He often uses that which is insignificant and weak. As Paul says (1 Corinthians 1 : 27 – 29) God chose 'the weak things of the world to shame the strong … so that no one may boast". A speaker was preparing for a meeting at which he was to use a projector, but it wouldn't work. He was getting frustrated, until his young son asked, "Dad, have you prayed about it?" Admitting that he hadn't, his son then prayed simply that God would make the projector work, so that his Daddy could tell about Jesus. And it did. God can use us whoever we are, so that His name can be glorified.

✝ *Almighty God, thank You that You use the insignificant and weak to fulfil Your purpose; use me as You desire. Amen.*

♥ It's not the reputation of the person that counts, but the greatness of our God that is really Important

---

22nd December Christmas

📖 Isaiah 9 : 2

"The people walking in darkness have seen a great light; on those living in the shadow of death a light has dawned."

☞ At this time of year we are accustomed to physical darkness, it's there when we get up in the morning, and comes round again in mid-afternoon. Thank God for electricity. Yet there are other kinds of darkness, the darkness of being oppressed, as the people of Northern Israel were by the Assyrians; the darkness caused by suffering or being alone to face life pressures, or of the occult, or the darkness caused by suffering or death. Back in Isaiah's time God promised to shine a great light in the region where the darkness was worst, namely Galilee. The coming of Jesus Christ was not only light for Galilee but also light for the whole world, and hence the light for every one of us. The dark path you tread may not be removed, but Jesus promises to walk through the darkness with us if we will but turn to Him daily in faith and trust.

✝ *Father God, Your light will never go out; shine on me and on those areas of life that are dark, that I might reflect Your light to all around me. Amen.*

♥ Arise, shine, your light has come...Jesus the light of the world has come. (G. Kendrick).

23rd December — Christmas

📖 John 1 : 9 - 10

"The true light that gives light to every man was coming into the world. He was in the world, and though the world was made through Him, the world did not recognise Him."

☞ What does John mean by 'true'? Not the opposite of lying. Rather the opposite of spurious or counterfeit. And what a lot of counterfeit there is in Christmas celebrations, cards sent because 'they sent us one', presents bought without thought because 'they'll expect one', or the false bonhomie of the office party...Yes, there are a lot of things done that will bring little lasting light into people's lives.

Yet there is genuine light in our world already, available for each of us. He has been around before any of us ever existed. He wants to bring light and meaning and joy to your world. Will you take off your blinkers, and so recognise Him as Your creator and Your redeemer? Will you put your faith and trust in Him today?

'Joy to the world!
The Lord has come:
Let earth receive her king,
Let every heart prepare him room...'
(I Watts)

✝ *Almighty God, I want to stop depending on the counterfeit, and to place the genuine in the midst of my life. I ask You to work in me that I might truly see and act on it. Amen.*

♥ To see the real meaning of Christmas, focus on Jesus.

24th December — Christmas

📖 Titus 2 : 11

"For the grace of God that brings salvation has appeared to all men."

☞ She was perhaps in her mid-40s, but her life style and its consequences gave her an older look. "Are you telling me that God could be interested in me? Surely He wouldn't want to have anything to do with me. I'll never be good enough for Him". How right she was, and yet how wrong. Right that she'd never be good enough. (She recognised that, whereas many others do not!) But she was wrong in thinking that God would have no time for her. For God's grace means that His love and forgiveness is for all men and women, young and old, upright citizen and down-and-out. It's His grace that can change people. And nowhere do we see that grace more clearly than in the coming of Jesus into our sinful world. The birth of Jesus is not a sentimental story. It is about a new power coming into the world, which can change lives and give us moral strength. It's for everybody, by faith and trust.

✝ *Gracious God, in Your love You desire all of us to know You. Sometimes I find that hard to understand. Work in me, deep in my heart, so that I'll really know it. Amen.*

♥ Jesus puts the joy in Christmas.

25th December Christmas

📖 Luke 2 ; 11

"Today in the town of David a Saviour has been born to you, he is Christ the Lord."

☞ Just as the Shepherds received the glorious news, so can we. 'A Saviour has been born **to you'**. They went to check it out and saw the child lying in a manager. They rejoiced in what God had done, and went back to their Judean hillsides unable to keep quiet about what had happened. Their lives would never be the same again.

That message comes to us as well, God's message of how He is offering hope for the future, real love and someone to have faith in, namely Jesus, who wants to be our Saviour today and everyday.

May our lives be different because of the coming of Jesus into our world. In the midst of fun and enjoyment may we take time to check the story, time to reflect, to worship and give praise and thanksgiving to God.

A blessed and a peaceful Christmas to you.

✝ *Father God, I've been so busy these last few weeks. Give me space today to stop and see all that Jesus' coming can mean to me. Amen.*

♥ 'O Holy child of Bethlehem,
Descend to us, we pray;
Cast out our sin, and enter in
Be born in us today'.
(Phillips Brooks)

Alistair Bill

26th December — Reward

📖 Genesis 15 : 1

"After this, the word of the Lord came to Abram in a vision: 'Do not be afraid, Abram. I am your shield, your very great reward."

☞ A friend who has suffered much in recent years and who is in constant pain told me recently that while she was not afraid to die, she was afraid to live, the future filled her with foreboding. What causes you apprehension?

On return from a successful military campaign Abram tried to settle down to the pastoral life but was prevented from doing so by feelings of loneliness, disappointment and depression which swept over him. Only a word from the Lord could help and it came. Believing people need to know that there is an impenetrable, invisible shield, which will protect them in every situation. God is that shield but He is much more. "I am …your very great reward". The reward of faith is God Himself. Someone once said, "To be destitute of God is to be bereft of everything: to have God is to have all." One of the great verses of the New Testament says, "Seek first the Kingdom of God and all these things will be added to you."

✝ *Lord there is no one I need more than You. Draw near to me and take away all my fears: fears of the past, of the present and of the future. Be my shield and my very great reward this day. Amen.*

♥ An interim minister had not gained a great deal of favour or approval from the congregation. Not even the portable microphone co-operated. Attempting hopelessly to fix it before the service, he mumbled to himself, "I wish they would get rid of this thing." The congregation dutifully responded, "And also with you".

27th December — Reward

📖 Matthew 5 : 11 – 12

"Blessed are you when people insult you, persecute you and falsely say all kinds of evil against you because of me. Rejoice and be glad, because your reward is great in heaven, for in the same way they persecuted the prophets who were before you."

☞ Even though Jesus set his standards high there were twelve young men who were willing to follow Him. Early on they had to get used to the idea that life with this man was not going to be a picnic. In this verse from the Sermon on the Mount, Jesus reminds them that persecution has always been the lot of God's faithful servants and it was going to be no different for them. Do you realise that there have been more Christian martyrs in the twentieth than in any other century since the first? When someone is called to suffer for Christ that is always a crucial moment. To have a share in such a moment is not a penalty but a glory. "Rejoice at such a moment and be glad" says Jesus. The Greek word he uses means to leap exceedingly. Spare a thought for heaven today because, after all, it's God's reward for those who are faithful to Him.

✝ *Lord, help me today to be faithful to You whatever the cost may be. Amen.*

♥ A minister was telling his grandson a thrilling bedtime story. The little lad was listening breathlessly. When grandfather stopped he asked, "Grandpa, is that a true story or were you just preaching again?"

28th December — Reward

📖 Luke 6 : 35

"But love your enemies, do good to them, and lend to them without expecting to get anything back. Then your reward will be great, and you will be sons of the Most High, because He is kind to the ungrateful and wicked."

☞ No command of Jesus has caused so much discussion and debate. People are uneasy with it and try qualifying it. We can think of a dozen reasons why we should not love our enemies. But it is uncompromising. Nor is it enough to refrain from hostile acts towards our enemies, we are to do good to them, even lend to them when there may not be a hope of ever getting anything back. That seems O.T.T. How on earth do you begin to do something that is so unnatural? Why not do what Jesus suggested on another occasion – pray for your enemies? When we pray for someone it may be that the person will not change but we will. Abraham Lincoln in response to urges to punish the South said "Do I not destroy my enemies when I make them my friends?"

✝ *Lord, I confess to You that I do not find it easy to love my enemies so please come and love them through me. Amen.*

♥ One winter evening during a violent thunderstorm a mother was tucking her small boy into bed. She was about to turn off the light when he asked with a tremor in his voice, "Mummy, will you sleep with me tonight?" The mother smiled and gave him a reassuring hug. "I can't dear", she said. "I have to sleep in Daddy's room". A long silence was broken at last by a shaken little voice saying, "The big sissy".

29th December — Reward

📖 1 Corinthians 3 : 12 –14

"If any man build on this foundation using gold, silver, costly stones, wood, hay or straw, his work will be shown for what it is, because the Day will bring it to light. It will be revealed with fire, and the fire will test the quality of each man's work. If what he has built survives, he will receive his reward."

☞ In Old Testament days a building was the temple or house of God, now it is God's people who are so called. A building is not to be a 'holy place', rather God's people are called to be a holy people. But God's building is still under construction and we are each building on a foundation that has already been laid (1 Corinthians 3 : 11). Take care how you build. Why? Because examination day is coming and examinations reveal everything, what is known and what is not known. What is the reward for passing this building exam? Paul writes to the Thessalonians, 'Are you not our crown of rejoicing?' I think the reward is simply joy, joy in knowing that your life has counted. So ask yourself, what is my life going to count for? Will my work last? Will it stand the test of time? On that great Day, will I be filled with joy because my life was invested in what was really worthwhile?

✝ *Lord help me to invest my life wisely and well. Preserve me from getting caught up with things which yield a quick, but no lasting reward. Amen.*

♥ An avid golfer wanted to know if there would be golf in heaven. After much search and prayer, God sent Gabriel to this man. "I have good news and bad news," said Gabriel. "The good news is that there will be golf in heaven. The bad news is that you have a tee time for 3 o'clock this afternoon.

30th December — Reward

📖 Hebrews 11: 6

"And without faith it is impossible to please God, because anyone who comes to Him must believe that He exists and that He rewards those who earnestly seek Him."

☞ People go to all sorts of ends to please God, to get on side with God when all that is needed is simple 'faith'! Have you heard of the little girl who wrote, 'Faith is trying to believe what you know isn't true'?' Of course this is a total misconception of faith. In our day–to–day relationships we exercise faith when we take someone at their word and there is nothing that pleases God so much as when people take Him at His word. Enoch did just that and by his daily reliance he pleased God. The Bible is full of promises. Why don't you claim one today? The moment you do, start praising Him and in doing so you indicate that you are taking Him at His word. Your reward will be an exciting life of faith.

✝ *Lord help me to walk with You today and every day in sure and simple trust. Amen.*

♥ The treasurer of the Ladies Aid Society went to the town bank to make a deposit for the society. Handing the money and book to the teller, she said: "Here's the Aid money," The teller thought she said "egg money" and desiring to be pleasant, remarked: "Well, the old hens certainly were busy last week, weren't they?"

31st December — Reward

📖 Proverbs 3 : 5-6

"Trust in the Lord with all your heart and lean not on your own understanding; in all your ways acknowledge Him, and he will make your paths straight."

☞ There is no better note to end the year and embark on a new one than that which is contained in this verse. There is no greater wisdom to be offered or received than that which is contained in it. The picture is of a squad of labourers, under expert supervision, preparing the route for the royal progress of a great king. Part of their task is to remove all the obstacles, which would block progress. All of us desire our paths to be made straight, but the Lord cannot do this for us until we forsake our own insights and inclinations, and trust Him absolutely. For some of us this might be very difficult and will involve some major re-adjustments to our lives, like enthroning Jesus Christ as King. But that is a small price to pay when you consider the rewards.

✝ *Lord thank You for Your faithfulness to me in the past: as I put my hand in Yours, lead me in Your way throughout the remaining years of my life. Amen.*

♥ The minister was ready to baptize the baby. "What name will you give to him? " he asked the parents. "You will be happy, Pastor, for we have picked a name from the Bible," the couple eagerly offered. "Wonderful", exclaimed the minister. "Is it Abraham or Moses or Caleb?" " No," the parents responded. "We named him Genuine Moroccan Leather".

Russell Birney

The world is passing through troubled times. The young people of today think of nothing but themselves. They have no reverence for parents or old age; they are impatient of all restraint; they talk as if they alone know everything, and what passes for wisdom with us is foolishness with them. As for the girls, they are foolish and immodest and unwomanly in speech, behaviour and dress. (Peter the Hermit; 1274)

The Lord bless you and keep you.
The Lord make His face to shine upon you.
The Lord lift up His countenance upon you,
and grant you His peace. (Numbers 6 v 24-26)

LIST OF CONTRIBUTORS

Agnew Noel: Minister of Bellaghy and Knockloughrim Presbyterian Churches. On Committee of Portstewart Convention. Hobbies and Interests: Golf, Motorbikes and Fishing Boats. January 21st – 25th

Bain Des: General Secretary, Methodist Home Mission Dept. Dublin and Belfast. Des is married to Valerie; they have 2 children Darren and Trevor. Hobbies and Interests: Woodturning, Fishing, Soccer (watching!) but especially doing things as a family.
November 1st – 5th

Bell Robert: Minister of Ballyclare Presbyterian Church. Robert is married to Christine, they have 4 children,: Kathryn, Suzanne, Louise and Alistair. Hobbies and Interests: Supporting Manchester United and Ballyclare Comrades! December 1st – 5th

Bill Alistair: Minister at Saintfield Road Presbyterian Church. Alaistair is married to Angela; they have 3 children, Sarah, Hannah and Andrew. Hobbies and Interests: Walking, D.I.Y and Sports
(From the armchair). December 21st – 25th

Bingham Derick: Teaching Pastor with Christ Church, Belfast. He is the author of 17 books and also a broadcaster, teaching across Europe weekly by satellite. Derick is married to Margaret, they have 3 children, Kathryn and twins Kerrie and Claire. Hobbies and Interests: Director of the New Irish Choir and Orchestra. January 26th – 30th.

Bingham William: Minister of Pomeroy and Sandholes Congregations, Co. Tyrone. William is married to Janet, they have 2 children: Stephen and Amy. Hobbies and Interests: Football (Liverpool) and Golf. December 11th – 15th.

Birney Russell: Minister of High Kirk Presbyterian Church, Ballymena. Russell is married to Arline, they have 3 daughters Emma, Sarah and

Claire. Hobbies and Interests: Walking in the Alps and watching sport! December 26th – 31st.

Boyd David: Irish Mission worker working with Dolebusters, an Adelaide Road Donore Presbyterian Church social action project in Dublin City Centre. David is married to Jenny and they have four children, Joel, Ethan, Cara and Jordan. His interests are every sport ever invented, computers and reading. May 10th – 14th

Bradley Doug: Minister at Ballycrochan Presbyterian Church, Bangor, Co Down. Lectures part-time in Belfast Bible College. Doug is married to Janice , they have 3 children, Caroline, Nicky and Michael. Hobbies and Interests: Music, Sport and Walking. February 20th – 24th

Bruce David: General Director, Scripture Union Northern Ireland. David is married to Zoe, they have 4 children, James, Anna, Ellen and Harry. Hobbies and Interests: Golf and Donegal. July 24th – 28th.

Burke Rev. Dr. David: Former Moderator of the General Assembly and Senior Minister of Hamilton Road Presbyterian Church, Bangor. David was married to Sheila (recently deceased) Hobbies and Interests: Enjoys walking, Family and Grand Children. March 31st – April 4th

Burnett James: Minister of Seskinore and Edenderry Congregations. James is married to Hazel, Hobbies and Interests: Reading, Cinema and Sport especially Manchester United. October 22nd – 26th

Burnside Mervyn: Minister of Ballyalbany & Glennan Presbyterian Churches, Co. Monaghan. Mervyn is married to Alison, they have 2 children Jonathan and Amy. Hobbies and Interests: Swimming and Walking. August 3rd – 7th.

Carroll Fr. Aiden: Curate of University Church, St. Stephens Green, Dublin 2. Hobbies and Interests: Reading, Walking and 9 hole golf in good weather!!! November 16th – 20th

Clarke Arthur: Minister of Glascar and Donaghmore Presbyterian

Churches. Retiring from the Parish Ministry 31st December 1999. Continuing as Editor of "The Herald". Arthur is married to Eileen, they have 3 grown children. Hobbies and Interests: Reading, Gardening and Obeying the commands of Grandchildren. November 11th – 15th

Clarke Ken (Fanta): Rector of St. Patrick's Church of Ireland, Coleraine. Fanta is married to Helen, they have 4 daughters, Alison, Tanya, Lynda and Nicola. Hobbies and Interests: Sport – especially rugby & football. Enthusiastic Manchester United supporter, Loves walking and Travel. August 18th – 22nd.

Clements David: Minister of Belvoir and Cairnshill Methodist Church, David is married to Niccy, they have 3 daughters Sarah, Ruth and Hannah. Hobbies and Interests: Squash and Golf. February 15th –19th

Conway Tom: Minister of Culnady & Swatragh Presbyterian Churches, Tom is married to Sheila, they have 3 children – Briony, Amy and Andrew. Hobbies and Interests – Playing Golf (very badly!) and watching sport on TV (very well!) April 30th – May 4th

Cordner Willis: Minister of 1st Presbyterian Church, Bangor. Willis is married to Iris, they have a son, Simon. Hobbies and Interests: Loves sailing and Hill walking. March 6th – 10th

Cupples David: Presbyterian Minister, Enniskillen. David is married to Rosie, they have a daughter Ellen. Hobbies and Interests: Reading, Playing the piano and 5 aside football. May 20th – 24th

Davidson Tony: Minister of First Presbyterian Church, Armagh. Tony is married to Christine, they have 3 children, Mark, Gemma and Ruth. Hobbies and Interests: Reading, Cinema, Watching all sport and Playing Golf Badly! December 16th – 20th

Dunlop Rosemary and John: Rosemary is a Relate Counsellor in Belfast and Antrim, John is Former Moderator of General Assembly, Minister of Rosemary Presbyterian Church, Belfast. They have a daughter and a son and a granddaughter. Hobbies and Interests: Reading,

Walking and Talking Politics. September 27th – 1st October.

Faris John: Presbyterian Minister in Aghada, Co. Cork and in Cork City. John is married to Heather, they have 2 children Naomi and Peter. Hobbies and Interests: Reading, Swimming, Walking, Painting with acrylics and stroking cats. July 29th – August 2nd

Fell Rev. Dr. Joseph: Minister of Ebrington Presbyterian Church, Londonderry. Clerk of the Derry and Strabane Presbytery. Joe is married to Sheila, they have 3 grown up children, Andrew, Rosemary and Jennifer. Hobbies and Interests: Caravaning, Boating and Reading Irish History. June 29th – July 3rd

Frazer Jim: Minister of Ballywillan Presbyterian Church, Portrush. Jim is married to Maureen, they have 4 children: James, Evane, Janice and Jonathan. Hobbies and Interests: Engineering and People. January 16th – 20th

Fyles Gordon: Rector of Crinken Church of Ireland, Bray, Co. Wicklow. Gordon is married to Yvonne, they have 2 children Maurice and Rosemarie. Hobbies and Interests: Fishing, Listening to Jazz and Reading History. September 2nd – 6th

Geoghegan Helen: Co-Ordinator, The Road Ahead Project. Helen is married to Shey, they have 4 children, Sandra, Brian, Paul and Matthew. Hobbies and Interests: Reading, Cross-stitch and craft work. March 11th

Gibson Drew: Lecturer in Belfast Bible College. Drew is married to Anne, they have 2 children Katie and Naomi. Hobbies and Interests: Football, Cooking and Bird Watching. November 6th - 10th.

Gillespie Stephen: Solicitor specialising in matrimonial matters and court cases. Member of Scrabo Hall, Newtownards. Stephen is married to Sonia, they have 2 daughters. Hobbies and Interests: Oil and water colour painting March 3rd.

Gilpin Edgar: Solicitor, specialising in Commercial property. Leader in an Independent Church in Belfast. Edgar is married to Winifred, they have 3 children and 1 grandchild. March 2nd

Glenfield Ferran: Rector, Kill O' The Grange Church of Ireland, Blackrock, Co. Dublin. Ferran is married to Jean, they have 3 children, Michael, Richard and Esther. Hobbies and Interests: Sport, particularly rugby, Hill walking, Theatre and Reading. January 6th – 10th

Hagan Jim: Minister of Donacloney Presbyterian Church. Jim is married to Eva, they have 4 children, David, Robert, Jane and Richard and 2 grandchildren. Hobbies and Interests: Walking and Caravaning. June 14th – 18th

Hamilton Norman: Minister of Ballysillan Presbyterian Church. Norman is married to Evelyn, they have a daughter Julie. Hobbies and Interests: Nature photography, Snooker and Tennis. April 15th- 19th

Hewitt David: Solicitor for 35 years with particular interest in welfare of the elderly. Member of the Northern Ireland Parades Commission. Former Rugby Irish International and British Lion. David is married to Margaret, they have 4 children (2 married) and 1 grandchild. Lives in Holywood and is Elder in Presbyterian Church. Hobbies and Interests: Watercolour painting and Walking Donegal Hills. March 4th.

Hill Rick: Minister of Cairncastle Presbyterian Church, Co. Antrim. Rick is married to Sandra, they have 2 children, Ethan and Bethany. Hobbies and Interests: Boating, Canoeing, Digital Media, Reading and Current Affairs. February 10th – 14th

Hyndman James: Minister of Glenwherry Church, James is married to Janice, they have a son John. Hobbies and Interests: Manchester United. March 26th – 30th.

Johnston David: Minister in Hamilton Road Presbyterian Church, Bangor. David is married to Olive, they have 4 children, Stephen, Mark, Heather and Laura. Hobbies and Interests: All kinds of music, playing piano and computers. August 13th – 17th.

Johnston Stephen: Minister of Carlow Presbyterian Church. Stephen is married to Ruth, they have 3 sons, Timothy, Philip and James. Hobbies and Interests: Soccer, History and Reading. October 12th – 16th.

Kennedy Neil: Medical Officer Embangweni Mission Hospital, Malawi. Neil is married to Sara, they have a son Ben . Hobbies and Interests: Attempting to play the guitar and supporting Manchester City. May 5th – 9th

Kingsmore Dr. Brian: Former Evangelism Promoter for P.C.I. Brian is married to Rona who is a lecturer in Linguistics in University of Ulster, Coleraine, they have 4 grown -up children living in the USA, Brazil and two in Scotland. Hobbies and Interests: 6 Grandchildren and Golf. January 31st – February 4th

Kirkpatrick John: Minister of Portrush Presbyterian Church. John is married to Joan, they have 4 children, Adam, Claire, Daniel and Cait. Hobbies and Interests: Chaplain to the Road Racing Motor Cycle Club. September 12th – 16th'

Lewis Howard: Associate Minister, Bloomfield Presbyterian Church. Howard is married to Elizabeth, they have a son Chris. Interests and Hobbies: Photography. June 24th – 28th

Lyle Peter: Minister in Ringsend & Second Dunboe on North Coast & Presbyterian Chaplain in University of Ulster at Coleraine. Peter is married to Heather. Hobbies and Interests: Travel, Music, Egypt, Meteorology, Motorcycle Racing and Football. May 25th – 29th

Little Alvin: Minister of Shore Street Presbyterian Church, Donaghadee. Alvin is married to Linda, they have 3 children, Joanna, Kerry and Christine. Hobbies and Interests: Horse-riding and Reading Christian Books! May 30st – June 3rd.

Mark Douglas: Field Representative in Ireland of 'Open Doors' which serves the suffering church worldwide. Douglas is married to Alison they have 6 children, Jonathan, Catherine, Olwyn, Andrew, Ruth and Peter. Hobbies and Interests: All sports especially Spurs! November 26th – 30th.

Mawhinney Samuel: Minister of Cahir and Fermoy Presbyterian Churches. Sam is a medical doctor. Married to Karen they have 3 children ,Andrew, Peter and David. Hobbies and Interests: Badminton, and spending time with family. July 19th – 23rd

McCarthy David: General Secretary of Evangelical Alliance Northern Ireland. David is married to Margaret, they have 3 children, Claire, Sián and Laura. Hobbies and Interests: Science Fiction, Films and Hill walking. October 2nd – 6th.

Mc Caughan Alison: Part –time teacher and editor of 'Wider World'. Alison is married to Jim, they have 3 children Jennifer, Christine and John. Hobbies and Interests: Local History, Walking, Reading and a King Charles Cavalier. December 6th – 10th

Mc Cullough Cecil: Professor of New Testament and Principal of Union Theological College, Belfast. Editor of the Irish Biblical Studies Journal. Cecil is married to Dorothy, a teacher in Victoria College. They have 2 children Judith and Stuart. Hobbies and Interests: Travel especially Europe and the Middle East. March 16th – 20th

McGeown Graham: Senior Lecturer in Physiology, Queen's University of Belfast. Graham is married to Eileen, who is a GP in Belfast, they have 2 children, Helen and Neil. Hobbies and Interests: Travelling, Reading, Gardening and Sleeping (not necessarily in that order). October 17th – 21st.

Mc Mullan Robert: Minister of New Row Presbyterian Church, Coleraine, Former General Director of Scripture Union in the Republic of Ireland. Robert is married to Christine, they have 3 children, Ross, Caris and Conor, and Molly the dog. Hobbies and Interests:

Playing golf, and is a life long supporter of Leeds United. April 20th – 24th.

Monaghan Paddy: Secretary, Evangelical Catholic Initiative and Part-time Financial Consultant. Paddy is married to Anne and they have 4 children, Ruth Anne, John, David, and Andrew. Hobbies and Interests: Promoting renewal in the Catholic Church, fostering reconciliation among Christians and building Jewish / Christian friendships. Co- Editor of 'Adventures in Reconciliation', featuring 29 Evangelical Catholic testimonies. Paddy also enjoys, Indoor soccer, Walking, Admiring God's beauty in nature and visiting Northern Ireland. July 4th – 8th

Montgomery David: Associate Minister of Knock Presbyterian Church Belfast and has served in churches in Liverpool, Dublin, Belfast and Vancouver. He has written on the Northern Ireland situation for ECONI, and his book on contemporary church worship 'Lift up your voice', is published by Rutherford House. David is married to Gwen. September 17th – 21st.

Moore David: Minister, Drum, Cootehill and Kilmount Presbyterian Congregations, Co. Cavan. David is married to Elaine, they have 3 children, Joshua, Hannah and Samuel. Hobbies and Interests: Sunderland AFC (Division one champions 1998 – 99, Record points 105), Dreaming of holidays and Surfing the net. October 27th – 31st.

Morrow Dr. Trevor: Minister of Lucan Presbyterian Church. Trevor is married to Carys, they have 2 children Peter and Ceri. Hobbies and Interests: Skiing, Dreaming Dreams and Reconciliation in Ireland. July 14th – 18th.

Murtagh Vivienne: works in education for ACET (Aids Care Education and Training) Originally from Co. Antrim. Now lives in Co. Kildare. Vivienne is married to Brian, they have 2 sons, Joshua and Nathan. Hobbies and Interests: Being fascinated by God, Enjoying books, Theatre and Music but mostly Brian and sons. August 28th – September 1st

Pantridge Gavin: Solicitor for 25 years, Former staff member of UCCF.

Gavin is married to Carol, they have 3 children. Member of Holywood Parish Church. Hobbies and Interests: Is a school governor and interested in Belfast Bible College and Crusaders. Used to play better golf than his current 10 handicap! March 1st

Poots Derek, OBE: Formally Minister in Trinity, Ballymoney, and Currently Deputy Clerk of the General Assembly and Secretary of the Home Mission. Derek is married to Mildred, they have 4 children, David, Catherine, Heather and Nicola. Hobbies and Interests: Reading, Music, Swimming, Ornithology, Sailing, Photography – gardening is a work of 'necessity' but not of 'mercy'. April 10th – 14th

Rea Stephen: Minister of Milford, Fannet (Kerrykeel) and Rathmullan Presbyterian Congregations, Co. Donegal. Hobbies and Interests: Philosophy, Music and Good wine. June 19th – 23rd.

Reid Cheryl: Assistant Minister in Railway Street Presbyterian Church, Lisburn. Hobbies and Interests: Enjoys France and all things French, Singing with a guitar, Walking in the mountains and Dogs! January 11th – 15th

Ryan Fergus: Leader of Fellowship Bible Church, Dublin. He was formerly a Captain with Aer Lingus, where he worked for 27 years, mostly on long – haul operations, but now works long-haul with FBC. Fergus is married to Sarah, they have four girls (Ryans' daughters!) and two grandchildren. Hobbies and Interests: Fergus is currently completing a theology degree, and also publishes a growing series of architectural drawings of Ireland's great buildings. February 25th – 29th

Samuel Joanna: Full – time Mum and Part-time General Practitioner, Joanna is married to John, who is Pastor of Grosvenor Baptist Church, Dublin. They have 3 children Tom, Clare, and Mark. Hobbies and Interests : Reading and Sport. September 22nd - 26th.

Searle David: Formally Minister of Hamilton Road, Presbyterian Church, Bangor before becoming warden of Rutherford House , Edinburgh. He is author of a number of books and has 3 children and 3

grandchildren. September 7th – 11th.

Sellar Frank: Minister of Adelaide Road Donore Presbyterian Church, Dublin 2, Frank is married to Claire, they have 2 children, Rebecca and Robert. Hobbies and Interests: Humour, Current Affairs and The Middle East. January 1st – 5th, March 12th – 15th, June 7th – 8th and October 7th – 11th.

Singleton Joan: Part – Time teacher at Irish Bible School, Joan is married to Stephen, who is Pastor of Thurles Baptist Church, Co. Tipperary. They have 2 children Paul and Clare. Hobbies and Interests: Parents Council at school, Gardening and finding good coffee shops! April 25th – 29th

Stanfield Mairisine and David: David is Chaplain at the University of Ulster. He is married to Marisine, also a Presbyterian Minister. They have 2 children, Jonathan and Daniel, and live in Ballynahinch, Co. Down. Hobbies and Interests: David keeps himself fit by coaching the ladies Hockey team at the University, Mairisine, by running after the three boys in her life. June 9th – 13th

Stirling Roz: Head of Youth Department for Presbyterian Church in Ireland, Hobbies and Interests: Walking, Enjoys the outdoors, Classical music and Irish folk music. August 23rd – 27th.

Stockman Steve: Dean of Residence, Derryvolgie Hall, Queens University Belfast. Steve is married to Janice, they have one daughter Caitlin. Hobbies and Interests: music, broadcasting, books, sport (especially golf and soccer)and training his daughter for the 2016 Olympics July 9th – 13th.

Symonds Fr. Paul: Spiritual Director, St Malachy's College, Belfast Hobbies and Interests: Home, Barnabas (cat) Music and Walking. April 5th – 9th

Thompson John: Chartered Accountant working in Dublin. John is married to Myrtle, they have 2 sons, Alfred and Peter. Hobbies and

Interests: Walking, Swimming, Liverpool Football Club and Formula One. August 8th – 12th.

Todd Ken: Minister of Cork Methodist Church. President – designate of The Methodist Church in Ireland. Ken is married to Frances, they have 3 children, Mark, Debby and Naomi. Hobbies and Interests: Golf, Stamp collecting and Bird watching. November 21st – 25th.

Tughan Clifford: Solicitor with 30 years experience in Law, including as Deputy Coroner for Belfast, Elder in Bethany Hall, Finaghy. Clifford is married to Carol, they have 3 children. Hobbies and Interests: Exploring the North Antrim Coast and Golf. March 5th

Watson Andrew: Minister of Donegal & Ballyshannon Presbyterian Churches. Andrew is married to Hazel, they have 4 children, Michael, Joshua, Sarah and Emily. Hobbies and Interests: Reading, Cinema and playing blues guitar. May 15th – 19th

Woodside John: Minister of Kilkenny Presbyterian Church, John is married to Sandra, they have 3 children, Andrew, Peter and Johnny. Hobbies and Interests: Formula One, Refusing to give up on golf. March 21st – 25th.

Woodside Sandra: Former staff member UCCF. Sandra is married to John. Hobbies and Interests: Family, Cross stitch, Hill walking and Inspector Morse! February 5th – 9th

Workman Sam: Evangelist, Formerly Congregational Minister, Sam is married to Una, they have a son, David. Hobbies and Interests: Golf and helping people out! June 4th – 6th

****

THE ILLUSTRATOR, - Robert G. Sellar.

Robert Gordon Sellar was born of Scottish parents in North Berwick, East Lothian and was brought to Belfast at the age of $4^{1/2}$, his father being then a draughtsman and subsequently a marine engine designer.

Following on school and College of Art days in Belfast, R.G went into the happy vocation of being a teacher of art, first of all in Technical and Grammar Schools in Larne and Belfast, and then on the staff of the College of Art wherein he had been a student.

In Autumn 1949 he became Art Adviser under the County Londonderry Education Committee in whose area he regularly visited all the Primary Schools. Closely linked in with this work, he devised and conducted, three evening classes a week in twelve centres in Co. Derry, classes for teachers in various aspects of Art Education. With the friendly co-operation of teachers, during school holidays, he put together a series of 24 filmstrips to support his lectures on 'The Pictorial Language of Children'.

During these rewarding days of School visiting, Robert met Roberta, a primary teacher, who became his wife in 1954. They became fully resident in Coleraine and when there, William and Frank were born to them. William is now an ophthalmic consultant in Cumbria, and Frank, (who even in his early school years showed signs of desire to become a minister of Christian teaching) is presently the compiler of this publication. So it has come that whilst Robert came into showing others how to appreciate what their eyes could see, his older son now restores sight to those whose eyes need physical attention and his younger son teaches and encourages those around him to read the Bible and to see, through eyes of faith, the greater world of Life that surrounds us, which, as yet, remains unseen to physical sight.

From his early years, Robert G, thanks to the influence of his father, had become much interested in the world around him - birds, insects, flowers and fossils - and the recording of them in drawings. The effects of water on stones, the wind among the trees, movement and colour, and the causes of sounds, all demand his interest in the physical creation all around and even within us.

Although, in his teens, Robert had been very aware of there being a spiritual dimension to his life, it was only at the age of 32 that he felt strong enough to make public his Christian commitment. That action very soon opened the door into his becoming a Bible class leader among teenagers, and this vocation continued, almost without interruption, first in Coleraine, then in Ballycastle, and ultimately in Castlerock, where, at the age of 73 he decided to leave others to 'carry the torch'.

Having been on Kirk Session, first in New Row, Coleraine; then in Ballycastle; R.G's love of the beauties of creation, his desire to communicate to other people through pictorial means the message of The Word, and his delight in the uses of pencil, brush and graver on paper, wood and other surfaces all fused together into his works, be they in the forms of paintings, woodcuts, lettering, or stained glass design; some samples of which are reproduced in this book. One of his most recent works was the design of the Marshall Memorial window in Castlerock.

He looks forward to the Life to come, but should that time be delayed, he is still full of enthusiasm for whatever art work he may be called upon to do, especially should it be in the almost international realm of Christian Symbolism.